W9-AQF-476

Acclaim for Laura Restrepo's

D e l i r i u m

"Lovely and daring. . . . [*Delirium*] is much more than a simple mystery. Laura Restrepo uses a shifting lens to take the reader into a world of madness, obsession and pain."

—*The Denver Post*

"*Delirium* is one of the finest novels written in recent memory. Restrepo has a total mastery over what she writes, an astonishing but absolute mastery. Yes, there's violence, narcotraffic, madness, perhaps even love itself as a form of total madness. The important thing is that we're talking about a truly great novel, of a kind that you seldom encounter anymore."

—*José Saramago*

"Restrepo writes with a sinister lyricism and a dry, leavening wit, detailing the ways in which money, power, and corruption have scourged the fragile Agustina and her city."

—*The New Yorker*

"Laura Restrepo breathes life into a singular amalgam of journalistic investigation and literary creation. Her fascination with popular culture and the play of her impeccable humor . . . save her novels from any temptation toward pathos or melodrama, and infuse them with unmistakable reading pleasures."

—*Gabriel García Márquez*

"Powerful. . . . A compelling, often beautiful novel. . . . *Delirium* starts slowly but builds in intensity and scope as Agustina's tormented life takes shape; indeed, it's the search for the cause of her mental deterioration that gives the book its energy."
—*San Francisco Chronicle*

"This beautiful and disturbing book haunted me during the days I read it and long after I put it down. Love, unknowability, loss, and even various forms of gain elide from one to another of its passionate, unnerving voices." —Vikram Seth

"A rich literary journey. . . . Laura Restrepo has created a diamond-hard vision that ultimately yields a layered, subtle, intelligent yet audacious sense of life."
—*The San Diego Union-Tribune*

"[Restrepo's] sense of erotic derangement is elaborately nuanced. Ultimately she seems to me an authentic descendent of the greatest New World author and seer of eros, Walt Whitman."
—Harold Bloom

"Vibrant and direct. . . . A complex, psychosexual family drama."
—*The New York Observer*

Laura Restrepo

Delirium

Laura Restrepo is the bestselling author of several prizewinning novels published in over twenty languages, including *Leopard in the Sun*, which won the Premio Arzobispo Juan de San Clemente, and *The Angel of Galilea*, which won the Premio Sor Juana Inés de la Cruz in Mexico and the Prix France Culture in France. She was also awarded the 2004 Premio Alfaguara and the 2006 Premio Grinzane Cavour in Italy for *Delirium*. A recent recipient of a Guggenheim Fellowship, Restrepo lives in Mexico City.

INTERNATIONAL

ALSO BY LAURA RESTREPO

PUBLISHED IN ENGLISH

Isle of Passion

The Angel of Galilea

Leopard in the Sun

The Dark Bride

A Tale of the Dispossessed

Delirium

Delirium

Delirium

a novel

Laura Restrepo

TRANSLATED FROM THE SPANISH BY

NATASHA WIMMER

Vintage International
Vintage Books
A Division of Random House, Inc.
New York

FIRST VINTAGE INTERNATIONAL EDITION, MARCH 2008

Translation copyright © 2007 by Laura Restrepo

All rights reserved. Published in the United States by Vintage Books, a division
of Random House, Inc., New York, and in Canada by Random House of Canada
Limited, Toronto. Originally published in Colombia as *Delirio* by Santillana
Ediciones Generales, S.L., Bogotá, in 2004. Copyright © 2004 by Laura
Restrepo. This translation first published in hardcover in the United States by
Nan A. Talese, an imprint of The Doubleday Broadway Publishing Group,
a division of Random House, Inc., New York, in 2007.

Vintage is a registered trademark and Vintage International and colophon are
trademarks of Random House, Inc.

This is a work of fiction. Names, characters, places, and incidents either are the
product of the author's imagination or are used fictitiously. Any resemblance to
actual persons, living or dead, events, or locales is entirely coincidental.

The Library of Congress has cataloged the Nan A. Talese edition as follows:
Restrepo, Laura.
[Delirio. English]
Delirium / Laura Restrepo ; translated from the Spanish by Natasha Wimmer.
p. cm.
I. Wimmer, Natasha. II. Title.
PQ8180.28.E7255D4513 2007
863'.64—dc22
2006020282

Vintage ISBN: 978-0-307-27804-3

Book design by Gretchen Achilles

www.vintagebooks.com

Printed in the United States of America
10 9 8 7 6 5 4 3 2

For Pedro my son,
this book which is as much his
as it is mine.

Wise Henry James had always warned writers against the use of a mad person as central to a narrative on the ground that as he was not morally responsible, there was no true tale to tell.

—GORE VIDAL

Delirium

Delirium

I KNEW SOMETHING irreparable had happened the moment a man opened the door to that hotel room and I saw my wife sitting at the far end of the room, looking out the window in the strangest way. I'd just returned from a short trip, four days away on business, and I swear that Agustina was fine when I left, I swear nothing odd was going on, or at least nothing out of the ordinary, certainly nothing to suggest what would happen to her while I was gone, except for her own premonitions, of course, but how was I to believe her when Agustina is always predicting some catastrophe; I've tried everything to make her see reason, but she won't be swayed, insisting that ever since she was little she's had what she calls the gift of sight, or the ability to see the future, and God only knows the trouble that's caused us.

This time, as usual, my Agustina predicted that something would go wrong, and once again, I ignored her prediction; I went away on a Wednesday, leaving her painting the apartment walls green, and on Sunday, when I returned, I found her in a hotel in the north of the city, transformed into someone terrified and terrifying, a being I barely recognized. I haven't been able to find out what happened to her while I was gone because when I ask she turns on me, it's incredible how fierce she can be when she's upset, she treats me as if I'm not me and she's not who she used to be, or at least that's how I try to explain it, and if I can't it's because I don't understand it myself. The woman I love is lost inside her own head and for fourteen days now I've been searching for her, wearing myself out trying to find her, but it's excruciating and impossibly difficult; it's as if Agustina were living on a plane parallel to reality, close but just out of reach, as if she were speaking a strange language that I vaguely recognize but can't quite comprehend. My wife's unhinged mind is a dog snapping at me, but at the same time its barking is a call for help, a call to which I'm unable to respond; Agustina is a hurt and starving dog who wants to go home but can't, and the next minute she's a stray dog who can't even remember it once had a home.

. . .

I'M GOING TO TELL YOU this point-blank because you have the right to know it, Agustina sweetheart, and anyway what do I have to lose talking about it all, when I've got nothing left anymore. Your husband is spinning in circles trying to find out what the hell happened to you and there's so much even you don't know, because listen, Agustina darling, all stories are like a big cake, with everybody's eyes on the piece they're eating, and the only one who sees the whole thing is the baker. But before I start, let me tell you that I'm happy to see you, despite everything I've always been happy to see you, and the truth is that after what happened you're the only person I wanted to see. Will you believe me if I tell you that this disaster started with a simple bet? It's almost embarrassing to confess, Agustina doll, because you took it all so seriously and were hurt so badly by it, but it was the lowest kind of bet, a dirty joke if we're going to call things by their true names, a prank that turned bloody.

We dubbed it Operation Lazarus, because the idea was to see whether we could breathe life back into Spider Salazar's pecker, which had been dead between his legs since the accident at the Las Lomas Polo Club. Do you remember the scandal, Agustina darling? The truth is, it was a stupid, ordinary accident, although later people tried to make it seem more heroic by spreading the story that Spider fell off his horse during a match against a Chilean team, but the rough stuff actually came later, during a drunken free-for-all, because the match was in the morning and Spider had watched it from one of the bottom rows of the stands since he's too fat to make it up to the top, and I can tell you that the closest he got to the action was betting on the Chileans and against the locals. The Chileans won and then were treated to a typical Colombian lunch that they probably choked down out of politeness, who knows what folk dishes were foisted on them—suckling pig, tamales, fritters, figs with caramel cream, or all of the above—and then they went back to their hotel to digest it while at the club the revelry went on, everyone getting drunker by the minute. Rivers of whiskey flowed, it got dark, and the only people left were the local polo players and the club regulars when Spider and his pals decided to saddle up, and I'm guessing, or actually I know, that when the happy pack rode into the night they were all as drunk as cossacks, a gang of juiced-up clowns; I don't know whether your brother Joaco was with them, Agustina doll, though probably he was, because Joaco never misses the chance for a spree.

They mounted the horses, which are high-strung to begin

with and don't appreciate overweight brutes squashing their kidneys and making them gallop in the dark along muddy paths, followed by a procession of Toyota 4x4s full of bodyguards, you know how it is, angel, because you come from that world and escaped it only when you'd had all you could stomach, but does the aftertaste ever go away?, no, sweetheart, the taste of shit lingers in your mouth no matter how many times you gargle with Listerine. Every fat cat from Las Lomas Polo is shadowed wherever he goes by five or six escorts, and Spider Salazar is even worse; ever since he struck it rich he's had himself protected by a troop of thugs trained in Israel, and that night Spider, who hadn't been on a horse for months because he was clogged with cholesterol and had to content himself with watching from the stands, that night Spider, who was completely plastered, ordered them to bring him the most spirited horse, a big, imperious bay called Parsley, and if I say "called," Agustina princess, it's because no one calls it anything anymore, since in the darkness, the mud, and the commotion, Parsley lost his temper and threw Spider, slamming him against a rock, and then some genius of a bodyguard, a guy they call the Sucker, had the brilliant idea of teaching the horse a lesson by blasting it with his machine gun, leaving it riddled like a sieve with its hooves pointing up at the moon, the most pathetic little scene imaginable. In a single burst the idiot pissed away the two hundred and fifty grand Parsley was worth, because that's life, Agustina sweetheart, fortunes go down the drain in a single binge and nobody bats an eye.

THE GIRL AGUSTINA hugs another, smaller child tight; it's her brother Bichi, who has a head full of dark curls, a Christ Child, the kind artists paint with black hair instead of golden. It's the last time, Bichito, Agustina promises him, my father will never hit you again because I'm going to stop him, don't hold your arm like that, like a chicken with a broken wing, come here, Bichi, little brother, you have to forgive my father's bad hands because his heart is good, you have to forgive him, Bichi, and not stare at him like that because if you do he'll go away and it'll be your fault, does your arm still hurt?, come here, it's all right, if you stop crying your sister, Agustina, will summon you to the great ceremony of her powers, and we'll do what we always do, she'll get the pictures from their hiding place and Bichi will spread the black cloth on the bed, you and me preparing for the service that will make my eyes see, Agustina calls up the great Power that lets her know when her father is going to hurt her brother, you're the Bichi I loved so much, Agustina repeats over and over again, the Bichi I love so very very much, my darling little brother, the beautiful boy who abandoned me a lifetime ago and is lost to me now.

I'll cure your broken wing, sings Agustina, rocking him against her, I'll kiss it and make it better. The only problem is that the powers of divination come to her when they feel like it, not when she calls on them, that's why the ceremony doesn't always work the same way even though the two children put on their robes and do everything right, step by step, carefully performing each step, but it isn't the same, Agustina complains, because the powers forsake me sometimes, the visions fade and Bichi is left defenseless, not knowing when the thing that's sure to happen to him will happen. But when they're going to come they announce their arrival with a flicker of the eyelids, the First Call, because Agustina's powers were, are, her eyes' ability to see beyond, to what's still to come, to what hasn't come yet. The Second Call is when the head tilts back of its own accord, as if it were descending a staircase, as if the neck were tugging it down and making it toss its hair like the Weeping Woman when she wanders the hills. I know Bichi is terrified by the Second Call, and he doesn't want to know anything about the Weeping Woman or the wild rhythms of her flowing hair, which is why he begs me not to roll my eyes back in my head and toss my hair because If you keep doing that Agustina, I'll go to my room, Don't go Bichi Bichito, don't go and I won't do it anymore, I'll control the shaking so I don't scare you, because after all this is a ceremony of healing and comfort, I'd never hurt you, I only want to protect you, and in return you have to promise me that you'll forgive my father even when he hits you, my father says it's for your own good and parents know things that children don't.

. . .

EVER SINCE MY WIFE has been acting so strange, I've dedicated myself to helping her, but I've only managed to irritate her with my futile selfless efforts. For example, yesterday, late at night, Agustina got angry because I wanted to take a cloth and dry the rug that she'd soaked, obsessed with the idea that it smelled strange, and the thing is, it disturbs me to see all the pots of water she sets around the apartment, she's taken to per-

forming baptisms, or ablutions, or who knows what kind of rituals invoking gods invented by her, washing everything and
scouring it with excessive zeal, my unfathomable Agustina, any
spot on the tablecloth or grime on a windowpane torments her,
dust on the moldings makes her miserable, and the muddy
footprints she claims my shoes leave make her furious; even
her own hands seem disgusting to her though she scrubs them
incessantly, her beautiful pale hands red and chafed now because she gives them no respite, and she gives me no respite,
and she gives herself no respite.

As Agustina performs her mad ceremonies she gives orders
to Aunt Sofi, who has volunteered her services as willing
acolyte, and the two rush about with containers of water as if
this is how they'll exorcise anxiety, or regain lost control, and I
can find no part to play in this story, nor do I know how to curb
the mystical mania that's invading the house in the form of
cups of water that appear in rows along the baseboards, or on
the window ledges. I open a door suddenly and upset a plate of
water that Agustina's hidden behind it, or I'm unable to go upstairs because she's set pots of water on each step. How can I go
up the stairs, Aunt Sofi, when Agustina's blocked them? Stay
down here for now, Aguilar, be patient and don't move those
pots because you know what a fuss she'll make. And where will
we eat, Agustina darling, now that you've covered the table
with plates of water? She's put them on the chairs, on the balcony, and around the bed, the river of her madness leaving its
traces even on the bookshelves and in the cupboards; wherever
she goes, quiet eyes of water open up, gazing into nothing or
the unknown, and rather than being upset I feel the anguish of

not knowing what bubbles are bursting inside her, what poisonous fish are swimming the channels of her brain, and all I can think to do is wait until she's off guard, and empty cups and plates and buckets and return them to their place in the kitchen, and then I ask you why you look at me with hatred, Agustina my love, it must be because you don't remember me, but sometimes you do, sometimes she seems to recognize me, vaguely, as if through a fog, and her eyes offer reconciliation for an instant, but only for an instant before I immediately lose her and the same terrible hurt invades me.

Strange comedy, or tragedy for three voices, Agustina with her ablutions, Aunt Sofi who plays along with her, and I, Aguilar, an observer asking myself when reason fled, that thing we call reason; an invisible force, but when it's missing, life isn't life and what's human is no longer human. What would we do without you, Aunt Sofi? At first I stayed home twenty-four hours a day watching Agustina and hoping that at any minute she would return to her senses, but as the days went by I began to suspect that the crisis wouldn't come to an end overnight and I knew I'd have to pluck up the courage to face daily life again. Maybe the hardest part is accepting the stretch of middle ground between sanity and madness and learning to straddle it; by the third or fourth day of delirium the money I had on me ran out and ordinary demands arose again, if I didn't go out to collect the money I was owed and do my weekly deliveries there wouldn't be anything to buy food with or pay the bills, but there was no way for me to hire a nurse to stay with Agustina while I was gone and make sure she didn't escape or do something hopelessly crazy, and it was then that the woman who said her name was Aunt Sofi rang the doorbell.

She showed up just like that, as if heaven-sent, with her two suitcases, her felt hat topped by a feather, her easy laugh, and her comfortable manner of a German from the provinces, and while she was standing in the doorway, before she'd been invited in, she explained to me that it had been years since she'd had anything to do with the family, that she lived in Mexico and had flown in to help care for her niece for as long as necessary. This struck me as odd, because my wife had never spoken to me about any aunt, and yet Agustina seemed to recognize her, or at least she recognized her hat, because she laughed, I can't believe you still wear that little cap with the goose feather, that was all Agustina said to her but she said it warmly, cheerfully, and yet there was something that made me uneasy, if this woman hadn't been in contact with the family, how had she learned of her niece's breakdown, and when I asked her, she simply said, I've always known, Wonderful, I thought, either something's not right here or I've just landed myself another seer.

The truth is, not only has this Aunt Sofi managed to lower the voltage on Agustina's frenzy, she's also gotten her to eat more, an enormous step forward because Agustina had been refusing anything except plain bread and pure water—those were her words, plain bread and pure water—so long as I wasn't the one who gave them to her. But she happily accepts the cinnamon porridge Aunt Sofi feeds to her spoonful by spoonful as if she were a baby. Tell me, Aunt Sofi, why does Agustina reject food from me, but take it from you?, Because when she was little cinnamon porridge was what I would make for her when she was sick, What would we have done without you, Aunt Sofi, I say gratefully, while asking myself who on earth this Aunt Sofi must really be.

·   ·   ·

TELL ME WHAT THE SKY looks like this summer, how the clouds pile up above us round and woolly as sheep, how my soul finds gentle rest deep in your eyes, Grandfather Portulinus persisted in asking Grandmother Blanca, referring not to any landscapes he could see but to those he dreamed, because by then he was mad, completely and utterly insane. She would take him by the hand and make him run until he was exhausted in order to tame the frenzy that otherwise could drag him down to the depths of hell, although to say he ran is a manner of speaking, since it was more the clumsy trot of a man who was by then a little fat and no longer young, and well on his way into the turmoil of dementia. Into, but also out of, of course, because sometimes he wasn't crazy, and then he was a musician, a German musician called Nicholas, last name Portulinus, who in time would be Agustina's grandfather and who had come from Kaub, a place with a river and a castle, only to end up amid the sugarcane fields of the scorching town of Sasaima, perhaps because the damp and elusive charm of those hot lands was so seductive for men like him, men with a tendency toward dreaminess and distraction. The matter of his origin was never entirely cleared up because it was something he rarely discussed, and if he did occasionally speak of it, he did so in that awkward Spanish of his, badly learned along the way, that never became more than the provisional language of someone who won't specify whether he's just arrived or whether he has yet to leave, and it wasn't clear why he'd settled in this precise spot, although he himself maintained that if he'd chosen Sasaima out of all the towns on the planet, it was because he knew of none other with such a melodious name.

• • •

WHAT WOULDN'T I GIVE to know what to do, but all I have is this terrible anguish, fourteen nights without sleeping, fourteen days without rest, and the determination to bring Agustina back no matter how much she resists. She's furious and dislocated and defeated; her brain has shattered into pieces and the only thing I have to guide me in putting it back together is the compass of my love for her, my great love for her, but that compass isn't steady now, because it's hard for me to love her, sometimes very hard, because my Agustina isn't nice and she doesn't seem to love me anymore; she's declared a war of tooth and claw in which we're both being torn to pieces. War or indifference, I don't know which of the two is hardest to fight, and I console myself by thinking that it isn't she who hates me but the strange person who's taken possession of her, that maniacal washerwoman who believes I'm merely someone who soils everything he touches.

There are moments when Agustina seems to accept a truce and scrawls pictures to explain what's wrong with her. She draws rings surrounded by bigger rings, rings that detach themselves from other rings like clusters of anxiety, and she says that they're the cells of her resurrected body reproducing themselves and saving her. What are you talking about, Agustina, I ask her, and she tries to explain by drawing new rings, now tiny and crowded, furiously shading them in on a sheet of notebook paper, They're particles of my own body, Agustina insists, pressing so hard with the pencil that she tears the paper, irritated because she can't explain, because her husband can't understand her.

It's the weight of my guilt working against me, guilt that I don't know my wife better despite having lived with her for what will soon be three years. I've managed to establish two things about the strange territory of her madness: one, that it is by nature voracious and can swallow me up as it did her, and two, that the vertiginous rate at which it grows means that this is a fight against the clock and I've stepped in too late because I didn't know soon enough how far the disaster had advanced. I'm alone in this fight, with no one to guide my steps through the labyrinth or to show me the way out when the moment comes. That's why I have to think carefully; I must order the chaos of facts coolly and calmly, without exaggerating, without dramatizing, seeking succinct explanations and precise words that will allow me to separate concrete things from phantoms, and acts from dreams. I have to moderate my voice, remain calm, and keep the volume low, or we'll both be lost. What's happening to you, Agustina darling, what were you doing at that hotel, who hurt you?, I ask, but this only unleashes all the rage and noise of that other time and other world in which she's entrenched, and the more worried I am, the more venomous she becomes. She won't answer me, or she doesn't want to, and maybe she doesn't know the answer herself or can't formulate it amidst the storm that's erupted inside her.

Since everything around me is collapsing into uncertainty, I'll start by describing the few things I know for sure: I know I'm on Thirteenth Road in the city where I live, Bogotá, and that the traffic, which is always heavy anyway, is impossible because of the rain. I know that my name is Aguilar, that I was a literature professor until the university was shut down because of unrest, and that since then, I've gradually become almost a nobody, a man who delivers dog food in order to survive, though maybe it's to my advantage that I have nothing to occupy me except my stubborn resolve to get Agustina back. I also know — I know it now, although two weeks ago I didn't — that any delay on my part would be criminal.

When it all began I thought it was a nightmare that we'd wake up from at any minute, This can't be happening to us, I kept repeating to myself and deep down I believed it. I wanted to convince myself that my wife's breakdown would last only for a few hours, that it would be over when the effect of the drugs had worn off, or the acid, or the alcohol, or whatever it was that had alienated her like this; that in any case the problem was something external, devastating but temporary, or maybe some brutal act that she couldn't tell me about but from which she'd recover little by little. Or one of those murky episodes that are increasingly common in this city where everyone's at war with everyone else; stories of people who're sold doctored drugs in some bar, or who're attacked, or who're given *burundanga*, an herbal extract that makes them do things against their will. At first I assumed it had been something like this, and in fact I still haven't given up the idea, and that's why my first impulse was to take her to the nearest emergency room, at the Country Clinic, where the doctors found her agitated and delirious, but with no trace of foreign substances in her blood. The reason it's so difficult to believe that they really found no evidence of foreign substances in her blood, the reason I refuse to accept that diagnosis, is because it would imply that the only problem is my wife's naked soul, and that the madness issues directly from her, without the mediation of outside elements, without mitigating factors. For an instant, the same evening this hell was loosed, her expression softened and she begged me for help, or at least she tried to make contact, saying, Look, Aguilar, see my naked soul; I remember those words with the sharp clarity that a wound remembers the knife that made it.

• • •

IN THE MIDDLE OF the drunken chaos, the polo players were shouting at Spider, who was still on the ground, Get up, Spider, don't be a pussy, while Spider was down there in the dark and the mud, at death's door and unable to move because, as we later learned, he had just shattered his spine on that rock. A few days later, when he came around to realizing he was still alive, he had himself flown to Houston in a private plane, to one of those mega-hospitals where your father was taken, too, in his time, Agustina kitten, because in this miserable excuse for a country anybody who gets sick and has some money makes a pilgrimage to Texas convinced that as long as the treatment's in

English they'll be cured, that the miracle will work if it's paid for in dollars, as if Houston were Fátima or Lourdes or the Holy Land, as if they didn't already know that livers blooming with cirrhosis couldn't be made right even by the technological God of the Americans. And no matter whether the doctors squeeze a fortune out of them in electrocardiograms, sonograms, or stress tests, or thread a stent through the kernel of their souls, they almost always end up the same as they would've here, six feet under and pushing up daisies; just look at what happened to your father, sweetheart, who took himself off to Houston only to return a little later in cold storage on an Avianca flight, just in time for his own burial in the Central Cemetery of Bogotá.

But to get back to Spider: as you must have heard, angel, that was what messed up your head and put an end to my lucky streak, and believe me I'm sorry you're sick, Agustina, you know better than anyone that if I ever hurt you it wasn't on purpose. What happened with Spider was that after four major operations and a pile of cash spent on rehab, the doctors in Houston, Texas, managed to save his skin but not his pride, because he wound up paraplegic and impotent, the poor bastard, shoveled into a wheelchair like a potted plant, and probably incontinent on top of it all, although Spider swears he's not, that not being able to screw or walk is humiliation enough and that the day he shits himself, too, he'll shoot himself without a second thought. When he's wallowing in self-pity, Spider says that that son of a bitch Parsley was the lucky one, since now he must be chasing mares up in heaven. What it all means, darling, is that this has been a chain of disasters and the first broken link was Spider; psychologically he was broken, is what I mean, although his huge fortune is still intact. Things happen the way they happen and whoever loses is lost, and in this three-way game Spider lost, you lost, and I lost, to say nothing of the supporting cast.

This was on a Thursday, I can tell you the precise day, an ill-fated Thursday when the five of us were having our usual dinner at L'Esplanade: Spider Salazar, Jorge Luis Ayerbe, your brother Joaco, the gringo Rony Silver, and I, the four of them smelling of Hermès and dressed in Armani, all wearing those Ferragamo ties with little equestrian prints imported straight from the Via Condotti, Spider's with little spurs, your brother Joaco's with riding crops, Jorge Luis's with saddles, and Silver's with something like tiny unicorns, as if the four had come to some kind of sissy agreement. They all arrived at L'Esplanade dressed up like respectable people, but I came straight to the restaurant from the Turkish bath, still steaming and radiating tan, healthy to the toes of my sockless Nikes, and shirtless under my raw wool Ralph Lauren sweater; you know how I dress, Agustina doll, I don't have to tell you, and I dress the way I do so that they never forget I've got them beat in the youth game, because any one of them could be my father, and any of their fiftysomething wives could be my mother, with those crocodile bags and big gold bracelets, and tailored pastel suits, while my thing is chicks by the dozen, top models, TV stars, architecture students, water-ski instructors, skinny little screwed-up long-haired beauties, Agustina, like you.

The truth is, if I'd chosen just one of them to set up house with, it would've been you, my little princess-in-waiting; it would almost certainly have been you, the one with the hottest little body, the prettiest and the craziest of them all. But never mind, why talk about setting up house, let Father Niccoló set up house for orphans and old people, let him shoot for sainthood; why should I care about homemaking, when it has nothing to do with me or my life, and I'm more than satisfied with what fate has seen fit to give me, a hot girl for every cold night, because if I've ever had a problem it's been lack of appetite, there's been so much sweet stuff that sometimes I get sick of it. And money-wise, too, I run circles around your hotshot brother Joaco, your dead father, Carlos Vicente, and plenty of the Bogotá old-money types, who know that when I'm paying they're served caviar wholesale, in a deep dish with a soup spoon, and, Eat, you bastards, I tell them, gorge yourselves on Russian caviar and enjoy, since in your fancy houses all you get is five little eggs on a piece of toast the size of a coin.

• • •

DON'T BE SCARED, Bichito darling, the girl Agustina says to the smaller boy she's holding close, this ceremony is to keep you safe and make you better. Like what happened to Achilles, Tina?, the boy asks, already half recovered from his panic, Yes, Bichi Bichito, like when Achilles the Wrathful, and he interrupts her to complain, I like it better when we say Achilles, he who is covered in golden down, All right, when Achilles, he of the golden down, is bathed in the waters of the Styx to make him invincible, I like it more when we say in the waters of the Infernal River, It's the same thing, Bichito, it means the same thing, what's important is to remember that since they're holding him by the ankle, that part of him is still vulnerable and they can hurt him there, No, Tina, they can't, because later, when he's big, Achilles the Wrathful returns to the Infernal River to dip his weak foot in and from then on his entire body is protected.

The problem is that their father is always after Bichi, he has it in for him because he's the youngest, not like Joaco, Joaco is my other brother, the oldest of us three, and my father never hits him or tells him he's done anything wrong, even when they call home from the Boys School to say that he lit a fire in the toolroom or did bad things to the caretaker's dog, and when their father finds out he orders Joaco into his study and then scolds him, but halfheartedly, as if he'd like to praise him instead and make him see that deep down he likes his oldest son to be badly behaved, to be known as an ace soccer player, and to get good grades, So long as you're at the top of your class, they'll let you get away with things sometimes, says Carlos Vicente Londoño to his oldest son, Joaquín Londoño, who unfortunately doesn't have the same name as his father but is just like him in spirit, and Joaco looks him boldly in the eye, Of the three of us, says Agustina, my brother Joaco is the only one who's never scared, because Joaco knows that my father's yellow eyes, his bushy eyebrows that come together in the middle, his big nose, and the peculiar way his index finger stretches longer than his middle finger are all traits they share, which is why father and son smile secretly, even when the vice-principal of the Boys School calls to say that Joaco will be put on probation because he's been drinking beer at break, but Joaco and my father smile because they know that the two of them are essentially the same, one generation after the next, studying at the same boys' school, getting drunk at the same parties, maybe even starting fires in the same place or tormenting the same old dog, the guard dog that hasn't died yet and won't die because its fate is to be there still when Joaco's son, Joaco's father's grandson, is born and grows big enough to extend the miserable dog's long agony over three generations. Listen Bichi, my pale-skinned little darling, we can't blame my father for liking Joaco better, because after all you and I perform ceremonies that we shouldn't, do you understand?, we commit sins and my father wants to help us be better, that's what fathers are for.

My father wanted his firstborn son to be named after him, Carlos Vicente Londoño, but because he was busy with work, he didn't make it to the christening in time, or at least that's what my mother says, and she's probably right because my father was never one of those people who arrive when you expect them to, so since he wasn't there, instead of giving the baby his father's name, his godparents named him after the Virgin Mary's father, that is, Joaquín, maybe thinking that he'd be better protected that way on his journey through this vale of tears, his godmother said that in the annals of the saints there is no Carlos Vicente because it isn't a Christian name, who ever heard of Saint Carlos Vicente the bishop or Saint Carlos Vicente the martyr, so they convinced themselves that it was better to call him Joaquín, and it was then that the story of my father's great frustration began. So that he would forgive her, Eugenia, the boy's mother, promised him that their second son would be called Carlos Vicente, but then I was born and since I was a girl they named me Agustina and so the long wait got longer, the wait for the chosen one who would be given the Name, until it was Bichi's turn to be born and by consensus and without discussion he was named Carlos Vicente Londoño, just as my father's obsession dictated, but life is so fickle that my father never wanted to call him that, and so we had to invent all kinds of nicknames, like Bichi, Bichito, Charlie Bichi, Charlie, all not-quite-real names, like names for a pet.

Why should it be your fault, Bichi Bichito, for not looking like my father, for looking exactly like my mother and me; she, you, and I with skin that's almost too white. Can you believe it, my mother was brought up to be proud of being Aryan, and who does she marry but someone who looks down on her for being washed-out and poor; whiteys, my father calls us when he sees us in our bathing suits at the pool at Gai Repos, the family estate in Sasaima, and before Bichi can ask her again what Gai Repos means, Agustina tells him: It means happy rest in one of the European languages that grandfather Portulinus could speak, he was the one who first came to Sasaima and bought the ranch; I've explained it to you a thousand times and this is the thousand and first time, but you never get it, you're such trouble, Bichi Bichito, sometimes I think my father is right when he says that you're the kind of boy who lives in the clouds and no one can make you come down.

• • •

THOUGH SHE'S NEVER MET ME and probably never will, my mother-in-law Eugenia won't forgive Agustina for living with me. Before the delirium, when Agustina hadn't yet forsaken reality, I never bothered to ask her about her past, her family, or her memories, good or bad, partly because I was so busy with teaching and partly, to be honest, because I didn't really care, I felt tied to the Agustina who lived with me here and now, not to the Agustina who belonged to other times and other people, and now, when that past might be crucial in helping to re-assemble the puzzle of her memory, I mourn the questions I didn't ask, yearning for those interminable stories that fell on deaf ears, about fights with her parents or past loves. I blame myself for everything I refused to see because I wanted to keep reading, because I didn't have time, because I didn't think it was important, or because I couldn't be bothered to listen to stories about strangers, by which I mean stories about her family, which bored me to death.

Those people, her family, have always refused to meet me because they think I'm a peon, Agustina herself confessed to me once that that was their word for me, peon, or in other words a bourgeois nobody, a third-rate professor, and that was before I was out of work; Agustina told me that there were other strikes against me, too, like the fact that I'm not divorced from my first wife, that I don't speak any foreign languages, that I'm a communist, that I don't make enough money, that I dress like a bum. It's no surprise that there's a wall of contempt between her people and mine, but the strange thing, the truly fascinating thing, is that the class Agustina belongs to doesn't only exclude other classes but also purges itself; it's always get-ting rid of its own kind, those who for subtle reasons don't quite fulfill the requirements, like Agustina or Aunt Sofi, and I ask myself whether they were condemned at birth or whether it was a consequence of their acts, whether it was original sin or some other sin committed along the way that expelled them from paradise and revoked their privileges; among her many faults, Agustina committed the cardinal sin of getting involved with me, because number one on the list of the internal rules that govern her people is not to fraternize with inferiors, much less sleep with them, although of course Agustina was already exiled when she chose to keep company with me, so who knows what other crimes she may have committed before.

I'd rather not think about my mother-in-law, but I can't forget the absurd phone call she made after Agustina's breakdown. Eugenia rarely calls here, and she hangs up if I answer, but the other day she deigned to speak to me for the first time in the three years I've been living with her daughter, and that was only because Agustina got extremely upset when she heard that it was her mother and refused to pick up the phone, I don't want to talk to her because her voice makes me sick, she repeated over and over again until she went into one of her nervous states, so Eugenia had no choice but to talk to me, though without ever calling me by name, twisting herself into knots to avoid mentioning my connection to Agustina and speaking in an impersonal tone as if I were an operator or a nurse, in other words as if I were nobody and she were leaving a message on the machine, which was how she informed me that from now on she herself would look after Agustina, Look, Señor, what my daughter needs is a rest, she said to me, or rather didn't say to me but to the nonentity at the other end of the line, This is to let you know that I'm coming today to take Agustina away to a spa in Virginia, What do you mean a spa in Virginia, Señora, what are you talking about?, I shot back at her, and since Agustina was next to me screaming that her mother's voice made her sick, I was having trouble hearing Eugenia, who was listing the healing treatments that her daughter would receive at one of the best spas in the world, thermal baths, floral therapy, seaweed massage, until I cut her off, Listen, Señora, Agustina isn't well, she's in a state of uncontrollable agitation and you come to me intending to take her away for some Zen meditation?, And who are you, Señor, to tell me what's best for my daughter, at least have the courtesy to ask her whether she wants to go or not, Agustina, your mother's asking whether you want to go with her to some hot springs in Virginia, Listen for yourself, Señora, Agustina's saying that all she wants is for us to hang up right now.

But Eugenia, who seemed not to hear, told me that the decision had already been made, and that when she came by in two hours her daughter should be waiting for her downstairs in the lobby, passport in hand and suitcase ready, since there wouldn't be anywhere to park and the neighborhood is so dangerous. And I said, Well no, Señora, Agustina is not leaving this house for any reason whatsoever, so go have seaweed plastered on yourself in Virginia if that's what you want, and immediately I regretted it, it would have been better to issue a firm but polite no, I let her see the worst side of me, I thought, This woman thinks I'm a boor and I've just proved her right.

Upset at having made such a mistake, I lost the thread of the conversation for a minute, and when I picked it up again, Eugenia was saying, You don't know how that girl has made me suffer, she's never shown me the slightest consideration, and I couldn't believe what I was hearing, now it turned out that the victim was Eugenia and she wasn't really calling to offer her help but to present a laundry list of grievances, and even though it was the first time that Agustina's mother and I had spoken, we ended up fighting over the phone with the assurance of old antagonists and what began as a brief, dry exchange, in which each word was weighed so as not to go beyond the strictly impersonal, gradually turned into a rapid volley of awkwardly phrased and poorly thought-out remarks, so full of mutual recrimination that the result was a repugnant intimacy, or at least that's how it seemed to me, as if a stranger had stepped on someone else's foot by mistake in the street and the two had dropped everything in order to spend the afternoon spitting in each other's faces. I said, What you want, Señora, isn't to help your daughter recover but to take her away from me, and she shouted, You stole my daughter, with a shrillness that she must still be regretting, because the pitifulness of a petit bourgeois like me is a matter of course, but it's unforgivable in a woman of her stature. I had worked myself into a nervous frenzy and I suppose she had too because she could hardly catch her breath, until I finally said no to her four or five times in a row, No no no no, Señora, Agustina is not leaving here, and then Eugenia hung up without saying goodbye and that was that.

* * *

BEING A MUSICIAN by profession, Grandfather Portulinus made a living by giving piano lessons to the daughters of the well-to-do families of the town of Sasaima, among them Blanca Mendoza, a slight girl who was hardly a promising pianist as

she had clumsy hands and little ear for music, and in fact Portulinus never even managed to teach her the scales, but instead
he ended up marrying her, although he was twice her age. If he
did, it was partly for love and partly out of obligation, because
he had gotten her pregnant through a thoughtless, inconsider-
ate act that was committed without her parents' knowledge
and probably against her will, an ill-fated start to any marriage,
but in the end what mattered most wasn't what was augured
but the way the man dealt with his fate, and twenty long years
of unswerving conjugal loyalty were proof that if Grandfather
Portulinus had married the girl who was now Grandmother
Blanca, it was because he loved her, not because he had to.

Besides giving piano lessons, Portulinus composed music to
order for marriages, serenades, and celebrations, certain folk
dances like *bambucos* and *pasillos*, which, as Grandmother used
to say, were catchy and lively despite his Germanness, and they
touched people's hearts even though their lyrics made refer-
ence to sky-blue summers, the snows of yesteryear, pine
forests, the ocher shades of fall, and other yearnings equally
unknown in equatorial Sasaima, where no one doubted that
Nicholas Portulinus was a good man, and if certain oddities of
character were noted in him, they were dismissed as being at-
tributable to his foreignness. But the truth is that every so often, as if in waves, Grandfather Portulinus suffered mood
swings of varying severity and for months he would give up
teaching, stop playing and composing, and only roar or mutter,
seemingly plagued by noises not of this world, or at least that's
what he complained to his wife. Blanca, sweet Blanca, your
name is enough to clear away the shadows, he would say to her

when she took him out into the countryside to soothe him, and he would run holding her hand and then trip and fall, rolling in the tall, sweet-smelling summer grasses, though it should be understood that this was not summer in Sasaima, since in Sasaima there's only one single continuous season all 365 days of the year, but that other summer, so far away now, lingering in a foreigner's mournful memory.

• • •

THE HOTEL ROOM was luxurious, or striving to be so; I remember yards of fabric in drapes and upholstery and a peach-colored carpet that exuded the smell of newness. At the far end was Agustina, sitting on the floor, as if trapped between the wall and a table with a lamp on it, a place where no one would think to sit unless they had fallen. She looked pale and thin and her hair and clothes were bedraggled, as if she hadn't eaten or bathed for days, as if she had been subjected to all sorts of humiliations. And yet her eyes were shining, I remember that clearly, at the far end of the room Agustina's eyes were shining, with an unhealthy gleam but they were shining, as if whatever was sapping her strength had been incapable of breaking the intensity of her gaze, in fact to the contrary, amid the sudden waste of her body I discerned a challenge in her eyes that filled me with fear, something disturbing, an excessive vibration that brought to mind the word *delirium*, Agustina was possessed by some delirium that simmered inside her with a slow, hostile shudder.

And yet it had been only four days since I'd gone away and left her painting the walls of the front room of our apartment a mossy green, a color she herself had chosen because, as she explained to me, feng shui advises it for couples like us, and to prevent her from spouting some complicated Eastern theory, I was careful not to ask her what she meant by couples like us or why moss green would be good for us. I had to drive my van to Ibagué on Wednesday to deliver an order of Purina, so I decided to take advantage of a free stay my health insurance offered at Las Palmeras Holiday Resort, tacky and middle class, as I informed Agustina, but it had a pool and cabins and was in a stunning mountain valley in the warm country, and ultimately why find fault when I couldn't have afforded anything better anyway. I wanted to spend a few days there with my two sons, Toño and Carlos, my children with Marta Elena, my first wife; for a while I'd needed some time with them to see how they were feeling, and to continue mending the family closeness that had been ruptured when I separated from their mother.

That was my reason for not inviting Agustina, too, although she gets along well with the boys and they get along well with her; in fact, I can't help but feel that there are moments when a generational bond is established among the three of them that leaves me out, or to put it another way, a slightly hypnotic and almost physical link, created when my two sons' eyes light up at the sight of Agustina's beauty, and she, in turn, gazes nostalgically at those sculpted adolescent bodies like someone relinquishing a place she isn't fated to visit. What I mean is, things cool a few degrees between my sons and me when she's there; our conversation turns a little stiff and we behave as though in the presence of company.

When I informed Agustina that I was taking the trip alone,

she threw one of those seismic fits that have led me to call her my rabid plaything, because Agustina is like that, witty and amusing but with a vicious temper. Afterward she refused to speak to me for several hours, and at last, when she was calmer, she asked how I could possibly not realize that she might like a break and some sunshine, too, that we had no time together during the week because I was at work and I spent Saturdays with Toño and Carlos. It broke my heart to hear Agustina's reproaches because in a way she's like an older daughter to me whom I sometimes neglect in favor of my other two children, and also because the sun and warmth make her even more desirable, cheering her up and toasting her skin, which is usually so excessively white that it's almost blue, and it broke my heart, too, because all her complaints were true, as true as they were inevitable: nothing in the world, not even my devotion to her, would prevent me from using those coupons and free days to go off alone with my two boys.

Upon seeing that I wasn't going to change my mind, Agustina pulled an old trick from her sleeve: she told me she had a feeling that something bad was going to happen, and only someone who has the dubious fortune of living with a visionary can understand the tyranny this represents, because by raising the alarm of impending danger, the visionary's premonitions freeze trips, plans, and impulses in such a way that you never discover whether the supposed mishap would have come about or not; or actually it does come about even when it doesn't, and the seer's will ends up being imposed on everyone else's. For example, Agustina warns, Don't go to Ibagué with the boys because something will happen to you along the way, although what she's really referring to is vague ill fortune, not a specific accident, but supposing she says, as she has before, Something bad might happen to you along the way, she has a high probability from the start of being right because life is hazardous in and of itself and likely to play dirty with us, but also because in a country like this, split from top to bottom by a mountain range, the highways, which are already in bad shape, twist and twine around abysses and as if that weren't enough, they're seized every other day by the army, the paramilitaries, or the guerrillas, who kidnap you, kill you, or assault you with grenades, beatings, gunfire, explosives, antipersonnel mines, or the massive detonation of propane tanks.

Another thing Agustina usually accomplishes with her doom-filled warnings is to make me cancel plans that for one reason or another don't appeal to her or aren't to her advantage, and on top of that I have to be grateful to her because I can't avoid the secret suspicion that it's thanks to her that I've been rescued from disaster. And finally, if I don't heed her warning and actually have an accident, even if it's something as insignificant as the engine overheating on the journey up into the mountains, then she can chant an "I told you so" that sounds triumphant even as she tries not to gloat, so when faced with this new premonition, I willed myself to keep my cool, telling her simply, No, Agustina, I promise, nothing bad will happen on this trip. And how wrong I was this time, my God, how disastrously wrong.

. . .

DO YOU HAVE A CIGARETTE, angel?, no, of course you don't, Agustina doll, you're not into that anymore; I, on the other hand, who used to be so healthy, the king of endorphins, lungs like brand new from so much exercise, have been smoking like a fiend ever since things fell apart, because believe it or not, nicotine's the only thing that keeps me halfway afloat.

That time at L'Esplanade, Spider was presiding from the head of the table propped up in his wheelchair, stiff as a frozen fish stick, the poor guy, and behind him at the next table were his two favorite lackeys, Paco Malo and the Sucker, who weren't waiting outside the way bodyguards should wait, steaming up the glass in those Mercedes that make guys like your father so proud and that don't do a thing for me, because I steer clear of heavy machinery, I ride easy, free as a bird, and full fucking throttle on my Bee Em Dubyoo bike, which is worth twice any of my friends' heaps in pickup and price, always moving smooth, with no bodyguards or hassle, my only protection my guardian angel, because I'm still the same today as I was when you met me fifteen years ago, baby, and I'll be the same till they bury me. And buried's the perfect word for this death in life I've been condemned to. But anyway, Paco Malo and the Sucker were shoveling in their rations shoulder to shoulder with the bosses, spoiling the show and giving everybody the creeps, all because Spider, who was paranoid about kidnappings, had the gall to sit a pair of thugs at the next table and let them order French wine and dishes with fancy French names, what a ridiculous sight, these two guys with pistols practically bulging out of their armpits, in scummy little ties, smacking their lips as they chewed, and if Spider wasn't so goddamn rich, that frog Courtois who owns L'Esplanade would never have permitted such a blatant show of disrespect.

At the head of the table was Spider, paralyzed from the waist down, with me to his left, and to his right your brother Joaco, who'd just socked away a fortune as a go-between in the privatization of Telefónica, and also Jorge Luis Ayerbe, who had the press after him because of a massacre of Indians in the Cauca region, which is where his ultratraditional, paramilitary-sponsoring family is from, because a few months back the Ayerbes had sent their little private troop of *paracos* to scare some Indians off state land that, according to Jorge Luis, had been the legitimate property of his family since the time of the viceroys; nothing unusual, since hiring mercenaries is what's done to control trespassing, except that this time the *paracos* started setting fire to the Indians' shelters with the Indians in-side, and as a result Jorge Luis was hounded by a raging pack of human rights defenders and an orgy of NGOs.

The other person present was, as always, Ronald Silverstein, the gringo we call Rony Silver, who poses in public as the man-ager of a Chevrolet dealership and operates under the table as a DEA agent, an open secret, completely fucking absurd, con-sidering that Spider, who can get away with anything because he's so loaded, always makes the same lame joke right in front of him, That Rony Silver, he's double trouble, wouldn't you say, boys?, and I myself used to take the liberty of calling Silver 007 to his face, the gringo smiling away, tolerating my rudeness be-cause he got a cut from me and those DEA people are more crooked than anybody, it wasn't just Silver who was getting down on all fours for me but every one of them, champions of the double standard, and your father and your brother Joaco, too, that's right, they may have been rich in pesos before, but it was me, Midas McAlister, who multiplied their profits and made them rich in dollars, because you know there's a reason they call me Midas, which is that everything I touch turns to gold, or at least that's the way it used to be, because now everything I touch turns to shit, including you, Agustina darling, I'm sorry, believe me.

• • •

AT GAI REPOS the three of us, my mother, Bichi, and I, slather ourselves with sunscreen and still we get as pink as shrimp the first few days of summer vacation while father and Joaco, who are naturally dark, tan right away and say, Be careful of the sun, it's too strong for you. Only I know, Bichi, how much you would've liked it if your first finger was longer than your middle finger and you never burned in the sun; only I know how anxiously you wished things had turned out that way, but they didn't, Bichi Bichito, you have to realize that, and you have to understand why my father scolds you for it, and scolds you with good reason. Your black curls and your pale skin and your big dark eyes like the Christ Child's are worth nothing to you, because you would much rather have been strong and a little bit ugly like them, like Joaco and my father. Angel Face, they call Bichi, because he's so pretty, and Aunt Sofi calls him Doll but our father doesn't like it, it makes him lose his temper.

Let's close the curtains, Bichi Bichito, so that it's dark in our temple, Agustina says, and the boy replies, I like it better when you say plunged into shadow, All right, so that it's plunged into shadow, and let's do it all secretly, so no one else will ever know. Each time her father hits her little brother there's a ceremony in the black night of a dark room, with a priestess who is Agustina and a novice who's you, Bichi; you're the sacred victim, the sacrificial goat, the Agnus Dei, and with your bottom still red from father's slaps, you, the Lamb, pull down your underwear to show me where it hurts and then you take your underwear all the way off, and I take my panties off, too, and I stay like that, with nothing under my school uniform, a prickly unease between my legs, a delicious little bit of fear that my mother will burst into the room and discover everything, because Bichi and his sister know very well, although they never say so, that their ceremony must be performed like this, without underwear; if it weren't, it wouldn't be sacred and the powers wouldn't be free to visit us, because it's they who choose me and not the other way around, and their visit is always connected to the tickles I feel down there.

This is the Third Call, this is our secret, although of course the true secret, the greatest mystery, the treasure of the temple, is the photographs, and that's why the real ceremony begins only when we bring them down from their hiding place on one of the ceiling beams, at the place where the beam meets the wall, leaving a small space that's invisible unless someone climbs on top of the wardrobe, but the only ones who can get up there are you and I, because that's the sanctum sanctorum, the place where the photographs are hidden and kept safe. You, Bichito, are in charge of lighting the wands of incense that make us dizzy with their threads of sweet smoke, and the two children laugh, huddled together with the joy of conspirators, because they know that never ever will anyone else find these photographs, nor will they know that I have them or that we celebrate our mass with them or that it's from them that I get my powers or that I found them by chance one afternoon after school, says Agustina, when I was rummaging secretly through the things my father keeps in his study, because although the children aren't allowed to go in, they do all the time, Agustina because she knows there are forbidden things there and her brother Joaco because he always finds some money to steal and invest in the business ventures of his friend Midas McAlister, who sells cigarettes, secondhand comics, pictures of soccer stars, and Amazonian amulets at the Boys School, anything for the idiots who hand over their allowances in exchange for junk.

After a period of astonishment, or rather several days spent examining the photographs, shut up in the bathroom, Agustina knew beyond a shadow of a doubt that he had taken them himself, my own father, not only because I found them in his study but because the furniture in them is just like his, the same window, the same desk, the same recliner, and also because my father's hobby, besides stamp collecting, is photography; my father is an excellent photographer and at home we have twelve or fifteen albums of pictures he's taken of us, at our first Communions, on our birthdays, on weekends at the house in the cold country and on vacations in Sasaima, on our visits to Paris, on our trip to see snow, and a thousand other occasions; all the pictures he takes of us prove how much he loves us, but there's nothing like these photographs, the most incredible thing is that the woman in them looks just like Aunt Sofi, is

Aunt Sofi herself, or rather at first Agustina couldn't believe it but in the end she finally had to admit that it was, because whoever sees them realizes immediately, just as Bichi realized when she showed them to him for the first time, It's her, said Bichi, it's Aunt Sofi but with no clothes on, what huge breasts Aunt Sofi has.

. . .

IT'S BECAUSE SHE'S SIMPLE, Agustina told me in a moment of calm, when I asked why she'd take food from Aunt Sofi and not from me. Aunt Sofi, who is simple, can understand why Agustina fills the house with containers of water while I, who am not simple, become upset over stupid things like something spilling, or tables being stained, or the rug getting wet, or Agustina catching a cold or going even crazier than she already is, or all of us in this house going crazy. Look, Aguilar, Aunt Sofi tells me, madness is contagious, like the flu, and when one person in a family has it, everyone catches it in turn, there's a chain reaction that no one can escape except those who've been vaccinated, and I'm one of those, I'm immune, Aguilar, that's my gift, and Agustina knows it and she trusts in that, whereas you have to learn to neutralize the charge, Tell me, Aunt Sofi, who is Agustina praying to with all this religious bustling about with water? The truth is I don't know, I think she's talking, not praying, Aunt Sofi replies, as Agustina, kneeling devoutly, covers a platter of water with a cloth and blesses it. And who is she talking to, Aunt Sofi? Why, to her own ghosts, And why does she need so much water? My understanding is that Agustina wants to clean this house, or purify it, says Aunt Sofi, and this gives me a start, as if I'd discovered shadows flickering in my wife that I'd never even suspected, And why does she want to purify the house? Because she says that it's full of lies, this morning she was relaxed as she was eating the egg I made her for breakfast and she told me that it was the lies that were making her crazy, And what does she say about her own lie, about going away for the weekend with a man to a hotel behind my back? With what man, Aguilar, what are you talking about? About the man who was with her that Sunday at the Wellington Hotel, you don't know how it torments me, You see? Now you're the one who's raving, Aguilar, that's exactly what I mean when I say that you're letting the madness contaminate you, But I saw him, Aunt Sofi, I saw him with my own eyes, Be careful, Aguilar, delirium can enter through the eyes, Then what was she doing with him, what can a man and woman possibly do in a hotel room but make love on the bed? Wait, Aguilar, wait, don't jump to foolish conclusions, because we're facing a more serious problem here, for the last few days Agustina has been talking about her father as if he wasn't dead, How long has it been since her father died? More than ten years, but she seems to have forgotten it, I don't know whether Agustina herself ever told you, Aguilar, but although she adored him, she didn't cry when he died and she wouldn't go to the funeral.

. . .

BLANCA, SWEET BLANCA, your very name clears away the shadows, says Grandfather Portulinus to his young wife, but it isn't true, because despite her efforts, Blanca isn't always able to ease his torments, on the contrary, it often happens that her very presence is a slippery slope toward all things that split and tangle, because nothing provokes a nervous person like being told to be calm, nothing troubles him like being asked not to worry, nothing thwarts his urges to soar like the charitable ministrations of a good samaritan. This is confirmed for Blanca day after day, and yet she still makes the same mistake over and over again, as if when faced with her husband's dark malady, she felt her ability to help reduced to a fumbling, clumsy distress.

There's the sleeping tree, says Portulinus, pointing to a myrtle that stands by the side of the road leading to their house, not a mango or a *ceiba* or a *caracolí* or a *jacaranda*, or any of the sumptuous, sweet-smelling trees that in the warm country crowd close together in exaggerated profusion, heavy with rain, fruit, parasites, and birds, but a myrtle, scraggly and stunted, though giant in Portulinus's memory, a myrtle that has accompanied him from the lands of his childhood and is therefore his, his tree, its shade the place where he chooses to lie down after his morning walk. He likes to repeat that the sleeping myrtle nourishes itself from airborne dreams imbibed through its outstretched branches, but someone less wrapped up in his own imaginings might simply notice that it's a tree bearing little yellow or red seeds, depending on the season or the particular efforts of each seed, something unrelated to the matter of interest just now, which is that Portulinus and Blanca have sat down under the tree to take up, once again, a certain difficult conversation, during the course of which he watches her intently, restraining his eagerness to ask her the burning question, Our tree?, and experiencing a momentary relief when he hears her confirm, Our tree. Yours and mine? Yours and mine. You and me? You and me. The two of us? Yes, my dear, the two of us.

The reassuring power of the number two, the first even number, repeated by Blanca day after day under the myrtle, brings back shreds of the tranquillity that was lost to Portulinus somewhere between Kaub and Sasaima, cities that would have little or nothing to do with each other were it not for the imaginary line that Portulinus has traced between them. For Portulinus, a man who knows alchemy and loves kabbalistic riddles, two is a number that makes it possible for him to shield himself, at least at the instant Blanca utters it, from the unbearable duality that interposes itself like a void between the sky and the earth, the beginning and the end, the male and the female, the tree and its shade, his love for his wife, Blanca, and his urgent need to escape her control.

What a burden you've become, Blanquita, Portulinus tells his wife, how fat and earthbound, while I fly over your head, light and unfettered, and comprehend the symmetry of crystals, the pathways of the blood, numbers and their analogies, the march of the constellations, the stages of life. Suddenly he sees her with new eyes, one the eye of compassion and the other the eye of scorn. How small and fat you look to me down there, my little Lard Ball, and how limited in your understanding, he says to his wife, who not only is naturally thin but has lost several pounds since his cosmic forays became frequent, forays leading her to oscillate painfully between the impulse to send him to a home for the mentally ill and the suspicion that Portulinus does in fact understand, that he understands better than anyone the framework of the constellations, the music of the spheres, the mysteries of numbers, and the unfolding of crystals.

Apparently this restlessness of his, the restlessness of a pining German, was related to a yearning to soar that drove him into a rage when it was frustrated, and that explains many of his attacks on Blanca, which were abandoned as quickly as they were launched, leaving him sunk again in the love bordering on idolatry that had tied him to her, and to her land, for more than two decades. You and me, Blanquita darling? The two of us?, he then would insist again, knowing that the only thing that could protect him from the onslaught of recklessness and the vertigo of flight was that number, the number two, which restored to him the rhythms of night and day and came as a refuge and a last chance, as absolution and the hope of a reunion between you, Blanca my love, life raft of my salvation, and me, Nicholas Portulinus, a castaway in the stormy waters of this deep unease.

•   •   •

RECONSTRUCTING THE HOURS preceding my trip to Ibagué, I remember that despite Agustina's annoyance at having been excluded from the excursion, she offered to help me prepare for it. Have you packed yet?, Yes, I've packed, Let me see, and against my will I showed her the suitcase where I'd put the few things I'd need, my bathing trunks and a novel by José Saramago. That's all? She threw up her hands, of course, and added pajamas, four T-shirts, my toothbrush, toothpaste, the flask of Roger & Gallet that she gives me for all my birthdays and that, according to her, is the cologne her father always used, the beeper in case she has to send me some urgent message, Not the beeper, Agustina, there's no service outside the city, All right, she agreed, not the beeper, but instead she slipped in a cap and several pairs of underwear, first labeling each item with the word *Aguilar* in big rounded letters, because one of her personal obsessions is that she labels everything we own, books, radios, rackets, suitcases, or overcoats, as if by stamping our name on things she were seeking to control them or make it clear that they must remain in their assigned places because, as people say, things have lives of their own. But Agustina, I protested, I'm not a schoolboy, and besides, who would ever steal the old rags I'm bringing with me, What do you mean who?, she teased, pulling my outdated trunks over her tight jeans, This little checkered number is to die for, with its triple-elastic waistband and two back pockets, blown up like a balloon for maximum comfort, nice and roomy in the legs so your balls can peek out and get a breath of fresh air.

And maybe it's true that things have lives of their own, because my rubber thongs were nowhere to be found and I insisted on taking them, why not, since things had gone this far already and at Agustina's insistence I was even saddled with pajamas, which I never wore, but since we couldn't find the thongs anywhere, I had to give up, Thank goodness, she said, thank goodness you lost those horrible thongs that made you look like an old spinster basking in the sun on her patio, But what will I walk around in, then?, Why you'll walk barefoot, Aguilar, don't even think about strutting around that resort in plaid shorts, lace-up shoes, and socks, although everyone there must dress that way, Las Palmeras Fashion.

Pretending to be a vacationer, Agustina started to shout things out like a cheerleader, prancing around the room with my trunks on, and making fun of my trip, nearly doubling over with laughter, With a B-B-B, with an A-A-A, with a B, with an A, with an L-L-S, let's all put on our thongs and head down to the pool, yaaaaay!, playtime at Las Palmeras under the supervision of specially trained staff, divide yourselves into groups by age, and hey, you old folks over there, cheer up, enter the raffle for a portable Walkman, do you remember, Aguilar, that's what it said in that pamphlet they handed us at the Supercenter once, a portable Walkman?, Think positive, friends, don't forget to pick up your personalized T-shirt with our I Love Las Palmeras logo, Yes sirree, sure as can be, Las Palmeras is the B-E-S-T! And she would have kept bouncing and shouting if I hadn't stopped her, That's enough, Agustina, stop clowning around, my resort may be tacky but Purina doesn't pay me enough for a suite at the Waldorf, Well, tacky as it may be, I would've liked to go, too, Agustina retorted, sounding gloomy again, and I said to myself, Let's not head down this path again because it'll be the same old story, so I left her alone for a while and walked down to Don Octavio's barber shop.

That evening I took her to the movies and then out for fondue at one of those vaguely Swiss chalets downtown; she decided that we should see Pasolini's *Decameron* again, and although we'd already seen it many times, we were happy, that I can say for sure. It was a quiet night and we were happy because Agustina, now that she'd gotten used to the idea of being left alone, took up her favorite sport again, which is amusing herself at my expense, this time making fun of the haircut I'd gotten from Don Octavio, a barber who shears you nearly bald so that you won't have to come back for at least three months, according to him. You look like Chiras the Chicken, Agustina told me, And who is Chiras the Chicken?, If you want to know all you have to do is look in the mirror, yes sir, Aguilar, that's quite a hairdo.

Since she already knows *The Decameron* by heart, Agustina paid no attention to it, instead spending the whole movie mocking my cropped head, and since she was still going strong when we stepped out into the cold, she began to play at covering my head with her scarf, supposedly so that I wouldn't catch cold, Let me take care of you, Aguilar, baldness is the Achilles' heel of senior citizens, and as we walked from the center of the city along Seventh Road at midnight, in other words at precisely the happy hour for muggings and stabbings, she fixed me a turban à la Greta Garbo, Bugs Bunny ears with the two ends of the scarf, and a Palestinian head covering à la Yasir Arafat, while I, tense and vigilant, watched every shape that moved on the lonely street, a couple of figures crouched over a fire on the corner of Jiménez de Quesada, sleeping in cardboard shelters in the doorway of San Francisco, a boy stoned out of his mind who followed us for a while and fortunately passed us by, and I wanted to say to my wife, who kept improvising caps, wigs, and headdresses for me, Not here, Tina darling, wait until we get home, but I didn't because I knew too well that for Agustina elation is just one step away from melancholy.

Then we climbed up to Salmona Towers, through the shadows barely dispersed by the yellow lights of Independence Park; before us was the hill of Monserrate and since its bulk was invisible in the dark, the illuminated church that sits at its summit floated in the night like a UFO. Sheltered in that church is a baroque Christ collapsed under the weight of the cross, the most beaten, broken, and long-suffering of gods, his body covered in bruises and sores and bloody wounds, poor Christ, so grievously mistreated, I thought, How plain your hurt is and how much this city of yours resembles you, this city that worships you from below and that sometimes, oh Lord, rails at you for having been marked with your fate and for being inexorably crushed by your cross. At the top of Guadalupe, the hill next to Monserrate, there rises a gigantic Virgin who tried to fold us in her embrace, and Agustina, watching how the enormous statue seemed to rise up with arms extended, radiating green light, said to me, Look, Aguilar, tonight the Virgen de Guadalupe looks like a plane. As we crossed the park I was on the alert for ambushes while she stepped on the little white buds that fall from the eucalyptus trees to make them release their scent, until sleepiness, which settled gradually over her, turned her features childish, slowed her reflexes, and made her hang from my arm and rest her head on my shoulder. Monserrate kept getting closer, and I thought, Who's left for you to watch over, old watch-post hill, when down here it seems everyone has been left to their own devices and forced to watch out for themselves.

EVEN SPIDER SALAZAR, who's so touchy he instantly pulls his ads from any media outlet that dares to mention him in any way, good or bad, even Spider allowed us to joke with him at those Thursday dinners at L'Esplanade about the most sacred thing of all: his masculinity. That night we'd already downed several bottles of Brunello di Montalcino during the main course, and then we got to joking about sex, you know, the whole macho routine, like whether so-and-so turned out to be a faggot, whether this guy is screwing that guy's wife, whether the president of the Republic appointed his lover the head of such-and-such an institute, you know how it goes, Agustina, you're nobody here if you don't claim to have screwed a long list of women, starting with your own mother.

And then Spider said, Don't be pigs, how can you talk about water around a man dying of thirst?, Spider my man, what the hell, don't tell me that little problem is still bothering you, I said, slapping him on the back, don't tell me you haven't been able to get it up yet, and if Spider let us get away with digs like that it was because deep down they made him feel better, deep down the jokes consoled him because they allowed him to believe, falsely, that his ordeal would come to an end, and anyway, we were only kidding around, mocking him slyly, making him think we weren't aware that there was no remedy for his impotence. Spider, man, there are some saints at my Aerobics Center who'd be happy to work a miracle for you, I said bluntly, like a challenge, and Spider, evasive, said, Believe me, old boy, don't think I haven't tried everything, cocaine on the dick, placenta cream, I even sent away for a Playboy bunny and all I did was make a fool of myself.

But I insisted, Agustina doll, I insisted, trusting in the girls who work for me and eager to boast, I'll bet you whatever you want, Spider my man, that the babes at the Aerobics Center will bring that dangler of yours back to life, and why did I ever open my mouth, when my ruin, and yours, too, my princess-in-waiting, began the moment Silverstein, Joaco, and Ayerbe called my bluff, because that was it, the three took the plunge, bet settled, everybody against Midas, If those chicks can make Spider happy, we'll all pay Midas; if not, he's the payola guy. And Spider? Under the circumstances Spider doesn't bet, he neither wins nor loses, Spider just puts up his best effort. Silver, Joaco, and Jorge Luis bet ten million a head, everybody against me and me against everybody, that if Spider got it up I'd pocket thirty big ones, but if he lost . . . and I knew he was going to lose. Not like that, no way, I'll be up against the wall, I said, pretending to back out even though I'd already decided to do it, to take the bet, do you see why, baby doll? Because even if I lost, I'd win in other ways.

They filled my glass thinking that if I drank enough I'd fold, and then, straight-faced, I said to Spider, Tell me the truth, Spider Salazar, swear it on the memory of your sainted mother, is it only mostly dead or dead for real?, and Spider swore on his mother that it wasn't completely dead, that sometimes he felt a tickle, something that might have been desire, and even a few times the stirrings of an erection. Then that's it, I said, I'm in, but you've got to give me three chances, which means that if the first try fails, there'll be a second, and if the second fails, I'll still have a third chance, so we can adjust our focus. Spider, old man, all you have to do is let me know what turns you on, what gets your juices flowing, and we'll go straight from there to the triumphant finale. Then Spider set his conditions, which were, most important, no whores or cheap sluts or women older than twenty-two, I want them to be white and daddy's girls, classy, the kind of college students who suit up in lycra and sweat buckets at your Aerobics Center and eat sushi with chopsticks and drink Gatorade, nice girls who speak English without an accent. And it shouldn't be just one, but a pair, though they've got to be girlie and the two of them have to work it out so that there's lots of stroking and tasteful little touches, all in front of me.

That was it, but the other three wanted to watch, know what I mean, sweetheart?, seeing is believing, witness with their own eyes whether the flag was raised. No problem, I told them, that big window in my office is a two-way mirror with a full-screen panoramic view of the gym, so we can watch and they won't see us. Amazing, a mogul like Spider, and he's as choked up as if we were really setting him on the road to salvation, Don't worry, Midas my boy, I won't let you down, and I say, Count on me, Spider, I'll arrange something deluxe with two first-class angels, and you just watch yourself lift off, and Spider, pathetic, embracing me, I'll be grateful to you forever, Midas my man, you're the best.

· · ·

SOMETIMES THE HUNCH, or the presentiment, comes to me suddenly even when we're not in the ceremony; in math class, for example, or some other class, or at Friday mass at school, when Ana Carola Cano, who has the highest soprano in the choir and who's in Agustina's class, sings the solo in the Panis Angelicus with that voice of hers that's so soaring it gives everybody goose bumps and those eyes that always seem to be full of tears, especially if the chapel is crowded and the nuns and the girls hover on a cloud of incense and can hardly breathe in the stuffy air because so many people, so many candles, and so many lilies hardly fit in the chapel, and it's there that the premonitory trembling comes over me most often, and so that no one will notice I bow my head and cover my face with both hands as if I'm burning with religious fervor, but what's really happening is that the powers are sending her the First Warning Call, shouting that their father is going to hit Bichi that night. I spend the rest of the day with a horrible migraine and can't pay attention in class because the echo of the Power that makes me act is still reverberating inside me, and it seems as if it will never be time for the four o'clock bell to ring so I can leave school, go home, and warn Bichi, since he's my little brother, after all, and I'm the one chosen by the powers to protect him.

Sometimes the voice is so insistent, so harsh, that Agustina skips school in the middle of the morning, running from Seventy-first Street and Fourth Road, which is where her school is, to Bichi's school, which is at Eighty-second and Thirteenth, just to tell him that my father is going to hit him, and since the guard at the Boys School won't let me in during classes, I make up a lie, please let fifth-grader Carlos Vicente Londoño come out because his sister is here to tell him that his grandfather is dying, and a little while later, Bichi arrives at the guardhouse all confused because he was in the middle of a geography test,

What is it, Tina, which grandfather?, and she, who realizes just then that what she's doing is ridiculous, and that it would have been better to wait until both of them got home that afternoon, nevertheless says, It's Grandfather Portulinus, the German one we never met because he went back to Europe, And what does that have to do with anything, Tina, did someone bring news that he was dying in Europe?, I guess they did, she lies, but never mind, go finish your exam, and when Bichi is already far away, she shouts, Lies, Bichito, Grandfather Portulinus has nothing to do with this, what I came to tell you is that tonight my father will hit you.

Once I've spoken these words I start back home, not paying the slightest attention to cars when I cross the street and not stopping even when I trip or step in a hole and then later at home, in the dining room, I sit at the table to have my chocolate milk and vanilla cookies with butter and jam that they always give me at five, and I make the little towers I like so much, cookie, layer of butter, layer of jam, cookie again, and back to the beginning until it's a stack this high; Agustina eats her tower of cookies and when Aminta, the cook, comes in, she asks Agustina, What happened to you, child, your knees are a mess, and when Agustina looks at them she sees that they're bleeding and that both knees are glistening with scrapes dotted with sand, scrapes that I don't know how or when I got.

And then Bichi isn't always grateful, because there are some corners of his life where he thinks he doesn't need me. Like a little prince, he says cockily to his sister, Not now, Tina, not now. That's enough, Tina, he yelled at her the last time, without coming to meet her, I don't want to talk about this now, But Bichi, it's for your own good and you're at recess, Yes, but I'm happy here playing tops with Montes and Méndez. Other times I've said to him, Bichito let's not eat in the dining room with everybody else tonight because the powers say that today for sure you'll get hit; and those times we ask my mother permission to eat in my room with the excuse that there's a television show we absolutely have to see, and my mother usually says all right, and makes Aminta bring up our food on the silver trays. When Agustina sees that Bichi's eyes are closing because he's so sleepy, she says, Now the danger is past, you can go to your room, but don't do anything to make Daddy angry on your way, The problem is I don't know what makes him angry, Tina, Everything makes him angry, Bicho, don't do anything because everything makes him angry. Then my little brother is grateful because I've saved him and the next day at breakfast he whispers in my ear, If it wasn't for you, Agustina, last night I would have suffered.

· · ·

THE LAST THING I thought about my wife before I left, watching her set about the task of painting the apartment walls for the second time that year, was how useless she was, and yet how much I loved her. I'm often struck by that dual thought, maybe because I don't feel she participates in my efforts to make a living in these difficult times; it's not easy for me, with my doctorate in literature, to resign myself to delivering dog food, and I fault Agustina for her innate lack of interest in productive activities, which simply don't suit her. She's very active, or, as it's fashionable to say now, creative; she'll knit, embroi-

der, bake, lay brick, shovel, hammer, so long as the end product has no practical or profitable purpose, and Wednesday, as
always, when I left Agustina alone at home, she was busying
herself at an arbitrary chore to disguise her inability to commit
herself to a regular job, with her hair disheveled and gathered
carelessly on top of her head in a way that always seems seductive to me even though it means that today once again she
won't be going out to look for work.

Her way of not fixing her hair means that she doesn't want
to be bothered with anything having to do with reality, and yet
it fills me with desire and, like everything about her, makes me
tremble at the privilege of keeping company with such a splen-
didly beautiful creature who so charmingly refuses to grow up,
a refusal that each day deepens the sixteen-year age difference
between us, she still so young and I no longer young at all.
Shoeless in red tights, and still in her pajamas at eleven in the
morning, she's perched on a ladder with the brush in her hand,
shouting, Ciao, amore, over the Rolling Stones at full blast, and
then at the last minute she runs to the elevator to ask me for
the millionth time whether I really think the moss green she's
chosen for the walls of our living room is a warm color. From
inside the elevator I tell her again, Yes, very warm, yes, darling,
it's a very pretty, cozy green, and at that moment the two
halves of the metal door close between us with the abruptness
of a way of life ended, because upon my return four days later,
a strange man in a hotel room gave me back an Agustina who
wasn't Agustina anymore.

I had called her Wednesday night from Ibagué to tell her
that no, despite her fears nothing bad had happened to us, and

yes, I really did think moss green was right for the living room, Thank goodness you like it, she replied, because it's looking greener than a frog pond in here, and I hung up with the peaceful sense that all was well. The truth is, I didn't call her again for the next few days, I don't quite know why, I suppose so as not to neglect my children, or in order to prove to them that the time we had together now, at least, would be devoted to them unconditionally and without interruption. I returned to Bogotá on Sunday at noon, having promised Agustina that I'd be back by ten in the morning at the latest so that we could spend the rest of the day together as we usually did, but it had been impossible to get the boys out of bed early enough, so we'd left Ibagué a few hours later than anticipated.

But what's important is that by noon I was in town, that the city was rainy and deserted, and that I left my sons at their mother's house, Hurry up and get out, boys, I said, betrayed by my impatience to see Agustina and give her the presents I'd brought her from the hot country, a sack of oranges, a bunch of plaintains, and a bag of arrowroot cakes. So that's over, I told myself, these few days with my sons were wonderful, but here we are back again, and it's Sunday. It so happened that my haste to return was due in part to certain questions sown in me by *Baltasar and Blimunda*, the Portuguese novel I'd just read about a woman who was also a seer, and those questions were, If Blimunda is a seer, why shouldn't Agustina be? What would've happened to Baltasar's soul if he hadn't trusted in Blimunda's powers? How is it that Baltasar can believe in his wife, and I can't believe in mine? All I wanted then was my quiet Sunday afternoon at home with Agustina, because our best times together had always been Sundays, free of tension, the two of us sheltered from the rest of the world and luxuriating in a glorious combination of sex, naps, reading, cold beer, and occasionally some Ron Viejo de Caldas.

I don't know why, but Sundays have always worked for me with Agustina; even at the rockiest moments they've been havens of concord and truce for the two of us, times when Agustina simply acts like what she is, a girl, a clever, pretty, naked, passionate, happy girl, and why Sundays? Well, according to her own explanation, it's because it's the only day I agree to shut doors and windows, unplug the telephone, and leave the rest of the world outside; she makes me laugh because she claims that if the universe were the size of our room and the two of us were its only inhabitants, her head would run as well as a Swiss watch. So after reading *Baltasar and Blimunda*, I couldn't wait to get home and find my own Blimunda there, she of the future-seeing eyes, still in her pajamas and perched on the ladder, brush in hand and singing along with the Stones at the top of her lungs, out of tune as always, because god knows Agustina can't sing to save her life and the funny thing is that she doesn't even realize it, maybe her family never pointed it out to her, or maybe the problem is hereditary and all of them are tone-deaf, for all I know.

I was happy and lighthearted knowing that the downpour that was already loosing its first volleys would soon burst in full over the city and that when I got home I'd watch it through the big windows from bed, with my girl in my arms, or later sitting in my cane rocker beside the heater with my feet up on the leather chest, safe from the deluge, reading the paper, and out of the corner of my eye checking every once in a while on Agustina, who would be doing exactly the same thing she'd been doing four days ago, which was painting the walls moss green according to the recommendations of feng shui for couples like us. And now it surprises me to remember that when I opened the door to my apartment that day, I was absolutely certain that the moment of my arrival would mesh perfectly with the moment of my leaving, in one continuous motion. Maybe that's why, although my first reflex was to lift my hand to press the buzzer, I changed my mind and decided to use the key, so as not to disturb what had been going on inside without interruption since my departure, which is why not finding Agustina made me so vexed and upset and even made me feel a stab of fear, and yet it wasn't the fear of someone who senses misfortune but the fear of someone who's been counting on a happiness that suddenly doesn't seem so assured. Only four days had passed, four days of absence during which anything might have happened. When I left for Ibagué, there was only half a green wall in the apartment, and upon my return the whole living room was green, by which I deduced that my wife must have stayed at home painting walls not only all of Wednesday afternoon but also all day Thursday. By the time I picked her up on Sunday at the Wellington Hotel, her mind had gone to pieces, so what I have to find out is what happened on Friday and Saturday. Not four days, but two; forty-eight hours of life erased from every clock in existence.

•   •   •

WHO KNOWS WHAT the people of Sasaima must say when they see Nicholas Portulinus sitting at the café in a corner by himself, a wool scarf wound tightly around his neck despite the heat, his gaze lost in space. But is there really a café in rural, rainy Sasaima, a remote mountain village? Of course not, it only shimmers amid the memories of a foreigner from another continent; it's probably a feed store or a bar, an ice-cream shop at best, and those who enter must say, It's the German, or It's the teacher, and then leave him alone with his bottle of beer in his hand, taking for granted that all Germans, or at least all German musicians, are like this, strange and unmoored.

Portulinus sips his beer slowly, his face puffy above his wool scarf, until Blanca comes for him and takes him away, angry at those who doubt his sanity and determined not to acknowledge his collapse before others. But in spite of her resolve, day by day the strangeness becomes plainer, the strangeness that's an ambiguous gleam in Portulinus's eye when he falls silent, a look as if he's walking lost in worlds he shares with no one, a birdlike nervousness of movement, a restlessness of swollen hands that leave damp marks on the surface of the table, hair that isn't quite right, as if he's forgotten to run a comb through it after a nap. It's also a kind of panic that comes from within and spreads like a minor contagion, but more than anything, Portulinus's madness is pain, the great pain living inside him.

Now, all these years later, two photographs of Grandfather Portulinus sit framed on the mantel at his youngest daughter, Eugenia's, house, one taken when he was twenty-nine and the other when he was thirty-nine, which make it possible to establish a before and an after, like in those advertisements for plastic surgery or weight-loss formulas, except that in this case instead of improvement there's pure decline, and the juxtaposition reveals how, in the space of ten years, the musician succumbed to an odious biological rhythm, a rhythm that must have been linked to his growing spiritual disquiet. Before: pleasant and seductive, curls that fall softly around the face, a gaze that scrutinizes while still remaining dreamy, an intense but balanced inner life. After: a flabby and long-suffering face, features recast, a dark and confused gaze, the swollen eyelids of an ugly woman who has cried for a long time, dull curls plastered clumsily against the left ear. Before, everything was still to be won, and after, everything is lost; the record is of irreversible damage to the spirit, a poisoning of the emanations of the soul.

• • •

DAY AFTER DAY following the dark episode, I park for a while in front of the Wellington Hotel, far enough from the front door so that my beat-up van won't rouse the suspicions of the doormen, and watch in the rearview mirror the movement of people on their way in or out, with or without suitcases, the flurry of bodyguards around some personage alighting from an armored Mercedes, the wariness of foreigners taking their chances on the streets of Bogotá, the bows of a bellboy in full regalia, the haggling of a street vendor selling sweets, the rapid steps of a woman crossing the street; in other words, the natural, predictable actions of all those who may be considered inhabitants of the land of the sane. They're so lucky, goddamn it,

I say to myself, and I wonder whether they can possibly be conscious of their enormous privilege.

I'm not sure what I'm waiting there for, parked outside the hotel. For Agustina's lover to return, for me to recognize him, launch myself at him, and smash his face in? I suppose not. To demand an explanation of what happened to my wife, or the hurt he inflicted on her? Maybe. But the truth is that I don't think the man will show up here, and anyway, deep down I don't even believe that he's her lover, since the only thing he did, as far as I know, was open a door; who's to say he wasn't the concierge. So I look out for vague signs, keeping watch with naïve and dim hope as if time might move backward and I could keep the dark episode from happening. Going over and over what's past has become my principal curse, reexamining it in order to formulate it in new terms, to imagine different paths than the one already taken, to retrospectively alter the course of events and prevent them from leading up to this point of extreme suffering that Agustina and I have reached.

Sometimes I step into the hotel, making sure that the older man with glasses who attended me the Sunday I came to pick up Agustina isn't on duty, then I sit at one of the tables in the lobby and order a tea with milk that a waiter brings me on a silver tray and for which I'm charged an exorbitant sum. I lie there in wait, among people hurrying about, waiting for the right moment to approach one of the desk clerks to ask for the guest register for that weekend; if they'd let me see it, I'd at least have a list of names, and behind one of those names would be a person who could tell me what I need to know, but of course I'm afraid to ask for it because they wouldn't give it to me, they'd tell me not to stick my nose into matters that don't concern me. But it does concern me, I'd shout at them, it's the only thing in the world that matters to me, though then they'd have even more reason to call security, seeing me as a potential kidnapper.

Although maybe not. Among the clerks on the night shift, I've noticed a girl with a lot of spirit, a fearless girl. I see it in the way she carries herself, like a woman fighting tooth and nail to make a living, in the way she has of looking people straight in the eye, in her skirt, four inches shorter than those of her fellow workers, in the brisk gesture with which her hand with its painted nails pushes back her ringleted hair. She shows every sign of being ready to ignore the hotel rules and risk her job in exchange for nothing, in exchange for helping someone in need; in fact she must already be irritating the manager with that disco miniskirt and nonregulation hairstyle, and all just because, because that's how she seems to be, strong and staunch and used to doing as she pleases. This country is full of people like her, and I've learned to recognize them in a flash. But what if it isn't true? I'm afraid of being wrong, and in the end I can't build up the courage to ask her anything, though of course the main obstacle is really the conviction that as soon as I return to the scene of events, what happened will repeat itself in a kind of unbearable replay; what's really holding me back, I mean, is the suspicion that those events are still pulsing in the place they occurred, and I'm afraid to face them. Tomorrow I'll do it, I tell myself as I leave the Wellington, tomorrow I'll be back, I'll wait until the Fearless Girl finishes her shift, I'll ask her to come with me to a café far from the hotel, far from the gaze of her supervisor, and I'll interrogate her.

•   •   •

OF COURSE I DIDN'T BELIEVE shit when Spider told me to bet with confidence because his pecker wasn't all the way dead yet; if I took the bet despite everything it was because ultimately I didn't mind losing, or at least that was how I explained it to myself, since after all I'd skim the money they won from the wad that Pablo Escobar sent them through me and they wouldn't even notice, how could they, when they were flapping their ears in delight at the rapturous and hygienic way they were getting rich, not sullying their hands in dirty business or being driven to sin or lifting a single finger, because all they had to do was wait for the filthy money to fall from heaven, already washed, laundered, and disinfected.

Or could you possibly have thought things were any other way, princess? Can it be that you didn't know where all those dollars came from, the dollars flowing to your brother Joaco and your father and all their buddies, and so many others from the Las Lomas Polo Club and the society circles of Bogotá and Medellín, the dollars with which they opened those fat bank accounts in the Bahamas, Panama, Switzerland, and every fiscal paradise in existence, as if they were international jetsetters? Why do you think your family welcomed me into their house like a sultan, Agustina kitten, why they dusted off the Baccarat crystal and the Christofle cutlery for me, and served me mousses and pâtés and blinis that your mother made with her own hands, even though I had gotten you pregnant and not even threats could make me marry you as your father demanded? Why do you think they treated me like a king despite it all, ignoring your rage and shame? Well, because it was thanks to me that they'd bought the lobster they were serving; don't look so surprised, sweetheart, don't tell me you hadn't already solved that little puzzle, because what would that say about your powers of divination.

The business I handled was bloodless and juicy, and had nothing to do with the Aerobics Center, which was just a front. To strip the veil from your eyes once and for all, Agustina doll, I'm going to give you a brief summary of the crooked dealings so that you see them in wide-screen Technicolor. Spider, Silver, Joaco, and a few others gave me X amount of money in checks in lowly Colombian pesos that I arranged to have delivered to Escobar, and when Escobar landed his shipment of cocaine in the USA, he returned their investment to them through me, but magic, oh magic!, now it was in dollars and had multiplied spectacularly, by three to one, four to one, even five to one, according to the blessed whim of Saint Escobar. And so, without tangling with the law or tarnishing their reputations, they became smug and invisible investors in drug-trafficking and fattened up their foreign bank accounts to the bursting point. Escobar was happy because he was laundering a fortune and I had no complaints, either, because I took a hefty cut.

The whole thing involved risks, of course, and to get mixed up in it you had to have steady nerves, because if the shipment didn't land, Pablo wouldn't even return the investment. The five-to-one deal made the old-moneys drool like crazy but it had its downside like everything else, which was that no tantrums were allowed, or in other words, the Olympian investors couldn't complain if the money was delayed or never reached them. Not to mention that any of them could be killed at any moment, according to the rights that Saint Escobar grants himself over the lives of those who get rich at his expense; I don't know whether you're following me, sweetheart, I know finances aren't your strong point, but what I'm trying to tell you is that the instant you put a dollar from Pablo in your pocket, you automatically become his pawn, a worthless lackey at his beck and call. By now you must be able to imagine who it was risking his hide in gringo-land, poking the balls of the DEA big boys over there, why who else but yours truly, Midas McAlister at your service. As soon as Pablo sent word that the oven was hot, I would fly to Miami, set myself up in an oh-so-discreet hotel in Coconut Grove, wait for the suitcases to arrive full of cash from the street sales of the drug, take what was mine and dispatch the rest to the spotless investors of Bogotá. Mission accomplished, I head back home, end of story.

. . .

TOMORROW, TOMORROW I'LL really do it, I said to myself each day, sitting in the lobby of the Wellington Hotel while I drank a cup of absurdly expensive tea. Until I did dare. Last Friday night I came into the Wellington at nine, knowing that I'd find the Fearless Girl in reception, with her long nails and stormy mane. And there she was, very businesslike and efficient, effortlessly improvising languages according to the nationality of each foreign guest, so I marched up to her, putting on my best face so that it wouldn't be immediately obvious that all I am is a poor bastard racked by despair because the woman I love went crazy on me, and in my best VIP voice I told her that I was there to make a reservation for a couple of friends who wanted to spend a few days in Bogotá, Bzz!, mistake, I made my first mistake, no one travels to Bogotá of their own accord; the only people who come here are those who have no choice, Anyway, I continued, these friends of mine are coming to Bogotá and they asked me to make a reservation for them, Of course, Señor, no problem, Well, yes, Señorita, there is a small problem, which is that they asked me to take a look at the room before I gave my approval.

At that point she seemed to glare at me with a policewoman's eyes; what if she worked for the police, like all receptionists in all hotels everywhere? You see, my friends were already here once, at this hotel, a few months ago, I was explaining more than necessary, And, well, my friends would like to have the same room they had last time because they liked the garden you can see from the window. She asked me which room it was, Room 413, I answered, and I felt sick saying that number, so intimately associated with my misfortune, I can't show you 413 because it's occupied right now, Señor, she said checking the screen and managing to hit the right keys on the computer despite her mile-long nails, each perfectly painted in stripes of red, white, and blue nail polish, like a miniature French flag, and I asked myself whether she painted the design herself, the nails of her left hand with her right, and the right-hand nails with her left?, she must be ambidextrous, this girl, to manage such a feat.

Instantly my thoughts swung to Agustina's lovely oval nails, always short and never painted, and to the mother-of-pearl case that once belonged to her grandmother Blanca, where she kept the files, tweezers, emery boards, and other tools for giving herself a *manicure*, Agustina pronounces the word in French, and when I hear her I grimace, The word exists in Spanish and it's almost identical, Agustina, we say *manicura*, see how easy?, in this country we get a *manicura* and not a *manicure*, the advantage being that we don't have to work so hard to pronounce it. Leaning there on the reception counter at the Wellington Hotel, I sweat in remorse when I realize how sharply I criticize Agustina for her rich-girl mannerisms, how cruel I am to her sometimes, but fortunately Agustina ignores my bitter remarks and keeps doing things her way, not only does she say *manicure* ten times over but she also impassively claims that the little orange emery board you use to expose the white half-moons of your nails must be made of orange-wood, my wife manages to live in a poor man's house like mine, where all we eat is hamburger because we can't afford sirloin, while at the same time she considers fussy things like those emery boards indispensable; exactly a year ago, when I was invited by a German university to travel to a symposium on the poet León de Greiff, I spent almost all the extra money I had at the duty-free shop at the Frankfurt airport buying the Clinique face creams Agustina had asked for; Marta Elena, my first wife, always made do with Pond's, which can be bought at any drugstore, but Agustina, like all her kind, has the unpleasant habit of systematically rejecting products made in this country and being prepared to pay anything for stuff from abroad, and now I'm thinking of her face, which has always seemed incredibly beautiful to me, and of her dark eyes, which no longer see me, which means that I've become invisible, ever since Agustina won't see me, I've become the invisible man.

At that moment, the Fearless Girl's voice interrupts my musings, But if you want I can show you room 416, which is practically the same thing, her voice bringing me back abruptly, Room 416, of course, thank you very much, Señorita, so long as it has a view of the acacia garden, too. It does, Señor, from a different angle, but I think you'll still be able to see the acacias, tell me when your friends plan to arrive, Aguilar makes up a date that she notes down, No problem, the little French flags confirm on the keyboard, room 413 will be available then and I promise you that those acacias won't have gone anywhere, My friends are the kind of people who pay attention to details like that, I say with a silly little laugh in an attempt to match her irony, Of course, Señor, the customer is always right.

The Fearless Girl takes me by surprise by asking me point-blank what my name is, and I tell her Sergio Stepansky, like an alter ego of the poet León de Greiff, which is the first thing that pops into my head, I'm not sure why I don't want to reveal my name to this woman I've decided to trust, Follow me, Mr. Stepansky, it's less a request than an order, so I walk behind her to the fourth floor. I was returning to the scene of events to re-live what had happened, to obtain information, to remember, to purge, to find solace, to torture myself, to have something to hold on to, for exactly what I couldn't say. My discomfort grew at each step and my breathing became agitated, so much so that the Fearless Girl asked me whether I was all right, It's nothing, I answered, I smoke too much and I get out of breath on the stairs, but since we had come up in the elevator, she gave me one of those looks that made it clear that she could see I was a little odd, and yet she said politely, Yes, smoking is no joke.

She was walking in front of me and even though some kind of death was lodged in my chest, I couldn't stop looking at her legs; she really was pretty, this girl enumerating the hotel's advantages for me, the merits that had earned it each of the five stars adorning its logo, If she only knew that I'm dying, I thought as she sang the praises of the Italian restaurant, the recently remodeled rooms, the gym with professional trainers on staff, the top floor bar open twenty-four hours a day, and there I was with my suffering on rewind, it was along this same seemingly interminable corridor, the same carpet muffling my steps, that the door that opened then opens again now; the tall, dark man who received me that day in room 413 looked more tired than upset, I still have a clear idea of his height and the color of his skin but I can't manage to fill in the rest of him, he becomes blurred in my memory or maybe I never managed to look him in the face, and I didn't hear his voice either because when I asked for Agustina all he did was let me in without a word, which means that I couldn't say whether the male voice I'd heard recorded on the answering machine when I returned from Ibagué was his, the voice that advised me to pick up Agustina at this hotel. The man opened the door for me and then must have left immediately because he wasn't there a second later, when I turned desperately to ask what had happened to my wife.

The minute I cross the threshold, I seem to see Agustina again in the corner on the floor, gazing intently out the window at the acacias; the Fearless Girl's handset rings and she answers, speaks to someone for a minute, and then says to me, Excuse me for a minute, Mr. Stepansky, but they need me downstairs, don't worry, I'll be back right away, soothing me because she suspects that something is wrong but my mind is on other things and I can't quite fathom what she's saying, Look around the room yourself if you want, adds the Fearless Girl, here's the closet and here inside is the safe, here's the bathroom, the television turns on like this, I'll be right back, excuse me for a second, Mr. Stepansky.

That day, there in her corner, my wife looked away from the acacias, then turned her head, everything happening so slowly that I had the impression that each of her movements was framed by a single, specific instant; upon seeing me she seemed to come back to life and her face softened as if suddenly bathed in relief, and she got up and came toward me like someone returning to her own kind after a long absence, You're here, she said and I held her as tight as I could, I felt her press against me and I knew that we were saved, I still didn't know what from, but we were saved, It's all over now, Agustina, as bad as it was, it's over now, let's go home, my love, I whispered in her ear, but all of a sudden I felt her whole body grow tense and push away from mine; if at first she had sought me, now she tore herself brusquely away, if before she had recognized me, an instant later she didn't know who I was; her gestures became theatrical and stagy, and she looked at me with deep dissatisfaction, Maybe it wasn't me she was waiting for, is the thought that pierces my mind now like a stiletto, I'm not going anywhere with you, she said, and her voice sounded false like that of a bad actor reciting her lines from memory, and turning her back on me and returning to her corner, she collapsed again on the rug like a broken doll and became absorbed once more in the movement of the acacia branches in the wind.

* * *

DO YOU REALLY THINK, Agustina angel, that your noble family still lives on the bounty of the land they inherited? Well, climb out of that nineteenth-century romance, doll, because your grandfather Londoño's fertile estates are nothing but pretty country today, and step down into the twentieth century and kneel before His Majesty King Don Pablo, ruler of the three Americas and absurdly rich thanks to the gringos' glorious War on Drugs, lord and master of yours truly and also of your brother, as he once was of your esteemed father. Don't you get it that the only things that flourish today on all those acres that Joaco inherited are polo ponies, country houses, and crimson sunsets, because the hard cash is slipped to him under the table from the crooks in the government and Pablo's launderettes? And do you think Pablo comes to your brother, to Spider, to any of us, because he really needs our money? In the beginning, maybe, but not anymore, darling, of course not; if he still uses us it's so he can control us, he came up with this arrangement to bring the country's oligarchy to its knees, he hinted as much to me in a single sentence the first of the two times I've seen him in person.

He'd made me catch a commercial flight to Medellín and

wait at a downtown hotel for his men to come and pick me up, then they brought me to a secret airstrip and from there I was taken to Naples in his private plane, a Cessna Titan 404 piloted by a gringo Vietnam vet. Naples? Naples is the whimsical name chosen by Pablo for one of his many properties, a place in the heart of the jungle with three Olympic-size pools and moto-cross courses and a gorgeous zoo with elephants, camels, flamingos, and all kinds of animals, because believe it or not, Pablo is a Greenpeace kind of guy and a sportsman and a liberal and a champion of animal rights.

When they introduced me to him I was disappointed, I was ready to meet the *capo di tutti capi* and what I see instead is a short fat guy with a mustache and a mop of black curls and a big paunch spilling over his belt. It was noon, it was hideously hot, and there I was, exhausted from all the traveling and stress, plopped down in the middle of a raging orgy, Pablo and his killers for hire wreathed in marijuana smoke and making out with some samba dancers in sequins and feathers that they had brought in on another plane straight from Rio, and as if the heat weren't enough, the girls were dancing the samba right on top of us, shoving themselves in our faces and making it impossible to talk, and I was sweating a river, trapped in that carnival of crap when all I wanted was to clear up the terms of the deal fast so that I could get out of there.

But Pablo, who was very attentive to me and almost shy, kept asking whether his good friend Midas wouldn't like more whiskey, how about a puff of Santa Marta Golden, how about a little roast goat, how about a samba girl to entertain me for a while, and I said, No, thanks very much, Don Pablo, I'm sorry but I'm on a tight schedule and I'd like to get back to Bogotá as soon as possible, while I was saying to myself that the last thing I needed in this godforsaken life was to get stoned and drunk in the infernal heat and gorge myself on goat and samba girls in the company of that gang of criminals in undershirts, My god, don't let them guess what I'm thinking, I thought, because they'll roast me over the fire, too.

And then Pablo brushes away the girls, calls me over to one side, and before he says goodbye speaks a single sentence, a sentence that opened my eyes once and for all, The rich men of this country are so very poor, Midas my friend, so very poor. Do you understand the implications of that, Agustina doll? It's the kind of thing that someone who's born poor can never understand, and here's this fat, monstrously intelligent guy getting it clear right off the bat, and that's why he's the one on top, baby, you better believe it; born in the slums, raised in poverty, always oppressed by the infinite wealth and absolute power of those who for generations have called themselves rich, he suddenly stumbles on the great secret, the one he was forbidden to discover, and the secret is that at this point in his short life he's already one hundred times richer than any of this country's rich men, and if he wants he can make them eat out of his hand and tuck them away in his pocket.

This oligarchy of ours still believes it controls Escobar when the exact opposite is true; to Spider Salazar, to your father, to your shark of a brother, Pablo Escobar is nothing but a lowlife who doffs his hat for them; they're making the same mistake I made, princess, and it's a suicidal one: the truth is that the fat guy has already swallowed us whole, and that's why his belly is so bloated. And me? You might say I was Escobar's waiter: I served up my friends to him on a platter, and added myself as dessert, then handed him an Alka-Seltzer as a chaser.

• • •

IF ONLY AGUSTINA would talk to me, if only I could get inside her head, which has become a space forbidden to me. Trying to get her to say something, I bring out the album of photographs from when she was a girl and leaf through it slowly, without seeming too interested, pausing as if by chance at the people in her family that I think I recognize. This tall, thin lady who must be her mother, Eugenia, surprises me because she's not as witchlike as I imagined; in fact, with that black hair, those red lips, and that white skin, she looks more like Snow White than a witch, Look Agustina, I say to her, see how much you look like your mother, but Agustina ignores me. This arrogant boy in a baseball uniform is clearly the kind of kid who's never up to any good; dark-skinned and older than Agustina, he must be her brother Joaco, always ready to perform some feat for the camera, like lifting a heavy object or plunging headfirst into the pool. This smaller boy with a pale face and jet-black eyes like his mother and sister must be the youngest, Carlos Vicente, the one they call Bichi, looking as if he's just been rescued from an orphanage. Here we see the whole clan sitting in a half circle and smiling at the photographer, and who is that pretty woman crossing an excellent pair of legs?, my God, it's Aunt Sofi, all those years ago Aunt Sofi was a knockout. And Londoño, Agustina's father, the tribal sheik? He's nowhere to be seen, unless he's the one taking the pictures; someone had to take them, of course, and everything indicates that Londoño is directing the farce but not acting in it.

There are other people, plenty of nice poses, ball games, celebrations in comfortable settings, predictable rituals of mass-produced happiness, happy birthday to you, the triumphal march from *Aïda*, should auld acquaintance be forgot, in all the old familiar places, Mozart's Requiem, the day you were born a little star smiled, the whole repertory of a life moving tidily through each of its stages, as if on purpose so the photographer can record it and stick it neatly in albums. And sometimes, never in the center, the girl who Agustina was appears, looking apprehensively at the camera, as if she doesn't feel entirely protected by this aura of well-being, as if she doesn't quite belong to this group of humans.

My intention when I brought out the album was to get Agustina's attention, to return her to a past that would disturb her and startle her from her isolation; I wanted to wrest a clue from her, or at least a comment, something that would give me a starting point. But her gaze slides over her own people as if she doesn't know them, as if I were showing her photographs of the floor staff at Sears or pictures from a two-year-old French newspaper. For the first time, I feel that something connects me to the people in her family, and that is our insignificance in her eyes; we're insignificant because we signify nothing, because we emit no signals, because Agustina isn't susceptible to the signs we make. When I return the photographs to their place on the shelf, I think that all I've managed to prove with my sad experiment is that delirium has no memory, that it reproduces by parthenogenesis, sparks itself, and shuns affection, but especially that it has no memory.

Then I look for other hints, new threads to grasp, asking myself, for example, what revelation might be had from a crossword puzzle, what fundamental combination of words or what clue might allow me to understand something that a moment ago meant nothing to me and that's suddenly of life-or-death importance. Because in her madness Agustina has developed a passion for crossword puzzles and to my surprise, on Sunday she got up early and said that she wanted to read the newspaper, something she's never done in her life because she's one of those people who doesn't concern herself with what's going on in the outside world, but on Sunday she got up early and I got up with her, nourishing some hope, because after all it was Sunday, which has always been a day of truce and harmony for us.

In fact, I'll go even further and say that I was almost certain that precisely because it was Sunday Agustina's madness would lift, or at least ease; in any case, I was prepared to interpret even the faintest sign as a symptom of the expected improvement. I watched her put a sweatshirt on over her pajamas and then, at her express request, the two of us went down to the drugstore to buy the Sunday edition of *El Tiempo*. When we returned Agustina climbed back into bed without taking off her sweatshirt and that was the first blow to my hopes because it looked as if I would never get her naked body back; that she didn't take off her sweatshirt could be understood as a warning, something akin to wearing a suit of armor, and she didn't start reading the paper we'd just brought back but instead began to fill in the horizontal and vertical rows of the crossword with an interest that for days she'd shown in nothing but her water rituals.

The armor thing requires particular emphasis, because before the dark episode, what we did on Sunday mornings was make love, and in my opinion we did it with impressive zeal, as if we were compensating for the hurried sex we were obliged to have during the week because I had to get up early in the morning and by the end of the day I was exhausted. On Sundays we'd make love from the time we got up until we were overtaken by hunger, then we'd go downstairs and eat whatever we could find in the refrigerator and come back up again and keep at it, then we would sleep or read for a while before moving again into each other's arms; sometimes she wanted us to dance and we would dance slower and slower and closer and closer together until we ended up back in bed. I don't know, it was as if Sunday really was a holy day and nothing bad could touch us then, which is why I woke up that morning full of hope, and in fact Agustina turned to me, seeking out my company again after days of icy indifference, though not to kiss me but to ask me to tell her what Spanish province begins with GUI, ends in A, and is nine letters long, and even so, that was like a gift; the sole fact that she recognized me and spoke to me was already like the difference between night and day.

Tell me the name of the salivary gland located behind the lower maxillary, Aguilar, this was the kind of question she asked me, which made me rack my brains and search the encyclopedia for the correct response that would elicit praise from her, a smile that for an instant would wipe from her face the almost blank expression that now marks it like a scar, reminding me that I loved this person once, that I still loved her, that I'd be able to love her again, this person barricaded inside her sweatshirt who got into my bed to solve a crossword puzzle and spent all day working at it with a fanatical obsession that undermined my hopes, until by evening I'd become convinced that if I asked her What's my name? she wouldn't be able to answer, though she'd be quick to say, What ancient Yucatán tribe is six letters long and starts with IT. I was afraid that if I could enter into her head, like a doll's house, and walk through the compressed space of the various rooms, the first thing I'd see, in the main room, would be candles the size of matches lit around a little coffin holding my own corpse, me dead, forgotten, faded, stiff, a Ken-size doll in Barbie's all-pink house, a ridiculous Ken abandoned in his tiny moss-green living room, I myself moss-green, too, because I've been dead for a while.

But again my head betrayed me, again the wound bled, Take off that sweatshirt and let's make love, I said to Agustina, with an ugly hint of aggression in my voice that undoubtedly sprang from my anger that she wouldn't do it with me but would with the man at the hotel. She hurled the crossword puzzle away and left the room, and when I went to find her she was rushing around with containers of water again and wouldn't speak to me or look at me, though I tried everything I could to undo my mistake and interest her once more in the crossword puzzle, Look, Agustina, who would've thought, the word that starts with P that we're missing here is palimpsest, look, it fits perfectly, but Agustina no longer wanted to have anything to do with me or the crossword puzzle or this miserable world. Could it be my fault that she's gone crazy? Or is her madness infecting me?

I'VE ACQUIRED ANOTHER POWER, says the girl Agustina, one that shakes me so hard it leaves me half dead, a power that sucks all my strength; looking back, she says, I think that's how I spent my childhood, gathering strength and accumulating power to keep my father from leaving home. Yesterday, today, many times, she's heard him fight with her mother and threaten her with the same words, do this and I'm out of here, do that and I'm out of here, and more than anything Agustina doesn't want her father to go because when he's here and he's happy it's the best thing in the world, and there's nothing, absolutely nothing like his laugh, like his clean smell of Roger & Gallet and his English shirts with blue-and-white stripes; sometimes, when the house is dark, I look at my father and it's as if he's shining, as if there's a halo around him of cleanliness, elegance, and good smells, I like it when he asks me to blow my nose or wipe some bit of food off my lips because then he hands me his white handkerchief drenched in Roger & Gallet cologne. I've seen how Maricrís Cortés's father sits her on his knees and I cling close to my father hoping he'll do the same but he doesn't, maybe if I ask him he will but I don't dare ask because it isn't really my father's way to sit his children on his knees, but I touch the gray wool of his pants, which is so soft because it's pure cashmere, my mother says, and it isn't really gray but *charcoal*, because the colors my father wears have only English names, and I idolize him even though he doesn't pay much attention to me because his favorites are Joaco, for spoiling, and

Bichi, for taunting, and because he has to work all day and when he's here he's busy with his stamp collecting.

But Agustina, who little by little has learned to be patient, waits for her turn, which always comes at nine on the dot, the time she calls the ninth hour, which is when we prepare for the night by closing all the doors and windows to protect ourselves from thieves, and my father says to me, Tina, shall we go lock up?, it's the only time he calls me Tina and not Agustina and that's when everything changes for a little while because he and I enter a world that we don't share with anyone, he gives me his heavy key ring that jingles like a cowbell and takes my hand, and we make our way around both floors of the house, starting on the top floor; we even go into the rooms that are dark and since I'm with him I'm not scared, the light that my father radiates reaches into the corners and chases the fear away, he and I are silent, we don't like to talk as we go about the sacred task of barring the shutters and bolting the doors, this is my old house, the one in the neighborhood of Teusaquillo, because the house after that was the one in La Cabrera, where it was never the ninth hour because it's a modern building that locks automatically and because by then my father didn't call me Tina anymore or give me his key ring to hold, because he had other things on his mind.

But this is the house on Caracas Avenue in Teusaquillo, and Agustina knows by heart which key fits where, the gold Yale with the notch at the top is for the door between the kitchen and the patio, the key that's stamped with a rabbit is for the back gate, the little square one that says Flexon is for the other lock, and the two longest are for the big door to the street;

LAURA RESTREPO

Agustina, who doesn't need to look at them because she recognizes them by touch, has them ready to pass to her father before he asks for them, at the moment he reaches out his hand, and she's overwhelmed with happiness when he says, Bravo, Tina, that's the one, you never get mixed up, you're even better at it than I am, When he praises me like that I think maybe he really does appreciate me even though he doesn't say so often, and I realize again that it was worth waiting for the ninth hour; whatever happens that night or the next day I'll just have to wait for it to be nine again, when my father says, Come on, Tina, and the fog lifts, because once again he'll offer Agustina his big, dark-skinned hand with its prominent veins, the wedding band on his ring finger, and on his wrist the Rolex that she was given when he died and that she started wearing herself even though it was enormous on her and hung like a bracelet; where must it be, the watch that was once her father's and is now hers, lost, the watch lost, the hand lost, the memory too vivid and the smell permanently lodged in her nose, her father's clean, cherished smell.

Agustina longs for that big, warm house, secure and brightly lit, with all of us safe inside and the dark street on the outside, so far from us that it was as if it didn't exist and couldn't hurt us with its perils, the street from which bad news comes of people who kill, of poor people with nowhere to live, of a war that's spread out of Caquetá, the valley, and the coffee-growing region, and is on its way here with its throat-slitting, a war that has already reached Sasaima, which is why we haven't returned to Gai Repos, news of roaming thieves and of corners where lepers crouch to beg, since if there was anything I feared, if there's anything I do fear, it's lepers, because pieces of their bodies fall off and the lepers don't even notice. But her father locks up the house tight, and Agustina says to him wordlessly, You are the power, you are the true power, and I bow down before you, and she focuses all her attention on handing him the right key because she's afraid that if she makes a mistake the spell will be broken and he won't say Tina anymore or hold her hand. On those nightly rounds, says Agustina, I avoid anyone who might annoy my father and make him leave us, whether it's my mother boring him, or poor Bichito, who irritates him so much, or especially her, Aunt Sofi, who is the main threat, it'll be Aunt Sofi's fault when my father and mother separate and we children are left at the mercy of the terrors outside. Or is it Aunt Sofi who keeps my father here? Do the powers visit her, too, especially when she undresses?

. . .

HOW CAN I WORK, Blanca my dove, Grandfather Portulinus would say to his wife, when the dead are making my blood run cold, when they're informing me of their sorrows with insistent little knocks on the table? Don't worry, Nicholas, let me stand between you and the dead so they can't come near you.

The preoccupations, or more accurately, obsessions, that plague Portulinus daily revolve around a multitude of puzzles and riddles that he makes himself solve as if they were matters of life or death. These include, for example, the orders sent to him by the spirits through something that Portulinus calls the letter board, and the spirits' imperceptible taps at the window, to say nothing of the jumble of words formed in crossword puzzles, the messages hidden in the notes of Portulinus's own compositions, the contents of the page of a book opened at random, the occult logic of the wrinkles in the sheets after a night of insomnia, the significant way handkerchiefs pile up in the handkerchief drawer, or even worse, the disturbing appearance of a handkerchief in the sock drawer.

One day, upon rising, Portulinus discovered a single slipper beside the bed and felt a shiver of terror at the tricks the fugitive slipper might be readying itself to play on him from its hiding place. You have to find it, he ordered Blanca, in a tone of voice that she found menacing. You have to find it, woman, because it's lying in wait. Who, Nicholas? Who's lying in wait? And in exasperation, exploding with rage, he replied, Why the cursed slipper! Cursed woman! I demand that you find the other slipper for me before it's too late!

When faced with such situations, Blanca usually maintained her composure and the customary assurance of a wife who considers the desire for symmetry to be normal—every slipper should be accompanied by its mate, according to the laws of equilibrium—and maybe her behavior was justified, since this could simply be the tantrum of a husband who refused to walk around the house with one foot shod and the other bare, a fundamental and understandable wish for any man and even more so for a temperamental, clearly gifted musician like Portulinus. After all, no one would question the sanity of Chopin if he asked George Sand to help him find his other slipper; on the contrary, it would be madness for him to walk half shod along

78

the corridors of that big, rambling Mallorcan house traversed by winds from every direction, a house that undoubtedly had icy marble or tile floors, surely hazardous for a feverish invalid who gets up for the sole purpose of going to the bathroom, so shaky and weak that it makes no sense to imagine him hopping on one foot, especially if he isn't trudging to the bathroom but rushing to the piano because a new nocturne has come to him in the throes of his fever. And why shouldn't what was true for the great Chopin also be true for Nicholas Portulinus, composer of *bambucos* and *pasillos* in the Colombian town of Sasaima?

Following the process of this logic, it's easier to understand how, despite everything, Blanca's domestic realism sometimes served as a bridge to normality for her husband, or as a parry of his frenzied thrusts, because although their approaches diverged—his unbalanced, hers obviously healthy—both ended up wanting the slipper to reappear, even if it was clear that it was always she, and never he, who took concrete action, asking the maid to come up to the room and rescue it from under the bed with a broom.

. . .

NO MORE. I CAN'T TAKE it anymore. I'm unable to contain myself, I know it's the stupidest thing I could do and yet I come right out and do it: when I get home I ask Agustina who the man in the hotel room with her was. Gesticulating like a Mexican matinee idol, I demand explanations, I throw a jealous fit, shouting at her, she who already has enough turmoil in her head, who cries at the slightest provocation, who defends herself by lashing out fiercely, who doesn't even know what's happened to her.

And since she doesn't respond I keep mercilessly insisting, I probably even shake her a little, So you don't remember? I'll make you remember then, I say and I play the man's voice recorded on the machine; third and last message (but first in order of appearance for someone playing back the messages, because on this ancient answering machine time is recorded backward), the speaker very abrupt, Isn't anybody there? Where the fuck can I call, then? Second message, same voice, which is beginning to sound impatient, Is anybody there? It's about Agustina Londoño, it's urgent, someone should come and pick her up at the Wellington Hotel because she's in bad shape. First message, same voice, still neutral at this early stage, I'm calling to ask someone to come pick up Agustina Londoño at the Wellington Hotel, on Thirteenth Road between Eighty-fifth and Eighty-sixth, she isn't well.

I really don't know why I need to upset Agustina by making her listen to this, my nerves must be shot, or it must be the urge to know what happened while I was gone, or the exhaustion of all these sleepless nights, or jealousy, jealousy above all, what a terrible thing jealousy is.

You know, Agustina, I asked myself a thousand questions that Sunday after I listened to the messages, as I sped in the van to the Wellington to pick you up, questions like why they were calling from a hotel and not from a hospital if something had happened to you, and is she really in such bad shape that she couldn't let me know herself? And why didn't the person who called identify himself? If it's a trap what kind of trap could it be? Could you have been hit by a car, kidnapped, could you have fallen, broken a bone, had a fight with your mother, could it have been a stray bullet, a mugging, but then why call me to a hotel? Someone else might have suspected that his wife had shut herself up in a hotel room to kill herself, but I never considered that possibility, I promise you, Agustina, it didn't even occur to me, because I know that suicide isn't part of your extensive repertoire. Do you know how many questions a person can ask himself over the sixty blocks that stretch from our apartment to that hotel? At least four a block, which means 240 questions, all pointless and absurd. But among them one question stood out, a doubt more pertinent than the rest, and that was whether you'd love me, Agustina, whether you'd still love me despite whatever had happened to you.

I press the repeat button on the answering machine, and Agustina, who has remained silent throughout, twists her wrist out of my grip, goes into the kitchen, brings back a jar of water, and pours the whole thing on the sofa. It's got to be cool, she says, hot things are bad, hot things hurt.

• • •

BUT LET'S GET BACK to our story, Agustina doll, let's get back to the bet that was made that Thursday at L'Esplanade. We were so carried away that we talked about nothing else all week, phone calls back and forth, big laughs at the expense of Spider and his limp dick. I made all the preparations for the first round, which was set for Friday at nine, and the others kept stopping by the Aerobics Center or giving me a buzz so I could bring them up-to-date. To refer to the matter without setting off any alarms we started to call it Operation Lazarus, after that resurrection thing.

In an unrelated turn of events, I get a visit at the Aerobics Center from a trio of fat harpies who step out of a shocking lime-green sports car as big as a boat, three dark-skinned blondes so brutally bleached it's as if they've tried to wipe out any trace of color, coconuts, they're called, I don't know whether I'm making myself clear, but I'm talking about a depressing threesome, my lovely Agustina, really cheap-looking bimbos. They show up in imitation leopard-print leggings, platform sneakers, and crap like that, all three of them bursting with enthusiasm at the idea of losing dozens of pounds and swearing to God that they're mentally prepared to start lifting weights, devote themselves to spinning, strictly follow the pineapple diet, practice yoga, and do everything they're asked, coming three times a week or more if necessary to get their figures back, because that's how they put it, their figures, so last-generation. What about stepping classes? Oh yes, wonderful, sign me up, And aerobic dance? Oh yes, how exciting, I'll take that, too, they were signing up for everything and once they had confessed their weights and ages to me and we were on intimate terms, when we were already practically like family, in fact, they hug me and come right out and tell me that they're Pablo's cousins by marriage and that it was Pablo's wife, their first cousin, who personally recommended my gym to them, and, annoyed, I say, What Pablo are you talking about, Why the only Pablo, who else, Pablo Escobar.

Just a minute, lovely ladies, I say cunningly to mask my utter horror, I have appearances to keep up here and it's obvious from the start that you've got too much money, that's what I say so I don't have to tell them to their faces that only narco whores like them would think of putting on false eyelashes to do spinning, that no amount of jogging will ever work off those hereditary spare tires, and that their massive thighs, flat asses, and short legs are signs of the lowest social origins.

So I got rid of them, Agustina doll, will you understand me if I say I have to keep a sharp eye out so that the level of the clientele doesn't plummet? And of course, letting in three mob lovelies like that, relatives of Escobar on top of everything else, would spell the end of the center, which ultimately is nothing but a front for the big money that comes from the laundering, so I kicked the coconuts out, Try the competition, darlings, Spa 92 or Superfigure at Fifteenth and 103rd, you'll lose weight faster there, I advised them, trusting that Pablo, a businessman first and foremost, would approve of my basic precautionary measures.

But apparently I was wrong. My analysis failed and I screwed myself royally, because Pablo turned out to be a man of honor first and a dealmaker second. But that's another story, Agustina angel; just hold on to it in a corner of your crazy little head, because it'll have a role to play later on. For now forget those three women as I forgot them at the time, watching them as they left in a huff and drove away down the street in their lime-green convertible, disappearing from my memory as soon as they turned the corner.

· · ·

SOMETIMES RAGE AT BICHI stirs in Agustina and she scolds him just like her father, Don't talk like a girl, she screams at him and immediately she's sorry, but she simply can't bear the idea that her father will leave home because of all the things that make him lose his temper, I hate it when my father raises his mighty hand against my little brother, says Agustina, I feel pangs in my stomach and I want to vomit when I see that each day my father is making Bichi more unhappy and withdrawn. But I also can't stand the idea of my father leaving home.

Come on, girlie boy, don't just stand there and take it, answer back, hit me harder, my father says mockingly to Bichi as he corners him with soft jabs, taunting him, and I say, Yes Bichito, hit him!, hit him Carlos Vicente Jr., show him you've got guts, if only you'd come back at him with all the fury of your manhood and testosterone and break that big nose of my father's, smash his mouth so that he bleeds even just a little bit and then maybe at last he'll be satisfied and feel proud of you and happy here with all of us, but Bicho is weak, he fails his sister when she needs him most, he only knows how to take it and take it until he's had enough and then he goes up to his room to bawl like a girl. Then all of my hatred is turned on my father and I want to shout in his face that he's a monster, a disgusting beast, a tyrant, that he's a coward mistreating a child, but in the end I don't say anything because the powers flee in disarray, and panic overtakes me, and then I think that maybe the same thing happens to my mother, who can bear anything so long as my daddy doesn't leave her.

But our ceremony is something else altogether, because during our secret ceremony Bichi and I become powerful beyond anyone's control, it's the supreme moment of our rule and command, our victory ritual. We climb up on the wardrobe, get the photographs out from the crack between the wall and the beam, and put them on my bed, first any which way, however they fall, while we organize everything else with the television turned up loud so that no one suspects. Bichi waits for me without his underwear, while I, with no panties on and that tickling feeling, go down the back stairs to the pantry and steal one of the linen napkins that my mother says used to belong to Grandmother Blanca, the German's wife. They're wide napkins, starched, that our mother puts out in the big dining room when guests come for dinner, and they have old-fashioned initials embroidered in one corner. During this part of the ceremony, Agustina must be very careful because her uniform skirt is short and pleated and if it sways the servants will realize that she's not wearing anything underneath. Taking the napkin would get me in trouble but that would be the least of it, the really bad thing would be if someone told my mother that I was running around with no panties on, because she'd be capable of killing me for that.

I bring a washbowl full of water from the bathroom, and once I'm back in my room we close the door, light the candles, and turn out the light, and with the water in the washbowl we perform our ablutions, which means that we wash our face and hands until they're free of sin, and then Agustina folds Grandmother Blanca's napkin into a triangle, makes her little brother lie on the bed and lift his legs, puts the napkin under him like a diaper, shakes on Johnson's baby powder and rubs it in well, then fastens the diaper with a safety pin. Next we dress ourselves in our vestments, mine an old burgundy velour robe of my mother's with the black mantilla that my grandmother used to wear to church around my shoulders; yours, Bichi, the diaper, and over the diaper a black kimono with white-and-yellow flowers from one Halloween when they dressed me up as a Japanese girl, we'd like to paint our faces but we don't for fear that afterward the traces of paint would give us away.

To put on their vestments, Agustina and her brother stand back to back and don't look at each other until they're ready, and then begins the most important part, the part with the photographs, the center of everything, the Last Call, because those photographs are our power cards: the aces of our truth. You and I know very well that the photographs are more dangerous than an atomic bomb, capable of destroying my father and ending his marriage to my mother and making our house and even all of La Cabrera explode, which is why before we lay them out on the black cloth we must always take the oath, speak the Words. Do you swear that you'll never reveal our secret?, I ask you in a low, solemn voice and you, Bichi, half closing your eyes, say, Yes, I swear. Do you swear that you'll never, under any circumstances or for any reason, show anyone these photographs that we've found and that belong to us alone? Yes, I swear. Do you swear that even if you're killed, you won't show them to anyone or confess to anyone that we have them? Yes, I swear. Do you know that they're dangerous, that they're a deadly weapon? Yes, I know. Do you swear by all that's most sacred that no one will ever find out about our ceremony, or anything that happens in it? Yes, I swear.

Then you make me take the same oath, with the same questions and the same answers, and we look at the photographs one by one and put them in their proper places on the bed, Aunt Sofi with her shirt undone, Aunt Sofi naked on the recliner in my father's office, Aunt Sofi sitting on the desk in high heels and silk stockings, Aunt Sofi lying on her back and showing the camera her behind, Aunt Sofi displaying her breasts as she looks at the camera with a shy smile and tilts her head in an old-fashioned way, Aunt Sofi in bra and panties, and the one that you and I like best, the one we always place highest on the slope of the pillow: Aunt Sofi in jewelry, with her hair up, and dressed in a long gown that's black and very elegant, but that leaves one breast covered and the other exposed, and neither you nor I can take our eyes off the enormous thing that Aunt Sofi has left out on purpose, fully intending for our father to fall in love with her and leave our mother, her own sister, who doesn't have awesome breasts like hers.

• • •

BUT HOW CAN I COMPOSE, sweet Blanca of mine, Portulinus asks his wife, when the living won't leave me in peace either? Relax, Nicholas, lie down here beside me on the grass, beneath the branches of our myrtle, and let the good sun warm your bones. Then he takes up the endless stream of urgent appeals again, Did you say our myrtle, our tree?, in an identical repeat performance that proceeds to the tremulous final sentence, The two of us?, and he even tries a third time to seek the assurances that will let him rest but she, who at this point knows that there's no rest to be had, is quick to say, Enough, that's enough,

Nicholas, you're making me tired, alert as she is to the rhythms and reiterations that open the door in him to wild ravings, although she'd like to say, That's enough, Nicholas, you're driving me mad, but she knows not to tread on that sensitive spot. Despite her youth, Blanca is as solid as a rock and on that rock her husband has built his life, My fortress on high, he says, or My castle stronghold, or in German, My *starkes Mädchen*, and she confirms this whenever she can, as the pages of her diary attest: "I feel that my courage is enough for what will come, and where my beloved Nicholas is concerned, that could be anything. But I live for him alone and he'll always have my love and support, whatever happens."

Blanca is *starkes Mädchen* but the one thing that makes her falter is harsh or accusatory words, and even more so on her husband's warm, fleshy lips, a feverish carnation red, as prone to revelation as to outrageous outbursts. I always believed that the difficulties Nicholas sometimes had in expressing himself in Spanish were because he was a foreigner, Blanca confessed to her two daughters, Sofi and Eugenia, when they were adults, until a cousin of his who was passing through Colombia on her way back to Germany and who came down to Sasaima to visit told me that in his native language, too, he was sometimes coherent and other times confused and stumbled over his words. From this same woman I learned that as a child, in the town of Kaub, Nicholas had serious difficulties learning to speak, and that he could scarcely stutter, if that, since he usually took refuge in a stubborn silence in which there was room only for his inner melodies. When he was four, his father, fearing deafness or mental retardation, took him to a neighboring city to have him examined by a language specialist, with the result that what he already knew perfectly well was confirmed, that the young Nicholas, a talented and precocious piano player, was slow-witted and hopeless when it came to speaking. Not even his father's threats and physical punishment could prevent him from obstinately closing his mouth and covering his ears to shut out the human voice, including his own, as if it was worming its way into his skull to burst inside him.

So in adulthood as well as in childhood, Nicholas Portulinus had a difficult relationship with words, which explains those deep silences that became more and more prolonged, If I talk to you too much, Blanca my dear, my love for you turns uncertain and slips away. That's why he made up for it by composing children's songs with simple lyrics that pleased her and made her feel that sometimes her husband was like a boy; she, who truly was a girl, saw her older husband as a sweet boy, silent and remote. But other times Nicholas would be moved to unleash a torrent of words and string together one sentence after another in bad Spanish, assembling mixed-up and dizzying trains of thought, and then Blanca was afraid and sought shelter beneath a black umbrella of inscrutability from the rain of syllables flooding her soul. At a breakneck pace and dragging out his *r*'s too much, he swears his eternal love to her, besieges her with promises of happiness, frightens her with jealous words and endless interrogations. He swamps her in speech: That's enough, Nicholas, I can't bear to hear another word, she implores him in a whisper and then a peaceful silence settles over the myrtle again. The pleasantness of midday stretches out around them, and the scattered pieces of the universe fall into place with no struggle or lingering bitterness.

At this point in their lives, resting together under the myrtle tree, they are as one, or at least that's what Blanca believes, because Portulinus is adrift, near and at the same time far. Portulinus thinks: Blanca is watching. If Blanca's enormous eyes weren't fixed on him he could recite his litany, but her vigilance prevents him from sailing as he pleases on the sea of his ruminations. In German and to himself, Portulinus begs Blanca to give him the space he needs and not to monopolize the air he breathes, that she not make all his worries her own or try to harness his thoughts, because Portulinus is and isn't with Blanca on that placid Sasaima midday under the myrtle, now that inside of him everything has begun to double and triple in meaning. The air is charged with confusion and has grown thick; the dreams in his head gradually impose themselves on the world around him, and in the middle of the radiant green of the tropics there appear before him, bleached and nocturnal, Greek ruins that have nothing to do with this time and place, the same Greek ruins he dreamed of the night before, and before and before, hearkening back in a continuous delirium to the mists of his adolescence. What am I doing amid these ominous ruins, since when did all color fade, why am I losing myself in smudges of blood, whose is all this blood that trickles on the cold smoothness of the marble and why is that boy wounded, what is he doing among the ruins and why is he bleeding, that sacred and ethereal being, that boy called Farax who exists only as a creature of my nights, that sweet, wounded Farax who has always lived in the annals of my memory?

Blanca suspects that behind Nicholas's apparent calm terrible thoughts are seething and her eyes grow huge and intense to prevent him from escaping, her gaze begging him please, by all he holds dear, to speak words that are sensible and prudent, as God intended, to renounce the too-many words and those words with a thousand meanings instead of one. Speak to me about things, not ghosts, Blanca begs her husband, not understanding that he's wandering amid ruins where things and ghosts are one and the same. Do you love me, sweet Blanca of mine?, Portulinus asks her, and she assures him that she does, I already told you I do, I love you so much it hurts, she promises him over and over again, not understanding that it's a different question that's troubling him. He wants, needs, to ask her to distance herself: Go away, woman, let me dream alone, don't talk to me about this tree here and the sun that's warming us now, don't trap me, I beg of you from the other side, where my soul has already fled. That's what he would like to say to her but he pleads for something else entirely, with equal sincerity: Don't leave me, Blanca darling, I'm nothing without you. And Portulinus's parched and spinning head isn't the only thing that's discombobulated; above all, it's reality itself, with the ambiguous weight of its double load.

* * *

WHAT I'M TRYING TO DO is this: reach into the quagmire of madness to rescue Agustina from the depths, because only my arm can pull her out and save her from drowning. That's what must be done. Or maybe not, maybe the right thing would be just the opposite, to leave her alone, let her make her way out on her own. I've loved Agustina so much; ever since I've known her I've protected her from her family, her past, the workings of her own mind. Have I alienated her from herself? Does she hate me for it, and is that why she can't find herself now, or me? I'm striving to liberate her from her inner anguish whatever the cost, refusing to accept the possibility that just now she might be better off inside than out, that behind the walls of her delirium, Agustina is perfectly happy.

Sitting at the window, Agustina is gazing out with such a lost air that she seems to exist out there, at the point of escape toward which she's directing her gaze, and not within the four walls of the apartment that enclose her. I look at her and re-member a phrase that suddenly takes on new meaning: the beautiful indifference of hysteria. Agustina is silent and indif-ferent, shedding language as one might remove a superfluous adornment. Aunt Sofi tells me that hours earlier she'd helped Agustina wash her hair with chamomile shampoo and that af-terward, upon seeing how calmly Agustina was drying her hair with a brush and the hair dryer, she left her alone for a minute while she busied herself in the kitchen. Minutes later she missed the sound of the hair dryer and went up to see what was happening and found Agustina sitting where she is now, dazed, as still as a statue, with her hair half dried. That must have been at around five in the afternoon and since then Agustina hasn't moved, or opened her mouth.

I beg Agustina to say something, a single word at least, but it's hopeless, then I sit next to her, imitating the way she's staring emptily into space, and after a while she opens her mouth and shows me her tongue: it's horribly injured, raw, as if it's been burned. Upon seeing this, a kind of howl escapes from my throat, alarming Aunt Sofi and making her come running. Feigning calm—I don't know where the woman finds such composure—she carefully examines Agustina's lacerated tongue, concludes that raw sugar is the only thing that's good for curing sores inside the mouth and brings some on a plate. Agustina sticks out her hurt tongue and lets the sugar be put on it with the docility of an animal that's been beaten, but no matter how many times I ask her how she'd done such a terrible thing to herself, she won't explain. Aunt Sofi apologizes to me for her inexcusable negligence. If only you'd seen her in the bathroom a little while ago, using the hair dryer as if nothing was wrong, as if fixing her hair was the most natural thing in the world, as if tonight she was going out to eat or to the movies, as if she wasn't sick or plotting to martyr herself as soon as I turned my back . . . I interrupt Aunt Sofi suddenly because a terrible thought has crossed my mind: Could Agustina have eaten glass? My God! Could she have eaten glass and be torn up inside, too? No, says Aunt Sofi, relax Aguilar, her tongue looks bad but it isn't cut or bleeding; it looks as if it was burned. But with what? What could she have used to burn herself so hideously? I can't take it anymore. I need to hide in the bathroom, cry a little. Cry without stopping for a day, two days, three.

Ever since she hurt her tongue, Agustina can't speak or eat anything, so her only sustenance has been Pedialyte, a serum for dehydrated children. But today she refuses even that. With a glass of serum in her hand, Sofi implores her to take a sip, but Agustina pretends that she can't hear her and when Sofi insists too much, she pushes the glass away sharply, then she comes to me, and struggling to speak the words, she says, I don't like the yellow Pedialyte, Aguilar, I want the pink kind that comes in cherry flavor. Don't make me laugh, Agustina, I tell her, and the truth is that I'm laughing as I haven't laughed since the Sunday all this began, and despite the horror of seeing the incomprehensible way she's hurt her tongue, I keep laughing to myself as I walk to the pharmacy to buy her the red cherry-flavored serum, because at certain exceptional moments, sometimes in the middle of the worst crises, normality seems to take pity on us and make brief appearances.

Last Tuesday, for example, after surviving a few horrendous days, Agustina and I had a period of quiet. It only lasted a little while, but it was heavenly. By seven I had finished making the day's deliveries and I came home with my heart in my throat, not knowing how I would find her on my return, and to my great surprise she greeted me neither with the aloofness of her prayers nor with the wrath of her attacks, but with a warm smell of cooking that misted the windowpanes in the kitchen. And in the middle of that smell, a youthful, carefree-looking Agustina was making soup on the stove, and she said to me, as if nothing had happened, It's a nice vegetable soup, Aguilar, I hope you like it. When I heard her I stood there frozen, paralyzed by surprise, not daring to move for fear that this incredible untroubled normality visiting my house for the first time in so many days would vanish; not kissing Agustina for fear of being rejected and at the same time fearing that her mood would change if I didn't kiss her; not telling her about the round of deliveries that day to avoid bringing up the subject of the lady from Quinta Camacho, a nice person who lives alone with her cocker spaniel and who calls each month to order a sack of Purina, and with whom I've never exchanged more than thankyous, she thanking me when I deliver her order and I thanking her when she pays me, and who nevertheless, I don't know how, gradually became a source of suspicion for Agustina regarding my faithfulness; all of this was before the dark episode, of course, I'm talking about jealous scenes and silly fights that until recently were a part of our life as a couple and that bored me terribly, and that I nevertheless miss now.

So that Tuesday, when I found Agustina making vegetable soup, I just stood there in the middle of the kitchen doing nothing, holding a package from Only Supercenter with the black velvet panty hose that Aunt Sofi had requested by beeper, as if nourishing myself on that amazing tranquillity sure to vanish at any moment and not return for who knows how long, and it was Agustina herself who spoke first to say that if I was tired why didn't I take a bath while she finished cooking, and she said it in the same cheerful voice she used to have before all this began. I went up to shower as she had suggested, and I stayed waiting in the bedroom, silent and trembling expectantly until she called me; she called me by my name, my last name, that is, with a shout that could almost be called happy. Soup's ready, Aguilar, she shouted from the kitchen, and I went slowly down the stairs, step by step, so as not to break the spell; she filled three bowls, one for me, one for Sofi, and one for herself, setting them on the table with hot French bread, and we sat down and ate in silence. But it was a silence without recriminations or tensions, a relaxed and benign silence that made me believe that we were finally beating it, that now we were almost home free, that Agustina was being cured of whatever it was that had come over her.

A little while later she climbed in bed on my side, entwined her legs with mine, turned on the television and said, How nice, *The Pest* is on, it's been so long since I've seen it, and she started to laugh at some of the characters' jokes and I laughed, too, cautiously, alert to any sign, any change, remembering that a few months ago I would have been annoyed if she had interrupted my reading by turning on the television, I wouldn't have said anything but it would have annoyed me, especially if the show was a mindless one like *The Pest*, and to think that the very same action that would have bothered me before now brought me back to life, as if this was all life needed to be, as if *The Pest*'s jokes were enough, and with Agustina still peaceful I surprised myself by being prepared to kneel down to give thanks, and I would have done it if I'd known to which god I owed the miracle. Agustina watched television and I watched her, her face familiar and beautiful again, as if the evil fog had cleared at last. But when *The Pest* was over and I asked her whether she wanted to turn the television off now, she looked at me again with a blank expression on her face and I knew that the respite was over.

The truth is, my wife's face has changed since she's been sick, to use a word I've heard her use to describe her own state these days. I miss her mocking look of a lost girl, the look that disturbed me so much the first time I saw it, outside of the film society, and that made me say something very gauche to her that I wouldn't have said if I hadn't been so naïve, You have the enormous eyes of a starving child, I told her, giving her fuel to make fun of me for a whole week, but in the end what I said wasn't so far off, and every once in a while there they are again, those eyes of a starving child, but only for a few moments, because when she looks at me without seeing me it's as if she no longer has eyelashes or retinas or irises or eyelids, and all that's left is hunger, a ferocious hunger that can't be satisfied. Agustina, my beautiful Agustina, is shrouded in a cold brilliance that signals distance, behind the barred door of the delirium that won't let her out or me in. Now she has a permanent look of having just spotted a hair on her plate, a grimace of simultaneous surprise and disgust, the opposite of a smile, a flutter of disappointment. And I ask myself how long this will last.

• •

MY MOTHER IS GETTING ready because tonight she's going out with my father, says Agustina, maybe they'll go to the movies or some party. She's happy and I'm keeping her company in the bathroom, a song is playing on the radio that I think is very pretty, my mother knows the words and I'm proud of her, she's singing along with the voice on the radio which she never does in front of my father because he makes fun of her and says she has a tin ear, anyway my father thinks listening to the radio is something only lower-class people do. Leaning over the sink, Agustina's mother is washing her black hair, and her only daughter, who is me, Agustina, is helping her rinse it with a jar of warm water, I pour the water over my mother's bent head and watch how it slides down her neck carrying the remains of the suds down the drain, my mother, tall and thin, dressed only in a grape-colored nylon slip trimmed with lace, I remember it clearly, says Agustina, because it must have been one of the few times in my life that my mother and I ever had a conversation.

Mother, I ask her, why don't girls wear nylon slips, Girls wear underskirts, she tells me, to show off their flouncy dresses. Now Eugenia, Agustina's mother, has pinned curls all over her head and she's drying them with the hair dryer as her daughter watches, No, I'm not looking directly at my mother, only at my mother's reflection in the mirror, I'm keeping her company in the bathroom because I like to watch how she puts her green wool dress on over the grape-colored slip, a very fitted dress because she's so slender, Mother, I don't want to wear the underskirt that makes my dress flouncy, I like dresses like the green one you're wearing to go out with my father, You'll have one when you're big, when you go out with boys, Not with boys, thinks Agustina, I'll go out with my father, For now you should wear your things, Eugenia continues, your dresses with embroidered bodices and full skirts, look at your friend Maricrís Cortés, she's lovely in the dresses that her aunt Yoya sews for her.

Tell me, Mother, what does your name mean, I've told you a thousand times already, Tell me again, Eugenia means of noble birth, And what does Agustina mean, It means venerable, Venerable?, I would rather have been called Eugenia, My mother puts on bright red lipstick and she tells me that when

I'm fifteen she'll let me wear lipstick, too, but it will be pearl pink, she doesn't like it when young girls wear red lipstick, she says that their parents shouldn't let them, that that's what pearl pink is for, it's more delicate and subtle. My mother dabs perfume behind her ears and on her wrists, the inside part, where there are little veins that carry the scent all over; she tells me that she only uses Chanel No. 5, which is what my father always gives her for her birthday, and she puts some on me, too, a little on my wrists and behind my ears, which is where it lasts. I ask her if she'll let me wear Chanel No. 5 when I'm fifteen and she says no, that the best thing for young girls is pure rose water because the stronger scents make them seem old. When her perfume is dry she fastens her pearl necklace around her neck, but not before; she warns me that perfume should never touch pearls, because it kills them. Are they alive, then? Yes, they come from the sea alive and you keep them alive with the salt of your body. And the smell of perfume kills them? It's the alcohol in perfume that kills them, silly.

The telephone rings and my mother puts down the hair dryer to go answer it, maybe it's my father calling to remind her that they're going out tonight, my mother turns down the radio so she can hear him clearly and runs to tell him that she won't be much longer, that she's practically ready now, from the bathroom Agustina hears that they're arguing on the phone and she knows that they're fighting. Aren't they going out after all, and won't her mother wear the green dress? What was the point of the pearls, the curls, or the perfume that she put on for nothing, for no one? Her mother is still in the bedroom and the hair dryer is within Agustina's reach on the bathroom cabinet, she turns it

---

on and lets the warm air blow on her face. I curl a wet lock of hair, like my mother, then I dry it and turn off the hair dryer because the noise prevents me from hearing the angry words that are being spoken, my mother's tearful voice, I look into the tube where the air comes from and I see that inside there's a coil of wire. I turn it on again and I watch the coil turn bright red, like candy. I feel the urge to touch that red wire with the tip of my tongue. My tongue wants to touch it, so red, so red, my tongue comes closer, my tongue touches it.

•   •   •

THE FRIDAY OF THE BET arrived at last, Agustina sweetheart, the day the coin would be tossed to see whether it came up erection or defeat, well, actually this would be the first attempt of three, and since Spider had made it clear that if anything in this world could touch his heart it was a pretty twosome, nice white girls with dirty minds, virginal dykes, bad kids from good families, I had set everything up according to his instructions, and I called him that morning, overcome by laughter, Everything's ready for tonight, you old rascal, and Spider at the other end of the line, stuttering in embarrassment because his wife must have been nearby, said, What's the story, Midas my boy, how's that business of ours, and I was fooling around, singing the song that goes Lady, lady of high birth and low bed; you can't imagine, Agustina darling, how worked up the man was. His manhood would be on the line that night, his pride or his humiliation in plain view of everyone, and still he was bragging on the phone, Put that deal through and don't you worry, Midas my boy, because lately I've been raring to go, and cheering him on, I said, Excellent, Spider my man, you keep your cool, because the two investors I found for you will get that business up and running in a jiffy.

Nine at night was the time set for the performance, and the place was the Aerobics Center, closed and empty by then; upstairs in my office were Rony Silver, your brother Joaco, Ayerbe, and I, hidden behind the two-way mirror in the best seats in the house, while below us the circus began with the two ballerinas doing their little number on the platform and the clown in his wheelchair, Spider all nervous laughter and prayers to God like a boy at his first Communion, and before him the pair of stark-naked girls weaving and making out to disco music under spotlights, pretty little things, giving their all, you might say, because the deal I made with them was for triple or nothing, triple if they got the client excited, nothing if they failed.

Everything was just right, five star, top ten, but the truth is, Agustina pet, that from the start you could tell the thing was a bust. Spider was writhing from the waist up, but downstairs there was still no one home, and seeing that what they were doing wasn't working, the two girls stepped up the swaying and exaggerated the touching, but nothing; they'd already taken off all their clothes, and nothing; they'd shown everything, down to their tonsils, and nothing; and somehow, back there behind the mirror, even the three of us fully functioning males lost interest after the thrill of the first fifteen minutes and began to talk politics, and Silver, who was good company that night, told us that at the American embassy, where he works, they have a machine that detects explosions and that just last Tuesday in Bogotá sixty-three bombs had gone off, Fucking stupid gringos, I said, they need machines to pick up blasts that slam us all against the ceiling, Pablo Escobar is in a bad mood, said your brother Joaco, all those bombs are because the Liberal Party has just expelled him from its slate for being a druglord, The man doesn't like being called the King of Coca, said Silver, he prefers Father of the Nation, Of course he does, it sounds more democratic, It may sound that way, but it means the same thing, Come on, Silver, man, tell us what else you pick up with that bomb-detecting machine at the embassy, your goddamn spy box must be able to let the Pentagon know each time the president of Colombia farts.

So there we were in full swing, Agustina doll, laughing at the gruesome national farce, when someone rings the bell outside, Who can it be at this time of night?, No one, I said, we won't let them in, that's all, but whoever it was had ideas of his own; tired of ringing he leaned on his car horn like he was trying to wake up the whole neighborhood, imagine, Agustina, a residential neighborhood and right there in front of the center some idiot decides to make a commotion like that, not caring who he disturbs, and Spider, who up until that moment had been a good sport, lost his temper, Tell that son of a bitch to cut the music, he shouted, because even God couldn't get it up with that racket going on, but the guy on the horn was at the door again and he was kicking it like he wanted to break it down, I'll be right back, I told the others, and high on adrenaline I took the stairs in two bounds, determined to tell the rude bastard off, and when I opened the door, Agustina doll, the blood froze in my veins; it was none other than Mystery, the bandit who was my contact with Pablo Escobar, and whom I would never in a million years meet at the Aerobics Center but rather on the outskirts of Bogotá, in the parking lot of Memory Gardens, what better place than a cemetery to meet Mystery, the walking corpse.

It's a good thing you opened the door, McAlister, he said in his eternal tone of veiled threat, I have orders from Don Pablo to give you a message, Mystery, my man, old buddy, I'm sorry about the wait, my friends and I were just having a little private party here and it never occurred to me it would be you, Shut up and listen, because I've got some big news for you, or I should say the Boss wants to do you a favor, Of course, Mystery, we can talk right here if you want, or even better in your Mazda so we're out of the cold, I suggested, doing my best to keep the wretch out of the Aerobics Center so that my esteemed partners wouldn't get a look at the kind of thugs I dealt with, it was best if they only saw the miracle and steered clear of the saint, because I'll tell you this much, Agustina princess, Mystery wasn't pretty, nothing holy about him, that's for sure, with his eyes bloodshot from crack, that skeletal look, foul breath, and greasy hair.

Mystery, my man, what brings you here, I said to him as we got in his car, but it gave me the creeps, Agustina darling, I swear, I got into that Mazda like I was headed for the electric chair, and I only did it to avoid a disastrous encounter between Mystery the sewer rat and my high-class Bogotá rat friends. Give me the news, then, Mystery, man, Nothing big, just a word from the Boss, And what is it?, Don Pablo wants you to get him two hundred million in cash by the day after tomorrow, Two hundred million?, You heard me, two hundred, and he'll return it to you in fifteen days at five to one, Five to one?, I repeated, Do I hear an echo?, Mystery retorted, with the nervous irritation of a desperate crackhead, Well, well, how generous of Pablo, I said soothingly, while mentally I calculated that a return that big would more than compensate for this god-awful little interval I was enduring, And why is that?, I asked Mystery, to conceal my eagerness, Could the great Pablo possibly have cash-flow problems? You know how things are, these are times of persecution. I imagined that Pablo, who had the Search Bloc, the DEA, and the Cali cartel on his heels lately, must not be hanging out with samba girls at his Naples property, but hunkered down in some hiding place, eyeball to eyeball with the grim reaper, And how will Pablo return it to me, if I may inquire, I asked Mystery, He'll pay it in *monitos*, that was what he said to tell you, *Monitos* are money orders, Agustina sweetheart, that's what they're called in money-laundering lingo, It'll be a great pleasure, my dear Mystery, but the tricky thing is that I can't come up with two hundred million in cash overnight, Well you see, McAlister, this is a take it or leave it kind of deal, I'll be back in fifteen days with the *monitos* in my pocket and it's up to you whether you come up with the pesos or not, oh, and one last thing, the Boss only wants you, the Informer, and the Cripple in on this, said Mystery and he vanished into the night, his tires squealing and his unhealthy aura lingering in the air behind him.

I stood there for a while feeling queasy, how the hell could I get that much money if I could only go to Spider and Silverstein, because you must realize by now, Agustina love, that it was those two Pablo Escobar meant when he referred to the Cripple and the Informer. Did Pablo know that Rony Silver worked for the DEA? well of course he did, that was why he licked his lips each time he could grease Silver's palm, and why it was Pablo himself who told me, when we started to do business together, that I should go after the gringo and get him involved, Those DEA guys are working both ends, Escobar had said, laughing, which is why when they fall, they go down twice as hard.

. . .

I DON'T KNOW, I think to myself, this tragedy is starting to take on shades of melodrama. Even Aunt Sofi, so calm and collected, sometimes talks as if she's in a soap opera. And what about Agustina, who seems plucked straight from the pages of *Jane Eyre*, and what about me, living with this anguish and these outbursts and this lack of understanding and selfhood, especially that, I feel as if my wife's illness has subjugated my identity, as if I'm a man who's been emptied out inside in order to be stuffed, like a cushion, with concern for Agustina, love for Agustina, anxiety about Agustina, resentment of Agustina. Madness is a compendium of unpleasant things: for example, it's pedantic, it's hateful, and it's tortuous. It contains a large component of unreality and maybe that's why it's theatrical, and I'm also on the verge of believing that it's defined by an absence of humor, and that's why it's so melodramatic.

Today I was bringing Agustina a cheese sandwich. I made it

for her with butter, toasting it in the waffle iron the way she likes it, and I was about to go into the bedroom when I heard Aunt Sofi ask to be forgiven, she was saying something like, Can you forgive me, Agustina?, and again, Will you ever be able to forgive me for what I did? So Aunt Sofi has a past and sins of her own. At last I'm going to find something out, I thought, and unnoticed, I waited outside the door for the conversation to begin, but the minutes went by and Agustina was still silent, neither granting forgiveness nor denying it, and then Aunt Sofi gave up, the sandwich got cold, and I went back to the kitchen to heat it up again.

Upon returning to the bedroom I found Agustina dozing and Sofi watching the news, and watching was the right word for it, because she had turned down the volume and was making do with the picture, and I shook my wife a little by the shoulder to make her eat but I only managed to get her to say, without looking at me, that she hated cheese sandwiches, and at that Aunt Sofi felt obliged to intervene, as she always does, Forgive your wife, dear, her problem is that she's suffering and she has disguised her pain as indifference, and as I chewed the rejected sandwich, I replied, Yes, I forgive my wife, Aunt Sofi, but tell me, what about you? who's supposed to forgive you?, Were you listening?, she said, then she asked whether I really wanted her to tell me and went on without waiting for an answer, I'll tell you for poor Agustina's sake, because it has to do with the involuntary role I played in this tragedy, and it involves something I did that hurt her badly, It would be better if we went downstairs, Aunt Sofi, I said, taking her by the arm, let's leave Agustina here asleep and talk in the living room, If I don't put my feet up for a while they'll explode, she said, sitting on the sofa, and I helped her settle her feet on a pile of pillows. Then I got out a bottle of Ron Viejo de Caldas, thinking it might smooth the way for a conversation that promised not to be easy, and there we were, each of us with a drink in one hand, I in the cane rocker and Aunt Sofi on the sofa with her feet up, A little music?, I asked to lighten the mood, and I put on Celina and Reutilio.

It was one of those things, Aunt Sofi said, as if she were about to start talking, but then she stopped, and was quiet for a good fifteen minutes, seeming to enjoy the relief of having her shoes off, savoring the Caldas sip by sip, and allowing herself to be soothed by the balm of Cuban *son*, and I let her be, the woman certainly deserved a moment's peace. Then she let out a laugh that was somehow lighthearted and at odds with the difficult story she'd announced she had to tell, and she asked me to listen to what Celina was singing, Listen to her, she'll explain everything, start the song over that's just finished playing, and I did as she asked and Celina began to sing the part of "The Old Horse" that goes "When love comes like this it's not your fault, when willing hearts meet love has no timetable or date." So willing hearts met and it wasn't your fault, That's right, Aguilar, willing hearts met and it was no one's fault, It's never anyone's fault, Aunt Sofi, now pour yourself another drink and let's focus on the matter of forgiveness, tell me why you were asking Agustina to forgive you, I was asking her to forgive me for some photographs that destroyed her family.

According to Aunt Sofi, her sister, Eugenia, and Eugenia's husband, Carlos Vicente Londoño, invited Aunt Sofi to live with them when they moved north, To a house that was enormous, Aunt Sofi told me, well, a house that still is enormous, because Eugenia lives there now with her son Joaco and his family; how to explain Joaco, he's someone alien to me, a man who has triumphed in life but who lives in a world that isn't mine, he's too big for his britches, as my mother would say, but he has one undeniable merit, which is that he has always taken care of Eugenia, and I tell you, Aguilar, it's a Herculean task, but that's my nephew Joaco's good side, he had to have some redeeming quality, you don't know how patient and gentle he is with his mother. My sister, Eugenia, so beautiful, because believe me she was lovely, but she's always been adrift in a kind of absence, Body without soul, city without people, Carlos Vicente would say when he looked at her, especially in the dining room, at dinner, when she was sitting at the head of the table under the slivers of rainbow from the chandeliers up above, her profile as perfect as a cameo, and just as still, just as stony.

I, on the other hand, wasn't delicate, Aguilar, I wasn't perfect, and unlike Eugenia, who was so slender, I had inherited the German frame you see today, and ever since I was young I've been big and heavy, like my father. But I was alive inside. The house was hers, the husband was hers, the children were her children. I, on the other hand, was a parasite, a freeloader, a spinster aunt they'd had to take in because I had nowhere to go, and everything I had in that house was borrowed. That's how it looked from the outside, but on the inside things were almost the reverse. Eugenia was the lonely one, the quiet one, the one who was always properly behaved and perfectly dressed, the one unable to love without suffering, the one who subsisted on appearances, and I filled the voids of affection she left. It was I, not she, who ministered to her husband in bed like a wife and who loved her children like a mother, I who did the children's homework with them and took them to the park and cared for them when they were sick, who handled the shopping and the housekeeping, because if it were up to Eugenia we would've eaten the same thing every day, not because she didn't know how to cook, she's a wonderful cook, but because of her sheer joylessness, because she left the servants to fend for themselves and never went into the kitchen, and because of the general lack of enthusiasm with which she got up each morning.

Carlos Vicente Londoño was a good man in his conventional and stuffy way, divinely well dressed, always in a dark suit, always freshly shaven and immaculate, hungry for affection, for someone to make him laugh a little; he certainly wasn't the most brilliant of men, suffice it to say that his great passions were stamp collecting and *Playboy* magazine. His tragedy was his youngest son, Bichi, a sweet, intelligent, imaginative boy, a good student, everything one might expect of a son and more, but with a certain tendency toward the feminine that his father couldn't accept and that made him suffer untold agonies. Carlos Vicente was convinced that the obligation to correct the defect and set the boy straight rested in his hands and whenever I tried to bring up the subject, he would lose his temper; he had no qualms about asking me what right I had to express an opinion when I wasn't the child's mother. To make matters worse, the boy was irresistibly beautiful, if your Agustina is lovely,

Aguilar, Bichi is even more so, and back then he radiated a be-
wildering kind of angelic light, but that only made things worse
with his father.

Eugenia had the habit of traveling for a week each year with
her three children to Disney World, in Florida, and she invited
me to come along but I refused on some pretext, unable to confess that I had my own Mickey Mouse at home, of course. That
week was the most important week of the year for me; you
can't imagine, Aguilar, what a good time Carlos Vicente and I
had, without ever having to pretend or hide because Eugenia
herself took the opportunity to give the servants their vacation,
Will you cook for Carlos Vicente, Sofi?, she asked me as she was
packing, and I said, Of course I will, don't worry, I'll see to it,
and see to it I certainly did! We danced at the cheap dance halls
or we went to see Mexican movies, always downtown or in the
south of the city, in those working-class neighborhoods where
there was no way anyone we knew would go, you know it's
farther from the north to the south of Bogotá than it is from
here to Miami, if you could've seen Carlos Vicente, always such
the society gentleman that he looked as if he'd swallowed an
umbrella, well, in the anonymity of the south he loosened up,
he was nicer to people, he danced like a dream in the dive bars,
we loved to go to the Swan, the Loose Screw, the Salomé, the
Pagan Delight; we found out where Alci Acosta and Olimpo
Cardenas were performing and we went to hear them sing,
tipsy and swooning until dawn, life only gave us a week each
year, but I swear, Aguilar, we knew how to make the best of it.

Well, it was while Eugenia and the children were away one
time that we discovered how much fun we could have taking

photos. I knew how much Carlos Vicente liked the *Playboy* bun-
nies, and I made fun of him, What strange kind of animal are
men, I'd say to him, that they prefer paper women to women of
flesh and blood, and since he was an excellent photographer, he
came up with the idea of photographing me naked and I was
happy to oblige; Now next to the fireplace, he directed, all right,
now on your way down the stairs, now on the rug, now do your
hair like this, now put that on, now take everything off, I swear
to you, Aguilar, I never saw Carlos Vicente so excited, he took
five or six rolls that he sent away to be developed, where I don't
know, far from the neighborhood anyway, and then we would
pore over the best ones, and make fun of the bad ones, in some
I looked too fat and I covered his eyes so he couldn't see them.
Incredible, I interrupt her, I bet that collection wasn't included
in the family album alongside the first Communion pictures, Be
quiet, Aguilar, let me finish telling you this before I regret it, a
day or two before the travelers' return we'd say goodbye to all
that and burn the photographs in the fireplace, but sometimes
there was one he liked a lot, and he'd say to me, Nothing can
make me burn this picture, because it's a work of art and you
look gorgeous, Don't be stubborn, Carlos Vicente, it'll cause
problems later on, Don't worry, Sofi, he'd soothe me, I'll keep it
in the safe at my office and no one knows the combination.

I stop the music and pour another round of Ron Viejo de
Caldas and just then Agustina appears in the living-room doorway in the same dirty sweatshirt that she has refused to take off
since the dark episode, with the bewitched expression of someone waiting for something that won't take place in the world
she shares with the rest of us, and she shows us the pair of

saucepans she's holding. Oh God!, sighs Aunt Sofi, lowering her feet resignedly from the cushions, she's starting up that water business again.

• • •

GRANDMOTHER BLANCA and Grandfather Portulinus leave the old myrtle and walk toward the river. Portulinus advances with difficulty through the dense weave of too-intense greens; he'd like to cover the pores and orifices of his body so that the clinging vegetal smell won't work its way into him, and he's dazed by the heat and the damp, stopping to scratch his ankles, swollen with mosquito bites. Just a little bit farther, Nicholas, says Blanca, we're almost there, and when your feet are in the water, you'll feel better. It's true, I can already hear the river, he says with relief, because the redemptive tumble of the waterfall has begun to reach his ears, the crash of clean water against the rocks of the precipice is nearby now. It's the Rhine!, Portulinus exclaims with barely contained emotion, and his wife corrects him, It's the Sweet River, dear, we're in Sasaima. In Sasaima, of course, he repeats with a fragile laugh to hide his confusion. Of course, my darling Blanca, you're right as always, this is the Sweet.

Before leaping into space, the water pauses docilely in a pool surrounded by smooth black stones; husband and wife sit on one of the stones and Blanca helps Nicholas roll up his trouser legs and take off his boots and socks, and he, more relaxed now, lets the pleasant coolness of the water rise up his feet, flood his body, and soothe his mind, How lovely it is, Blanquita, how lovely it is to watch the water flow, and she tells him that she's worried about the chronic flu that Nicasio, the steward, has. It must be consumption, says Portulinus. Not consumption, Nicholas, don't say such things, God forbid, it's just the flu, but the problem is that it's chronic. Chronic flus are called tuberculosis, says Nicholas. In German, maybe, she replies, laughing, and he says, I like when you laugh, you look so pretty. Then she tells him, The Uribe Becharas loved the *bambuco* you composed for them for their daughter Eloísa's wedding. They liked it?, he asks, I thought it would bother them because of the part about love bleeding out slowly drop by drop. And why would that bother them, when it's so pretty. Yes, but you're forgetting that the father of the groom died of hemophilia. Oh Nicholas!, you're obsessed with illnesses today. Come here, Blanca my dove, let me hold you and together let's watch the innocent way the water idles in the pool before it falls. There you have the lyrics for another *bambuco*, she jokes, and they continue on in the same vein, speaking about the things that make up their daily lives, about how many eggs the hens are laying, the lateness of the long rains, their daughter Eugenia's love of birds and their daughter Sofía's passion for dance, and Portulinus's speech flows smoothly and coherently until Blanca sees that the river, which lulls and calms him, has put him to sleep.

The Rhine, says Portulinus from his doze, and he smiles, half closing his eyes. Not the Rhine, my darling, the Sweet. Leave me be, woman, let my memory drift, what's the harm in that?, the Recknitz, the Regen, the Rhine, he repeats, speaking slowly to savor the sonority of each syllable, and he doesn't mention the Putumayo, the Amazon, or the Apaporis, which are also melodious though real and in this hemisphere, but the Danube, the Düssel, and the Eder, which are very far away if they're anywhere at all, making Blanca realize that it's time to go home. She dries his feet with her skirt, rubs saliva on the mosquito bites so they don't sting, slips his boots back on him, tying the laces well so that he won't step on them, takes his hand and leads him away, because she knows that she must prevent Portulinus's dreams from chasing after the sounds of the water. On one of the pages in her diary, Grandmother Blanca will write, "When he's tired and nervous from too much work, it soothes Nicholas to watch the river, but if he stays too long, he begins to get excited and then we must leave as soon as possible." What Grandmother Blanca doesn't say in her diary is that when Grandfather Nicholas repeats the names of the rivers of his country, the Aisch, the Aller, and the Altmülh, the Warnow, the Warta, and the Weser, he does it in strict alphabetical order. A madman's habit, manias destined to send him to his grave, or to put it another way, tics and repetitions that help him disconnect from reality, or at least from what's real for someone like Blanca. The Saale, the Spree, the Sude, and the Tauber, intones Nicholas like a prayer, and inside of him a noise begins to echo and carries him away.

That same day, upon the couple's return home after their walk to the river that Blanca knows as the Sweet and Portulinus sees as a compendium of all the rivers of Germany, Eugenia, their younger daughter, a mute creature, pale and lovely and in the flower of adolescence, gave them the news that while they were away a boy who wanted to take piano lessons had come on foot from Anapoima in search of her father. If Por-

tulinus then asked his younger daughter, What boy?, it was
merely out of courtesy to her, to Eugenia of the long face, Eugenia the muddled, the daughter with her head always in the
clouds, because the hunger assailing Portulinus just then ren-
dered him more interested in the smell of pork coming from the
oven than in listening to his daughter tell him about the boy,
since he knew in advance that what she told him would be
vague, because everything his daughter said was vague, while
Blanca, as is known from what she would later write in her diary, was already in the kitchen, dealing with the pork roast and
ignorant of their conversation. And yet Eugenia answered her
father in a more spirited way than usual, saying, A handsome
blond boy, with a knapsack on his back.

Portulinus, friendly and hospitable so long as he wasn't
muddled—and anyway why not welcome a handsome blond
boy who has arrived exhausted after traveling by foot from
Anapoima?—asked whether his daughter had invited the visitor in, whether she had at least offered him some lemonade,
but no, the boy wouldn't accept anything, he'd just announced
that if the piano teacher wasn't there, he'd return the next day.
That settled, the family sat down at the table with Nicasio, the
steward with the perpetual flu, Nicasio's wife, and a pair of
salesmen from Sasaima, and were served the pork roast with
golden creole potatoes and steamed vegetables. Portulinus was
clearheaded and charming and questioned those present about
the state of his or her health, and in the middle of the boister-
ous conversation, the girl Eugenia said, though no one was listening, that the blond boy had brought some lead soldiers in his
knapsack. He let me play with them while he was waiting for

you to come, Eugenia told them, but they didn't hear her, and we set them up in three rows in the hall and he whistled military marches and said that we had staged a great parade; he also told me that the soldiers were just a few he'd brought with him since they were his favorites, but that he had left many more at home in Anapoima.

•   •   •

WHO'S OUTSIDE, MOTHER?, asks Agustina, Who's outside, Aminta? She's talking about her first house, the one from before the family moved north, the white-and-green house in Teusaquillo, on Caracas Avenue, and there's someone outside and they won't tell her who it is. The school bus comes to pick me up early in the morning, someone blows the horn, and Aunt Sofi laughs and says, That poor bus moos like a sick cow. Where are my notebooks, Aminta, where are my pencils? But they won't let me go, they refuse to open the gate, they look out the peephole, the day had to come when even Aminta was scared of something. Mr. Leper, stand aside and let the girl by!, shouts Aunt Sofi, who doesn't live with us yet but who's the only one who knows how to fix things, Stand aside, please, Mr. Leper, Señor. Let me go, Aunt Sofi, I'm on my way to school, but she hugs me tight against her, covering my head with her white orlon sweater, the one with fake pearls instead of buttons, and we hurry out into the street like that, so that I can't see. So that I can't see what? So that I can't see who?, but Aunt Sofi isn't here anymore to answer me.

So that you don't see the leper man, says Aminta, Who is

he? A poor sick man. And why can't I see him? Your mother says you shouldn't see him, because you'll be scared. He's horrifying, the poor thing, deathly white, with rotting skin and cemetery breath. My head has managed to escape from Aunt Sofi's sweater and my eyes see him, a little, or they dream of him at night, he's a bundle of dirty rags and he's holding a piece of cardboard in his hand, a sign. The writing is clumsy, like that of a child who hasn't learned to write yet, the writing of a poor person: my mother says the poor are illiterate. That's dirty, child, What's dirty? I already know the answer, everything that comes from the street is dirty. But I want to see it, I have to see it, the leper has written something for me to read. What does it say, Aminta? What does it say, Mother? Will someone read me what it says on his dirty piece of cardboard? That we should give him money because he's from Agua de Dios, they answer, but I don't believe them. What's Agua de Dios? Hurry up, Agustina, the bus will leave without you, Let it leave, I want to know what Agua de Dios is, Agua de Dios is the leprosarium where they keep people with leprosy locked up so they don't come to the city to infect us. Then why is he here, why has he come to stand outside my house, not my house now but the one from before, did he escape from Agua de Dios to come looking for me?

Now I know why my father bars the doors at night; it's so that the Agua de Dios contagion doesn't creep in with its stinking white flesh that falls off in pieces. Tell me, Aminta, what is he like, what does he smell like, who says he has death written on his face? I want to know what he sees with his empty eye sockets, do his eyes turn to wax and melt? Aminta says his eyes turn to pus, Be quiet, stupid, don't say that! Mommy, Aminta is scaring me about the leper, you'll be sent away for lying, do you hear me, Aminta?, my mommy said she'd fire you from your job if you kept scaring the children. Now I don't have to ask anyone, because I know: I have the Power and I have the Knowledge, but I still don't have the Word. They think I don't understand but I do; I know the face of the horrible thing waiting in the dark, outside the door, quiet in the rain because it escaped from where it was locked up, the thing that stares with vacant eyes into our lit-up house. Turn off the lights, Aminta!, but she pays no attention to me. This is our house from before, the white-and-green one on Caracas Avenue where my two brothers and I were born, I'm talking about the old days. After my father closes the shutters, I go around covering up all the holes in them with my finger, one by one, because my mother says that what happens in families is private, that no one should go around sticking their noses into other people's business, that dirty laundry should be aired in private.

When faced with the Leper my powers are small and flicker out like a dying flame that hardly sheds any light anymore. Does he know he'll be victorious in the end? Does he know that one day my father will go away and won't be here to lock the doors? When we're abandoned, the Leper will triumph, Oh, Father, take my hand and let's go lock the doors, because if he's escaped from Agua de Dios it's because he already knows. Mr. Leper, stand aside and let the girl by! I don't like it, Aminta, I don't like it when Aunt Sofi shouts that word so loud, that word *girl*, because that's me, and if he learns my name he'll infect me, he'll make my name his own and crawl inside of me, he'll burrow deep in my head and make his cave there, in a nest of panic. Deep in my head there lives a panic called Leper, called Leprosarium, called Agua de Dios, that has the power to change its name whenever it wants. Sometimes, when I speak in Tongues, my panic is called the Hand of My Father, and as I grow up I realize that there are other threats.

The little holes in my house's shutters are round, splintered around the edges, like eyes with eyelashes on the wood's green face. What are those little holes, Mother? What are those little holes, Father? They always answer me, They're nothing, They're nothing. What they mean is that the shutters have holes in them and that's all, that's just the way it is, like people having eyes. One night, while we're making the rounds with the keys at the ninth hour, my father confesses that it was the April 9 snipers. I understand his words: the April 9 snipers made those holes in our house's shutters. And how did they make the holes, Father? By shooting, Were they shooting at us?, No, at the people, he tells me, but that's all he'll say. At what people, Father? People, people, these things happen and there's no point in discussing it. And were we scared?, I ask him then and he answers that I wasn't born when it happened. The number of harmful beings against whom we must protect ourselves keeps growing, the Agua de Dios lepers, the April 9 snipers, the students with battered and bloody heads, and especially the guerrilla rabble that took Sasaima; and that killed Grandfather Portulinus? Mother, did the rabble kill Grandfather Portulinus? No, Grandfather Portulinus left Grandmother Blanca and returned alone to Germany.

There are other threats that my fear seizes on because it

won't stay still; my fear is a growing beast that must be fed and that swallows everything up, beginning with Ben-Hur's mother and sister, who become lepers and wander paralyzed by shame, hiding from people's gazes in an abandoned courtyard where leaves blow in the wind. And also Messala, Ben-Hur's enemy, who is trampled by chariot wheels and the hooves of galloping horses until he's the bloodiest wreck imaginable. The theater was almost empty during the matinee and I didn't dare move in my seat, it was Aminta who took me, I think, because that afternoon my mother was sick, Leave your mother alone, she's depressed, said Aunt Sofi who didn't live with us yet, and I see Messala smashed and bloody and those two women with pasty white skin broken out in blisters who cover themselves up with cloaks and rags. Aminta tells me, Don't be afraid, child, these are things from the Bible. But I'm afraid of the Bible, it seems a terrifying book to me; my mother, who is religious, has put one in each bedroom but at night I shut mine up in the garage, because it's full of lepers.

No matter how well those two women cover themselves, the stink of their sores gives them away and that's why they take shelter in the abandoned courtyard of the house that used to be theirs when they were well, a grand house. My old house in Teusaquillo, where no one lives now, had a courtyard, too, and I ask my father whether dead leaves are blowing there. My mother says that the rabble who've risen up in the south won't come to our new house, but I know they can because they live in my memory, or in my dreams, and all dreams come from way back, from biblical times. Aunt Sofi went to the school to complain, Don't read the girl these things, she doesn't understand them and her head is already full of nonsense, that's what she said and I'm repeating it because I like how it sounds, I laugh when I remember it because I realize it's true, ever since I was little I've lived the way Aunt Sofi said, with my head full of nonsense. At school they told Aunt Sofi that it was spiritual instruction and that it was required that we read such things in religion class. Don't worry, Mommy, I know they won't be able to get into our house, that's the message I receive each night from my father's hallowed hand. And if my father leaves us? When he leaves, the great panic will begin.

In the morning I shout for Aminta to bring me breakfast in bed, on the silver tray, as my mother has taught her. Orange juice, hot milk with Milo, yucca rolls, poached egg; Aminta brings me good things. But she also brings news: That man has been standing outside the house all night, waiting. Don't lie to me, Aminta, did you see the horrible hole he has instead of a mouth? Did you see his arms, all raw? Tell me, Aminta, tell me what his sign says, how can I protect myself from him if I don't understand his message. I think I dreamed of his rotten voice coming in my window, saying: I'm infected with Lazarus's disease. Who was Lazarus, Mother? Leonorita Zafrané, the teacher who's in charge on the school bus, swears that she's seen the leper in front of my house, too. I ask her what's written on his piece of cardboard but she doesn't know either, and instead she scolds me, You're not being fair to Ben-Hur's mother and sister, she tells me, because in the end Christ the Redeemer grants them the miracle of healing. Then they don't drag themselves through the dead leaves of the courtyard at night anymore? No, not anymore. They don't hide in the courtyard of my old house in Teusaquillo? No, and they never did, you made that up, you make up too many things. Thank you, Leonorita Zafrané, thank you for erasing that nonsense from my head, my problem, Leonorita, is that my head is full of nonsense.

This afternoon my mother, Bichi, and I are out in our yellow Oldsmobile with the black convertible top, my mother driving and the two of us sitting in the backseat. We like to ride in the Oldsmobile because all you have to do to open and close its tinted windows is push a little automatic switch, and because it smells new. We've just bought it, it's the latest model. There's lots of traffic, we're stuck in the crush of cars, and then my mother gets strange, she's talking a lot and very fast. It's hot, Mommy, let me open the window, but she won't let me. Because of muggers? Yes, because of muggers. The other day a mugger yanked off Aunt Sofi's gold chain and hurt her neck. The chain is the least of it, said Aunt Sofi, who was just visiting because she didn't live with us yet, it can be replaced, but my mother's Saint Angel medallion was hanging from the chain, Well, we'll get you one just like it, promised my father, Impossible, said my mother, that medallion was an old gold coin, where will we ever find another one like it, It doesn't matter, said my father, the important thing right now is to have her seen by a doctor because she has a nasty scratch and it could get infected. Two of the mugger's fingernails left a mark on Aunt Sofi's neck, the scars are still there and my daddy tells her it's a Dracula bite, but her Saint Angel and her gold chain are gone and today she's not with us in the Oldsmobile, but we still keep the windows shut tight despite the heat, just in case. If no air comes in I feel sick, Mother, Well don't open the window even if you feel sick.

The Oldsmobile is trapped in a tight knot of cars. My mother checks again to see whether the doors are locked; she already checked but she does it again. Are you angry, Mother?, I ask because when Bichi and I are noisy she gets annoyed, but she says she isn't, it isn't that, and she tells us to come up to the front seat, beside her. Cover your eyes, children, cover your eyes tight with both hands and promise me you won't look, no matter what happens. We obey her. She clutches us as tight as she can with her right arm while she holds the steering wheel with her left; she won't let us lift our heads and we can't see what's happening outside. But we can hear shouts in the street, shouts that come closer, and we know that, although we can't see them, there are people passing the car, shouting. What's happening, Mother? Nothing, nothing's happening, those are her words but her voice is saying something else entirely. Now she tells us to get down, huddled on the floor of the car, where you put your feet, and here all I can see is the plaid of the kilt she's wearing, the pedals, the rugs, which are gray, a lost coin, some trash, Bichi's shoes, which are red and almost round they're so small, like little wheels. My mother's shoe has a very high heel and it pushes one pedal and then the other and then the first one again, accelerating and braking, accelerating and braking, and I hear her heartbeat, the ticktock of my own fear, and some little words that Bichi is saying, happy down here playing with the coin he's found under the seat. I hug him very hard, Keep playing, Bichi Bichito, nothing's going to happen to you, my powers tell me that you're safe, and I play with the coin to distract him, but I know that things are happening. What is it, Mother? Nothing. Then can we get up now and sit on the seat? No, stay down there. My mother wants to protect us, from something, from someone, I realize that, I know that things are happening around us that she can see and I can't. It's the lepers, isn't it, Mother? What makes you say that, what a ridiculous idea. They escaped from Agua de Dios and now they're here? My mother tells me not to say silly things because I'll scare my little brother. But he's already scared and he's crying!

I know it was the lepers even though later, at night, when we're home and everything is over, my father tells me a thousand times that what happened today on the street was a student protest against the government. It doesn't matter what they tell me, I don't believe them, and the next day my father shows me the pictures of the student revolt that were published in the papers, but even the pictures don't make me believe him. My father tries to explain that my mother didn't want my little brother and me to be upset, and that's why she wouldn't let us see the students running between the cars, bleeding, with their heads smashed. But I know it isn't true, I know that the lepers have come at last. Thousands of lepers have left Agua de Dios and invaded Bogotá; Sacred Hand of my Father, protect me from the invasion of the lepers. Though I know you shouldn't really trust the Hand too much.

. . .

I JUST MANAGE to hit the brake so I don't run over the beggar who suddenly appears out of the rain and crosses in front of my van, what the fuck is this suicidal lunatic doing, I almost killed him but apparently he couldn't care less, it's just part of his routine, a hazard of the trade, and before I realize what's happening he sticks a begging hand in my window, Give me something for coffee, brother, I'm freezing my balls off out here, his voice is casual as if two seconds before I hadn't nearly mowed him down and he seems satisfied, even proud of having achieved the practical and premeditated goal of stopping me by any means necessary to ask me for change: here you are again, dementia my old friend, wily bitch, I recognize your chameleon-like methods, you feed on normality and turn it to your own ends, or you mimic it so well you supplant it.

When my son Toño was seven he asked me once, Is it true that people are crazy inside, Dad? Now, pondering his question, I remember something from the day I met Agustina. I mean in person, because back then she was famous all over the country as the seer who had just used her telepathic powers to find a young Colombian hiker who'd been missing for days in Alaska, and since he was the son of the then-Minister of Mines, his fate had captured the attention of the press as the rescue mission proceeded, with the joint efforts of a group of marines there on the frozen tundra and, oh!, who but Agustina Londoño here in Bogotá, coming up with parapsychological clues, intuitively sticking pins into a map of the Arctic, and issuing paranormal predictions from the very office of the Minister of Mines. When the lost boy was finally found, the whole country, from the cabinet ministers on down, flamed with patriotic fervor as if we had qualified for the Copa América, and the press didn't hesitate to give full credit to Agustina's visionary powers, discount-

ing the will of God as well as the efforts of the marines, who in
the end were the ones who rescued him from who knows what
kind of avalanche, glacier, or northern peril.

A few days after the denouement, I was introduced to her as
we were leaving a film club. All I was told was, This is Agustina,
and not making the connection with the Alaska story, I saw only
an ordinary Agustina, though a very beautiful one, who couldn't
stop talking about how wonderful the film was and the first
thing that occurred to me was, What a pretty girl, though she's
completely crazy. But the word *crazy* didn't have negative asso-
ciations for me at the time. In the days that followed I was able
to establish that Agustina was sweet and fun, and, according to
my son Toño's theory, that she was crazy inside.

Agustina dressed all in black, like a cross between a Spanish
belle and a witch in lace mantillas, astonishingly short mini-
skirts, and cutoff gloves that left her long, gothically white fingers bare; Agustina made a living reading tarot cards, telling
fortunes, casting the I Ching, and playing the lottery, or at least
that's what she said but she really lived on a monthly allowance
from her family; Agustina had very long hair and smoked marijuana and traveled each spring with her family to Paris and
hated politics and intoxicated her admirers with a bold, barbaric
perfume called Opium; Agustina lived alone in an apartment
with no furniture, but with candles and cushions and mandalas
drawn on the floor; she rescued stray cats and was a disturbing
mix of orphan and daddy's girl, rich kid and Woodstock grand-
baby. Whereas I, a middle-class professor, sixteen years her senior, was a Marxist of the old school and a dyed-in-the-wool
militant, and therefore I scorned crazy chic in all its permuta-

tions and was uncomfortable with the phenomenon calling itself magic realism, so fashionable at the time, because I considered myself far removed from the superstitions and miracle worshipping of those around us, of whom Agustina was the prime representative.

But it was enough that she could make me laugh with her sharp wit and irreverence; it was enough that she would take my hand in hers to read my palm and ask me why I was so hard on myself when I was a good guy, a nice guy, meaning why did I take everything so seriously. It was enough that she called me an old man because I smoked Redskins, because I wore a wedding band and talked about the class struggle; it was enough that she taunted me by claiming that there was no such thing as proles—that was the word she used—and that she didn't say, as I did, stockings instead of nylons, and brassiere instead of bra, and that she didn't wear pants like the ones I had on, muddy-colored, made of synthetic fabric, bell-bottomed. They weren't exactly muddy-colored or bell-bottomed, but she'd hit the mark with the synthetic fabric and she's merciless when she finds an opening through which to get in her digs. It was enough that upon letting go of my hand she left it impregnated with a penetrating and sensual smell that I, who know nothing about drugs, thought was marijuana, and when I told her she laughed and explained that it wasn't marijuana but a perfume called Opium; and it was enough, too, that a few months later, when I went to buy her a flask of Opium as a present, I found out that French perfume cost what I made in two weeks. It was enough that she began calling me simply Aguilar, erasing my first name with a single stroke and leaving me reduced to my last name, but above all it was enough that one sunny morning in Independence Park she bent down to tie one of my shoelaces which had come undone; just like that, with no warning.

We were both sitting on a bench and I was trying unsuccessfully to get her off to a real start on one of her many enthusiastically planned and rapidly abandoned projects, an autobiography that she'd asked me to help her write, and just then she saw that my shoe was untied, and she bent down and tied it for me, and when I asked her whether an Opium girl's reputation wouldn't be tarnished by tying the shoelaces of a prole in synthetic fabric, she made a face. It was pure demagoguery. And yet it wasn't demagoguery, and that's why I fell in love; nor was it deference or submission but simply the kind, unpremeditated gesture of someone who notices an untied shoe and leans over to tie it, whoever the foot in it belongs to.

When I told Marta Elena, the mother of my children, from whom I was already separated, that I had fallen for a pretty girl because she'd bent down to tie my shoelace, she surprised me by responding, You're so Christian. Anyone else would have pegged me as a chauvinist, but Marta Elena knows me well and realizes it's not that; she's well aware of the subliminal and devastating effect on me of bishops washing the feet of the elderly, saints offering their coats to beggars, nuns devoting their lives to the sick, all those who give their lives for something or someone: the kind of excessive or exalted gesture that today seems so anachronistic. So it was that, and her astonishing beauty, that were enough to make me think, What a pretty, crazy girl, and to fall hopelessly in love with Agustina, without even suspecting that madness, not the way it was then but the way it is now, isn't beautiful at all but petrifying and horrendous.

• • •

HOW TO PUT THIS, Agustina doll, I'm not good at explanations, but do you believe in that silly thing the gringos call a winner?, well it does exist, and that's what I am, a born winner, a natural at coming out on top, which is something you should know better than anyone else, since each time we've been up against each other you've lost, and yet look at me now, down here biting the dust of defeat.

What happened was that Mystery's visit left me with a bad taste in my mouth, don't ask me why, when he'd come to offer me the deal of the century, after all, and I've never been superstitious because for that I have you, my pretty little witch-girl, but as soon as I opened the door and saw that sinister bird standing there, burning with crack fever and polluting the air with his corpse-sucking breath, I, King Midas, golden boy, superstar of the highlands, felt an uncomfortable prickle run through me. And I don't have to tell you, Agustina kitten, that Spider didn't get it up that night, it was the first failed attempt, as was to be expected, chronicle of a failure foretold, and the truth is, I was ready to quit the game right then, settle my ill-fated bet, and tell Spider, We had our fun, Spider old man, let's not fuck around with this anymore, you might as well settle for making money because lovemaking isn't in the cards now.

At this stage in the game I had hit rock bottom, and even though I'd just landed the deal of the century, I felt miserable, like I'd had enough, and what I desperately wanted was to go to bed all alone and sink into a quiet, bottomless sleep with the lights out and the blinds hermetically sealed, total blackout against the onslaught of the sun in the morning, but good old Spider, who couldn't figure out why I was suddenly so down, was whimpering, convinced it was his fault, asking me over and over again to forgive him for failing, It's not over yet, Midas my boy, he tried to console me with pathetic and groundless enthusiasm, his insistence only sending me deeper into my funk, I failed you in the end, but I swear we were millimeters from success, we would've won the bet if those two girls you brought me hadn't been so limp and lifeless, next time I want some real women, some hot pussy, no more little china dolls.

But Spider, old man, I replied, I brought you exactly the kind of girls you asked for, bilingual and ladylike and sushi-fed, Not quite, Midas my boy, I think there's some kind of generation gap here, you missed the fact that men my age like women with a little meat on their bones and you set me up with a pair of anorexics, the kind that have to be kept in the freezer, men like me want ripe, juicy flesh, and you, Midas my boy, present me with a pair of forlorn, malnourished little girls who might be nice to adopt but not to fuck. Don't worry, Spider old man, things will be looking up soon, that's what I told him, because I can be the biggest ass-kissing bastard when I have to be, and at the same time I was pretending not to be in a foul mood so I wouldn't screw up the serious business that had to be done, Don't leave yet, Spider, old man, let me send Joaco and Ayerbe home, and you stay in my office with Silver for just fifteen more minutes, because I have word from Escobar.

When I told Spider and Silver the big news, leaving out unflattering details like the fact that the Boss calls them the Cripple and the Informer, both of them sat silent, as if at first they weren't sure they liked the sound of the thing, then they started asking questions and getting caught up in doubts, like why was Pablo asking us for cash now when he'd always taken checks before, and why had he come looking for us again when so little time had passed since our last encounter, and they were right to worry, Agustina baby, because Escobar always lets at least six months go by before he comes to you again, he's not the Boss for nothing and he knows how to rotate his paid beneficiaries, I knew that perfectly well and I don't know how I could have forgotten it, I guess greed and Alzheimer's go hand in hand, what's worse is that the deal smelled bad to me from the start, but the payoff was so juicy that I decided to ignore the stench.

Something didn't smell quite right to Spider and Silver either, so they vacillated between scratching their heads and squirming at the slightest excuse, complaining, for example, about the difficulty of getting so much cash together overnight; they were acting like people who find out they've won the lottery and then gripe because they don't know what they'll do with all the money, but after a while they'd shrugged off any concerns or misgivings and were taking their Montblancs and little Hermès notepads out of their pockets to do the math, calculating deposits here and investments there, and that was when we all started to get carried away by excitement, because after all, making eight hundred million in one fell swoop is something that doesn't happen every day. But don't be late, boys, remember Pablo's condition, the hard stuff has to be here in my hand by the day after tomorrow at the latest, I warned them as we said our goodbyes out there on the pavement in front of the center, by then it was almost two in the morning, and before taking off, we were hugging and slapping one another on the back like schoolboys on graduation day, the three of us bonded in the sweetness of the coming windfall.

The next day, as I'd predicted, I woke with no desire to get up and with the feeling that I'd had a bad dream, I dreamed that somebody was chasing me, it was a paranoid kind of thing, I can't be more specific because it was hazy in my mind, Agustina princess, hazy but so terrible that I felt weak when I woke up that morning, if you can call it morning when you open your eyes and the sun is already halfway across the sky; the covers felt heavy on me, as if I'd be trapped under them forever, and I couldn't tell whether I was coming down with some kind of Asian flu, whether it was shock at the massive amount of money that was about to fall into my lap, or whether I was just shitting myself at the possibility of things turning out badly, or probably a combination of all three; the truth is that the only thing I wanted was to hibernate, I mean I didn't even have the strength to pee, because I knew that out of bed I would be slobbering and ridiculous like a helpless snail without its shell.

And when that happens to me you won't believe it but I think of you, Agustina darling, and you should take that as a fucking earth-shattering declaration of love, because I've never been the kind of person to dwell on memories, the past is always erased from my hard drive, and anything outside the present moment is the land of the forgotten, as far as I'm concerned; of course you may ask what good my declarations of love have done you when in practice I act like a pig, but it's true that I think of you when I'm alone in my bedroom, which is essentially my place of worship, and it's also true that for a scum like me, the only prayer that counts is the memory of you. That's why sometimes I think about what your life and mine might have been like if they weren't what they are, and the thought makes me tired and I sink deeper and deeper into lethargy and that's when I'm least interested in the world outside my bedroom, which in the end has become my only kingdom; you visited it on your night of horrors, Agustina doll, after you made the fuss that wrecked everything, but you were so out of it that you probably don't even remember, and don't think I blame you, Agustina my love, that family of yours has always been a collection of crazies, but the funny thing is, while it's only too plain in your case, your mother and your brother Joaco hide it beautifully, it's amazing how coolly Joaco rides his madness without being thrown, like it's one of his polo ponies, and meanwhile you, Agustina baby, are tossed back and forth and jolted up and down like in a Texas rodeo.

But I was talking to you about my bedroom, because although the outside world may have gotten too big for me, you should see me within the four walls of my room, I'm even astonished myself at how my will reaches into all eight corners without hindrance or difficulty; when I'm in my room, standing firm on my own ground, it's as if time slows down or speeds up to suit me. I showed you, Agustina, but you didn't see how slickly I turn everything on or off just by pushing a button on the remote, that pretty little toy; I smoke a joint, holding the remote like a ceremonial staff, and from the bed I dim the lights and adjust the temperature, I make my Bose stereo thunder, I open and close the curtains, I brew coffee as if by magic, I make a fire spring up instantly in the fireplace, I start the sauna or the Jacuzzi to cleanse myself with gushing water and steam myself until I'm free of dust and grit, and then I spend a while in the shower designed especially for me, with multiple jets so powerful that they could put out a fire, but which couldn't calm you that night, my pretty little lunatic, although I took turns drenching you with icy and scalding water. Everything in my room is extremely clean, Agustina doll, you don't know how much cleanliness money can buy, especially if your mother is a saint like mine and like all middle-class mothers, a saint who can warble detergent jingles and who picks up your dirty clothes and returns them to you impeccable the next day, washed and ironed and organized in perfect stacks in your closet.

The rest of my apartment doesn't interest me and that's why I didn't even try to show it to you, it's immense and boring and I've declared it part of the vast outer wastes, which must be why I haven't bought furniture for the living room yet, and why I haven't once sat down to eat in the dining room, which seats twelve, because eating alone makes me sad and the idea of having to invite eleven guests makes me feel like passing out, but the most pathetic thing of all is the terrace, which has a red-and-white-striped umbrella in the center of its eight hundred square feet, an umbrella that has yet to shade anyone from the sun, and around it there are six dwarf palm trees in pots that could grow as high as the sky for all I care; I don't think I've ever set foot on that terrace, or maybe I did once, just once, the day I came to look at the apartment to buy it. The living room, the study, the big dining room and the little one, the terrace, the kitchen, all of that is across the border; my bedroom is my kingdom, as far as I'm concerned, and the king-size bed where I sleep with pretty girls whose names I don't even ask for is a replica of the maternal womb.

It was in that very bed that I was dozing the morning after my encounter with Mystery when the telephone rang at about ten, propelling me into a sitting position, I, who had come to the firm decision to lounge lazily between the sheets until one, then to get up and go jogging, shower for a full half hour, have some granola and carrot juice for breakfast, and finally go blasting out to find the money for Pablo. But the telephone rang and it was Spider's voice saying, Come to my office, I have some gossip for you, and I said, Spider, my man, tell me whatever it is on the phone because I'm not in the mood to get up, but in his best ministerial voice, Spider let me know that the matter was private and top priority and I sped out to see him, giving up the jogging and the granola and the endless shower for fear that there might be some problem in getting the money for Pablo.

When I arrived, Spider poured me a whiskey, steered me into an empty conference room, and there, the two of us sitting alone at the end of the mile-long table, he leaned over as if to whisper some secret in my ear. I really thought he was going to tell me that he wanted out of the deal with Pablo, and I started to shake, the possibility frightening me more than anything in the world, first because my craving for the stunning profits had already taken root and second for fear of revenge, because everybody knows the Boss doesn't take no for an answer. Do you know when it was, Spider asked me, puffing his moist breath in my ear, and I replied, bewildered, When what was, When I almost managed it, Managed what, Spider my man, Well what do you think I mean, you sleepy-headed fool, I'm asking you whether you know when it was that I almost got an erection last night. And I couldn't believe the man had dragged me out of bed for something so idiotic, so I said to him, Of course I know, you old bastard, you almost got it up when you heard how much money you were going to make with Escobar, I'm serious, Midas my boy, do you know when it was? It'll be the day hell freezes over, I would have liked to answer, but instead I gathered my patience and asked with a conspiratorial air, So, old boy, tell me when it was.

Then Spider said that the night before he'd felt the stirrings of an erection each time one girl did something naughty to the other one, Do you mean like them smacking each other's asses? That's right, when they went like this and like that with the little whip, too bad it was all fake, and Spider informed me that for the second phase of Operation Lazarus he wanted the emphasis to be on the rough stuff, but this time for real, without all the pretending and toys. So you mean you want me to find you a professional masochist, one of those women in black leather and chains? Figure it out for yourself, Midas my boy; I'm giving you some general guidelines and you take care of the details, the only thing I'll spell out for you is that ever since last night I've been in the mood to see a girl suffer for real. All right,

I said to play along with him, but inside, Agustina doll, I made the decision to hold the session in private, without Joaco or Ayerbe or the gringo as witnesses, so they wouldn't find out about this new failure. Because we didn't want to waste our second shot, which after all would be the next to last, and even though I'd shaken on the bet knowing I couldn't win, deep down it drove me fucking crazy to have to lose, because a bet is a bet, Agustina baby, and in the end you want to win no matter how stupid it is.

You're staring at me with those big black eyes of yours, Agustina darling, and you're thinking that I didn't go along with Spider's idea to win the bet but out of obsequiousness. Why didn't I tell Spider the truth, why didn't I tell him that not even a crane could give his poor pecker a lift? Are you thinking that it was for the same old reason and that if I let Spider have his way it's because I'm incapable of breaking the hold that he and all the old-money types have over me? That it's because even though I try to hide my admiration for them, it's stronger than my pride, which is why sooner or later I always end up rolling over for them? If you come straight out with that moralistic crap, sweetheart, if you tell me that my worst sin is obsequiousness, I'll have to accept it even though it pains me greatly, because in the strictest sense it's true; there's something they have that I'll never have, no matter whether I give myself a hernia trying, something you have, too, and you don't realize you have, Agustina princess, or you do but you're crazy enough not to care, and that is a grandfather who inherited land and a great-grandfather who brought in the first streetcars, and diamonds that belonged to your great-aunt and a library of books in French that your great-great-grandfather collected and a christening gown of embroidered batiste kept in tissue paper for four generations until the day your mother removes it from its chest and takes it to the Carmelite nuns to have them scrub away the marks left by time and starch it, because it's your turn and you're going to wear it, too, to be baptized.

Do you understand, Agustina? Can you understand the stomach-churning agonies and the character weaknesses that not having any of that inflicts on someone like me, and what it's like to know that what you lack will never be forgotten by *them*, the people with the christening gowns starched by Carmelite nuns? Consider the syndrome. Even if you've won the Nobel Prize in Literature, like García Márquez, or you're the richest man on the planet, like Pablo Escobar, or you come in first in the Paris-Dakar rally, or you're a fucking amazing tenor in the Milan Opera, in this country you're nothing compared to one of those people with the starched christening gowns. Do you think your family appreciates a man like your husband, good old Aguilar, who's given up everything, including his career, to fight your craziness? Your family doesn't even register Aguilar, Agustina princess; to say that your mother hates him is to flatter him, because the truth is your mother doesn't even see him, and when it comes right down to it, you don't either, and that's just the way it is, no matter how he martyrs himself for you, Aguilar will always be invisible because he didn't have a christening gown. And me?, well it's the same story, princess, they kneel down and suck my dick because if it wasn't for me they'd be ruined, with their fallow lands and their diamond pendants that they don't dare take out of their safes for fear of thieves and their embroidered christening gowns that stink of mothballs. But that doesn't mean they see me. They suck my dick, but they don't see me.

Now I'm going to spare you the details of the next chapter in Operation Lazarus because it was a dirty business. All you need to know is that for the second phase of the bet I didn't try hard at all, no careful attention to detail or subtleties, I just looked in the newspaper for an S&M ad, picked up the phone, and hired a showgirl calling herself Dolores who had a little private act with her pimp involving mild torture; once we'd come to an agreement about the fee and set a date, I washed my hands of the whole affair. On the agreed-upon night, Dolores arrived at the Aerobics Center with her whip, gear, and instruments of punishment and the thing was pathetic, Agustina my love, like a small-town circus. She was perfunctory and uninspired, what you might call a bureaucrat of torture, and he was a hustler with slicked-back hair and a burgundy dinner jacket, and I swear to you, princess, that all I felt at the sight of them was gloom, so I did my duty and turned on the gym lights, then I left them down there performing for Spider and his two escorts, Paco Malo and the Sucker, who follow Spider like evil shadows, while I went up to my office, sat down with my calculator, and started to do some math because by then it had been a few days since I'd sent all the money to Escobar through Mystery and we were waiting for the miracle of the multiplication of the loaves and the fishes. I told you that the S&M woman was called Dolores, well, remember that name, Agustina doll, because Dolores's unlucky star is still shedding its fucking black light on us.

IT HAPPENED IN THE sixth month of Agustina's only pregnancy, her only pregnancy with me, that is, because she'd been
pregnant once before, and that first time had ended in a volun-
tary abortion, she'd told me about it herself and in passing let
fall the name of a Midas McAlister who was the man she'd been
sleeping with. The name, Midas McAlister, was stamped on my
brain, not only because it wasn't the first time I'd heard my
wife mention it but because it sounded familiar from somewhere else, too, probably the society pages of *El Tiempo*, or even
more likely, gossip in which he was labeled a money launderer.
But to return to our story, we'd spent five months waiting for
the baby when the doctors told us that a condition called
preeclampsia would probably cause us to lose it. From that moment on, Agustina once again devoted herself entirely, as she
had when I first met her, to that convoluted form of knowledge
that makes me so irritated and suspicious and that consists of
interpreting reality from the wrong side of the cloth, or in other
words guided not by clear and obvious signs but by a series of
secret winks and hidden manifestations that she settles on at
random and that are nevertheless invested not merely with the
power of revelation but also with the power to decide the
course of her life.

The doctors told us that only something like absolute rest
might eventually make the pregnancy go smoothly and save
the baby, and my Agustina, who clung to the child with all her
might, chose to lie in bed day and night without moving, nearly

petrified, afraid of any movement that might trigger the loss, and it was then that she began to notice the creases that formed in the sheets. Wait, Aguilar, don't move, she'd say when she woke up, lie still for a minute, I want to see what the sheets look like this morning. At first I had no idea what was happening and just watched the way she smoothed her fingers over the creases and wrinkles of the bedclothes, taking great care not to disturb them, The message is that everything will be all right and when the child is born I'll call him Carlos after my little brother, she'd inform me in relief, and then she'd be plunged into a torpor from which I couldn't wrench her even with breakfast, which I brought to her in bed every day because I knew it comforted her. What message, Agustina? What message are you talking about? The one that was written here last night in the sheets. For God's sake, Agustina, what do the sheets know! They know plenty about us, Aguilar, haven't they been soaking up our dreams and moods all night long? Don't worry, Aguilar, the sheets say the child is all right for now.

But the sheets didn't always bring us encouraging news, and more often it would happen that after studying the nonexistent map traced on the bed, Agustina would begin to cry inconsolably. The baby is suffering, she'd tell me between sobs, gripped by a despair that I didn't know how to ease, certainly not by mentioning the lab tests, which indicated stability, or by reminding her of the doctors' optimistic appraisals, or appealing to common sense. Like the sentence of a cruel judge, the folds in the sheets determined our fate and that of our child, and there was no human power that could make Agustina realize how irrational it all was.

Unfortunately, neither the doctors' efforts nor Agustina's heroic dedication did any good. We lost the baby and as a result the divinatory powers of the sheets were simply confirmed and their tyranny over us was strengthened. But this didn't happen right away. On the contrary, a few weeks after the loss, Agustina, who never mentioned the affair again and who seemed recovered in body and spirit, threw herself energetically into a business exporting hand-stamped batiks. It was a happy era, in which the apartment was turned into a full-fledged factory, and I kept stumbling into stretching frames, rolls of Bali cotton, and buckets of vegetable oils. We couldn't cook because the stove was the place where the wax was heated, so we made do with sandwiches and salads, or with fried chicken that we ordered from the restaurant on the corner, and in order to bathe we had to remove yards of cloth that dripped indigo and cochineal and who knows what other organic dyes from the shower, and I remember with particular horror a sticky yellow mass that Agustina called *kunyit*; the cursed *kunyit* stuck to everything, to the soles of our shoes, to my students' papers, to the rugs, especially the rugs, because when *kunyit* attacked a rug, it had to be left for dead.

The batik phase was one of our best times. Because you were radiant, Agustina, inventing designs and testing blends of colors. You painted a red dot on your forehead and wrapped yourself in saris, sarongs, pashminas, and pareus, and we spent all day listening to records by Garbarek, Soeur Marie Keyrouz, and Ravi Shankar. Do you remember Paksi, Agustina?, Paksi, the woman who sold crafts from Java and who looked like she was from the mountains of Boyacá, but said that she was born in Jogjakarta, the one who offered to teach you the technique and who we then had a hard time getting out of the house. But at the end of that year the batik business started to go under. Agustina, who had invested a fortune in materials and hadn't managed to export anything, grew sad and listless, so disheartened that she couldn't even get rid of the paraphernalia still cluttering our space, now simply junk and the dreary evidence of failure. Don't worry, Agustina darling, I tried to console her, minimizing the importance of the fiasco, but nothing helped, and she sank into a deep depression.

It was then that she began talking to me once more about the dictates of the sheets, which this time were telling her that the time had come to try to get pregnant again. I replied in exasperation that I couldn't care less what the sheets said, If that's what you want, if you're prepared to run the risks again, then you can count on me and we'll try, but I warn you that I'm sick of this whole business, and I refuse to accept that you have to consult the sheets, or the Ouija board, or the saints even to sleep with me, but of course Agustina wouldn't listen, Agustina has never listened to me, she wouldn't hear my protests and she kept waiting for messages and signs to appear telling her how to act and think. It was as if she'd lost the ability to form an opinion of her own, and she became paralyzed by the prospect of having to make any decision for herself. All she could say was, The doctor says . . . , the sheets indicate . . . , according to the horoscope . . . , last night you told me . . . , since you refuse . . . , my mother thinks . . . , the woman who reads my cards . . . Agustina was like an automaton, and she clung to outside opinions and random signs that sunk us neck-deep in a swamp of indecision. But this wasn't madness yet. And if it was, it had just barely announced itself.

• • •

SOME THINGS ARE BEYOND the control of my Sight, says Agustina, because they're stronger than my gift of seeing. Not even the secret photographs of Aunt Sofi have the power to control these things, and of all of them, it's the blood that disturbs me most. She means the Spilled Blood, which surprises and overwhelms her each time it escapes from where it should be, which is inside of people. When it obediently flows in its hidden pathways, blood doesn't bother me because it's invisible, it has no smell, and the rush of its many white and red globules isn't noisy at all. One would think God created it to be quiet and secret, but that's not true, since blood, like steamed milk, is always waiting for the chance to spill over, and when it starts it won't stop.

Come, Bichi Bichito, little boy, come here and let me cut those fingernails of yours that are black from playing in the dirt, and Bichi, trusting, holds out his hand to his sister Agustina; my little brother's hand is so sweet, he's such an adorable boy with those black curls, and so defenseless, the two of us sit on the bed, with my left hand I hold his hand tight and in my right I hold the nail clippers, and meanwhile, with his free hand, he plays at making a little pile of the bits of lint on the wool bedspread, Bichi's mind is elsewhere as I cut his fingernails, or maybe he's not thinking of anything, maybe he's so small that his thoughts are full of the bits of lint, making him forget his own hand as Agustina, who is hardly any older, cuts the finger-nail of his little finger with a click.

A tiny piece of nail springs away and falls to the floor, and it's the tiniest thing on the planet, if Bichi himself is as small as can be, imagine how tiny the nail on his little finger is. Says Agustina: At the time, I don't think my little brother even knew how to talk yet. Stay still, baby, don't wiggle so much, this fin-ger is called the ring finger because you wear rings on it, I make another click and a tiny sliver of crescent moon flies through the air, That's two nails, Bichito, only three left and if you don't move we'll be done very soon, this bigger finger is the middle finger, stay still or I can't do it, there's another click and the first unexpected thing is that this last bit of nail doesn't spring into the air but falls softly straight down onto my skirt, the second thing, though not right away but after a long silence has passed, is the inexplicable howl that Bichi lets out seemingly just for the sake of it, and he doesn't even pull away his hand, which is still caught in mine, his little hand offered up and exposed as if that cry had nothing to do with it.

Only after a while, when Bichi's cry breaks and turns into sobs, only then do Agustina's eyes see, for the first time since they opened to the world, how something warm and red is ooz-ing out and staining the bedspread, by now Bichi has pulled his hand away and he brings it to his face which now is also sticky and stained, Let me see, Bichi, please, I try to look at his finger to understand what's happening, but my head goes fuzzy be-cause I'm shaking, fear takes away my powers, and so many voices bombard me that I can't understand any of them, the worst of the voices, the one that paralyzes me most, is the one that keeps repeating that I've hurt Bichi, that I've done him harm, just like my father, I'm sorry, Bichito, please say you forgive me, and he shows me his hand red with blood and his eyes are full of tears, Quiet, my love, quiet, baby, if you cry like that I can't see anything.

A faint voice reaches my mind and reveals to me that the soft nail I just cut isn't a nail but the little piece of fingertip that his finger is now missing, I'll fix it for you, Bichito my love, but don't cry like that because they'll punish me for hurting you, and Bichi tries not to cry, he's still whimpering but very quietly, it's incredible how his finger matches up with the tip that has come off, they could be stuck back together if it weren't for the blood that keeps coming out, because this is the Blood, Bichi Bichito, this is what's called the Spilled Blood, and now I can hear the Big Voice, which warns me Your little brother will die because all the blood inside of him will come out the tip of his finger, then I don't care if they punish me or if Bichi screams and goes running to tell my mother because more than anything I don't want Bichi to die, and I think I remember that I cried all that night and that some brown spots were left on the bedspread as a reminder of the bad thing I did, and when my brother Bichi and I were older, his finger was still a little bit short because the tip never grew back, he was missing the tip of his middle finger and he must be missing it still, each time I think of that I start to cry and can't stop thinking that I was the last person you would've expected to hurt you, wherever you are, Bichi, little brother, I'd give anything to make what I did to you stop hurting. After that the thread of blood was hidden again and ran inside, waiting for a new chance to confuse me and blur my special sight.

La Cabrera was a modern neighborhood, with private streets to protect us and guards in ponchos stationed twenty-four hours a day in little huts with bulletproof windows in front of each house, and we children were never left on our own because my mother or Aminta or any of the other maids, if not Aunt Sofi, who by now had come to live with us, were there to watch us, but one afternoon Aminta snuck away to see her boyfriend, and Agustina doesn't know where the other adults were, but she and her two brothers were left alone and someone rang the doorbell, Don't open the door, Agustina, don't open it, Bichito, we're not allowed to open the door, but I looked out the window and saw that it was the neighbors' guard, he was wearing his black wool poncho and from outside he made me understand that he wanted a glass of water, Look, Joaco, it's a watchman and he just wants water, and I ran to the kitchen to get it and opened the door to give it to him and he drank it in two swallows, but the third time he tried to bring the glass to his mouth it fell to the ground and shattered, then he leaned a little against the wall and slid slowly down it, he must have been hot because he took off the poncho without saying a word and then he was on the floor clutching it.

Bichi came out to see what was happening and he stood there beside me and after a while the security-guard man asked me from the floor to please give him more water, and that thing had already started to happen: the Blood was slowly coming from him, making its way out of his body, and a voice told

Agustina that only water could control the will of the Blood that is Spilled, the guard asked me to bring him water and I understood what he meant, he was letting me know that he wouldn't die if I gave him water so I ran to the kitchen to get him another glass, What are you doing, Joaco shouted and she said, I'm bringing him more water because he's thirsty, He's not thirsty, he's dying, can't you see that somebody hurt him and he's dying?

But he was thirsty, he tried to sit up and he stretched his hand out toward me, toward the glass that I was giving him, his fingers brushed mine, which still retain the memory of that touch, but he didn't take the glass, instead he slid down again on his side, slowly, like his blood, which was now a big dark puddle on the white marble of the entranceway, the tips of Bichi's shoes were at the edge of the puddle and I pushed him back with my arm, Don't touch that blood I told him, but Bichi didn't listen, Did you think, brother of mine, that the blood that day was like the waters of the Styx and that touching it would make us invincible?

The rest of the afternoon was very long, sunny at first but then less so until the air turned violet and each thing grew a precise shadow, as if cut out with scissors, and the cold started to come down from the mountains but I didn't feel it because I was standing at the edge of that man's blood, unable to take my eyes off it or move, my eyes wide open and my sight growing sharper and sharper, standing there like a pillar of salt because the sight of blood freezes my powers and traps me, Bichi wasn't with me anymore and neither was Joaco and even the guard himself seemed to have gone, maybe the only part of him left before me was his body, his black poncho, and his blood but I kept standing there, motionless, my presence required by what was happening, which was that a man was dying, for the first time in my life someone was dying.

At some point during that long afternoon two men in gray coats arrived in a police van, one of them putting on rubber gloves and kneeling down in front of the dead man, who by then seemed to belong to me after all the hours I'd spent watching him, or maybe keeping him company if he was aware of my company. I had already memorized his thin mustache and the blank gaze of his one open eye and the two shoes that had fallen off leaving his feet in plain sight, and later in life I learned that it's a kind of law that the dead always lose their shoes. Agustina thought, This dead man is mine because I was the only one with him when he died, I'm the only one here staring at his socks which are brown with little white dots, and I'm surprised to discover that even the dead wear socks; Agustina swears that back then she believed men were split into two groups, on one side were those who wore black or charcoal-gray socks, like her father, and on the other side was everyone else, those who wore socks that were essentially brown with light-colored dots.

The man with the rubber gloves tried to move the dead man but he wouldn't budge, as if he preferred to stay clutching his poncho in that uncomfortable position, then the man in the coat started to search the dead man's pockets and found a small battery-powered radio that was still playing, turned down low but playing, emitting music and commercials and torrents of words as if the guard could still hear it and Agustina thought:

The radio is the only part of him that's still alive. From another pocket they took four coins and a small comb that the man in gloves put in a plastic bag with the radio, which he'd turned off so that it wouldn't keep playing, and then the other man who was with him also put on gloves, extending the index and middle finger of his right hand and curling the other two fingers and thumb under the way priests do when they're blessing the faithful from the altar, He's going to bless him so he doesn't go to hell, I thought, but no, it wasn't that, what he did with the upraised fingers was probe my dead man's wounds; one by one he stuck his two fingers into each wound while saying, Sharp instrument, left armpit, six centimeters; sharp instrument, four centimeters, right intercostal gap between the seventh and eighth rib, counting all the holes in the body while a woman in blue made notes in her pad until they reached nine and he said: Nine stab wounds, one perforating the liver.

As they walked back and forth to the police van, the two men and the woman stepped in the guard's blood and left red footprints in the marble entranceway until my father and mother came home at the same time but in separate cars and there was a terrible uproar, Agustina could hear their words but she couldn't understand them, How could this happen, the children shouldn't be seeing this, Joaco, Agustina, Bichi, go to your rooms immediately, How can it be that neither Aminta nor Sofi are here, how could they be so irresponsible. Father, there were nine stab wounds with a sharp instrument, Mother, there were nine stab wounds with a sharp instrument; we tried to tell them about the little radio and the glass of water but they wouldn't listen, Father, what does perforating the liver mean, Mother, where is the liver, but my father double-locked the door to the house with us inside and my dead man was left outside, I never found out what his name was and I still wonder whether the water I gave him trickled out through the holes in his body, too.

I've already said that before things happen, I get three calls, and the Third Call of the Blood sounded in my ears at the pool at Gai Repos, in Sasaima, and sounded again in the reproachful look my mother gave me, how many times have I seen her face twist at the things I do or say or the things that happen to me, it's an expression of such disgust, and this time it was because the Spilled Blood came out of me, running down my legs and staining my bathing suit, and my beautiful mother with her horrified face, so thin and pale in her white summer dress, took me by the arm and said, You have to get out of the pool now.

She tried to wrap me in a towel but I, who was playing cops and robbers with my cousins and brothers, I, who was a robber, was only interested in not being caught, Let me go, Mother, they'll capture me if I don't jump in the water, the water is the robbers' hideout, Mother, can't you see they're going to catch me. But she wouldn't let me go, she squeezed my arm so hard it hurt, It's come, Agustina, she told me, it's come, but I didn't know what had come, Cover yourself up with the towel and come in the house with me right now, but I threw away the towel and yanked my arm out of my mother's grasp and jumped in the water and it was then that I saw it, coming out of me with no one's permission and tinting the pool a watery blood color.

This is the Third Call, I thought, and I don't know what happened next, all I remember is that finally, inside the house,

Aunt Sofi gave me a Kotex, I already knew what they were because we stole them from my mother's bathroom and used
them as padding in the baskets for the little live chicks colored
with aniline dye that we were given for our first Communions,
chicks with green, lilac, pink, or blue feathers, chicks that only
lasted a few days and then had to be buried; my father said it
was wrong to dye them because the color poisoned them. Put
this in your panties, Aunt Sofi said to me, handing me the Kotex, Come on, I'll show you how, but Agustina was crying and
didn't want to do it, it seemed horrible to her that her blood
should come out there and stain her clothes and that her
mother should give her that reproachful look, the kind of look
you give someone who does something dirty, who dirties-
things-with-her-blood.

Then Aunt Sofi said, Poor girl, so young and she already has
her period, and since outside my cousins and brothers were
shouting for me to come back and play cops and robbers, I dried
my tears and I said to my mother, I'll go tell them what's happened to me and I'll be right back, and my mother's eyes glit-
tered and from her mouth came the Ban: No, Agustina, we
don't talk about these things. What things don't we talk about,
Mother? Things like this, do you understand, private things,
and then it was she who went to the window and said to my
cousins and brothers, Agustina isn't coming out now because
she wants to stay in here with us and play cards, What cards,
Mother, no one's playing cards in here, I want to keep playing
cops and robbers, but my mother wouldn't let me because she
said the sun would make the hemorrhaging worse, that's what
she said, the hemorrhaging, it was the first time I'd heard that

word, and when Bichi came in to ask me what was wrong my mother told him that nothing was wrong, that I just wanted to play cards. It was then that I understood for the third time that my gift of sight is weak when confronted with the power of Blood, and that the Hemorrhage is uncontrollable and unspeakable.

. . .

I COULDN'T HAVE CHOSEN a worse place to fall apart. Even though the last thing I wanted was to collapse in public, I couldn't wait until I got to the van, my heart sinking right there in the hotel room when I looked out the window and glimpsed those black acacias swaying in the wind against the brightly lit night, those same acacias that Agustina was watching so intently the Sunday of the dark episode, as if she was hypnotized by them. The little that remained of my reserves of courage suddenly vanished as if down a drain, and it wasn't so much the weight of my wife's illness that crushed me as it was the distinct memory of her first lucid moment, that instant of recognition in which her face relaxed and she ran to me, throwing her arms around me and clinging to me like a drowning woman to a scrap of wood, that one unrepeatable minute when everything was solved, when the tragedy halted just before it sprang itself on me, as if it had repented of the intention to destroy us, Let's go home, Agustina, I said to her, but it was already too late, the instant of possible salvation had passed, she was numb once more and no longer paying attention to me, her gaze fixed again on those acacias that waved their branches as if to say to her, You aren't from here, you're not of this world, you have no memories, you don't know this man who's claiming you, the only things binding you to him are scorn and rage.

So as soon as the Fearless Girl left to deal with the call she'd gotten on her handset, I could no longer remain standing and sat on the edge of the bed, scorched inside by the blaze of that memory, and when the girl returned, a few minutes later, she found the client she'd left alone in room 416 flat on his back, Mr. Stepansky? Mr. Stepansky, is something wrong? Yes, something is wrong, Señorita, I'm the husband of a woman who lost her mind in room 413, What do you mean? she asked, and I confessed that my name wasn't Stepansky and I didn't have friends who wanted to stay at the hotel, My name is Aguilar and I need to find out what happened to my wife; her name is Agustina Londoño and she's a tall, pale young woman who dresses in black, this was twenty-eight days ago exactly, I gave her the dates and got mixed up trying to explain that I'd picked her up that Sunday but that I didn't know who she'd come here with or when exactly she'd arrived, A gorgeous girl, like an artist, or an actress, but strange somehow, all dressed in black and with long hair? That's a good description of my wife, I said, and of course, the Fearless Girl did remember her, I wasn't here when they checked out, but I was the one who checked her in the night before, when they arrived, When who arrived? Why the woman you say is your wife and the man who was with her, wasn't it you? That's the problem, it wasn't me.

Then the Fearless Girl excuses herself saying that if this has to do with cheating she'd rather not get involved, The thing is you never know, Mr. Stepansky, It's Aguilar, That's right, you told me, but what I'm trying to say, Mr. Aguilar, is that it's a bad idea to take sides in this kind of thing because you never know, It has nothing to do with cheating, it's a very serious mental health problem and you have to help me, it's your duty as a human being, Wait, wait, Mr. Aguilar, first calm down a little, stay here with me for a second, and, oddly, she closed the door to the room as if to allow me a moment of peace in my suffering and then she sat down beside me on the bed, so close that our legs touched, Look, Mr. Aguilar, in a hotel like this all kinds of things happen, and every so often strange people arrive and do strange things, but believe it or not, all the strangeness is predictable in ways that you end up recognizing; the different kinds of strangeness can be reduced to five types, and I tell you this as someone who's paid careful attention, it's either sex, alcohol, drugs, beatings, or shootings, that's what it boils down to, life is like that, even strange behavior can be monotonous, for example there've never been any stabbings or suicides here, Yes there have, I corrected her, a professor even in the worst of circumstances, No sir, there haven't been, a Romanian committed suicide in another hotel on the same block but here at the Wellington we haven't seen anything like that, and the girl in 413, the one you say is your wife, all I can say is that she might have been on drugs, or she might have been crazy, or just extremely nervous, it was hard to tell, but whatever it was, she was worked up, anyway, the suitcase that she left is still here, but when I asked her for it, the Fearless Girl answered that they couldn't give it to anyone except the person it belonged to, management's orders, But the person it belongs to is crazy, I said raising my voice and getting up, how can you expect her to come and claim a suitcase when she's crazy, she went crazy here, in room 413 of this hotel, you yourself just admitted that you were a witness, and the Fearless Girl, pulling on my pants leg to make me sit down, said, No, Mr. Aguilar, she didn't go crazy here, when she got here she was already crazy, or sick, or at least extremely upset.

We agreed not to talk any more at the hotel, the Fearless Girl only had forty-five minutes left until the end of her shift, if the gentleman liked they could make a date for later, at some café, Yes, the gentleman liked, of course the gentleman liked, and then she suggested that we meet at five past ten at a cheap restaurant on Thirteenth Road and Eighty-second Street, a place called Don Conejo; the Fearless Girl, now bringing a little bit of toilet paper from the bathroom for me to blow my nose with, told me that the empanadas there were excellent and that it was where she went when she got off work, starving. Don Conejo was nearby but not so near that anyone from the reception desk would see them, and anyway she was the only one who liked it because the others didn't like to leave the place with their clothes reeking of grease, Look, Mr. Aguilar, I understand how worried you are about your wife and I'd be happy to help you any way I can, it broke my heart to see her like that, but we have to leave here now because if they find me like this they'll fire me, just relax and we'll talk later, I promise you that if you wait for me at Don Conejo I'll help you, or at least I'll keep you company in your sorrow, you know, when you work at a hotel in some ways you end up becoming a nurse; lots of lonely people with problems come to stay here, you're not the first, believe it or not, but we should go now because the manager will kill me if he sees me having some strange conversation with a guest, I'm not a guest, No, you're not a guest, which makes it even worse, who knows who you might be. That's what the Fearless Girl said but as she said it she was smiling as if to let me know that she didn't mind not knowing, I was a stranger who had cried as he looked out the window of one of the rooms in her hotel; in other words, I was the kind of man she was prepared to be friendly to and help and probably also sleep with, because that's the way she was.

We returned to the lobby separately, she in the elevator and I by the stairs, and from a public phone I called Aunt Sofi to check on Agustina and let them know I'd be late, She's sleeping, she told me, and I went out to walk the streets aimlessly in the cold with my hands in my pockets and the collar of my raincoat turned up, a third-rate Humphrey Bogart among the fierce transvestites and the college-girl prostitutes in skintight jeans. I looked at my watch every few seconds as if that would make the time go faster, needing it to be five past ten so that I could barrage her with the many questions that were swarming in my head, but also because her nearness was a relief in the midst of the hell I was going through.

When it was almost time I walked to Don Conejo and discovered that it was closed, so I crossed the street and sat in the café there, near the entrance so I could watch for her arrival; asking for a cup of tea, I burrowed even deeper into the collar of my raincoat, on the verge of collapse and not wanting to run into anyone who wasn't her, but of course two old activist friends of mine happened to be sitting at the next table, and they came up to me because they were gathering signatures to protest the forcible disappearance of someone, I didn't know who because I paid no attention to what they said and didn't read the petition before I signed it, I have to get out of this place, I thought, and paying for the tea and waving goodbye to them, I went out just as the Fearless Girl was crossing the street, heading toward Don Conejo.

Except that at first glance I didn't recognize her, because she'd taken off the short-skirted navy blue suit and now she was wearing black pants which for some reason didn't look right on her, maybe because they were too tight, and she had put her hair up in a ponytail and now she didn't seem as attractive to me, in fact I was almost convinced that she was someone else, but what settled the matter were her nails, there could only be one set of nails like that in the known world, and it wasn't until she was a few feet away that I noticed that the suitcase she was carrying must be Agustina's, You brought it for me!, I shouted, Yes, I brought it, let's hope it doesn't get me in trouble.

We went walking along Fifteenth Road, which was torn up for some construction project, and the movement of the dump trucks and the deafening noise of the drills drowned out my questions, so I walked quietly along, thinking only about the suitcase I was carrying now, which was the proof that everything had been premeditated; my wife hadn't come to that hotel room by chance or accident but had packed her things and left the apartment voluntarily and with a specific purpose, and her purpose was her meeting with that man, who knows how long she'd been planning it, and on and on, a flurry of similar speculations that I prefer not to recall, I was so intent on endlessly working myself up over the whole thing that I didn't even know where I was walking, with the Fearless Girl running after me perched on platform shoes that made it hard for her to step around the gaping holes in the pavement and trying to shout over the roar of the drills, telling me who knows what about her life, something about her mother's varicose veins, about the cost of schooling for her brothers and sisters.

As we were passing the Country Clinic she took me by the arm and pulled me in, Come on, she shouted, there's a little cafeteria here where we won't run into anyone, the empanadas didn't work out, so keep me company while I have a doughnut and coffee because I'm starving to death, and I wasn't quick enough to say that this wasn't the place, not this clinic, because it was the only souvenir I had yet to collect on my horrible memory tour, so by the time I realized what was happening I was already sitting and eating a pink doughnut in front of the sign that said EMERGENCY ROOM in cold blue letters, the same emergency room where Agustina was examined the night of the dark episode . . . You didn't eat a thing, the Fearless Girl said, I did, I ate half a doughnut, Not you, your wife when she was at the hotel, You're saying she didn't eat at all? No, the man who was with her came down to the restaurant for dinner by himself, ordered his meal and arranged for the same thing to be taken to her in the room, but then the tray was left untouched in the hall, and when I tell you untouched, I mean untouched, she didn't even lift the covers to see what was on the dishes, I know because the next day, Sunday, the same thing happened, he came down for breakfast alone and ordered breakfast to be taken up to her, and she didn't eat that either, and when these things happen the waiters let us know, because it can be a sign that something weird is going on in a room, I don't know, Mr. Aguilar, honestly, it didn't seem like a lovers' meeting, There are lovers' meetings that end badly, I said, Oh, Mr. Aguilar, you're hopeless, I'm telling you frankly that the two of them weren't very romantic, now if I were spending the night with a boyfriend . . .

It was so difficult, everything that's happening is so difficult, I said to her after a long silence, though the silence was mine alone because she had continued speculating about what she would've done with a boyfriend in a hotel like the Wellington, You don't know how hard all this has been, I repeated and realized that I still didn't know her name, My name is Anita, I've told you three times already but all you care about is your own suffering, I also told you that I support my mother and my brothers and sisters and that besides working at the hotel I run a little business with a photocopy machine and a fax service in my garage, what else can I do, I can't make ends meet otherwise, Where do you live, Anita, I asked, thinking to myself that it was good to be with this Anita, that it was good that her name was Anita, but that I liked her better with her hair down, If you want to make me feel better, Anita, let down your hair, I said to her but she ignored me and continued on with her extremely long story, of which all I retained was that Anita lived in Meissen, a working-class neighborhood that I knew well because decades ago I had gone there to organize meetings and sell copies of the newspaper *Socialist Revolution*, Meissen, my dear Anita, is a long fucking way out, Yes, Señor, tell me about

it, each day I spend an hour and a half on the bus from Meissen to the hotel and another hour and a half getting home.

It was funny to watch how Anita managed to balance her
pink doughnut on the tips of her ten little French flags and
bring it to her mouth, and like the doughnut, her generous,
pouting lips were pink and round and oh so sweet, coming too
close to mine with the excuse of telling me any old thing, but
not even the lips of a desirable girl could make me forget the
suitcase that was under the table, the source of my unhappiness
and resentment, I'm going to open it right here, in front of you,
Anita, because it would kill me to do it alone, and Anita, who
had begun to speak to me more casually but who occasionally
seemed to think better of it and become more formal again,
said, Go ahead, Mr. Aguilar, open it, who cares, people will
think they're personal belongings that we're bringing to a sick
relative.

I began taking out one thing after another, placing each on
the Formica table, a few white cotton undergarments, a T-shirt
of mine that says Bean Man and that Agustina likes to sleep in,
two shirts that she must never have worn because they were
clean and ironed, How odd that your wife arrived at the hotel
looking like such a mess when she had clean clothes in her suitcase, said Anita, when I saw her I couldn't believe such a beautiful woman would be out looking like that, like she'd been
chewed up and spit out. I kept removing things, a case with a
toothbrush and toothpaste, Clinique facial cleanser, Pablo
Neruda's *Heights of Machu Picchu* that I'd given her myself soon
after meeting her, What's Machu Picchu, Anita wanted to

know, Some Incan ruins in the Peruvian Andes, and since she grabbed the book and saw the inscription from me on the first page, "To Agustina, atop the tallest mountain on earth," she asked me whether I'd been up there with my wife, No, the truth is I haven't, Then what did you mean when you wrote this, Well I don't know, I must have liked her a lot, And who is Pablo Neruda, she persisted but I didn't answer because I was absorbed in those objects, a hairbrush, a few other Clinique lotions, a cortisone skin cream, And what's that for, For allergies, Agustina's skin is so pale that sometimes she gets rashes and she uses skin creams.

Don't worry, Mr. Aguilar, Anita said to me, suddenly grabbing my hand, if the man who was with your wife was her lover, she wouldn't have worn plain panties like these but black lace ones or red low-cut ones and a more exciting bra, You don't know her, Anita, my wife is the type who always wears plain white underwear, I see, then you must be married by the Church, No, Agustina and I live together without anyone's blessing, Then, asked Anita, why do you wear a wedding band on your finger, It was given to me by my first wife, the mother of my children, look, her name is engraved inside, Mar-ta E-le-na, and upon seeing this, Anita said, sweetening her voice and lowering her eyelids, What a character you are, Mr. Aguilar, you live with one woman and wear another woman's ring, I think you need a third woman to set things straight, and, moving too close, she said, Tonight something is going to happen, as if insinuating that something sexual was going to happen between us, but I pushed abruptly backward, and she, taking the hint, hastened to clarify, I mean in the country, I have the feel-

Delirium

ing that something big is going to happen tonight in Colombia,
And why not, I replied, after all something big happens almost
every night, but nothing happened last night or the night before, so the odds are that we're in for it today, and as I was
halfway through the sentence I was suddenly curious to know
what her hair smelled like, Let it down, Anita, I asked her again
and since this time she listened to me, all that curly hair tumbled down on us, and grateful and softening inside, I pushed
my nose into it and inhaled the sickly sweet perfume of her
shampoo, Peach?, I asked, Incredible, Mr. Aguilar, you guessed,
it's L'Oréal Silky Peach.

Without moving my nose from her hair I told her about an
afternoon when I was fifteen and I rode too fast down a hill on
a borrowed bicycle and ran into a barbed-wire fence that cut my
right forearm badly and ripped a piece of skin from my neck, I
still have both scars, look, Anita, you can see them, and she ran
the tip of her index finger over the ugly mark across my throat
and asked, Why are you telling me this, I'm telling you because
of what happened afterward, in the neighborhood clinic where
Doctor Ospinita, who practiced on a good-faith basis since he
didn't have a medical degree, disinfected my wounds and gave
me twenty-seven stitches, all of this while I was fully conscious
because anesthesia was an inconceivable luxury in a poor
neighborhood like mine, Uh-huh, said Anita trying to look as if
she were following me though she didn't understand what this
had to do with her, Look, the reason I'm telling you this is because it's one of the sweetest memories of my life, I mean what
happened to me with a lady at the clinic, she was a young
woman and in my memory she's very beautiful although I've

163

forgotten her name and what her face looked like, or maybe I never knew her name or saw much of her face, she wasn't the nurse, she was simply someone who happened to be there at the clinic, probably waiting for her turn, and when she saw me frozen in panic at the sight of the curved needle and the nylon thread that Ospinita was aiming at my neck, she amazingly sat at the head of the operating table and rested my head on her thighs, not caring that her clothes were being drenched with blood, in one hand holding up the bag for the transfusion that Ospinita was giving me to replace the blood I'd lost, and here comes the really important thing, Anita, the part I can't forget, which is that with her free hand this woman stroked my hair, and her caresses put me in such a trance that I could only think of her hand, so I closed my eyes to concentrate on her touch, which allowed me to forget the pain and the fear and the sight of my own blood, and I just drifted there in the immense plea-sure of those fingers stroking my hair; whenever I feel like I'm going to die, Anita, which is how I've been feeling every day lately, the memory of that woman keeps me going, or rather the memory of her hand, and if I tell you this it's because your pres-ence has a similar effect on me, and since this made Anita begin to purr like a cat, I leaned back again and changed tone, And speaking of fingers, I said in order to say something, my God, girl, what long nails you have, do you paint them yourself or do they do it for you at the salon, I'll bet you don't know, lovely Anita from Meissen, what emery boards are for.

I stepped away for a minute to call Aunt Sofi again and tell her that I was on my way, and when I returned to the table I said to the Fearless Girl, Look, Anita, if I were fifteen I'd ask you to stroke my hair for a while, but I'm old and a mess and in the middle of a crisis so we should leave instead, come on, I'll give you a ride home. Do you have a car? she asked incredulously, as if I didn't look like a car owner or as if she couldn't believe her luck at being saved for a night from her hour-and-a-half bus ride, Do I have a car?, more or less, I've got an old wreck that barely deserves to be called a car, but it will get you home safe and sound.

Now it seems funny to me to remember how confidently I spoke that last sentence, because it almost didn't come true, by which I mean that on the drive south down Thirtieth Road past Nemesio Camacho Stadium with Anita in the passenger seat, the road nearly deserted at that time of night, we were shaken by a violent jolt that actually lifted the van from the pavement, while at the same time a blast of air hit our eardrums and a sharp noise, like thunder, came from the bowels of the earth and then gradually faded away, in successive layers of echoes, until an absolute silence fell over the city, and in the midst of this deadly quiet I heard Anita's voice saying, A bomb, a big fucking bomb, it must have gone off nearby, I told you, Mr. Aguilar, I told you something horrible was going to happen tonight. But all I could think of was Agustina, wondering if she was all right.

Anita turned on the car radio and that's how we found out that someone had just blown up the police station in Paloque-mao, about twelve blocks from where we were and eight blocks from the place where the explosion would surely have woken Agustina, terrifying her, if the blast hadn't actually blown out the windows of my apartment, that is, and I was struck by the image of her getting out of bed in a state of shock and stepping on the broken glass, and the picture was so vivid that it became a certainty, I literally saw Agustina walking barefoot on the floor covered in shards, and I was overcome by the urgent need to be with her.

I don't know how long I was silent, lost in my obsession, driving to Meissen as fast as the van would go to drop off the girl beside me and return home without losing an instant, preoccupied by the idea that Agustina might somehow be hurt, while at the same time I surprised myself by turning over and over the possibility of such a thing happening; I don't know, it was as if something not quite right were shifting inside me, something like the unspeakable notion of an eye for an eye, so deeply had I been hurt by her rejection of me. So when Anita spoke, I had forgotten her so thoroughly that her voice took me by surprise, Mr. Aguilar, she said, you won't like what I'm about to say, you'll be thinking what right do I have to get involved, but in my opinion it's too hard on you being married to that crazy woman.

BEGONE FROM ME all remorse, Nicholas Portulinus said out loud after the lunch of roast pork. Once he'd had a cup of herbal tea for his digestion and a long swallow of valerian extract, he repeated, Begone from me all remorse!, like a plea or a command requesting that the sleep-inducing properties of the valerian bestow upon him the brief bliss of a nap. Then he asked Blanca to unlace his boots, because his bloated body wouldn't bend enough to permit the maneuver, and he lay down on his high bed protected by the gauzy cloud of a mosquito net, letting himself be lulled by the dull boom of the Sweet River, which tumbled into falls outside his window, and he saw again, in a certain kind of light that he himself would describe as an artificial glare, the polished surfaces of an ancient stage—at other times he will call it Greek ruins—on which two boys are fighting, wounding each other, and bleeding. "In the dream, I'm standing there bolted to the ground"—he will write later in his diary—"struck dumb by the metallic gleam of the blood and deaf to the call of the torn flesh. I don't care about one of the fighters, the one whose back is to me so that I can't see his face. I don't know his name, either, but that doesn't trouble me. I dream that his name doesn't matter. The other boy, however, affects me deeply; I see that he's the younger of the two and maybe the weaker, of that I'm not sure, but I do know that he's whimpering and licking his wounds in a pitiful way."

Portulinus wakes up at five in the afternoon and gets out of bed, although his mind is so scattered that it would be more accurate to say that he gets up without having completely awoken. He's wearing a silk robe printed with a tangle of black branches on a forest-green background and the slippers that tend to lose themselves, which angers him so; his hair is plastered sideways from being pressed sweaty against the pillow and he's still floating amid the passions of the dream that visited him during his nap. As if obeying an order, he takes up pen and staff paper and sits down at the piano, spending a few hours composing the song that for months has been buzzing in his ear, evading capture. From the garden, his wife, Blanca, spies on him through the latticework, happy to discover that Nicholas is composing again after months of idleness, "At last his creative energy is reborn"—she'll write later in a letter—"and once again I hear the harmonies that spring from the depths of his soul." Blanca, who also believes that her husband's gaze has cleared a little, asks herself, Am I not the happiest woman in the world?, suspecting that at this moment she really is. That's why, entranced, she watches her husband through the latticework as he fills one page of paper after another, pretending to set down notes and beats to make his wife happy, or to convince himself of his own happiness. But he's really only scrawling flies and fly tracks, black dots and wild strokes that are the exact transcription of his painful internal clamor.

There's no point in asking what the bloody fighter boy he dreamed of was like, but rather what he is like, because Portulinus dreams of him often and has for years, which is what he tells his wife that night when the frogs, crickets, and cicadas pierce the darkness with their song. Blanca, my dear, he confesses to her, I dreamed of Farax again. Who is this Farax, Nicholas?, she asks, visibly upset, and why does he always accost you in dreams? He's just my inspiration, he answers, trying to calm her, Farax is the name I give my inspiration when it visits me. But is it a he, or a she? It's a he, and he grants me the intensity of feeling that I need for life to be worth living. Tell me, Nicholas, she insists, is it someone you know? Have I ever seen him? Is he a dream or a memory?, but Nicholas isn't up to answering so many questions. His name is Farax, Blanquita darling, content yourself with that, and just then they're interrupted by their daughter Eugenia, the quiet one, but she's radiant now, bringing them the news that the piano student from Anapoima has knocked at the door again, asking for the Maestro.

The blond boy is back, she tells them, her heart pounding. What boy are you talking about? The one who came yesterday with the lead soldiers in his knapsack, he wants to know whether Father will give him piano lessons. To receive the visitor Portulinus went down to the spacious parlor with chairs set around the Blüthner rosewood grand piano that Portulinus had had sent from Germany and that today, a whole lifetime later, stands in Eugenia's house in La Cabrera, in the capital, now an enormous, silent white elephant. Portulinus entered the parlor and saw that the visitor from Anapoima had sat down at the piano, though no one had given him permission, and was running a reverent hand over the precious dark-grained red wood, but instead of irritating Portulinus, this boldness struck him as a sign of character, and skipping the usual pleasantries he got straight to the point. If you want lessons, show me what you know, he ordered the boy, and the boy, although he hadn't been asked, said that his name was Abelito Caballero and presented the list of references he had memorized, explaining that he'd come on the recommendation of the mayor of Anapoima and that he'd studied at the School of Music and Dance in Anapoima until he knew more than the only teacher, Madame Carola Osorio, which was why he wanted to receive more advanced training from Maestro Portulinus, but since the latter seemed uninterested in his story, the boy stopped volunteering information that hadn't been requested and rolled up his sleeves to free his arms, shook his head to clear it, rubbed his hands to warm them, recited a prayer for God's help, and began to play a creole waltz called "The Greedy Cat."

Although timidity caused the boy to stumble here and there, Portulinus, who had begun to breathe heavily as if he were choked by some powerful internal trauma, could only murmur, Good, good, good, no matter if "The Greedy Cat" slid gracefully by or faltered. Good, good, good, sighed Portulinus and he couldn't believe his eyes, that shimmering golden hair, those hands still a child's and yet already skilled, that black silk bow the newcomer wore knotted around his neck as if he were a doll, the tanned leather knapsack still on his back. Nor could Portulinus's ears believe what they were hearing, music that seemed to descend sweetly from on high to gradually inhabit the parlor's shadows; all that was certain was that his heart as well as his senses were telling him that what was happening had to do with an old prophecy, that this was the longed-for fulfillment of a promise at last.

Trying to guess whether he would be accepted as a student or not, the boy lifted his eyes from the keyboard from time to time to cast a sidelong glance at the famed German teacher, who was sweating and puffing beside him in his robe and slippers, but he couldn't decipher the teacher's expression or understand the meaning of those good, good, goods that the Maestro muttered indiscriminately, whether he played well or made mistakes. When the piece ended, it was with apprehension that he sensed the great musician coming up behind him, brushing his shoulder with his hand, and saying, almost into his ear, I must call my wife; and then the Maestro made a great show of leaving, inclin-

ing his bulk forward and not watching where he was going, as if
he were in a hurry to be somewhere else.

Abelito Caballero, left alone in the now silent room, suddenly became aware of an excessive weight on his back and
realized that he hadn't removed his knapsack, which he proceeded to do, and then blew his nose to clear the stuffiness
brought on by the smell of damp that permeated the parlor.
Folding his arms, he settled down to wait, until he spotted the
flicker of a small presence in one of the corners. Getting up, he
discovered, crouched behind a chair, the thin, shy girl who had
come to the door yesterday and today. If you want, we can set
up the military parade again, he said, and when she nodded, he
took the lead soldiers out of his knapsack and they got to work,
the two of them kneeling on the floor. I'm Abelito, I don't think
I told you my name yesterday. And my name is Eugenia, I
didn't tell you mine, either.

Meanwhile Portulinus went looking for Blanca all around
the house and found her at last in the larder, What the devil
are you doing in the larder, confound it Blanquita, come at
once! there's a prodigy in the parlor, he announced, dragging
her by the hand, Come, Blanquita darling, come and meet
him, it's the boy, he's playing "The Greedy Cat" on the piano,
hurry, it's the boy!, it's Farax!, and she, alarmed to see her husband in such a state, tried to calm him and allay the intensity
of his outburst, Don't make things up, Nicholas, how can it be
Farax when Farax only exists in your dreams, Quiet, woman,
you don't know what you're saying, come, you must meet
Farax.

SO THIS, AGUSTINA princess, is how we came to the end of the farce, because life sets the stage, and we little puppets dance to whatever tune they play for us. What happened was that this Dolores and the loser with the whip put on their act, a pretty vile spectacle but since there's no accounting for taste when it comes to sex, I bet you can't guess who was thrilled out of his skull by the cheap violence, well who but Spider, I don't think I'd be exaggerating if I told you that nothing had ever sent him into such ecstasies, I swear I saw him turning purple in his wheelchair shouting at the pimp, Hit her harder! Stop playing, get serious! Hit her for real! and obnoxiously egging him on like a paralytic Nero sending the lions in to wreak havoc, drunk with delight.

It was then that I decided to go up to my office and wash my hands of that miniature Roman circus, because although you may say, Agustina doll, that I'd put up with anything for Spider's sake, this was so depressing that even I had to draw the line. His little squeals of glee, not to mention all that giggling and squirming, overrode my sense of duty; he may have been baptized in a starched christening gown and his great-grandfather may have brought civilization to our country, but he's still a yokel with no scruples who struck it rich, and I promise you, Agustina doll, that that night he was like a happy Neanderthal, but since everything changes from one minute to the next, and when you least expect it what's white turns to black and what's black turns to white, in that same way Spider's satisfaction with Dolores's tricks began to turn to annoyance, The thing isn't working quite right, Midas my boy, he told me, puffing so hard he could barely get the words out, this woman is 80 percent swindler and 20 percent actress, and there's plenty of moaning and fake wailing and crocodile tears, but almost no true feeling; it's been rehearsed so carefully that there's hardly anything real about it. And how could I explain to Spider that this wasn't the moment to be picky, since after all the woman wasn't Our Lord Jesus Christ, about to let herself be crucified for some random Christian's sexual salvation.

But you know how far Spider is willing to go to satisfy his urges, Agustina doll; it was more than clear that his thirst for the pain of others wouldn't be satisfied with ordinary pantomime, so he demanded that the woman be submissive and docile, and questioned the pimp's professionalism and dedication to his duties as whip-wielder, and since neither of the two paid much attention to him he started getting on my back, hinting that it was my fault for not lining up a real show, a more convincing scenario, so right then and there, I, Pilate McAlister, washed my hands of it all; Spider had already laid the blame for his erectile dysfunction on me once, to give a scientific name to the problem afflicting his floppy dick, and as obsequious as I may be, Agustina kitten, I wasn't going to take the rap again.

So I shut myself up in my office, lowered the blind of the window that overlooks the gym so I couldn't see anything that was going on down there, took a hit of weed, and immersed myself in Pac-Man, which is what I do to take my mind off things that irritate me. Pac-Man, adorable Agustina, is the greatest invention of the century; when you're playing Pac-

Man there's no pain or love or regrets, and your thoughts are no longer your own, so I turned on the monitor, hooked up my electronic toy, and let myself be hypnotized.

I wasn't myself anymore, Agustina darling, just a little ball all mouth and teeth, a ball roaming the labyrinth and eating pellets to give me strength to wipe out the little ghosts that crossed my path, and I started to win bonus points and my score went through the roof, because you're looking at the world champion of that stupid game, Agustina princess, I swear the bastard hasn't been born who could beat me at Pac-Man, I can gobble up the entire pellet supply in a single round, and if every so often I could hear Spider bellowing for blood from downstairs, I pretended it had nothing to do with me, I was remote from it all and looking out for number one, pac, pac, pac, eating pellets and darting around my labyrinth, I was just a little ball with a wild craving for pellets and a primal hatred of ghosts, and if any female cry reached my ears, I pretended not to hear it, I'm sorry, Dolores my girl, I can't help you, you're off my radar, but of course sometimes she would make some frightening noise and then I would get nervous and distracted, letting the ghosts take over, and Pac-Man lost lives like crazy.

It's not that I'm sentimental, but I made the mistake of talking to Dolores before the show, I had brought her up to my office to settle the bill and we chatted a little, just the usual small talk, and when I gave her the money, I added a tip that she thanked me for on behalf of her little boy and that was when I committed an inexcusable error: I foolishly asked her what her son was called and it turned out that his name was John Jairo, or Roy Marlon, or William Ernesto, one of those double-barreled bilingual names, but the problem was that the boy crept into my consciousness, because putting a child at risk by torturing the mother is hardly my style, and that's why I was so jumpy.

Then the great performance, that vaudeville of lashes and hooks and skewers and pinches and butt-slapping, reached its climax, and suddenly everything was quiet and from down below, the noise of the gym machines started up, the old familiar hum of the pulleys, the sharp clang of weights falling into place, the clatter of the presses, and I relaxed, thinking that the two escorts, Paco Malo and the Sucker, having had their fill of sado-masochism, were warming up on the machines now, Go for it, you flabby pair of thugs, let's see you lose those little bellies you started at L'Esplanade, I thought, putting some disco music on full blast for them to work out to, and I submerged myself in Pac-Man with maniacal concentration, I don't know how many hours I spent like that, Agustina doll, I swear that when I'm playing I lose all track of time, pac, pac, pac, opening and closing my big mouth and devouring pellets, pac, pac, pac, around and around the labyrinth overrunning ghosts, and I would've kept it up all night if the Sucker hadn't stuck his head in my office to say that there was a problem and Mr. Spider needed me downstairs. Holy Mary Mother of God, I sighed, stopping the game and trying my best to be patient, because who could bear Spider whining and begging forgiveness for his latest erotic-sentimental defeat and demanding that I set up the next extravaganza for the next day, and when I got down there he was looking very old and very fat and infinitely weary in his wheelchair, So what's the problem, Spider my friend, I asked condescendingly, The problem is that the little woman kicked the bucket, Midas my boy, God save her soul.

I won't even tell you what I felt, Agustina darling, or rather I will tell you; at first I didn't understand what Spider was saying, but when he pointed toward the other end of the room, where the machines are, there on one of the multipurpose stations, the Nautilus 4200 Single Stack Gym, my most beloved and recently acquired machine, equipped with a pec deck, leg extension station, abdominal bar, ankle cuff, side tower, and 210-pound weight stack, there I saw Dolores lying all disjointedly, as if they'd broken her neck by strapping her down and pulling the cable back too far, as if they'd drawn and quartered her, as if they'd turned my Nautilus 4200 into a torture rack, as if they'd gone too far and something had snapped.

Is she dead?, I asked Spider and his two thugs, and now I understood what the sound of weights and pulleys had been that I'd heard a little while ago, and that had made me think the worst was over when it was precisely then that things were getting hideously out of control, Is she dead? She's fucking dead, said Spider, dead, dead, dead and gone, but get a move on, Midas my boy, don't stand there with that long face, the mourning and condolences will have to wait until later because now we have to get rid of the body, And the guy who was with her?, I asked, He went for a stroll, Don't fuck with me, Spider, tell me where he is before it's too late, I'm telling you, Midas my boy, we got rid of him because he didn't want to play along with us; before the girl up and died on us we told her boyfriend that he'd better go home if he didn't want to play rough, that he should just go and not worry, that his fiancée would be fine with us, Get out, Velvet Hands, this is a man's game; Spider thought that his two sidekicks, Paco Malo and the Sucker, could do the job with more zeal than that lightweight, How was I to know, Midas my dear, that these two would turn out to be such bungling clods, and anyway the other guy was so yellow that he didn't say a thing when we suggested that he leave us alone with the lady, says Spider, at first he made a little fuss but he gave up looking out for his partner when the Sucker advised him not to get touchy because he might end up with an extra asshole, You do the best you can on your own, baby, I'm out of here, that was his gallant farewell, and right there he took out a little comb to smooth down his hair as if that might restore his ruffled pride, then he wrapped himself up in his magician's cape, and shazam, he disappeared as if by magic into the Bogotá night.

And now Dolores's little son was an orphan and there she lay as if surrendered to her fate, resigned to dying; maybe after all those fake rehearsals she was ready for her last and only true performance, as it turned out to be, This time it really was for real, I said to her as a kind of tribute.

And what came next, Agustina doll, was purely procedural and technical, lifting the girl off the machine, rolling her up in a rug, and at an order from Spider to his thugs, watching her leave for parts unknown in the trunk of the Mercedes, Don't come back until you're 100 percent sure she's gone forever and won't be heard of again until Judgment Day, those were Spider's curt instructions, and when the two killers and their victim were gone, I went up and turned off the disco music, which through all of this had kept thundering like a noise from hell, and I lovingly cleaned my Nautilus 4200 and polished the steel until there were no marks left on it, because after all the machine was innocent, then I turned out the gym lights and sat in silence on the floor at the foot of Spider's chair, and I buried my head between my knees and I started to think of you, my glorious Agustina, which is what I do when I'd rather not think about anything.

. . .

I SMELLED IT as soon as I opened the apartment door: it was the acrid scent of strangeness. It suffuses the house when Agustina isn't herself anymore, when she's in the middle of one of her crises, and I've learned to recognize it and make it part of my own sadness, which smells just like it; I know I've begun to exude the same scent.

After leaving Anita in Meissen the night of the Paloquemao bomb, I'd returned to Salmona Towers along Twenty-sixth Street, listening to the sirens of ambulances made invisible by the thick dust cloud of the disaster, the radio reporting forty-seven dead as well as an unspecified number of bodies in the wreckage, but I could only think about the shards that had surely cut Agustina's feet. Miraculously, the explosion hadn't shattered any of the windows of my apartment and I realized that nothing had happened to her feet because when I finally arrived, she had shoes on; she was fully dressed and wearing high heels and that surprised me. I interpreted it at first as an encouraging sign, because since the dark episode my wife had succumbed to slovenliness in matters of appearance, everything yielding to the pure centripetal force of her introspection except for the brief moments when she recovered some degree of consciousness of her physical existence. Madness is navel-gazing, my wife spends day and night in pajamas, or at most a sweatshirt, forgetting to eat, to listen, to look, it's as if her entire horizon of events is contained within herself. That's why I was surprised to see her in dark pants, high heels, and a jacket again, with her hair up, as if she were ready to go out but had to take care of a few things around the house before she left, these being essentially a compulsive transferring of objects from one place to another and back again, although what was happening now wasn't the familiar hauling of containers of water, but rather a kind of domestic reorganization that obeyed no visible logic but that required all of her concentration and energy; anyone who hasn't lived with a crazy person has no idea what boundless energy they can expend, the number of movements they make per second.

On her niece's orders, Aunt Sofi is standing in a corner of the living room, afraid to move because each time she tries, Agustina gets angry and won't let her; Agustina also orders me to stay where I am and establishes the rules of a new ceremony that we don't understand, a fresh epiphany of dementia that involves Agustina exerting relentless control over her territory. We live on this side, Agustina on that side, and she is as careful as a goalkeeper or a customs agent to make sure no one crosses that imaginary boundary, My father is coming to visit me, she announces suddenly, my father warned me that if you were in my house, he would cancel his visit because he doesn't want to

see you here, stay over there, goddamn it, that's where you bastards live and this is where I live, get back, you, get back, she
shouts at me.

• • • •

MEANWHILE I WAS THINKING of you, which is what I do
when I'd rather not think about anything, Agustina sweetheart,
you might say I'm fascinated by the texture you take on in
memory, smooth and slippery with no hint of responsibility or
regret, it's something like stroking your hair, the pure pleasure
of stroking your hair, so long as there are no consequences; God
played a dirty trick on us with the whole idea that one thing
leads to another until it becomes some fucking unstoppable
chain reaction, I swear that hell must be a place where they
lock you up with the consequences of your actions and make
you duke it out with them. That's why I'd rather remember you
the way I saw you the first few times that your brother Joaco
invited me home after school and there you were and it was as
if the air stood still, you were like nothing I'd ever seen before,
the fanciest doll in the most expensive store in town, my rich
friend's gorgeous sister, which is maybe why you've gone
around acting crazy ever since, to force us to remember that
you're flesh and blood and make us accept you with all your
consequences.

Your brother Joaco is one of those people who never had to
wear hand-me-downs, but I'm the kind of guy who only today,
after all kinds of struggle, has the means to dress like Joaco
Londoño, but I don't, anyway, Agustina baby, because I allow

myself the luxury of doing my own thing. So I'm a true phenomenon of self-improvement, a champion of self-help, but I'll
always bear the stigma of having shown up at the Boys School
on the first day of classes looking all wrong, despite my efforts,
and especially the efforts of my sweet mother, who bought me
everything new, combed my hair the best she could, and sent
me out with my skin shiny from soap and scrubbing, but she
missed a few details, and after all how could she not, when the
woman was a widow who had just arrived in the capital with
barely enough money to live respectably, which more than explains the countless errors she made regarding my appearance
and attire on that critical first day of school: for example, a
cheap leather briefcase, a green wool cardigan she'd knitted
herself, and scratchy wool pants, but among all these outrages,
my lovely Agustina, there was one, the white socks, that was
fatal, because to the cry of "White socks, black pants, homo
alert," your brother Joaco, young leader of the pack, came after me and beat me to a pulp, which I thank him for to this
day because he walloped the whole fatherless-boy-from-the-
provinces identity out of me once and for all, and that same afternoon I stole money from my mother's purse to buy myself
black socks and a pair of jeans, then I made her cry by an-
nouncing that she'd better not knit me any more cardigans because I wasn't going to wear them, and I had scarcely recovered
from the thrashing that Joaco gave me when I went after him
myself and kicked the shit out of him, and I really did kick the
shit out of him, even breaking a bone or two.

So then we were even, and from that moment on I devoted
myself to imitating my friend Joaco in every way. Because at

the Boys School, my pretty pale princess, I didn't learn algebra or discover trigonometry or develop any kind of interest in chemistry; at the Boys School I learned to walk like your brother, to eat like him, to look at people the way he did, to say what he said, to despise the teachers for being of inferior social status, and, in a broader sense, to radiate contempt as a supreme weapon of control; how could Joaco not be my beacon and guide when my father was a stone in a graveyard where my mother and I left carnations on the Day of the Dead, and meanwhile his father had given him a brand-new Renault 9 with an incredible sound system when we were just kids in ninth grade; it was in Joaco's Renault 9 that my ears were opened to the miracle of meesees braun yugotta lobleedotta by Yairman Yairmees, and how we admired Joaco because he was the only one who could pronounce Herman's Hermits and sing Mrs. Brown you've got a lovely daughter with all the syllables; everything was dazzling, a revelation, when Joaco let me step into his world.

Blasting along full fucking throttle in that Renault 9 we blew through stop signs and red lights, showing off our alpha-male status by tossing coins at the prostitutes on the corners and parking at the Icy Cream, wild-haired and triumphant as young cannibals, to order hot dogs and malteds from the car, and how could I have suspected, recently arrived from the provinces and living in a dark little apartment in the respectable neighborhood of San Luis Bertrand, tell me, Agustina doll, how was I to know that there existed such a thing as a vanilla malted, that glorious invention, and that if you asked for it over the intercom they brought it to you in the car. The albums that

Joaco had sent to him from New York, and the new smell of his
Renault 9, and the golden freedom of boys without a license
whizzing along the Northbound Highway, it was all too much
for me, my heart beat with a strange, wild anxiety, and all I
could do was repeat to myself, Someday this will all be mine,
mine, mine, and meanwhile they sang Jesterdei by the Beekles
and also the Sowns of Seilens by Simonan Garfoonkel, always
cursing Simonan for having stolen the song from the Indians of
Latin America, ending with the ultimate apocalyptic explosion,
the cosmic orgasm that was Satisfackchon by the Roleen,
AICANGUET-NO! SATISFACK-CHON! Those words became my
battle cry, my wish, my mantra; my credo was Anaitrai!, my secret Anaitrai!, my magic spell Anaitrai! Go on, Joaco, tell me
what Anaitrai means, what a powerful, amazing fucking word,
but he was very conscious of the superiority that his command
of English gave him over us and was happy to leave me hanging, It means what it means, he declared pompously, and then
he sang alone, with his perfect accent, I can't get no satisfaction
'cause I try, and I try, and I try, and then I asked again, practically dying, Come on, man, don't be a jerk, tell me what
Anaitrai means, tell me what Aicanguet-no is or I'll bust your
face, but he, unyielding and remote, knew exactly what to say
to put me in my place, Don't beg, McAlister, you can only understand if you're meant to understand it.

Of course I invented my own desperate tricks for social sur-
vival, like the time I discovered a Lacoste shirt among my father's old clothes, worn out and faded from use and too big for
me, but that didn't matter, nothing could dim the glory of my
discovery and with fingernail scissors I set myself the task of de-

taching the little alligator logo, and from then on I went to the trouble of sewing it each day to the shirt I was going to wear, you laugh, Agustina princess, and I'm laughing, too, but you have no idea how going around with that Lacoste alligator on my chest helped me have confidence in myself and become the person I am today.

Through the process of my systematic spying on that world of yours I came to realize the particular skill that I had and your brother Joaco lacked, and it was at your house and the Boys School that what I'll call the divine paradox was revealed to me, the lowly boy from the provinces with the mother in house-slippers, the cramped apartment in San Luis Bertrand, and the crocheted doily on the television: I knew how to make money, princess, it was as easy for me as breathing, while your brother, the son of rich men and the grandson of rich men, himself raised with money, had lost the knack, and my insight was to understand early on that the Joacos of this world weren't going to have anything but what they had inherited, and that it meant something when people here say, "Great-grandfather a mule driver, grandfather lord of the manor, son a man of leisure, grandson a beggar," in other words, there's a slow spiral downward, Agustina princess, with past splendor gradually losing its luster without anyone noticing and the original fortune dwindling until all that's left are the mannerisms, the pomp, the sense of superiority, the grand gestures, the alligator on the Lacoste shirt conspicuous on the chest. Whereas I, who came from nothing, was acquiring a talent, Agustina darling, a skill born of necessity and despair: the gift of making money, cold hard cash.

But I was still lacking the most important thing, Agustina angel, the truly important thing amid all that lesser detail, and that was coming to my friend Joaco's house and finding you there, doing chores with your mother, because then a sigh of truth rose from the very depths of my being, bursting from my chest, Oh, Mrs. Londoño, yugotta lobleedotta! Because year after year, growing up alongside us but out of reach, there you were, Agustina my love, Joaco's incredibly beautiful sister, the farthest and strangest star, so slender and white, always lost in your own head like someone hiding with the junk in the attic, you were the gold medal, the grand prix reserved for the best of us, the only trophy that your brother Joaco could never snatch, because he might be the richest and get the best grades and wear name-brand clothes, he might be the shit at tennis and waterskiing, the one with the spring vacations in Paris and the eternal tan, but there was one thing your brother Joaco couldn't have, Agustina angel, and that was you.

The second time I saw you was in the dining room of your house in La Cabrera, which to me seemed like a sultan's palace, and there you were making little towers of cookies with butter and jam, Joaco and me at one end of the table and you at the other end alone under the big crystal chandelier absorbed in your towers, so little, so transparent, with your huge black eyes and your insanely long hair, your hair was so long, Agustina baby! Back then I think it almost reached the floor, and when I tore my eyes away from you at last, I looked around and realized that this room contained all the elements of my happiness, what I mean is that just then something clicked in my head and I knew that everything I needed to be happy was right there, those too-high ceilings, like they were meant for giants not humans, that chandelier of crystal prisms that sent bits of rainbow dancing over the white tablecloth, those vases so crammed with roses that it looked as if a whole rose garden must have been cut to fill them, that porcelain as delicate as eggshells, those heavy knives and forks that were nothing like the light, tinny utensils we used in San Luis.

They're silver, you shouted at me from one end of the table to the other and that was the first thing your mouth ever said to me, your mouth with its thin lips and perfect teeth. I'm not kidding when I say that I understood more things that day than you'd expect of the twelve- or thirteen-year-old boy I was then; for example I took careful note of your teeth, because thanks to orthodontia, yours were as perfect as your brothers', and that same afternoon, snooping around in your bathrooms and trying to find out what this world was made of, this world that was so different from mine and that was driving me crazy with wanting, I found out that your family didn't brush their teeth with toothbrushes like other mortals but with a gringo device called a Water Pik, and I came up with the plan: to begin to save money by selling pictures of naked girls at school, first to buy a Water Pik and then to have my teeth fixed. And that's how the world works, Agustina princess, I was precocious enough to realize from an early age that you don't get anywhere with yellow, crooked, rotten teeth, while perfect smiles like the Londoño children's smiles and the one I bought for myself later were worth as much as or more than a college education.

Of course it was also a revelation to me that the food served by two maids dressed perfectly for the part on those eggshell dishes at the table for twelve at your parents' house, a table that by the way is almost identical to the one I have today in my own apartment, that food, as I was saying, the chocolate with corn-flour buns, the cheese rolls, and the cream cookies, was exactly the same as the food my mother served me on our unbreakable plastic Melmac dishes in our living-dining room in San Luis Bertrand; that detail amused me, Agustina princess, it amused me to see that although you called it tea and we called it a snack, at five in the afternoon the two families served the same down-home food, the very same cheese rolls in the heart of Bogotá's most fashionable neighborhood as in San Luis Bertrand, and from that I deduced that the unbridgeable gap between your world and mine was only a matter of appearances and surface polish, which amused me but also encouraged me to fight for what I wanted.

Well, if it's just a question of packaging, I said to myself that day (and I've already told you that I was only thirteen), then I'll be able to bridge that seemingly unbridgeable gap, and in fact by the time I was thirty I had bridged it and your mouth had already been mine, and I had two authentic Baccarat crystal chandeliers, a never-used dining table seating twelve, twenty-four silver place settings, and an impeccable smile, and yet look at me today, a shadow of my former self, brought down by the mistaken perception—it was too much to expect of a child's intelligence, after all—that the difference was merely a question of packaging. It wasn't, of course it wasn't, and here I am, paying for my mistake in blood.

MY SKIN STILL CRAWLS when I remember the episode of the dividing line because perhaps never before had my wife rejected me so ferociously. With her teeth clenched and hatred in her eyes, Agustina ordered me to stay behind the line and I did what I could to obey her, hoping she would calm down, but the geographic division she imposed wasn't fixed and that made things even harder, which is to say that the line shifted depending on her whim; at one point I sat on one of the chairs in the dining room, which strangely had remained on my side, at which Agustina hurried to annex that peninsula to her own territory, reclaiming the dining room as hers and throwing me out.

If you tried to take a step in any direction she was on you like a tiger, Out, you bastard, she said to me, my father doesn't want to see you in any way, shape, or form, and that goes doubly for you, you filthy pig, she said to poor Aunt Sofi, whose face was screwed into an expression of guilt, anguish, or utter exhaustion; she who up until that moment had shown such fortitude and presence of mind now seemed shaken by the exceptional virulence of this development, she hadn't seen anything like it since she'd come to stay with us and to tell the truth I hadn't either, what was happening now was really serious, Go do your dirty business elsewhere, you disgusting pigs, Agustina was raving so madly and her abuse was so over the top that it couldn't just be abuse, or hyperbolic use of language, it had to be true that she felt an enormous urgency to get us out of the house, it had to be true that the supposed presence or arrival or return of this father of hers was an earth-shattering event that split things in two, leaving Agustina with her father on one side and all other despicable mortals on the other.

Watching her, I wanted to bang my head against the wall thinking of everything I never asked her about this Mr. Carlos Vicente Londoño, who, despite having been dead for years, now turned out to be the mysterious guest in the wings, the person turning me out of my own home and driving me from my wife, the man who was the living incarnation of everything I hated, and yet who was the object of baffling, almost religious worship for Agustina. The hardest thing of all was to witness the control that Mr. Londoño exercised over his daughter, to the point that it brought to mind the word *possession*, which doesn't even form part of my vocabulary since it belongs to the realm of the irrational, which is of no interest to me, and yet it was that word, and none other, that kept occurring to me that night. I couldn't help feeling the conviction that my wife was possessed by her father's will; the split in her manifested itself so intensely that I was having a hard time reining in my own thoughts and remembering that it was my wife's sick mind that was molding itself to her father's purported wishes, and not the other way around.

I've always had the feeling that during her crises my wife goes through patches of devastating isolation, it's as if she's brutally alone on a stage while I observe her performance from a seat where I'm surrounded by the rest of humanity, and yet this time I knew that I was the solitary one, while she was accompanied by a force greater than herself, the will of her late father. Agustina talked endlessly about her father and his approaching visit, speaking so quickly that it was hard to understand her, something that was made even more difficult because half of the time she was talking to herself, aspirating the sentences as if she were plucking them from the air and wanted to swallow them, Agustina, my love, don't swallow your words because you'll choke, but my voice couldn't reach her; between us there was only estrangement and distance, we were two exhausted creatures unable to draw near each other even though we were in the same cave, while down below the city throbbed silently, cowering and broken, as if the horror of that night had crushed it and now it was waiting for the start of the next round. Agustina darling, let's not let madness, that old foe, extinguish any spark of hope, but Agustina isn't listening because tonight she and the madness are one.

My wife is crazy, I acknowledged to myself that night for the first time, and yet the thought wasn't enough to convince me, it can't be, Agustina darling, because you're still there behind your madness, despite everything you're still there, and probably I'm still there deep down, why should I be gone, do you remember me, Agustina?, do you remember yourself? I'd never been afraid that she would hurt me physically, how could she when I was five inches taller and twice her weight and mass, but that night the fear was there; everything about her indicated a desire to assault, to wound, and her way of grabbing things and brandishing them showed determination, even an urgent desire, to hit with them. The last thing I ever wanted was to come to blows with the woman I love, but she was doing everything she could to start something, seeking by any means possible a kind of des-

perate final outburst of physical violence that would put an end
to my decision not to attack her no matter what. It was as if she
were trying to rob me of the infinite love for her that lets me systematically evade all her provocations and keep our coexistence
peaceful; maybe Agustina understood that this was the only
way she could do away with the main obstacle to her father's arrival, because I was that obstacle.

Who had this Mr. Londoño been, what had his relationship
to his daughter been, where had his power over her come
from? I would've given anything to know. When I got to the
apartment that night with the suitcase that Agustina had
brought with her to the Wellington in my hand, sad trophy and
resounding proof of my defeat, I was obsessed with the man my
wife had spent one night with—well, just one night that I knew
of, God knows how many others there might have been—and
I set the suitcase in plain sight on the dining-room table so that
she would come upon it suddenly, I needed to know what her
reaction would be, whether she was capable of looking me in
the eye, but what she did was hurl it furiously toward my side
of the apartment, Who left this shit here, she asked and then
she immediately forgot about it; the delirium induced by her father's imminent arrival made her hyperkinetic, stricken by a
fever that caused her to nearly emanate light, and I began to realize that even if the story of her lover was true and behind my
back Agustina had one hundred other lovers, the true, inde-
structible rival, the one anchored in the depths of her disturbance, and possibly also her love, was the ghost of this father
about whom I couldn't form the vaguest idea, apart from the

caricaturish notion of the Bogotá landowner that I'd had from the start, The man has that advantage over me, I thought, the advantage of being an unknown quantity.

Shut behind the wall of rejection that my wife had erected, I remembered the crazy autobiography that at some point she'd wanted me to help her write, though we never made it to the first page, now I'm convinced that it was really a plea for help, that she needed to go over the events of her life with someone to make sense of them and put her mother and father in their proper place, bringing them out from inside where they tormented her, but back then how was I to know; the truth is that I thought the ludicrous idea of the autobiography was another one of those stabs in the dark that she was making simply because she refused to take note of what direction she was really headed. This was how it happened: after I was introduced to her that time at the film society, I left feeling awed by her beauty, which honestly struck me like a lightning bolt, but like a lightning bolt that dazzles and then disappears, by which I mean that it left me without the slightest sense of nervous anticipation of a second chapter to follow that first encounter, sure as I was that this strange, delectably lovely girl was one of those shooting stars that crosses one's path and speeds on, so it came as a great surprise when I found a note in my cubicle at the university signed by none other than her.

• • •

MY FATHER TOLD ME to be back by midnight, says Agustina, and I don't want to be even a single minute late; I must obey orders, especially because they come directly from my father. It was out of the goodness of his heart that he let me go to the movies with the boy in the Volkswagen on the condition that I be home before midnight, and as I turned my key in the lock at the agreed-upon time, there was my father, wide awake and waiting for me in an armchair in the living room. Is that you, Father?, and in the dark came his deep voice and the puff of his pipe, glowing like a watchful eye. Who were you with in that car?, It was just me and the boy who brought me home, Never again, thundered my father, You'll never ride alone in a car with a boy again because I forbid it.

She is surprised that he sounds so impassioned, so upset, nothing I'd done before had ever shaken him, in the past few years I'd been disobedient and rude and a bad student, and my father had severely reprimanded me for all of that, but never like this, up until that night my father had always been distant with me, and even when he scolded me it was in a blank kind of way, but suddenly this was all I had to do to attract my father's attention and scrutiny, to make him quake, to wipe everything from his mind but my date that night and my strict obedience of his orders, When you come home late it shows a lack of respect for me, I do respect you, Father, and if that's your rule, I'll always obey it, I was here by midnight, Father, as you ordered, But you were alone in that car with a boy, make sure it's the last time it happens.

Then Agustina went to bed and she couldn't stop wondering whether her father might possibly have guessed what had happened, that the boy in the Volkswagen had invited me to the movies but didn't take me there; we stayed in the car and talked, eating hot dogs at the Icy Cream, until he pulled his Great White Candle out of his pants. Agustina couldn't see it in the dark of the deserted street; she didn't see it with her eyes, which refused to look, but she saw it with her hand and she discovered that it was enormous and felt like wax, then she had to let go of it so that she would be home by midnight just as she and her father had agreed, and there I found him waiting restlessly for me in the dark living room, his pipe smoldering.

Her father had never waited up for her before, nor had he spoken to her in a voice so charged with emotion, almost deranged, Agustina thinks, Why were you alone with that boy when I told you to go out in a group, He just gave me a ride home, Father, she replied, not wanting to confess what she'd discovered, and wondering whether her father had one, too, and whether it was the Great Staff with which he ruled, And then, in bed, I couldn't sleep, says Agustina, and what kept me awake wasn't the car or the night or the first date on my own, not even the thing that came out of the boy's pants and felt like wax, but knowing that my father hadn't gone to bed because he was worried about me, it had never happened before, says Agustina, never.

When I was invited to the movies again I said yes because I knew that it would bother my father and keep him up, and this time Agustina didn't come home at exactly midnight but a little later in order to push her father a few inches further, she would bait him, but just a little, not so much that he'd hit her, just a little, to see whether what she thought she'd noticed that first time was true, that if she went out at night with a boy her father couldn't ignore her, at last Agustina had learned to do something that would get her father's attention, and this second time that she went out with a boy, a different boy, who did take her to the movies, Agustina asked him to let her touch the Great Candle, And he let me and this time it burned, it didn't feel like wax but instead it burned and stung my palm, and Agustina went home knowing that her father, who maybe could guess what she had done, would be there waiting for her seething with rage but in the end there would be no explosion because he had no evidence, he could only brood over what he suspected she might have done in that car, unable to prove it, but it would hurt, it would hurt him, it would have to hurt her father whether she'd done anything or not, and he himself, with the palpable pulsing of his fears, had been the one to reveal the secret to her, grant her this power over him, give her room for maneuvering that she would know how to take advantage of from now on, while the question of who profited from this agony and who endured it, father or daughter, was something that chased in circles and couldn't be decided.

Then comes the third time in her life that her father pays attention to her, But this time his suppressed fury has grown, says Agustina, although just by a few more degrees, not enough for him to hit me—he never hit me, only Bichi—but enough so that his voice quivers when he scolds me for having come home fifteen minutes late, my father forbids me to go out again with the new boy and this serves me as proof of his affection, of his intent, vigilant affection, I forbid it, Agustina, do you understand me?, you're never to go out with that boy again, and it was then that Agustina swore to God that she'd never go out with him again, If you don't like him I won't, You're right,

Agustina, I don't like him, there's something strange about that boy, the way he looks at you, I have no idea who his parents are and I don't want you hanging around with strangers, Yes, Father, yes, Father, yes, Father.

Once in bed, Agustina burned with fever and pride at being the object of her father's disapproval and in a little solitary ceremony, secret and in the dark, she promised him never to go out with that boy again, This is my offering to you, Father, she prayed to herself, I'll never go out with him again because you asked me not to, and I won't go out with anyone who looks at me that way either, or anyone whose parents you don't know, or anyone who you for any reason don't trust, which in the end is everyone, And I kept my promise, I kept it every time, says Agustina, I was true to my word, I never went out with that boy or any other boy more than once, I always found new ones. As a gift to my father, who demanded their heads, I shunned the ones he shunned and offered their heads up to him in exchange for his presence in his armchair, waiting for me with his pipe, checking his watch over and over again to monitor when I returned.

Minute by minute, my father kept watch over my nights, and I went out with a different boy each time and I asked each of them to let me touch the Great Candle, and that was how I learned that there were many different varieties and sizes, some burning hot and some cold, some swift and some slow; only with my hand, only my hand, never letting them get close to other parts of my body, never between my legs, or at least that's how it was for the first few months, doing it with my hand was enough to make Father guess it from the shadows on my face, though he couldn't say anything to me because he didn't have proof, shadows and expressions are almost the same as nothing, and just by putting my hand on the Great Candle of every boy who took me to the movies or the Icy Cream on 100th Street, I could be sure that my father's attention would be fixed on me until midnight, the trick of arriving fifteen or twenty minutes late worked well and it thrilled me to know that he would be suffering agonies.

Never before, says Agustina, had I held the keys to my father's love, and to think that I only discovered them when boys started asking me out to the movies; never before and never again would my father pay so much attention to me. This is the last time you go out with that boy, he would demand, which was his way of punishing me, and especially of punishing himself because I had arrived twenty-five minutes late, You're not letting him take you out again, because he's from Pereira or Bucaramanga or Cali, my father only likes boys from established Bogotá families, and when it comes down to it, he doesn't even like them if they chew gum or handle their silverware clumsily, Father always finds something wrong with them, and I know that the possibility of pleasing him is in my hands, I just have to make a small sacrifice, says Agustina, I have to sacrifice the boys, who aren't worth much anyway, in return for the great reward of my father's attention, his unwavering concentration on me until midnight, Yes, Father, I'll give them up; for you, I'll give up those who came before and those who have yet to come, one by one and all at once, so long as you stay up waiting for me and so long as when I come in you look at me with that terrible question mark in your eyes, eyes that want to be sure I didn't do anything in the car, and I swear to my father that I didn't but I know how to say it so that I sow poisonous seeds of doubt in him, and the truth is that I did it at the movies but only a little bit, and I did it for you, Father, to keep you alert and on guard, because at last I'd learned how to wield my powers over you, but I don't know whether it was your love I won in the cars of my thousand and one boyfriends, Father, whether it was your love or only your punishment.

• • •

LIKE A "GIFT OF THE NIGHT" is how, in his diary, Nicholas Portulinus describes the boy from Anapoima who came asking for piano lessons from the great musician of Germany and Sasaima, the apparition who, with hands still soft but already skilled, played "The Greedy Cat" for the Maestro with a professionalism that seemed at odds with his long golden girl's hair, with his voice that oscillated between the high peaks of childhood and the valleys of a deepness that was already gaining ground. In the presence of this unexpected guest, this lovely, talented boy who'd arrived from out of nowhere, as if he'd dropped from the sky or escaped from a dream, the great Maestro was left transfixed and utterly vulnerable, like someone who'd just witnessed a miracle. But unlike the fighters in the Greek ruins, the cherished spawn of delirium, the young performer of "The Greedy Cat" was real, real as could be, most definitely of flesh and blood, almost cruelly beautiful, childlike, overflowing with talent. It was as if this Farax were invented by Nicholas in one of his reveries, but Farax isn't wounded like the marble youths, he's not bleeding from any wound, he's surprisingly alive and healthy, and he can be touched, or he could be touched, or one would like to touch him; one can see how much Nicholas would like to touch him, and in fact he dares to touch his shoulder, or if it's too much to say touches, if the verb must be qualified, he scarcely brushes his shoulder the day everything begins.

And now Blanca appears onstage, with Nicholas dragging her by the hand, to behold the prodigy with her own eyes. Come, Blanca my dear, Nicholas has told her, you're going to hear music like nothing you've heard before, and Blanca comes, annoyed and disbelieving, inured long ago to surprises and worried about the ripples of delusion that again crease her husband's forehead. Blanca seeks strength that she no longer possesses to tackle once again the tiring task of deflating Nicholas's fantasies and reducing them to their proper proportions, and yet, as she confesses in her diary, when she sees the child sitting at the piano she's overcome by a strange feeling, "Suddenly I felt that I'd been given back the capacity to forgive," to forgive life its rigors and herself her mistakes, to forgive Nicholas his terrors and start over again. "If I had to explain the strange, deep-seated feeling that came over me when I saw and heard Abelito, whom Nicholas has called Farax from the beginning, I would have to say that he struck me as the living image of the Nicholas I knew years ago, when everything was still promise and possibility, with no hints of shadow," in other words, when her husband was still the sturdy man recently arrived from Germany whose visions seemed merely a poetic touch and whose twisted nature had yet to reveal itself.

Suddenly, seeing this boy playing "The Greedy Cat" on the piano, Blanca has before her again an immaculate, unburdened, carefree Nicholas, and she reproaches herself for allowing the flutter of a pleasant but unfounded feeling that life is granting her a second chance. As for Farax, as soon as he sees the fine-featured woman with dreamy eyelashes and dark circles under her eyes coming into the parlor hand in hand with the Maestro, he has the feeling that his hands will be paralyzed by fear and he won't be able to play his best, but this proves untrue; his hands respond with joy and confidence because Farax feels at home before this woman with the somber gaze, as if he is with his mother or his sister, as if he is with someone he could love, or maybe someone he already loves from the first instant.

To listen to the visitor, Nicholas and Blanca sit together holding hands, he all aquiver with expectation, barely perched on the edge of the sofa and smacking his lips as if he's hungry and about to be served a great delicacy, she trying to do two things at once, watching the boy with one eye and following her husband's gaze with the other. Farax, meanwhile, gives himself over to the rhythm of the dance, forgetting his distinguished audience, rocking on the stool to keep time and accompanying the melody with an unconscious crooning, sweet and innocent. When "The Greedy Cat" comes to an end, one of those famous sentences is spoken, of the sort that is seemingly simple but loaded with hidden meaning and that seals the destiny of the speaker as well as the recipient. You and I understand each other, Nicholas says to Farax, using the casual *tú* instead of the formal *usted* although they hardly know each other, although there is an age difference of almost twenty years, although one is the master and the other the apprentice. Farax doesn't know how to react to this unexpected form of address, to the Maestro's smoldering gaze, to the brush of the Maestro's hand on his shoulder, but he understands that his life will change in the wake of this *We understand each other* that wafts past his ears like a damp breath. Could we hear something else?, asks Blanca, moved, in a voice that isn't quite hers, and Farax, as if understanding the transcendent nature of the moment, starts to play the *Blue Danube* waltz with all the requisite solemnity.

Beyond the euphoria revealed in Nicholas's and Blanca's respective diary entries, one might ask whether this was really the "sweetest of sweet" instants that Blanca describes, and if it was, was it so for all three of them?, for two of them?, did anyone have a foreboding of pain and future shadows? During that first meeting, which of them was jealous, and of whom? What did Nicholas see in this Abelito to whom he gave the name Farax: a promising disciple?, a rival in the trade?, a rival in love?, an object of desire?, did he see his heir, the continuer of his art and in a certain way also of his life?, or rather did he see in him the one who would trigger his ruin, the bringer of the silent news of his approaching end? In her diary, Blanca asks herself the question in broader terms when she speculates whether decisive moments are decisive from the instant they occur, or whether they only become decisive in light of what comes after them and what they bring about. Meanwhile, there's no diary or letter to explain what Eugenia was doing in the big parlor that exuded dampness, what corner she'd been

relegated to when her father, her mother, and Farax all forgot
her, leaving her alone with the lead soldiers lined up in march-
ing order.

Farax came from far away and to judge by the modesty of his
clothes and the battered state of his knapsack, it seemed un-
likely, even impossible, that he would have money to pay for
room and board in town, so the Portulinuses invited him to dine
with them that night and to sleep there if he so desired, and in
fact he did so desire, not just that night but all the following
nights for the next eleven months. If only silence were white!,
Nicholas shouted at dawn the first time Farax spent the night
with them, If only silence weren't so damnably filthy and
tainted, he said with a sigh, bursting into his wife, Blanca's, bedroom and waking her up. What are you talking about?, she
asked, sitting up in bed and struggling to see where such a
thorny topic would take them at this hour of the night. I'm saying, Blanca, that I wish silence wasn't polluted. Polluted how,
she asked just to gain time, at least enough to put on her robe.
With noise, with noise, what else?, can't you hear it?, the silence is riddled with sounds that hide in it like creaks in the
joists, and that eat away at it from within; you'd have to be deaf
not to hear the humming and buzzing, or are you still asleep and
that's why you can't understand me? Nicholas shook her, grasping her by the trim of her nightdress, while she begged him to
lower his voice so he wouldn't frighten the children and the visitor, and at the same time tried surreptitiously to find the drops
for the tinnitus, or chronic ringing, that her husband suffered
from in both ears. To compose I need pure silence, Blanca, the
way poets need blank pages, or do you think Lord Byron could

have written anything worthwhile on a sheet that was already full of words; and seeing that his wife was deathly pale from being shaken he let go of her and smoothed her crumpled nightdress and disheveled hair. It's all right, Blanquita my dear, it's all right, he said, sitting down beside her, it's all right, nothing's the matter, don't look so frightened, I just want you to understand that despite what people think, silence isn't beneficial or restful.

Now melancholy instead of frenzied, he explained to her that there were basically two kinds of noises that plagued him and drove him to distraction, or that actually there were many but these two were the worst and most persistent, one sibilant and sly, like the sound an old woman with no teeth might make whispering an interminable secret in your ear, and the other rasping, sometimes like the purr of a cat and sometimes mechanical, like the clatter of a waterwheel or a millstone. When the whispering noise takes possession of my ears I can compose but I can't think, and with the other noise the opposite occurs. It's all in your head, Nicholas, go to bed, darling, I don't hear any old ladies or cats, and then he left the room cursing her and slamming the door.

The next day at breakfast, as the young guest busied himself serving oatmeal to Sofi and Eugenia, the couple's two daughters, or rather the two surviving after the early deaths of five other children, Nicholas repeated at the table the same description he'd given Blanca the night before of his auditory woes. The difference, he says, is that now the rasping noise doesn't sound like a waterwheel or a millstone but like a chair being dragged along a very long passageway. You're right, Professor, Farax replies in that disturbing voice of a child who minute by minute is leaving childhood behind, and who at the instant he speaks is already a bit more of a man than he was when he was serving the oatmeal, You're right, Maestro, that's why I go high up into the mountains, where I seek the inner and outer peace I've lost. These words seem wise and profound to Nicholas, who has the look on his face of someone who has heard the ultimate truth revealed, and he smiles placidly. You do understand me, he whispers to Farax, you and I understand each other, a statement that Blanca interprets as an indirect reproach for the clumsy words she spoke a few hours earlier on the same subject, and for the first time she experiences what from then on will become a constant, that anything she says will sound coarse to her husband when contrasted with the angelic and extraordinary pronouncements that issue from Farax's lips.

A few days later it's Blanca's thirty-fourth birthday, and the trio and the two children celebrate what is unanimously pronounced a perfect day, a time that Nicholas describes in his diary in English as "domestic bliss," spent walking along the river, collectively analyzing a Bach fugue, taking turns reading aloud passages from Shakespeare and Goethe. Heaven, as Blanca put it, smiled on them again that day, enabling Nicholas to rise in the morning with the swelling of his body sufficiently reduced so that his good looks were partially restored and to wake Blanca with a bouquet of daisies that he'd cut himself from around the stone fountain, and also that night at dinner to give her a pearl necklace with a note reading, Take these, my tears. Enraptured by this message, Blanca ran to her diary and wrote "Am I not the happiest woman in the world?", but something bad, something she didn't want to record, must have happened later on in the festivities, because the next sentence in her diary, written in different ink now and in a different spirit, says "Today I turned thirty-four and I was immensely happy, and yet the house is plunged into a strange silence . . ." Nicholas's diary gives no clues to what happened, either; the only thing set down on the page corresponding to that date is "Today, which is her birthday, Blanca is wearing her hair up, gathered on top of her head, which accentuates the elegant shape of her face and makes me desire her greatly. I ask myself how it's possible that such a woman could love me."

. . .

THE NOTE THAT WAS slipped under the door of my cubicle was written in the kind of adolescent, absurdly rounded handwriting in which the *i* is topped with a horrible little circle instead of a dot. I still have that note, and I keep it with me in my wallet because it was the starting point of my relationship with Agustina; this was ten or twelve days after I met her and it went like this, "Professor Aguilar, I'm the person you met the other day at the film society and I need to ask you a favor, which is that I want to write my autobiography but I don't know how, you may ask whether anything memorable or important has ever happened to me, anything that deserves to be told, and the answer is no, but it happens to be an obsession of mine anyway and I think you could help me with it, since you're a literature professor, after all."

Instead of including her telephone number so that I could reply, she gave me her address, and then she continued on in a second paragraph that was even odder than the first, and that kept me awake that night tossing and turning as I tried to gauge the precise degree of her flirtatiousness. What could such a la-di-da girl want with a man like me? Could she really be making a pass at me? "Listen, Professor, before we start working on the autobiography I'd like to see your hands, that's the first thing I notice in a man, his hands, you don't know how fascinated I am by men's hands, when they do fascinate me, of course, because although I always notice them I hardly ever really like them because they're never the way I imagine them. When we met as we were leaving the film club I couldn't see yours because you had them in your pockets, so I thought that maybe you could send me a photocopy of your hand, either of the two, really, but make sure it's both sides, the palm side and the other side, maybe you can tell me what that other side is called, I mean the reverse-palm, but anyway, put your hand in the photocopier like a piece of paper, and make the copy and send it to me, although of course my other fascination is hair, the hair of any mammal but especially the hair of the human male, and when I see a man with nice hair I can hardly stop myself from reaching out to touch it, although actually I couldn't see your hair either because you were wearing that little black wool cap, I hear that you're a lefty and I'd like to know why lefties are always wearing stocking caps no matter what the weather's like, but don't think I didn't notice your eyebrows, your eyelashes, and your beard, because I did, and I liked them all because they were silky and thick and dark though I especially liked your mustache, with those little gray hairs that make it glisten, but I realize that asking you to cut a lock of your hair and send it to me would be going too far, so if you'll let me have that photocopy of your hand and your answer to my other question, I'll be satisfied, Agustina Londoño."

In the literature department at the National University there's only one photocopier, and it's in the dean's office, where besides the dean and the students who mill around filling out forms or asking to see their grades, there's the secretary, Doña Lucerito, a permanent fixture and a nice lady except when it comes to anything having to do with the photocopier, which she presides over with a stinginess maddening to us professors who need to use it, because not only does she give us a reproachful look when we come more than once a week but she also makes us keep track of how much paper we use, which meant that I couldn't see how I would manage to sneak in and photocopy my hand. But I left my cubicle and strode decisively toward the dean's office, firmly resolved to succeed and prepared to have it out with the dean or Lucerito herself, or even look like an idiot in front of my students if I had to in order to win the affections of the lady charging me with such strange feats, laughing to myself at the things a gray-haired man in his forties could end up doing clandestinely. My crowning achievement was pressing the buttons with my right hand to take a picture of my left hand, front and back, or reverse-palm, to use the term coined by that strange creature Agustina, and I put the two photocopies into an envelope along with a reply in the negative regarding my collaboration on her autobiography, explaining that it was called autobiography and not plain biography precisely because it was oneself and not anyone else who should write it, and in closing I gambled everything by asking her to meet me the following Sunday in the hydrangea garden in Independence Park at ten thirty in the morning.

I waited for her in the park from twenty past ten until after eleven, convinced that it was a miserable waste of time because there wasn't the slightest chance she'd come, and yet, just when I was about to leave, she actually showed up, bringing me some popcorn as a gift, which we sat on a bench to share and which she ended up eating herself while I told her about the seminar I was teaching on Gramsci, Lukács, and Goldmann's theories of the novel, and then she showed me what she'd done with those photocopies of my left hand, and it made me laugh because it seemed a flagrant assault on my rationalist core; Agustina had shrunk the images down and turned them into a reversible card, palm on one side, back of the hand on the other, and laminated it, I call it the Hand That Touches, she told me, I gave it to one of those street laminators who'll laminate your name if you don't watch out, and look, he did a perfect job, I carry it in my wallet and it's my amulet.

And now Aunt Sofi and I were standing in the corner of the living room where Agustina kept us corralled crying, Back, pigs!, and there was something terrifying about it all, something demonic. As Agustina occupied herself by dragging away the furniture and objects on our side and moving them to her side, we were able to talk a little about the bomb. Aunt Sofi told me that through the window she'd seen a mushroom cloud two hundred feet tall rising over the city, and when I asked her whether it had affected Agustina much, she told me that after the tremor had woken her, she'd gotten up in a state of excitement saying that this was the sign, What sign, child? The sign that I must prepare for my father's arrival, Do you want me to help you?, Aunt Sofi asked cautiously, If you want to help, get out of the house this instant.

The imaginary line that divided the apartment in two began to firm up and stopped fluctuating so much; Aunt Sofi and I were assigned to a corner that had no access to the door, the telephone, the bathroom, or the kitchen, and everything else, including the second floor, became the exclusive property of Agustina, Don't sit on the sofa, damn you, that's for me and my father, or Into your pen, you scum, that side over there is for pigs and this side over here is for us, and of course this Us referred to Agustina and her father, because not a trace was left of the us that she and I had been, In that sense my niece is just like her mother, says Aunt Sofi, always seeking Carlos Vicente's love, always forgiving him, in life and now in death, too.

I didn't see it at the time, but every tragedy has its humorous side, and today I can remember what happened with a sort of fondness and even laugh, because Agustina really had us pigs screwed, not even letting us have a glass of water or make a telephone call. Aunt Sofi was getting impatient and she said that she was going to step over the line no matter what because she had to go to the bathroom and she couldn't hold it any longer, Even if Agustina is furious, I have to pee, she said and she managed to slip away and run up the stairs, heading for the upstairs bathroom since it would have been impossible to make it into the other one without Agustina seeing her, and a few minutes later she came down with a shawl for herself and a poncho for me, because the icy fog that comes down from Monserrate each night was descending on us now.

I watched Aunt Sofi sneak into the kitchen and I thought, Clever woman, she's going to smuggle us some food, remembering just then that the only thing I'd had in my stomach for hours was those few bites of Anita's pink doughnut, sweet, pretty Anita, would Anita, the girl from Meissen, be asleep now?, and yet it wasn't food that Aunt Sofi brought from the kitchen, hidden in her pocket, but the little battery-powered radio so that we could listen to the news, What must have happened to all those poor people who were hurt, asked Aunt Sofi, and she hadn't finished the sentence when Agustina discovered us and snatched away the shawl and the poncho and turned off the radio; still, we managed to hear that Pablo Escobar was claiming responsibility for the attack.

IT WAS A SIMPLE TURN of the screw that catapulted me from glory to ruin, Agustina darling, I swear. It started with the back-and-forth of gossip and secrets in the gyms, dressing rooms, and bathrooms at the center, one of those conspiracies that builds up underground until it explodes and shit flies everywhere, and I suspect that the person who set off the bomb was this woman Alexandra, who is physically a goddess but mentally not all there, though I don't know, the truth is I can't be sure it was her, she's someone who's been coming to the center for years to work out and at first she was kind of a girlfriend of mine, I told you I sleep with the prettiest ones and she was no exception, so we were more or less together for a while, but I extricated myself from that fast, because as I was saying, she's a chick with an outstanding body but a fucked-up mind, and on second thought maybe it's paranoid of me to blame her for something that happened so long afterward.

When it comes down to it, it could have been anyone, because anyone could've read *El Espacio* and started the rumor, although it's strange, very strange, Agustina sweetheart, that someone from this side of town would pick up that trashy tabloid; in general my clientele thinks there's no point wasting time on bad news, especially if it involves people they don't know, and if they ever feel like reading, they read *El Tiempo*, which lets them know what's going on the way they like to hear it. But it was my bad luck that a story in *El Espacio* about the mysterious disappearance of a nurse had to make its way to the Aerobics Center, especially since Dolores's vanishing was an unremarkable occurrence if ever there was one, the kind of thing that goes completely unnoticed in this country, I mean, if no one complains when a whole hospital is robbed and plundered, who's going to get worked up about a single missing nurse, but you know how it is when your luck turns.

El Espacio went after the story of the phantom nurse and released a statement by her boyfriend which said that the last time he saw her she was entering a gym on the north side of town. So far not great, though bearable, Agustina doll, but the next day *El Espacio* runs a longer story and bingo!, specifies that the gym in question is Midas McAlister's Aerobics Center, and publishes a picture of Dolores, alive and smiling, a younger and less worn-down Dolores than the one I met, but definitely Dolores, no doubt about it, although *El Espacio* doesn't call her that, they call her Sara Luz Cárdenas Carrasco, and they don't describe her as a whore specializing in S&M who died fulfilling her true destiny as a professional shit-eater, but as a registered nurse whose colleagues say they've heard nothing from her, and there's also the testimony of the man who claims that he's her boyfriend and that his name is Otoniel Cocué, who, as you'll have guessed, Agustina darling, is none other than the pimp, although he doesn't share that bit of information and instead identifies himself as an accountant because he certainly couldn't reveal the nature of his miserable illegal profession, and as a result his accusations are only half-truths, the kicking and squirming of a man in over his head; for example, he claims that the nurse Sara Luz, his fiancée, exercised at the Aerobics Center, and that she went in one night and never came out.

But the women in the 7:00 a.m. super-rumba class catch wind of all of this—from Alexandra, if my suspicions are correct—and they tell the women in the noon spinning class, who tell the women in the five o'clock spinning class, who pass it on to the eight o'clock class and the women in the massage rooms and the women in the tanning booths, in other words by evening the story has taken on Hollywood dimensions and when they see me stroll by, some women clam up, others laugh, and the most brazen come up to me to ask what happened; and then of course there's the flirt who tells me straight out that if I'm Bluebeard she volunteers to be the next victim. Certain games become popular, like getting spooked, hearing moans, spotting the killer, or pointing out suspects, and so it goes, the Aerobics Center brimming with rumors, fears, ghosts, jokes, and teasing, and one thing leads to another according to the inexorable law of consequences until I get a visit from the police, who have a warrant to search the place and question me, but as you might expect, sweetheart, they find nothing and I don't let anything slip, Women come in and out of here all day, Sergeant, I tell a lieutenant who immediately reminds me of his rank, Of course, Lieutenant, excuse me, I was saying that at least three hundred women come through this door every day, and three hundred leave by the same door, and then the lieutenant performs some routine procedures, like checking the attendance records to verify that in fact there is no Sara Luz recorded, and I very calmly pass him the sign-in book, Go ahead, Lieutenant, take a look if you want.

And now prepare yourself, Agustina doll, because the story is about to take a turn for the surreal, imagine my surprise when I see that on one line, in grandiose handwriting in blue fountain pen, the lieutenant has found the signature of one Sara Luz Cárdenas Carrasco, her name written out in full and with all the i's dotted and t's crossed, I swear I almost fell over backward, it must have been that idiot Dolores the night of her tragic performance, the fool probably saw the book where gym members signed in and thought it would be cool or trendy to sign her name there, too, after all why not, she probably thought of herself as an artist or a model, so I had to smooth things over by explaining to the lieutenant that there was nothing strange about someone attending one of our free promotional sessions, This is a public place, Lieutenant, anyone can come in, maybe the girl did stop by but that means absolutely nothing, I repeated several times, though also and most important I slipped the man enough cash to make him keep his mouth shut and leave me in peace, or relative peace because the whole business was getting me down and it was starting to look like there was no way out.

If I don't give you a detailed account of what came next, Agustina sweetheart, it's because in the end there were no further police or legal repercussions for me beyond that routine inspection ending with the usual bribe to the authorities; the lingering problem was more subjective, or emotional, maybe, because the gym clientele didn't want the excitement to be over and they kept adding to the story and updating it in their imaginations, with talk about Ms. X passing by and the neighbors hearing music until late the night before, a sobbing woman bricked up in the wall, cars coming in and out of the parking lot, a creepy vibe in a certain room, and speculation as to who that poor girl must have been.

Anyway, Agustina darling, I won't bore you much longer, but the honest truth is that the ghost of Dolores, or Sara Luz as she was called now, started to grow and suffocate me and give the Aerobics Center a bad name, to the point that even I, each time I smoked a joint to relax a little, was plunged into the most unpleasant fantasies in which my own gym became an Inquisition torture chamber and my beloved machines were turned into racks and Dolores was crucified on the Nautilus 4200, What the fuck, I thought, this is her revenge, and I tried to kick-start a dialogue so that we could come to some kind of agreement: I promise you, blessed soul of Dolores, that as soon as the scandal dies down I'll send money to your John Jairo, or Henry Mario, or whatever your kid's name is, so he can go to school, I promise you, my dear Sara Luz, that if you help me stop the gossip, I'll bankroll a technical-school degree for your William Andrés some day.

On top of everything, while all this was going on, time was passing, and the date went by on which, according to Mystery, Pablo had promised to make good on our investment, so as you can imagine, Agustina baby, Spider Salazar and Ronald Silverstein were all over me, Has it come yet, What's the meaning of this, What the hell is going on, and there I was taking the blame and saying how sorry I was in an effort to put out this second blaze, I understand, Spider my friend, it's the pits, Silver old man, you're both right, it's shit, I realize this delay is shit, but everything will work out in the end, you'll see; that's what I told them, Agustina princess, but the truth was that I had no idea what might be going through Escobar's head since Mystery wouldn't even keep his appointments with me. I spent hour after hour waiting for him at the cemetery hoping he'd show up with the money at last, or at least with an explanation, but there was nothing, the days passed and nothing. Go on, Midas, Spider commanded imperiously, find Pablo and let him know that this little delay is putting us in a tight spot, Relax, Spider old man, as soon as his messenger shows up I'll pass on the complaint, You never told me, Midas my boy, that you weren't in direct contact with Escobar, Well, yes, or I mean, no, I used to be but now the situation has changed a little, try to understand, Spider my man.

That week our Thursday dinner at L'Esplanade was extremely tense; since Spider and Silver couldn't pester me in front of Joaco and Ayerbe, who didn't know what was going on, they satisfied themselves by making merciless fun of me, and I was feeling awful, so that even though I ordered my favorite dish, partridge in a chestnut chocolate sauce, I couldn't eat a bite, and the truth is, my stomach wasn't up for partying, what with my friends fucking with me, Dolores's hounding of me, the crisis at the Aerobics Center, Pablo's delay, and on top of it all, the stranglehold of the loans I'd had to take out to get together all the cash for Pablo.

This was a Thursday, Agustina princess, and the very next day, bam!, there was that bombing at L'Esplanade and we all survived in one piece, those of us who weren't at the restaurant, that is, because anyone who was there came out in multiple pieces; I escaped by twenty-four hours, sweetheart, it was my amazing luck that the bomb went off on Friday, because if it had gone off a day earlier I wouldn't be here to tell the tale. It was a massive explosion, and the diners, the cooks, that frog Courtois and his incredible wine cellar, the ladies with crocodile purses and crocodile skin, and even the cat were blown up, and when Escobar claimed responsibility for the attack, everyone asked what reason he could possibly have had to break his truce with the Bogotá oligarchy, planting a huge bomb in a restaurant full of rich people right in the heart of the residential north side of town. Some said that he was furious and blinded by pride because he'd been blackballed at a country club, or because the DEA was putting the squeeze on him, or because of the extradition threats, or because he was banned from running for office, or because the government wasn't abiding by its agreements with him, or all of the above, but whatever it was, the residents on the north side of the city started to shake because until then they'd thought that Pablo's war wasn't with them, but the dead and the wounded and the rubble of L'Esplanade proved otherwise. Escobar's problem, I tried to explain to them without success, is that he got tired of the balancing act, of us taking his money with one hand and trying to kill him with the other.

And Spider, like a pesky fly on a noble steed, was after me constantly, Explain this to me, Midas my boy, now that Pablo has come unglued, what the fuck is going to happen to our investment?, who's got an answer for me?, and Rony Silver chimed in, too, and then there was Mystery, vanished into thin air, and finally I sank into a state of profound melancholy and retreated alone to my bedroom to turn off everything that I possibly could from my bed with the remote control and sleep twelve or fourteen hours straight with the blinds shut in a single long peaceful night.

And there in my room in the dark, Agustina princess, with the telephone unplugged, I thought about Pablo, remembering our second and last meeting, which wasn't at his Naples estate this time, no samba dancers or giraffes or Olympic-size pool, but in a shabby house that smelled like the den of a rogue tiger, I never knew which of the neighborhoods of Medellín it was in because they brought me there with my eyes blindfolded, but anyway the Boss's hiding place this time was only furnished with a few chairs and beds and there he was in a T-shirt and baseball cap, fatter than before, and he made me laugh because he showed me a picture that had been taken a few months earlier; guess where, Agustina darling? In front of the White House in Washington, if you can believe it, because according to what he told me he could enter and leave the United States whenever he felt like it.

The picture was really incredible, Pablo Escobar, the most wanted man in history, in a white shirt and with his face bare, no dark glasses or cap or fake beard or plastic surgery, just standing there, as he is, leaning like any tourist against the railing around the White House, which you could see behind him with its Greek columns and the triangular pediment of its north face, so as I looked at that picture, Agustina angel, I said, Unbelievable, Don Pablo, President Reagan is looking for you everywhere and there you are right at his front gate, and he replied, Reagan's problem, Midas my friend, is that he's the one behind bars.

And yet things had changed for Pablo since that carefree afternoon in the capital of the empire, because in this dark, empty place that was his hideout he didn't strike me as his usual self; there was even one silly detail that made me think the end might be near for him, and it was a cardboard box holding the remains of some fried fish he'd been eating, I'm sure one of the gunmen guarding him had bought it for him at some stall, which was fine, but what I couldn't understand, Agustina princess, was why Pablo hadn't ordered for those cold, greasy leftovers to be taken away. I don't know if you follow me, it was nothing, really, just the sort of thing I always notice, carelessness that I tend to interpret as a sign of decline.

Pablo doesn't waste time, he gets straight to the point, so in twenty minutes we had settled the four business matters on the table and then he went on to question me about what has always been his great concern: he wanted to know what was being hatched in Bogotá with regard to the Extradition Treaty that would surrender drug traffickers to the United States, and when I told him it was almost certain that Congress would enforce it, I saw him tremble with righteous fury and heard him speak a momentous sentence, the same sentence that later echoed in my memory when the bomb exploded at L'Esplanade, and take careful note, Agustina princess, because what he said was the historic proclamation of his vengeance: I'm going to spend my fortune making this country weep. Do you realize what that means, doll?

Since Pablo is a phoenix and has the nine lives of a cat, he had soon overcome the difficulties he was in at the time of our second meeting and was the master of the universe again, and there were more samba dancers and armies of hired assassins and bloodbaths all over the nation, and meetings with ex-presidents of the Republic and giraffes and airplanes and Olympic-size pools, and so two years had gone by since I'd heard him utter his threat, and then the other night, when the bomb went off at L'Esplanade, I remembered it and thought: The time has come, goddamn it. I'm going to spend my fortune making this country weep, that's what Pablo said to me, Agustina darling, and his fortune must be the biggest in the world, so if the man manages to squeeze one tear from us for each dollar he's got, think how much crying we still have left to do.

• • •

WHEN WAS THE LAST TIME you saw your sister, Eugenia, I ask Aunt Sofi, a more or less routine question with no notion of the kind of answer it will elicit, The last time? Why it was the day of the final judgment, the day the family was destroyed, What are you talking about, Aunt Sofi, About precisely that, Aguilar, about the day the family became simply a memory, and a bitter memory at that, I'm talking about a Palm Sunday thirteen years ago, A Sunday, I say, why is it that everything has to happen to us on Sunday?

Agustina was seventeen and finishing high school that year, Aunt Sofi tells me, and Joaco, who was twenty, was already in college, and Bichi had turned fifteen but he was still a child, though he was very tall, probably already as tall as he is now, which is six foot two, but he was childish and shy, too, a boy with few friends, desperately attached to home and especially to Agustina. It was six thirty in the evening, says Aunt Sofi, when it happened. Like every Sunday when they were at their house in La Cabrera, lunch consisted of banana–passion fruit sorbet, a proper chicken-and-potato *ajiaco* soup, and custard for dessert, and at three o'clock everyone was home, a fairly un- usual occurrence, Joaco in tennis shoes and white shorts be- cause he'd spent the morning playing sports at the club and the other two children, Agustina and Bichi, still in their pajamas, because on Sundays Carlos Vicente Senior made the special concession of allowing them to come to the table like that. My sister, Eugenia, and I had taken palm branches to be blessed at the twelve o'clock service at Santa María de Ángeles and on the way home we stopped at a little street market to buy avocados for the *ajiaco*, and since it was a beautiful afternoon we sat for a while in the sun on a low wall, although the real reason we sat there was because my sister, Eugenia, had broken a shoe strap, isn't life incredible, Aguilar, if she hadn't broken that strap we probably wouldn't have started to talk, which we almost never did although we'd lived together all our lives except for a few brief intervals.

Do you remember what you talked about?, I ask, Yes, of course I remember, it began with the strap, the two of us discussing how the shoe could be fixed, Tomorrow, if you want, on the way to the Areneras clinic I can leave it at a shoe-repair place for you, I'll take in the pair so that both can be reheeled, that's what I said to my sister, Eugenia, At the time, Aunt Sofi says, I'd been working for several years as a volunteer nurse at a clinic for the children of the workers in the sand pits north of the city, and though I don't recall what paths our conversation took, we ended up talking about Sasaima, a subject that we usually avoided because of the many unspoken things that had happened there, but that day, as luck would have it, we wound up discussing the eternal mystery of Farax's passage through our childhood, Farax?, I ask, it sounds like a dog's name, No, Aunt Sofi answers, he was a handsome blond boy, a piano student, his name was Abelito Caballero but we called him Farax, Where did the nickname come from, I ask. That I couldn't tell you, nicknames are like sayings, you never know who came up with them. Anyway, that afternoon, for the first time in our lives, Eugenia and I began to approach the edges of the mysterious chasm of Farax's stay in the house where we grew up, the brutal way things changed between my parents from the time Farax first appeared.

Eugenia and I were coming closer and closer to the heart of the matter, Aunt Sofi says, and it was I who adjourned the meeting, reminding her of the *ajiaco*, I who prevented us from going any further, Maybe you were afraid, I say, Yes, I might have been, maybe I believed that all secrets are kept in the same box, a single box of secrets, and that if you reveal one you risk exposing all the rest, And you were keeping a big secret from your sister, I say, Yes, well, I already confessed that to you, Aguilar, let's not go over that again, All right, I agree, but tell me more about your conversation after the Palm Sunday service. Let's go, Sofi said to Eugenia, your husband and children must be hungry, and Eugenia smiled—sadly, I think now— You've been living with us for how many years, she said to Sofi, and you always say it that way, your husband and your children, I wonder whether I'll ever hear you say my brother-in-law and my nieces and nephews, and it was precisely because of words like these, which stung me so, that I always avoided conversations with my sister, Aunt Sofi says to me and then confesses that she was afraid of what might happen, On the one hand I felt the urge to reveal everything to Eugenia and beg her forgiveness a thousand times over, a forgiveness I knew that she could never give, but on the other hand some part of me rebelled and I felt a terrible urge to say to her face, *My* husband and *my* children, Eugenia, my husband and my children, because they're more mine than they are yours, but the conversation took another turn and nothing more was said about Farax or the other, even pricklier, matter; it was left at that because they never had a chance to speak of it again.

It's been one of our rules for living, Aunt Sofi says to me, that way of taking refuge in silence when the truth is about to surface, We're paying a high price for that strategy, I say, I know, says Sofi, you're talking about the tangles in Agustina's head, That's right, Aunt Sofi, that's exactly what I'm talking about. Anyway, the day was still glorious and the rest of the way home Eugenia and I laughed, and that was even more un-usual, hearing my sister laugh, the two of us laughing because the broken strap was making her limp, and then during lunch Eugenia sat at the head of the table, beautiful, silent, and re-mote as always, while I served the *ajiaco*, running in and out of the kitchen to make sure that everything was ready, the trays of chicken and the ears of corn, the cream, the capers, and the avocados in their respective bowls, and the *ajiaco* with the green herb *guascas* piping hot in the big earthenware tureen, because on Sundays the food was served with a wooden spoon from black clay Ráquira dishes, just as it had been all our lives in my mother's house, despite the fact that the local cuisine was never to my father's taste, since he was Colombian when it came to composing traditional dance tunes but still German when it came time to eat, but as I was saying, Aguilar, in Car-los Vicente's presence my sister, Eugenia, fell silent.

And Agustina?, I ask, Agustina, too, she was so entranced by her father that she couldn't utter a word. After lunch every-body went off on their own, Carlos Vicente and Eugenia shut themselves in their bedroom, Joaco left in the car, and what Agustina was up to I don't know, Try to remember, Aunt Sofi, I'd like to know what Agustina did after lunch, I don't know, Aguilar, anything I told you would be a lie, and yet I remember perfectly that I went out into the front garden to prune the roses, and that Bichi put on a sweater and socks and boots over his pajamas and said that he was going to ride his bike around the neighborhood, although he really only rode around the block, over and over again, always clockwise, I saw him pass the house at least seven or eight times, so tall that the bike looked comically small and the cuffs of his pajama bottoms riding up over his ankles, with those black curls still uncombed, that beautiful face, those eyes that already had such depths, and an almost feminine delicacy of features, and I remember asking myself, When will that boy change, he's such a solitary child, it must be fear of his father that keeps him from growing up and making friends, I remember all that with horrible clarity, Aunt Sofi says, I've read that when the atomic bomb fell on Hiroshima, shadows were etched on the walls where they were cast, and everything that happened during our family atomic bomb has been chiseled into my memory, too, my pupils even retain the image of the long-stemmed yellow roses that I cut that afternoon for the dining-room vases.

Around five thirty in the afternoon the maids brought hot chocolate with cheese buns and yucca rolls to the television room and one by one we all gathered there, even Joaco, who on Sundays didn't usually come home until late at night, and, odder still, Carlos Vicente Senior was there, which really was strange because except at mealtimes he was either out or shut up in his study, not being a man who devoted much time to family life, but I tell you Aguilar, we were all there as if we'd been summoned, as if someone directing the scene had made sure that no one was missing, by which I mean to say that it was written that everyone be in attendance that Sunday. We'd probably all been drawn into the television room by the scent

of the fresh-baked yucca rolls but that would be an easy explanation; the only real answer is to acknowledge that the scene
had been scripted by fate long ago. Aunt Sofi was serving the
hot chocolate, the two younger children were in an argument
over which channel to watch, Carlos Vicente and Joaco had
started a game of chess, and Eugenia was knitting a lilac-
colored shawl, You may ask what the significance of these minor details is and I tell you again that they mean everything,
because this was the last time for us.

Though no one was expecting her, Aminta came to visit; she
was a maid who'd worked in the house for years, since she was
very young, in fact, until the day, some eleven months before
that Sunday, when she told us that she was pregnant; this is
what's terrible about Eugenia, her dark side, when she heard
that Aminta was expecting a baby she fired her, the children
cried, I tried to intercede, but Eugenia stood firm, maybe it was
the same horror she's always had of other people's sexuality
surging up in her again, a horror that's probably also loathing of
her own sexuality, I wouldn't be surprised, but most important,
this compulsion to censure and regulate the sex life of others
was something she shared with Carlos Vicente, the two were
united by the joyless pursuit, they coincided in it, they were ac-
complices in it, and it was the pillar of their authority, maybe
even the mainstay of the family honor, as if by hereditary training they knew that whoever controls the sexuality of the rest of
the tribe is in command, I don't know whether you understand
what I'm talking about, Aguilar, Of course I do, I say, if I didn't,
how could I ever understand this country of ours.

But Aunt Sofi continues to overflow with explanations as if

she's addressing them to herself, It's a kind of force more powerful than anything else, something in the blood, a pitiless and
indignant condemnation of sexuality in any form as something
repugnant, Eugenia was insulted by couples who kissed in the
park, to the extent that she complained because the police
wouldn't prevent them from doing *that* in public, *that* being
anything having to do with sexuality, with sensuality, two
things that she always refused to name, reducing them to a *that*
uttered with a grimace as if merely mentioning them soiled her
mouth. I don't know where she got the phobia because neither
my mother nor my father were like that, they had other fixa-
tions but not that one, nor did anyone else in Sasaima, in such
matters Eugenia is more like Carlos Vicente, and I'd say that she
learned the phobia from him and then developed her own extreme version; viewing people's sex lives as a personal affront
must be a hereditary trait of the families of Bogotá, or maybe
it's the very quality that gives them their stamp of distinction, I
couldn't tell you, Aguilar, but what I do know is that it's there
that the heart of the suffering lies, suffering that's inherited,
that spreads and is transmitted, suffering that people inflict on
one another; in Eugenia's case I suspect she's just as hard on
herself privately, but in the case of Carlos Vicente I know for a
fact that it was only a front.

Let's go back to that Sunday with Bichi riding his bicycle
around the block, you pruning the roses, and Agustina holed up
somewhere in the house, I suggest but then immediately ask, Or
had Agustina gone out? No, no, she was still there, I just don't
know what she was doing, but of course she was there, Aunt
Sofi assures me, the scene was set, the actors were ready, and

now all that was lacking was the trigger to set things off, which wasn't long in coming. It was a quarter past six that evening when Aminta arrived; it had been a while since we'd seen her and she'd brought her newborn daughter, intending to announce that in honor of my sister and me she would be called Eugenia Sofía, and to ask them whether they would be godparents at the baptism, To ask whom? Why Eugenia and Carlos Vicente, the baptism would take place in a few weeks and the baby was a little doll, Aminta had dressed her all in pink, the bonnet, the dress, the mittens, the booties, even the shawl she was wrapped in was pink, then Eugenia hugged Aminta as if to say, Now you're pardoned, and although she didn't say it I know she was thinking it, because for her, giving birth was like forgiveness for a great sin; my sister, Eugenia, said, and I'm repeating this word for word, With the yarn I have left when I finish this shawl I'm going to knit this little darling an outfit to keep her warm at night, that was exactly what she said, this was thirteen years ago but as I told you, Aguilar, I remember every gesture, every word, like the shadows etched on the walls of Hiroshima, and I'm sure that Agustina remembers it, too, step by step and word by word, because it's emblazoned inside all of us who were there, throbbing in our hearts and memories.

Everyone wanted to hold Aminta's new baby, except for Carlos Vicente and Joaco, who watched the scene from the remove of men who're playing chess and who don't involve themselves in women's things, and it was Agustina who made the next move, with everyone, in my memory, repeating their actions as if following to the letter a script from which there is no escape, as if playing carefully choreographed parts; Agustina, who was sitting on the floor in front of the television, got up, still in her pajamas, you know, one of those huge T-shirts, the same kind she still sleeps in, though now she wears yours and then she wore her father's, Agustina got up, went over to Aminta, and asked her if she could hold Eugenia Sofía, taking the baby with the kind of maternal instinct that makes it possible for a woman to cradle a baby in her arms even when she's never done it before, and she starts to cuddle it and talk baby talk to it, making the kind of noises that are repeated as if the adult were trying to imitate the child's cooing, you know what I mean, says Aunt Sofi, and I say that I do, I do know, but that she shouldn't stop, she should keep going. What Agustina said to Aminta's baby was precisely this: Oh my goodness what an adorable little thing, as she smiled lovingly at it and stroked its cheek with the tip of her index finger, and at that moment Bichi, who was also sitting on the floor, got up and went to stand behind Agustina, looking at the baby over his sister's shoulder, and he stroked its cheek just as she'd done and repeated, in the same tone of voice and in exactly the same way, what she had just said, Oh my goodness what an adorable little thing.

At that instant Carlos Vicente Senior, who as I told you was present but not participating in the family scene, got up abruptly from his armchair, his eyes inflamed with rage, and kicked Bichi violently in the back near the kidneys, a blow so sudden and ferocious that it knocked the boy down, making him stumble first against the television, which also fell; we all felt our hearts leap in our chests and for a few seconds we weren't able to react, paralyzed by the horror of what had just happened, and then we watched Carlos Vicente Senior approach Carlos Vicente Junior, who was still facedown on the ground, and kick him a few more times in the legs as he mimicked him, Oh my goodness what an adorable little thing, Oh my goodness what an adorable little thing, Talk like a man, for God's sake, not a queer!

• • •

THEN CAME THE DAY of the Father's great wrath, says Agustina, and the younger brother was the scapegoat, Per sua culpa, per sua culpa, per sua maxima culpa he's on the floor and the Father is kicking him, how many times did I warn you, my sweet pale-skinned brother, my little lost boy, not to do anything to annoy the Father, Talk like a man!, he ordered you and as he said it he turned into a powerful beast looming over you, you, a child lying beaten on the floor, and my powers eluded me, they weren't able to protect you, they couldn't reach you, Talk like a man, he ordered you and his wrath was just and terrible and it filled the house, then he fell back of his own accord, the Father stunned by his own strength and the cruelty of the punishment, And the younger brother got up, says Agustina, and his face, or what could be seen of his face hidden behind a tangle of black curls, blazed with a strange light, Were you crying, Bichi, or begging for forgiveness? No, you weren't crying, you weren't trying to say anything, you weren't speaking out at last in the man's voice that the Father had demanded, you just got up, awkwardly because your back was hurt, pressing one hand to the spot of the Great Blow and picking up the machine.

What machine, Agustina, Aguilar asks her, The machine that had been broken, Do you mean the television?, Yes, that's what I mean, And what did your brother do with it, He put it back in its place, And why do you think he did that, He did it out of pride, says Agustina and her voice changes, she begins to talk to herself again, pontificating so that it seems as if all her nouns are capitalized, as if she's addressing people who aren't actually there, It was your pride that made you pick up the machine, you wanted to show the Father that he hadn't cowed you, didn't you?, the rest of us watched you from the depths of despair, Come on, Agustina, says Aguilar, don't talk like you're preaching a sermon, let's just have a conversation, the two of us, Leave me alone, Aguilar, let me continue with my sermon, because it's important for you to know that now the Father is just staring and puffing and panting from his Great Exertion, if you interrupt me I won't be able to tell you that the Father is exhausted after performing the sacred duty of punishing his son, now he's no longer in the spotlight and has lost his leading role because it's the younger brother, the Lamb, who is moving among the pillars of salt.

Tell me the name of the lamb and the names of the pillars of salt, says Aguilar, The Lamb is called Bichi, his name is Carlos Vicente like my father but we call him Bichi, and the pillars of salt are Eugenia, Joaco, Agustina, Aminta, and Sofía, Who is Sofía?, Sofía is my aunt Sofi, Your father's sister or your mother's sister?, Not my father's sister, my mother's sister, and it's my little brother, the one we call Bichi, who gets up from the floor and, despite his hurt back, he bends down and lifts the full weight of the machine, Hadn't we agreed that it was the television?, All right, the television, which is now a broken machine, and he puts it back where it was although the screen is smashed, Do you remember what you and your brother were watching on television before your father got angry?, What stupid questions you ask, Aguilar, we were watching He-Man and She-Ra, we'd fought over the channel for a while and finally settled on He-Man and She-Ra, and then we were happy, actually it is nice to remember, I wonder whether Bichi remembers, too, because a few minutes later there came the blow and the television crashed to the floor, sparking inside because it was still plugged in, it was Bichi who unplugged it.

You were moving slowly, Bichi Bichito, says Agustina, and you stood very tall, taller than my older brother, much taller than the Father and you looked at all of us, one by one, letting your gaze linger on each of us, and I fell to my knees to beg forgiveness with my inner voice and to summon my powers, which after the Event wouldn't come to me, and Bichi half turned, his hand holding his hurt back again, and with the other hand he finally pushed his hair out of his face so we could see that he wasn't crying and he went walking out very slowly, I'd seen you cry so many times, Bichi Bichito, after the Father hit you, but not this time, this time you were the unscathed victim who walks away after the sacrifice, What sacrifice are you talking about, asks Aguilar, your father kicking him?, If you already know, why do you ask, Agustina says, I can still see Bichi as if the picture of him is stamped on my brain, What was he wearing?, asks Aguilar, Our ceremonial robes, I heard otherwise, that he was in his pajamas, That's true, says Agustina and her voice lightens and grows steadier, he was still in his pajamas but he looked incredibly tall to me, so that I thought he wasn't going to fit through the door, and his hair, which was a mess, was the only fierce thing about him, the rest of him was moving slowly, without the slightest hesitation or uncertainty, and since from where we were you could see the big stone staircase that curves up to the second floor, we were able to watch how you climbed step by step, little brother, stopping for a moment to arch your back and close your eyes slightly before immediately beginning the Ascent again, then I tried to follow you and was stopped short by a shout from the Father, Leave him alone, maybe he'll learn something this time, he ordered and Agustina obeyed, she stayed where she was, on her knees, Your Will is my command, Father, don't unleash your wrath on me, too; now that the Lamb who had angered the Father was gone, the Father could sit down again and return to his chess game with the older brother, picking up where he'd left off to carry out the Punishment.

He'll be crying now that he's up in his room, says Agustina, telling Aguilar what she'd been thinking at that moment, speaking to the bearded man who's sitting across from her, listening to her, Agustina likes his beard because it's thick and silky, she likes his graying mustache, That's what I thought, Aguilar, but Bichi had shut himself in my room, not his, although I only learned that later, I thought he would have shut himself in his room to cry after the Punishment, as he always did, and that I was the only one he would let in, to bring him Consolation, but this time she didn't go to him for fear of the Father who said, What are you looking at, all of you keep doing what you were doing, a command that it was impossible for me to obey, because I'd been watching television and now I couldn't; Father kept issuing orders as if nothing had happened, You, Aminta, can go now, I congratulate you on your daughter's birth and I agree to be her godfather, Eugenia, you keep knitting, and you, Sofi, pour me another cup of hot chocolate, please.

Was that what they were having, asks Aguilar, hot chocolate?, I don't want to talk about it, says Agustina, don't say that word, chocolate, I don't like it, You don't like the word, or chocolate itself?, I don't like it, I mean it, Aguilar, I don't want you to ask me about it anymore, what matters is that the Father's orders demonstrate that everything is still the same in the house, but his hands suggest otherwise, because they're trembling, I can see them tremble, Aguilar; although the Father tries to hide it he's shaken by the ferocity of his actions, just now he's still unaware of the Repercussions of his actions, or maybe he senses something but he doesn't have a clear idea of what's about to befall him, then we see you, Bichi Bichito, my little brother whom I'd so much like to see again someday, we witness your Return, now you're coming down the stairs and you look huge and your face is shining with righteousness and beauty and there are no tears in your eyes, just a determined look that makes the Father quake and that prevents his hand from setting down the knight that he has ready for his next move, the Father never played that piece, Aguilar, the knight remained in the Father's hand forever, you were the Knight, little brother, because in your hand you held the real playing piece, the great destructive token that would bring down the house and everything around it, too, remember Bichi Bichito, you who forgot, remember what we used to repeat in our ceremonies, that we wouldn't use the Power, satisfied in the knowledge that it was infinite and that even though it rested in our hands we wouldn't use it because that's where our strength lay, in keeping it hidden and not making use of it.

Bichi came down the stairs radiating light, Agustina says to Aguilar, the younger brother turning toward us resplendent, purified by suffering, brandishing in his right hand the keys of destruction, Do you mean the photographs of your aunt?, Yes, Aguilar, that's exactly what I mean, Bichi came in holding them high and I shouted to him with my inner voice, the one that can't be heard but that reverberates, I shouted to him from inside with all the strength of the powers that had fled me, Don't do it, brother, remember the Oath, remember the Warning, if you show them what you've got, if anyone else sees, the pictures will lose their value, if you show them my powers will slip through my fingers like water, because they're hidden powers and light makes them melt away, and I repeated the Warning: the keys of destruction only shine bright and instill terror so long as they're hidden, you'll vanquish me if you reveal them and once I'm vanquished no one will be able to protect you from the hand of the Father, forgive me, Bichi, a thousand times forgive me.

Why did you ask him to forgive you, Agustina?, says Aguilar, Because that was the Terrible Time my powers slept but from now on Agustina won't let it happen again, she swears to Bichi that she'll be more careful, more vigilant, I swear to you, Bichi Bichito, trust in me again and don't do what you're about to do because I'll be left helpless, and also because you swore in our ceremonies that you would never do it, that you would never let them know we had them. But Bichi did it: on the little table in the middle of the room, with everyone watching, the Father, the mother, the aunt, the older brother, and me, Agustina, the sister pleading silently for what was about to happen not to happen, the thing that split our story in two, Bichi, the younger brother, ten feet tall, He couldn't have been that tall, Well, maybe not quite, then almost seven feet tall, That sounds more likely, Almost seven feet tall and with a halo of black curls that brushed the ceiling, he dropped the Photographs and all of us saw them, and the air kindled, the void opened beneath our feet, do you understand, Aguilar?, says Agustina in a different voice, her everyday voice, What I'm trying to tell you is that from that moment on our lives were never the same again, now I see it that way but sometimes I forget.

My eyes were fixed on the floor, says Agustina to the man with the beard who's there to listen to her, I wasn't present in my body when my little brother turned his triumphant gaze on my mother, waiting for her to set the crown prince's circlet on his curls because he had just overthrown the Father; there they were, before my mother's eyes, the proofs of the Father's failure to love, the Father's betrayal, Tell me what that proof was, Aguilar insists, Proofs, proofs, Agustina repeats, I already told you, the Photographs, Tell me what photographs, Ask Aunt Sofi, I want you to tell me, Some photographs of Aunt Sofi's breasts that my father had taken, slutty Aunt Sofi the slut, and my father was a slut, too, that was why now the mother would embrace her hurt child, the Lamb, why she'd fold him in her loving arms, he a victim, she a victim, and at last justice would be done and the unfaithful Father would be expelled from the kingdom, and the youngest son, the Lamb, fixed his huge eyes on his mother waiting for her warm welcome but I knew it couldn't be, I knew it, Aguilar, I knew that no support could be expected from the mother because my powers, although they were gone, whispered with their lesser voices in my ear, telling me that it couldn't be, that the bond between the mother and her youngest child couldn't be cemented that way, that the bond between the mother and her daughter would never be cemented.

Do you mean you?, asks Aguilar, I mean the daughter, Agustina, and that's why I shouted, No, Bichi, don't do it, that's why I begged him with my inner voice, the one that makes no sound but that reverberates, Don't do it, Bichi, you don't know what the mother is capable of, you shouldn't trust her, you should fear the mother's extreme weakness, the mother's weakness is more dangerous that the Father's wrath, but the younger son didn't believe it and that's why the photographs fell there for everyone to see, the photographs that the Father had taken of the Naked and Willing Aunt, the usurper of her sister's husband, the Terrible Aunt who would be expelled with the Father so that the mother would no longer be so sad and distant, the younger brother wanted vengeance for himself and also for the mother, so that she wouldn't be the snow queen with the shard of ice in her heart anymore, he wanted to defeat the Father's authority and melt his mother's icy heart, and Bichi the Lamb, He of the Hurt Back, gazed at us all from the lofty summit of his towering height, the reign of the Lamb lasting for a single minute, the kneeling family bowing their heads at the evidence of betrayal, the sister alone remaining apart, with her eyes closed, because she was the only one who already knew,

knew that the Great Revelation of the photographs had just taken place, that the mystery had been laid bare, that Pandora's box had been opened and the Furies unleashed, and Father was transformed, for the first time Father was smaller than a dwarf, tinier than a mouse, and Aunt Sofi, she of the big breasts, covered her face with her hands, while the older brother was the only one who dared to touch the photographs and look at them one by one, and Father didn't even try to stop him because Father was a dwarf, a mouse who could only watch for the reaction of the mother, Father was waiting for the mother to let her sword fall on him, the younger brother was waiting for the mother to let her sword fall on Father's neck, and only I knew that it couldn't be, that we wouldn't seal our Pact with the mother and that on the contrary our powers would be annihilated forever and the Great Revelation would become meaningless drivel, a pathetic children's game.

Agustina looks at me and laughs. You make fun of me, Aguilar, because you say that when I'm raving I talk like Tarzan, You talk like the Pope, I say, Yes, it's true, sometimes I can't help talking like the Pope when he blesses the crowds from the balcony of Saint Peter's.

. . .

AND YOUR MOUTH, AGUSTINA?, I learned a few things about your lovely mouth, too. It was unnerving, believe me, to see you sitting at the other end of the dining-room table again, like when we were children, though not at your house in La Cabrera this time but at your cold-country place, which is where you Londoños have always looked your best, or shone in your full splendor, lordly and at ease in old corduroy pants and high boots for riding your own horses, casually wearing tweed jackets or baggy sweaters hand knit from the new, strong-smelling wool of sheep that, like the horses, also belong to you, and I'm certainly not talking about those tight sweaters that my own mother knitted for me with green and gray skeins of yarn bought at the variety store on the corner; you have to under-stand that there's a world of difference between the one and the other.

The clothing you Londoños wear in what you yourselves call the cold country is especially impressive when you pair it with a languor that nicely matches the mood of your surround-ings, as well as with the reading of books in French by the fire and the presence of the dogs that you treat better than humans, and here we come to another key point, the kinship with dogs, which is something you have to be born with, like christening robes; I, for example, have to scrub my hands after touching a dog because the smell clings to me and drives me crazy, but that doesn't happen to any of you Londoños, who no matter what you do or what kind of people you get mixed up with, always play for the squeaky-clean team of Roger & Gallet when it comes to smell, except for you, Agustina darling, who prefer some kind of suspiciously Oriental scents that exasperate your brother Joaco and make him sneeze.

I remember how impressed I was each time Joaco would say, On Friday we're going to the cold country, meaning your house in the highlands, or Today my mother is in the hot country, which meant at the Sasaima estate, or if not, We're going to stay here, and here was the house in La Cabrera, and how could I not be dazzled, when each morning I listened to my mother thank the Holy Father for having granted her a loan at the Central Mortgage Bank to pay for that 200-square-foot apartment in San Luis Bertrand where I slept almost every night from the time I was twelve until I was nineteen, the apartment that was an unspeakable embarrassment for me and to which I never wanted to bring any of my friends, least of all Joaco; I duped them all with the story that I lived in the penthouse of a building in El Chicó, telling them that they couldn't visit me there because my mother was terminally ill and even the slightest disturbance might be fatal, my poor mother, if she'd only known what lies I spread about her, so respectable and selfless in her little black suit and worn-down shoes, always holding her rosary, making pilgrimages from store to store in search of the best prices on lentils and rice.

My mother was right at home in a neighborhood where everyone was more or less the same, you might say that she fit the prevailing pattern of mothers in San Luis Bertrand, but there was no way I could ever bring her to school for my friends to see, these are delicate problems I'm talking to you about, Agustina angel; you, who've actually met my sainted mother, know that she ties her stockings above the knee with a tight knot that shows when she crosses her legs, terrible, I've always told her that if she limps from phlebitis it's because those stocking tourniquets cut off her circulation, but anyway, neither my neighborhood nor my blessed mother are fit to be seen, and you can't imagine, Agustina princess, the schemes I've had to come up with to keep them both hidden from everyone, as if they didn't exist.

To meet Joaco and the rest of the gang at the building where I supposedly lived in El Chicó, I first had to take a bus from San Luis to Parallel and Ninety-second Street, and then hurry eight long blocks in order to arrive a few minutes beforehand and slip a tip to the doorman, so that there was no chance he might give me away; thanks to this early practice, I became a master in the art of pretending. To this very day, baby, no one from your side of the world has met my mother or knows of the existence of this apartment in San Luis Bertrand, well, no one except you; how I must have loved and trusted you to bring you here for an afternoon snack on unbreakable plastic dishes with my dear mother, under sacred oath not to reveal the secret, which incidentally you've kept religiously for me ever since.

I believe that the traumatic living circumstances of my adolescence must be the reason I was hypnotized, and still am hypnotized, by the idea that the Londoños could split their week among three different houses and do it without traveling, because traveling meant something else entirely to your family, you took trips, you flew to faraway places, but that side of things was less interesting to me as a child; what really blew me away was the idea that you could have a regular life simultaneously in three different houses, without carrying suitcases back and forth, because you had clothes in all three places, and LPs and televisions and a cook and a gardener and toys and slippers, everything three times over, even pajamas waiting for you under the pillow wherever you went, or in other words family life beautifully contained within an equilateral triangle, with an amazing house at each corner, each in a separate climate and only an hour and a half away from the other two; that's all there was to it, Agustina princess, for me that was the height of elegance, the holy trinity, the ultimate in geometric perfection.

And now, in the dining room again, Agustina still has those ridiculously huge eyes and that insanely long hair, her fingers still extend through the holes of those gloves, gloves like a cyclist's or a junkie's that irritate her brother Joaco, and her slender body is still lost in the black clothes that her mother finds highly inappropriate for a sunny day in the country. From the start they were a little put off by your presence, Agustina darling, you've always made a habit of violating their dress code and making them feel uncomfortable. The place?, your family's highlands estate; the time, Saturday noon; the action, the devastating chain of events that would culminate in our respective downfalls, but to introduce it properly let's say that it all began the day before, on Friday, at six in the afternoon, with me alone in bed in my dark bedroom while the rest of the world tumbled down around me, my Aerobics Center overrun by the ghost of a dead woman, my finances collapsing because of Pablo, and my friends Spider and Silver embarked on a personal crusade against me as if the unpleasant consequences of their own greed were my fault, and just then the telephone rings and it's your brother Joaco inviting me to spend the weekend at his house in the cold country. I turn him down flat and I'm about to hang up and sink back into my self-imposed blackout when he drops your name, Agustina is coming with us, he says, What?, I ask, startled and suddenly interested, because this is the first thing anyone has said in days that manages to capture my attention, Yes, that's right, Joaco confirms, I said Agustina is coming with us, and when I ask him how this miracle came about he explains that your husband is in Ibagué on who knows what kind of business, and then I change my mind about this trip to the cold country: All right, I'll come.

I accepted Joaco's invitation, Agustina doll, because not even the worst funk could prevent me from taking advantage of this once-in-a-lifetime opportunity to spend a few days with you, with those big dogs lying at our feet in the silent galleries open to the rippling of the eucalyptus trees in the afternoon, the scent of manure, and the comforting sight of inherited lands stretching off into the distance, what a fucking pretty thing, Agustina princess, if I'm lying when I call it nirvana, let my hand be chopped off. And suddenly there we were, back in paradise with the eucalyptuses and the dogs and all the rustic trappings, and you were as quick and teasing as you'd ever been, your smiles so easy that I, who hadn't seen you for months, started to believe that you were cured; we had a few Heinekens and you whipped me at Scrabble, you've always been a fiend at Scrabble, and also at solving crossword puzzles and playing charades and instantly picking up on double entendres and riddles, in general your thing is making clever use of language and playing mischievously with words.

It was a gorgeous day, you were astonishingly beautiful, and there was just one problem, Agustina sweetheart, and that was that your eyes got even bigger than they already were and your hair grew a tiny bit longer each time your mother opened her mouth to utter one of her usual interpretations of things, so

plainly counter to any evidence, and then, in that dining room
so lavishly hung with paintings of colonial saints that it looks
like a chapel, I realized that each lie was like torture for you and
that each omission was a snare for your fragile mind, and you
sat there quietly, while your mother, Joaco, and Joaco's wife
snatched the words from one another's mouths as they discussed the big news, that Bichi had called from Mexico to say
he'd be coming to the country for a few weeks before year's
end, after all those years away, Bichi, who left as a child, would
return as an adult, and I see how you're shaken and overcome,
after all, your little brother must be the only person you've ever
really loved, and who knows what crazy kind of birds must
have started flapping around inside your head with the an-
nouncement of his return.

But the rest of the family is also in a state of excitement and
your mother keeps approaching the subject and retreating from
it, glossing over things with that amazing gift for concealment
she's always had and that Joaco plays along with so well because he's been practicing since he was little, and the plain
truths keep getting caught in the honeyed ambiguity that
smoothes and civilizes everything until there's no substance left
to any of it, or until it produces convenient historical revisions
and lies as big as mountains that are gradually transformed into
realities by mutual consensus, I'm referring to gems like this:
Bichi left for Mexico because he wanted to go to school there,
not because your father was always beating him for acting like
a girl; Aunt Sofi doesn't exist, or at least she doesn't exist so
long as no one mentions her; Mr. Carlos Vicente Londoño loved
his three children equally and was a faithful husband until the

day he died; Agustina left home at seventeen because she was a rebel, a hippie, and a pothead, not because she'd rather run away than confess to her father that she was pregnant; Midas McAlister never impregnated Agustina or abandoned her afterward, and she never had to go alone to have an abortion; Mr. Carlos Vicente Londoño didn't die of heart failure but from moral distress the day that he was driving along a hippie street and happened to see his only daughter, Agustina, sitting on the sidewalk selling necklaces of colored beads and seeds; Joaco didn't cheat his siblings out of the family inheritance but instead is doing them the favor of managing it for them; there is no man named Aguilar, and if he does exist he has nothing to do with the Londoño family; darling Agustina isn't stark raving mad, she just is the way she is—that's how Eugenia and Joaco put it, not specifying what way that is—or she's nervous and needs to take Equanil, or she didn't sleep well last night, or she needs psychoanalysis, or she's difficult for the sake of being difficult, or she's always been a little strange.

That's the Londoño Catalog of Basic Falsehoods, but each one of them branches out into a hundred shades of fabrication, and meanwhile I'm watching you, Agustina sweetheart, sitting there at the other end of the table, and I realize that while listening once more to that whole repertory of half-truths you haven't been able to eat a bite and your food is growing cold on your plate, and I see your lovely white hands twisting as if they'd like to pull each other apart, your hands in those strange gloves that you never take off and that soon, around dessert time, maybe, will make Joaco say to you, in an irritated way, that it would be nice if you could at least take them off when you sit down at the table, and when he says that you'll turn pale and you won't say anything and you'll be on the verge, the verge of the thing that has no name because your mother has taken it upon herself to erase the word from the list of words permitted in your house.

And Joaco talks animatedly, my adorable little nutcase, about how they'll go riding with Bichi when he comes, and your mother announces that she'll have a big pan of caramel cream *arequipe* for him to eat all by himself, and she predicts how thrilled Bichi will be when he sees that his room in the house in La Cabrera is still intact, I haven't touched a thing, says your mother, moved, because she really is, almost to the point of tears, His clothes and toys are still there, your mother says, and her voice breaks, everything is just as it was when he left, as if no time had passed. As if nothing had happened, right, Eugenia?, because in your family nothing ever happens, that's what I want to say to her so that Agustina will stop wringing her hands, my poor girl, who keeps drifting further away and growing paler, while I ask myself what I can do to wipe that panicked expression off your face, that look of impending doom, of something drawing nearer that has no name. When Bichi comes, Eugenia is going to organize a trip to Sasaima, the first in years ever since the property had been left in the hands of the estate agent because of the violence, But we're going to arrange a return to the hot country, says Eugenia, her eyes wet, I'm going to have the whole house painted and the pool repaired and we'll celebrate Bichi's arrival with a big family trip to Sasaima, and Joaco nods, he makes it clear that this time, too, he'll bow to his mother's wishes in small matters, as he always does.

Neither of the two mention the fierce argument they had just before lunch, shut up alone in the library, which doesn't have thick enough walls to have prevented the others from hearing them from outside and flinching, but even Joaco's wife, who is clueless and dumb as a brick, catches on that they have to pretend they didn't hear Joaco shouting in the library as he warned his mother that if Bichi came to Bogotá with that boyfriend he has in Mexico, neither Bichi nor his faggot boyfriend would set foot in this house; not this house or the one in La Cabrera or the one in the hot country either, Because if they come I'll throw them out, and your mother, who's shouting too but not as loud, repeats the same sentence over and over again, Hush, Joaco, don't say such a terrible thing, the terrible and unspeakable thing being, to her mind, that Bichi has a boyfriend, not that Joaco will throw Bichi and his boyfriend out, but anyway, the rest of us outside pretend not to hear, and keep our mouths shut. As if they'd already forgotten what they were shouting about in the library a moment ago, as if Bichi didn't have a boyfriend in Mexico or as if by not mentioning the subject they were willing it not to exist, over lunch your mother and Joaco go on planning the improvements they'll make at Sasaima for Bichi's visit.

When everyone's finished eating, one maid gathers the plates, another brings in dessert, and just as you reach out your hand to take an apple from the fruit bowl, your brother Joaco, who has been making an enormous effort to contain himself, suddenly snaps and demands that you remove those filthy gloves this instant.

ON THE RIVER, Nicholas Portulinus saw Ophelias floating, child Ophelias like his sister Ilse, who was older than Nicholas and never left Germany, or if she did, it was because the river carried her away to other lands. During the wet season, when they had to spend long hours in the open galleries of the big house in Sasaima talking as they watched the rain fall in sheets, Nicholas told Blanca and Farax about Ilse, about how in his hometown of Kaub she brought such shame on the family that it threatened to fall apart. In words veiled by decorum and sorrow Nicholas revealed to them the extreme tension generated around the sad figure of Ilse, even translating two letters from the German, one in which his father urges him to keep watch over his sister's moral conduct and another in which his forbidding mother alludes euphemistically to certain "improper" and "very distasteful" acts that Ilse performs in front of company and that disgrace the rest of the family. Regarding the nature of these embarrassing acts, Nicholas disclosed that it had to do with a certain prickling; Ilse was afflicted by an itch so relentless that it led to her undoing.

Though it's often said that no one is lost because of stigmas that can be borne with resignation, discretion, and in secret, it became clear that this was not Ilse's case on the day that a group of relatives dressed in black arrived at the Portulinus house in Kaub to offer their condolences upon the death of a great-aunt. Circumspect and recollecting the deceased in a hushed silence, they sat in a circle of chairs around a rug and a small table; it was as if they were waiting before an empty stage, hands in laps, for a show to start, although of course they knew that there would be no show, and that in fact the show bringing them together had just ended, in other words the long death throes of the great-aunt, dead of some nameless illness, unmentionable like all illnesses that send great-aunts to their graves. Those present kept their eyes fixed on some small object, perhaps a ring, a bit of paper, or a coat button that they fingered as they waited for the ritual of paying their respects to be completed and for the moment to arrive at which they could say their farewells, until one of the chairs began to creak and everyone turned and saw, to their astonishment, that the girl Ilse, also dressed in black and almost a woman now, not to mention very pretty, as the relatives had just told her parents, had her hand under her skirt and was rubbing her crotch spasmodically, with vacant eyes, as if she were alone, as if decency were not imperative at wakes, as if her parents, ashamed and confused, weren't pulling her by the arm to drag her out immediately.

According to Blanca, who transcribes in her diary words that she claims to have heard Nicholas speak, Ilse's behavior resulted from a stinging that "poisoned the most precious parts of her body," or to put it in medical terminology, an itch affecting the genitals, which, as anyone who's suffered from such a malady knows, not only requires one to scratch but also to masturbate, because it arouses as well as torments, producing an agitation similar to desire but more intense. After trying various treatments, the parents declared themselves unable to control their daughter and chose to lock her in her room for hours at a time, hours that little by little became days. In her confinement she sank into a slow mental decline that the doctors diagnosed as quiet madness, or a progressive retreat inward so that what she displayed on the outside was a disconcerting and, in the view of many, intolerable combination of introspection and exhibitionism, catatonia and masturbation.

Ilse was in gradual retreat from the world, consumed by the burning itch in her crotch that derived from the scrofula or blight or rash that covered her sex, making it aggressively present but not fit to be seen, fevered with desire but at the same time undesirable, disgusting in the eyes of others and especially disgusting in Ilse's own eyes. Meanwhile, Nicholas grew in splendor, as full of grace as a Hail Mary, according to his own mother, with the ability to recite long poems from memory and a gift for playing the piano. Nicholas, the fortunate child, the pride of parents for whom Ilse was an undeserved punishment, listened as his father, beside himself, shouted at Ilse, Don't do that, you filthy girl, it's disgusting, and watched him resort to brute force, half out of his mind and half racked with pain, to stop her from reaching her hand down there, which was the worst thing that could happen to the family. Anything would be better, wept his mother, anything, even death.

Nicholas was scorched by these reproaches as if by a red-hot poker, reproaches that Ilse bore with resignation as well as stubbornness, not altering her behavior one bit; there was something voracious and insatiable about his sister's silence that at once terrified and fascinated the boy, and when he found her with her hands bound behind her, a measure that was imposed on her with increasing frequency, he would wait

LAURA RESTREPO

until his parents were away to untie her, and when she returned to her usual habits, he would whisper in her ear in the
most persuasive tones, Don't do that, Ilse, because Father will
come and tie you up again. Who can say how many hours
young Nicholas spent leaning against that locked door, feeling
beat for beat how his sister's ferocious welts throbbed on the
other side. Then the snow fell, the snow melted, the birds sang
in the blooming cherry trees, and the boy Nicholas gradually
developed tastes and manifested talents while the girl Ilse
brooded over conundrums, cloistered in her room and caught
up in her own rhythms, and began to look increasingly like a
shadow of herself.

Then Nicholas learned to steal the key, penetrate the chamber of mysteries, and make his sister's martyrdom his own, sitting beside her and pretending that he, too, had his hands
bound behind his back. You see, Ilse?, he consoled her, they've
punished me just like you, you aren't the only bad one. But she
didn't seem to hear him, always preoccupied with the itch that
was devouring her, first her insides, then her legs, her torso, her
breasts, her ears, her nose; all of her, including her eyes and
voice and hair and presence, were consumed by her inner
hunger, all except her sex, which radiated inflammation and
neglect, sad agent of her downfall; and also of her brother
Nicholas's downfall? Because it happened then that Nicholas's
mother gave her beloved son a little piano in recognition of his
precocious talent, a white piano, as Portulinus specifies in his
diary, and Nicholas, as well as complying with maternal expectations by impressing everyone at family gatherings, played
Ländler and waltzes in secret just for Ilse, Dance, my pretty sis-

ter, and Ilse came out of her lonely corner and danced, ungainly dances but dances all the same, and as if that weren't enough, sometimes she even laughed as she danced, and it was then that Nicholas realized what music was for and wished with all his heart to someday become a professional musician.

But in the middle of the night during an endless winter, Ilse threw herself into the Rhine in a paroxysm of fever and drowned, and then Nicholas realized something else that as an adult he would confirm in the flesh, which is that before the onslaught of madness, sooner or later even music succumbs. It could be said that the itching of his sister's sex settled in her brother's soul, since Portulinus now spent his days repeating the names of rivers in alphabetical order, the Hase, the Havel, the Hunte, the Kocher, the Lech, and the Leide, perhaps to accompany Ilse on her long journey, Ilse, who drifts under the old stone bridge of Kaub in her hurry to go nowhere, while on the other side of the ocean Blanca sits on a black stone on the banks of the Sweet, watching the river run.

• • •

AUNT SOFI TOLD ME that she had savings in Mexico, and she offered to pay whatever it took to give Agustina the necessary medical treatment. After the incident of the divided house, from which we emerged exhausted, battered, and badly shaken, she told me point-blank what she had probably refrained from saying for days out of respect for my intimacy with Agustina and for what she cryptically called Your Methods; Aunt Sofi exploded at last, scolding me for not seeing that Agustina received the proper professional attention, Anyone can see that love and patience aren't solving the problem, she told me, and for the first time since she'd been with us she seemed exasperated, although she excused herself by explaining that she felt close to the end of her strength, that her nerves were frayed, that she couldn't imagine how day after day I could stand the state of extreme tension in the house. If I may say so, Aunt Sofi went on, asking permission to speak but continuing before I granted it, It seems criminal not to have the girl treated by a specialist, for her sake and yours, too. Doctors, hospitals, drugs, treatments, I replied, in the three years we've been living together there's nothing we haven't tried, and when I say nothing, I mean nothing: psychoanalysis? couples therapy? lithium? Prozac? behavior therapy? Gestalt?, you name it, Aunt Sofi, and you'll see that it's already been crossed off the list, that we've been down that path before.

Since she looked at me in astonishment, I made an effort to provide her with a reasonable explanation, The thing is, Aunt Sofi, when Agustina is well she's such an exceptional woman, she's so delightful that sometimes all the times that she's been sick are wiped from my mind, and each time we get through a crisis, I'm convinced that this was the last manifestation of a passing problem; to put it another way, Aunt Sofi, I've always refused to acknowledge that Agustina is sick, but that doesn't mean I haven't tried everything within my means to cure her, I even left my job as a professor, well, at first it was because they closed the university, but as everyone knows it reopened months ago, and Purina leaves me enough free time to give her the attention she needs, and yet I have to confess that I've never been through anything as serious as this; there have certainly been ups and downs, of every variety and magnitude, attacks of melancholia in which Agustina withdraws into a silence charged with secrets and woes, frenetic periods in which she pursues some obsessive, excessive activity to the point of collapse, yearnings with a mystical slant in which prayers and rituals predominate, voids of affection in which she clings to me with the desperation of an orphan, and periods of distancing and indifference in which she doesn't see me or hear me or even seem to recognize me, but until now no spell has been so deep, violent, or prolonged as this.

In the previous episode, which was five months ago, she took to listening to Schubert's trios and crying along with them for hours on end; in the morning, when I left, she'd be calm and busy at something else, and when I returned in the afternoon I would find her desolate again, assuring me that Schubert was the only one in the world who understood her troubles; the funny thing is that this harmonic accord only involved the trios, or the trios and *Death and the Maiden*, because she could listen unmoved to the rest of his complete works, And why didn't you hide the trios?, Aunt Sofi asks, I didn't need to, I answer, one day she simply forgot about them.

. . .

AND THEN YOU AND I were on my motorcycle hauling ass out of there, no helmets, Agustina baby, fleeing your mother and your brother Joaco and especially your own craziness, which was hot on our heels; fortunately a BMW R100RT like mine is the only machine in the world with enough pickup to escape that kind of horror show. In the dining room of your house in the cold country all the alarms had gone off, first your hands twisting, then that ugly grimace contorting your face, and finally the maximum red alert, the ultimate SOS, which is when your voice turns metallic and you start to preach, and this time you were snottily warning about some legacy, and I'm sorry, Agustina doll, but I have to say the whole thing was a little freaky, because when you start talking that way it's actually scary to see, like the voice coming out of you isn't yours anymore.

You got very upset about the legacy thing, but there was something else, too, I'm trying to remember, I think you were also talking about dominion, you were saying something about how you couldn't escape the legacy, or that we were living under the dominion of the legacy, I don't know, Agustina baby, I really couldn't say exactly because there's nothing to be exact about, since when you're raving you start talking in this nervous, complicated gibberish and you get extremely angry, making pronouncements that must seem like matters of life or death to you but that don't mean anything to anyone else; of course it isn't your fault, and I'd guess you don't even have much to do with what's happening to you, but the truth is that when you let loose I get goose bumps, everything you do slants suspiciously toward the religious, if you know what I mean, you start to use fancy words and predict things like a prophet, but a whiny, annoying prophet, know what I'm saying, baby?, an out-of-it, fucking crazy prophet, so that even now, at this very moment, when you're here talking to me relaxed and in your right mind, even now I'm afraid to say certain words in front of you, like *legacy* or *gift of sight*, because I know from experience that they work on your brain like a code that triggers the craziness and opens the door to disaster.

That's why there in the dining room in the cold-country house, in the middle of Eugenia and Joaco's planning for the welcome-home parties and festivities for Bichi, when you started talking in that metallic voice, I prepared myself mentally to take action as soon as necessary. Here it comes, here it comes, here it comes, I said to myself, and when your brother Joaco ordered you to take off your gloves I knew that was the last straw and I got up from the table, having already decided to get you out of there and take you far away; I grabbed your hand and said to you, Come on, finish your coffee and let's go, Please excuse us, Eugenia, please excuse us, Joaco, I need to get back to Bogotá in a hurry because I have to be who knows where, I don't even remember anymore what excuse I concocted for us, all I know is that I took you by the hand, that you offered no resistance, and that we climbed onto the motorcycle.

Be careful, Eugenia advised us, having come out to see us off, accompanied by her pack of friendly dogs, Don't stay out past dark, it's dangerous, Of course, I promised her, don't you worry, we'll be back early, but I knew that Eugenia knew that we wouldn't be back, how could she not when we'd taken our bags; if you and I were leaving, baggage and all, it meant that we considered the weekend plans abruptly concluded, which was how your mother understood it and which came as a great relief to her, because by getting you out of there, Agustina baby, I was defusing the time bomb that had been activated by the subject of Bichi's boyfriend, by Joaco blowing up, and by the spark of delirium that already shone in your eyes. When she saw that we were going your mother secretly approved and was even grateful and pretended that nothing was happening, Don't forget to bring yucca rolls for breakfast tomorrow, she shouted as we were at the gate, Of course, Eugenia, how many yucca rolls do you want?, I answered her, which translated into Londoño language meant, I know that you know that something isn't right here but don't worry, I'll let it pass, don't worry, I'm not going to rub it in your face, because I know how to play that game, too, the game called I don't think about it therefore it doesn't exist, or So long as no one talks about it, it's as if it never happened, Certainly, Eugenia, of course we'll be back early, and on and on, blah blah blah, you know what I'm talking about, Agustina sweetheart, that exchange of words that mean exactly the opposite of what they say, and yet despite it all I feel sorry for your mother, have you ever stopped to think, Agustina baby, how different your poor mother's life is than she dreamed it would be?

And meanwhile you, my pretty little lunatic, were sitting behind me on the motorcycle still issuing your apocalyptic warnings, droning on about the famous legacy, until we shot off along that unpaved road and each time I showed signs of braking, you wouldn't let me, Make it go faster, Midas, hurry, don't stop, and then you were off again with the whole dominion and legacy thing, and I swear, Agustina baby, God help us when your head tilts at that weird angle. I don't know how we managed not to kill ourselves on that road, me clinging to my motorcycle, you clinging to me, your madness clinging to you, and the four of us flying along blindly at a thousand miles an hour, until we reached the tiny town of Puente Piedra and there you informed me that we should stop for coffee, and I agreed; we went into a store and asked for two black coffees, and you burst out laughing, back to normal now and even finding it all funny, like you were your real self again, and not inhabited by that other person, Well, well, you said to me, giving me a hug, we escaped just in time, before things got ugly, What a tease you are, Agustina, I said, I think you wear those hideous gloves just to drive your brother Joaco insane, It's true they're nasty, you admitted, and you came up with the idea of burying them somewhere, so we got back on the motorcycle and found a field by the side of the road that seemed right to you.

You took off your gloves, threw them into an irrigation ditch, and we stood there watching as the soupy green water swallowed them up. Since the day was still beautiful and the sun was inviting, we decided to lie down in the grass and suddenly everything seemed very amusing, Agustina doll, there you were, the owner of countless acres, and here we were, trespassers on someone else's land, keeping a careful eye out in case they set the dogs on us, but happy, adolescents again, great friends, partners in crime; it must be true that those who've shared a bed never completely grow apart. We started to talk about Bichi's return and you shivered with emotion at the news, When my father returns . . . , you said, You mean when Bichi returns, I corrected you, and I corrected you again the second time you said it, but by the third time I suspected that it would be better to change course, steering us away from that particular minefield.

You don't know what an uproar there's been at the Aerobics Center, I said, and you had already heard about it because a few hours ago, in the cold-country house, Joaco's wife, who was a gym regular, had brought it up, asking me whether the mystery of the disappeared woman had been solved. And in the middle of the conversation your brother Joaco suggested, either to mock you or to mock me, that I should bring you to predict the nurse's whereabouts; Joaco was on a roll, With any luck Agustina will find her in Alaska, where she found the minister's son, and that way the girls at the center will relax and stop blaming Midas. And later, in the field, I brought the subject up again as a way to distract you and stop your neurons from whirring, and I was happy when you took the bait, mysteries and stories about people who vanish have always been your thing, and I got you going by inventing silly versions of the drama for you, imitating the ghost of Sara Luz and the hysterical gym members who let themselves be scared by her, and I clowned around as much as I could, Agustina doll, trying to keep your hands from starting their wringing again, doing my best not to let that dangerous glow light up your eyes, and you got excited, you said that there was a connection between you and that woman, and that you felt that she had a message for you; I think she needs to tell me where she is, you said and I was alarmed, because no matter which way you looked at it, this seemed off base, so I insisted that we go to the movies instead, I wanted to see *E.T.*, you were set on *Flashdance*, and since neither of us would give in, we settled on smoking a joint there in the coziness of the late-afternoon sun, and then we somehow started in on the whole nurse business again.

I was seeing everything in a positive light now, thanks to the excellent weed, and so I went along with it, calculating that maybe it wasn't such a bad idea after all, it would get colder soon anyway and we couldn't agree on a movie or stay in that field forever, and Joaco might even be right when he said that one of your flashes of intuition could have a positive effect on the girls at the center, or positive from my point of view, that is, in the sense of throwing everybody off the scent with your visions, which if you'll excuse me, sweetheart, I've always thought were a joke; I started to imagine you in the grip of your prophetic powers, half closing your eyes, breathing deeply, going into a trance, and coming up with a verdict that pinpointed the whereabouts of the alleged nurse in some faraway place; in other words, I visualized something like the following: me coming in with you just before the five o'clock super-rumba class, which is crowded enough on Saturdays, Listen up, please, listen up, I would shout, I know that everyone's been concerned lately about a woman who unfortunately disappeared, and since we sincerely want to help find her, and since no one is more interested than we are in seeing that she appears so she can return home safe and sound to her loved ones, I've brought you the famous seer Agustina Londoño, and as soon as I mention your name everyone would recognize it and exclaim, It's her, the girl who finds lost people!, and I'd call for silence, then you'd run your fingers over the signature that the poor woman apparently left in our sign-in book and put your mental powers to work trying to find her, that was more or less what I had in mind when I approved the crazy plan to bring you to the center.

Once you were there, you'd do your thing and say with total conviction something like, I see her, I see her, I see a woman named Sara Luz Cárdenas Carrasco who's run away with her Dominican boyfriend to San Pedro de Macorís, and they're living there happily ever after, or, version number two, Where are you, Sara Luz? Sara Luz? Oh yes, now I see you, my sixth sense tells me that you're in prison in New York City, oh no!, you went to work as a drug mule, Sara Luz, the stewardess gave you away because she thought it was suspicious that you weren't eating the chicken and carrots that she'd served you on a cardboard tray, they arrested you with Baggies of cocaine in your stomach at John F. Kennedy Airport and now you're locked up and sentenced to 127 years of prison in a windowless cell, or version number three, maybe even better than the first two, No, ladies and gentlemen, this signature isn't hers, my great gift of sight tells me that it's a fraud, a fake, a name scrawled by someone who wasn't the real Sara Luz Cárdenas, someone playing a stupid joke; I don't know, Agustina doll, forgive me again, please, it was just another one of my stupid pranks, another pot trip, another one of those silly but amusing ideas that I let myself get carried away by; I really believed that for you it would just be a game and that it might help me or at least not hurt me, and how could I know it would end the way it did, when after all you're the expert at guessing games.

∙ ∙ ∙

BEFORE THE WEEPING over Schubert, maybe three months before, things had become unbearable and I'd turned to Social Security, discovering that because of my restricted policy as a university professor, my wife only qualified for treatment at the charity hospital La Hortúa, where she was assigned to a doctor named Walter Suárez, who subjected his patients to sleeping cures, shooting them full of sodium amytal. She was admitted to one of the halls in the psychiatric ward and put to bed, and all I could do was watch her sleep, and accept that as soon as she opened her eyes, or moved her lips to try to say something, Doctor Walter Suárez's assistants would appear with another dose of the barbiturate, a yellowish powder with a sulfurous stench that they dissolved and injected intravenously, and that's how I spent my days and nights, in contemplation of that sleeping beauty who glowed pale and distant on the worn hospital sheets that had seen so much human suffering, her hair like a creeping vine that had claimed the pillow centuries ago; I couldn't take my eyes off the soft and slightly trembling shadow that her eyelashes projected on her cheeks as if she were an old doll forgotten on a shelf in an antiques store, and I looked for hidden messages in the rhythm of her breath, the tone of her skin, the temperature of her hands, the silence of her organs, the ripple of time over her still body, Are you dreaming, Agustina, or just swimming in a sea of fog? Are you barricaded alone in your little death, or is there a crack I can slip through to keep you company?

As I watched over her to make sure that, helpless in her unconsciousness, my wife wouldn't make an involuntary movement and tear out the needle through which the sleep-inducing drug entered her vein, so that she wasn't bothered by drafts or caught uncovered by the early-morning chill or tormented by nightmares or possessed by who knows what incubuses, as I sat

waiting for the ghostly hours at La Hortúa to pass, I often re-
called the terrible stories of the Japanese writer Yasunari Kawa-
bata, peopled with naked girls lying drugged, girls in whom no
trace of love, shame, or fear was left. Three times a day the ef-
fects of the drug wore off and I had to feed her and take her to
the bathroom, and then for a few minutes her body came back
to life but her soul was still lost, her gaze turned inward and her
movements became mechanical and remote, like a marionette's.

Six other patients shared the room with Agustina, all of
them also there to find rest from guilt, hallucinations, and worries with Doctor Walter's famed sodium amytal, and one of
them, the one in the next bed, was an old woman as light as a
breath of air, whose husband, a man as old as she was, brushed
her hair, massaged her legs to stimulate her circulation, and
rubbed lotion on her hands because, as he would say, My Teresa
doesn't like her hands to be dry, Have you seen how white my
Teresa's hands are, young Aguilar?, Look, not a mark, and that's
because they've never seen the sun, since whenever she goes
out she puts on gloves to protect them. This gentleman had an
unusual name; he was called Eva, because, as he explained to
me, Eva was short for Evaristo, and I played endless chess games
with Don Evaristo as our respective girls sank down to regions
very close to death, and sometimes Don Eva would bring a gui-
tar and sit next to his Teresa singing old boleros in her ear in a
ruined but impeccably modulated voice, the voice of a professional singer of serenades, and over and over again he'd sing her
the song that goes "pretty little girl with locks of gold, pearly
teeth, ruby lips," and he'd say to me, It's Teresa's favorite, ever
since we got married I've sung it for her on all our anniversaries,

of course there are other songs that she likes, too, like "Acacias," and "Sabor a Mí," "Bésame Mucho," and "Pardon Me Young Man But Don't Presume," Don Evaristo told me, My Teresa is a very discerning woman, a lover of good music and all fine things, but wait, come here, come closer, see how she smiles when I sing "Pretty Little Girl," I don't know whether you can tell because it's just the faintest hint of a smile, but knowing even her subtlest expressions as I do, I know that a smile lights up her face each time I sing that song.

Don Evaristo stayed religiously by his wife's side from the time he arrived at the hospital at eight on the dot in the morning until the clock struck eight at night, and when he got up to go he always asked me to look after her in the same words, I'm off to work and I leave the heart of my heart in your care, he'd say patting me on the shoulder; on one of these occasions, I asked him what he did, and Don Eva replied, I work nights singing boleros at the Blue Star, a popular, reputable bar near here, and once when I was walking to the hospital along Twelfth Street near Tenth, I happened upon the famous Blue Star, which actually turned out to be a roadhouse and brothel of the lowest sort, and since it was seven thirty in the morning and they were cleaning the place, the woman who was sweeping had the doors wide open so that I could peek in and see a row of wooden tables with clay candlesticks in the middle, dusty curtains hiding dismal little rooms with cots and washbasins, red lightbulbs that by night must have disguised the shabbiness, and a wooden platform with a single microphone where I imagined Don Eva singing "Pretty Little Girl" so that the whores and their clients could dance while he pined for his Teresa, who lay next to my Agustina, the torments of her madness lulled with sodium amytal, and a minute later, Don Eva emerged from one of the tiny rooms, and behind him came a fat girl who by all indications seemed to be one of the women who worked there; at first Don Eva tried to avoid meeting me, but since it was inevitable, he greeted me warmly and introduced me to the woman who was with him, This is Jenny Paola, he said, and shrugged his shoulders in apology, doing his best to explain, I take care of my Teresa and Jenny Paola takes care of me, what's to be done, young Aguilar, human beings are vulnerable creatures in desperate need of companionship . . .

The days passed identically from the first to the fourth, and then on the fifth, when we were in the middle of one of our interminable chess matches, I announced to Don Eva that I wasn't going to let them drug my wife anymore and that I was taking her away tomorrow, I couldn't stand the agony of seeing her this way, blank, lifeless, nonexistent, Anything but this, I said, Don Eva, anything but something so much like death, You're doing the right thing, boy, take her away, what you say is true, And what about you, Don Eva, why don't you bring Teresa home with you, you could watch over her there by day and find someone to take your place at night while you're working, Oh no, Don Eva said, I couldn't do that to my Teresa, you can't imagine how frightened she gets when she's awake.

Hours later, as Agustina and I were leaving La Hortúa, we were welcomed by one of those Bogotá afternoons that are beyond compare, I'm referring to the high-altitude sky of an intense hydrangea blue and the smell of mountain vegetation,

and unlike Teresa, my Agustina wasn't terrified to be awake
again, in fact she seemed happy and ready to return to the
world of the living; The sun is so nice, she said, leaning on a
stone wall where the rays fell, her head slightly tilted, half puz-
zled and half amused, as if she hadn't seen me for a while and
now I seemed slightly different but she couldn't quite say why,
Your hair is shinier, she said at last, stretching out her hand to
touch it, and you've gotten some gray hairs, Please, Agustina,
I've had gray hairs since you've known me, Yes, but it isn't the
same, she declared without taking the time to explain, and she
didn't want to go straight home, so we walked with our arms
around each other along the streets of the city center, as dazzled as Bogotá's founder, Don Gonzalo Jiménez de Quesada,
must have been the first time he set foot on this high plain
more than four centuries ago and thought it blessed.

The city responded to our enthusiasm by displaying the hu-
mility of a newly established town and the Plaza de Bolívar
welcomed us with the golden glow of a slanting light; at
Agustina's request, we went into the cathedral, where I showed
her Jiménez de Quesada's tomb, Look, Agustina, we were just
talking about him and here's his tomb, then she walked to the
vestry, where she bought six big red candles, lighting them and
setting them beside the tomb, Wouldn't you rather offer them
to some saint?, I asked her, Look, over there is Saint Joseph
with the Christ Child in his arms, and in that chapel there's a
saint ascending among cherubim who must be the Virgen del
Carmen, and there's the Dolorosa with beams of light shooting
from her crown, any one of them would work, whereas there's
no guarantee of the saintliness of the founder of Santa Fé de

Bogotá, who knows how good he really was, Good enough, because once they get to heaven they're all alike, Agustina assures me, And why six candles?, I ask her, One for each of my five senses, so that from now on they don't betray me, And the sixth?, The sixth is for my sanity; let's see whether by some miracle this Don Gonzalo brings it back.

• • •

THOUGH IT'S NOT CLEAR just when, Abelito Caballero, alias Farax, gradually becomes the center of the Portulinus household: Nicholas's beloved piano disciple, Blanca's companion in the tasks of feeding the rabbits, collecting the eggs from the henhouse, letting the dogs loose at night, shooing away the bats that nest in the rafters, and taking Nicholas on walks to clear his head, confidant of Sofi, who is just beginning to have secret loves, and accomplice in Eugenia's slow, mute games. Writing regularly and at length in her diary, Blanca tells how she spends her days, without altering the general shape of things or omitting details, while Nicholas, in his own diary, shows a notorious lack of precision in his stories, which are sometimes cut off in the middle and other times lack a logical order, often becoming so tangled that it's impossible to understand what they're about, but this complete chaos, on a level that might be called literary, contrasts with a curious and obsessive tendency to quantify certain events; for example, in the upper left-hand corner he writes "m. r. B"—marital relations with Blanca—each time he has them, which occurs with astonishing frequency, or to be more specific, almost every day. The longest period of ab-

Delirium

stinence recorded is scarcely five days long and corresponds to a week when he was severely depressed; another of the regular accounts he keeps in the margins is "dreamed of F last night," or "dreamed of F during nap," with the F definitely standing for Farax.

Although husband and wife had vowed to respect the privacy and secrecy of each other's diaries, there's no doubt that Blanca regularly leafed through Nicholas's, perhaps less out of an unhealthy curiosity than as a means of obtaining clues to her husband's state of mind that would allow her to anticipate major attacks of rage and melancholy, and Nicholas was undoubtedly aware of this systematic spying, because when he didn't want her to know something he would write it in German, as on the page for a day in the month of April, when the customary "dreamed of F last night" is followed by parentheses and in tiny, cramped, almost illegible handwriting "Ich bin mit auffälliger Erektion aufgewacht," or I woke up with a considerable erection.

Not only did Nicholas give the boy piano lessons but he also made an effort to teach him to compose, unveiling the musical structure and lyrical secrets of *bambucos* and *pasillos* and introducing him to English and German poetry so that it might serve as a source of lyrical inspiration for his future compositions, and as if all that weren't enough, he gave him, one by one, most of his own books, much to the surprise of Blanca, who watched entire shelves disappear from the library, their contents later appearing scattered across the floor of Farax's room. Tell me why you're giving the boy all your books, Nicholas, she asked him, but she received only vague replies like, So he can educate himself, woman, a musician without knowledge of the classics is nothing. Little by little he had given up all contact with his daughters, contact that had never been particularly close anyway, and whenever either of them required his attention he would reply, Ask Farax, he knows, or Get it from Farax, he has it, or Go with Farax, he'll take you.

As the boy grew physically and spiritually stronger, as if nourished by the love and care of his adopted family, Nicholas was deteriorating, each day becoming more bloated, lost in his own musings, detached from everything around him, and prone to confusing real people with imaginary ones, especially Abelito with Farax, and vice versa. More painfully than in other instances his mind seemed to go to pieces at the spectacle of Abelito, the real boy, and Farax, the dream boy, battling each other on the smooth white marble of ancient ruins and wounding each other, bleeding, and in the process wounding Nicholas, too; or rather wounding only Nicholas, because he was the real victim of this imaginary combat, the one bleeding to death in the temple crumbling into dust amid the greatest splendor. I see a polished surface, Blanquita darling, I see a spotless expanse, I'm dazzled by the metallic gleam of blood on that expanse, I'm overwhelmed and transfixed by the enigma of spilled blood. What are you talking about, Nicholas, look, your lunch is getting cold, stop thinking about blood and unpleasant things, the girls and Farax are already at the table. Farax or Abelito?, he asks her, perturbed. Please, Nicholas, you know very well that they're the same person. Yes, Blanquita, but only one of the two is real, only one of the two is strong, and I don't know which it is. You're dreaming, Nicholas, you got up from your nap but haven't woken yet. I'm sorry, Blanca my dove, but it's only in dreams—daydreams?—that I'm able to understand the true nature of things, and today I realized that the one who's licking his wounds is bleeding to death. These are fancies of yours, Nicholas, you're just hungry. You refuse to see that something terrible is going to happen, woman, because I can't tell which one really exists, whether it's Farax or me, Farax or Nicholas, one of the two will prevail and the other is fated to disappear, because there's no room for both on the face of the earth.

In an attempt to keep track of Portulinus's ravings, the following outline of several steps might be drawn up: first, Nicholas builds a bubble or a parallel world in which what he imagines acquires real-world worth, as when he meets Abelito and identifies him with the Farax of his dreams; in the second step, the bubble is divided into opposing halves, Abelito and Farax, for example, or Farax and Nicholas, that polarize Nicholas's mind, making him flit unbearably fast between two extremes; third, Nicholas transfers his deepest feelings to the bubble, making everything inside it a matter of life or death, in such a way that after he's built up an impossible conflict between the opposing forces, he crucifies himself on his own creation. I'm a helpless and horrified witness, Blanca laments, to the way he is caught in the pincer of opposites and driven to destruction. Fourth, once the parallel world is perfected in every detail, Nicholas detaches himself, breaking contact with the real world, and is left sealed and alone inside his bubble; fifth and last: during the course of his ravings, Nicholas is swept away by an anxiety that feeds on itself; he's like a man bewitched, unable to escape his delirium, though he doesn't want to escape, either, because the relationship he's established with it is that of a slave to his master.

This is more or less the state of things inside Nicholas Portulinus's head, but not entirely, of course, since nothing can ever be quite so precise, and anyway, it was taken for granted at the house in Sasaima that he should rave or be queer, as his daughters put it. The odd thing lately is that Blanca seems a little unbalanced, too; nothing has been the same since Farax knocked at the door with his old alpaca jacket and his knapsack full of lead soldiers. Farax has become the dream and the nightmare of both Nicholas and Blanca, the love object and the rival of both in an ascending spiral, a spiral that rises to where the air is so thin it's impossible to breathe. Does Nicholas suspect that if Blanca had to choose between the two men living in the house, deep in her heart she would choose the younger one, even if her lips professed otherwise? I liked the number two, Bianchetta darling, Nicholas confessed to her one afternoon when the world was flooded with rain, two made it possible for me to get along, two filled the void between you and me, but three makes my head explode into a million pieces.

⋅ • ⋅

BUT AT THE CENTER you didn't say anything you were supposed to say, Agustina my love, you didn't choose version number one, in which Dolores, or Sara Luz, goes with her boyfriend to the Dominican Republic, or version number two, in which she's been working as a drug mule and is behind bars in the

United States, or even version number three, which was by far the easiest, because how hard would it have been to declare that the signature in the sign-in book was a fake, and if the positive options were limitless and the number of possible destinations infinite, why couldn't you reassure the five o'clock super-rumba class by telling them that the nurse, as she claimed to be, had ended up in Puglia, in the south of Italy, for example, or in Nunavut, in the north of Canada?

No, of course not, because true to yourself you chose extremism, irrationality, and melodrama, as always; you started waving your arms and shouting wild things in front of fifty fitness fans who watched you in horror, quite a spectacle you made of yourself, my lovely Agustina, it would've made you blush if you hadn't been so demented, and speaking in your worst metallic voice, the one that sounds like it's echoing in a tin can, you started to say, Something happened here, something happened here, and from the moment you uttered that very first sentence my blood ran cold and I knew that there was no way to stop you now, that disaster was already imminent, Something happened here, you insisted with touching conviction and you went sniffing around the gym like a bloodhound, searching for clues here and there as I tried to convince you that we should go somewhere else, Come on, Agustina, I said to you under my breath so that the super-rumba class wouldn't hear me, Come on, why don't we forget about all of this, and instead I'll take you to see *Flashdance*, that movie you wanted to see a little while ago, are you listening to me?, *Flashdance*, Agustina, does it ring any bells?

But no, nothing could stop you, you were determined to

ferret out that Dolores, even if she was hidden at the end of the earth, and you wouldn't give up until you had found her dead or alive, you were becoming more agitated and upset, and finally you blurted out, Something terrible happened here, and I didn't know what to do with myself, there before all my clients, when the seer I myself had brought to put out the blaze started to fan the flames instead, and next you were seeing blood, I see lots of blood, you said, and I did what I could to discourage you, No, Agustina, not blood, I tell you honestly there was no blood, and that was true, princess, I don't know what that whole blood thing was, because Dolores didn't lose a drop, the poor thing was all broken up inside but there was no blood to speak of, I swear to God, why would I lie to you, and still you insisted, you'd already started down that path and there was no stopping you, I see blood, I see blood, terrible blood flooding the channels, But please, Agustina, what channels are you talking about?, That woman was killed here, you said, she was kicked to death, Not kicked to death, Agustina, I broke in, get a hold on yourself, sweetheart, try to keep your voice down, and I wasn't lying to you about that either, angel, the whole kicking thing is a scene from a different movie, but in your cocktail shaker of a brain everything turns into the same slush, it was your monster of a father and your brute of a brother who wanted to kick Bichi to death for acting like a faggot, but as far as I know getting kicked was the only thing that didn't happen to Dolores that night, and yet you, Agustina darling, were deep in a stubborn trance and no one could bring you out of it, but why bother to keep telling you about the massive disaster you caused, what point is there now in totaling losses and damages.

What I do want to talk to you about is what an ordeal it was getting you out of the center once you had reached the final stage of full-blown delirium, because you weren't seeing or hearing anything, much less prepared to listen to reason; I tried to take you back to my apartment on my motorcycle but I don't know if you realize how hard it is to get someone who's convulsing onto a motorcycle, so with great sorrow I left my cherished R100RT at the center, called a taxi, brought you to my refuge and opened its doors to you, thinking that maybe in the calm of my bedroom and with another little toke of weed you might relax, Come on, Agustina darling, get in my bed and I'll cover you with my blanket of vicuna-pup skin, see how soft?, yes, I guess you're right, vicuna-pup skin is probably banned by all kinds of animal protection societies, but there's no need to worry, because those societies don't generally have access to my bedroom, and what if I bring you a Baileys with a few ice cubes and we watch a movie on the Betamax, how does that sound?, I understand, Baileys is too sweet and the picture quality is no good, well fuck Baileys and the Betamax, there's no point arguing about that, wait a minute, I've got the hottest new song right here, Michael Jackson and Paul McCartney, "The Girl Is Mine," haven't you heard it?, but sweetheart, you're out of touch, this song has conquered the planet and the two guys who sing it made millions, what's wrong, you don't like it, you want me to turn it off?, shit, Agustina, this is getting old, that fucking psychic crap makes you really impossible.

I didn't know what to do with you anymore or how to deal with your fit, so I took you into my bathroom, doll, which to me is like the quintessence of hedonism, almost everything good that's ever happened to me has happened in that bathroom, which itself is as big as a small apartment in San Luis Bertrand and completely done in Kalopa black granite imported from Malawi, its Finnish sauna suffused with the smell of birch, its huge window with the morning sun pouring through, its pile of *Newsweek*, *Time*, and *Semana* magazines beside the toilet, and especially its twin sinks, one next to the other, the truth is I've never understood what the point is of having two but it gives me almost orgasmic pleasure to have both. So I try to introduce you to the joys of steam and water, convinced that this will do the trick, but you don't agree at all and put up an epic resistance that leaves us both soaked from head to toe, And now what do I do with you, you spoiled brat, you wild thing, you're going to die of cold and fever in those wet clothes, but suddenly I had an idea, or more than an idea, it was as if a lightbulb had come on in my head, Wouldn't it be nice to be alone, I thought, and I felt an infinite relief at the mere possibility, it would be so nice to be alone in the quiet of my room, and as I let myself be swept away by this radical desire for solitude, I realized that my Christ-like patience and compassion had been entirely used up, and in an instant I had called Rorro, Who's Rorro?, What do you mean who's Rorro, for God's sake, Agustina, you know perfectly well who Rorro is, good old Rorro, my right-hand man at the gym, giant with a quarter-inch of forehead, not too bright but as decent as they come, the person in charge of all the stretching classes, weight training, and spa treatments, I didn't have to think twice because I knew there was nothing the man wouldn't do for me, so I called him and said, Come on over, Rorro, do me a favor and bail me out here.

At that moment of utter anarchy only a single thing was perfectly clear to me, Agustina darling, and that was that I wanted you out of my bedroom, out, vanished, gone, you were shouting in the only place where I demand perfect silence, you were wreaking havoc in the only corner of the world that I like to keep neat, you had spun out of control precisely within the four walls where I keep everything under control, Enough, angel, chaos in my private paradise is more than I can stand, Rorro can't take you away a minute too soon, I need to get back into a healthy rhythm, work out the kinks with a good soak in the Jacuzzi and then turn on the fireplace with a click of the remote control, and naked by the fire like the first man in his primeval cave, smoke a blunt of Santa Marta Golden and do my best to forget, let my mind go blank and soar in the placid void of blue vastness.

I managed to establish that the first step was to call Rorro to come and get you, but problems arose with step number two, where to send you. Return you to your mother, batty as you were, defenseless and exposed?, no, certainly not, you would never have forgiven me and even I'm not capable of something that cruel. Send you alone to your apartment, where Rorro could keep you company until your husband came back from Ibagué, good old Aguilar, who is apparently the most self-sacrificing loony-bin keeper in the city?, that wasn't a bad plan, in fact, it was clearly the best, or the only good one, but it wouldn't work because I had no idea where you lived, you'd never told me where your apartment was and considering the level of mental chaos you were operating on, asking you would have been a waste of time. To a hospital, then?, I suggested it to you, wanting to know whether you thought it might be a good idea for me to send you to a psychiatric clinic and you, instantly grasping every word, as if you'd gone from speaking only Sanskrit or Russian to a sudden comprehension of Spanish, threw your arms around me and begged me please not to send you to a hospital, anything but a hospital, maybe you were afraid that they would lock you away forever, fry your brain with electroshock therapy, give you pills that would put you to sleep for all eternity like Sleeping Beauty, I don't know what it was that terrified you so much, but the forlorn, despairing look on your face made me abandon that idea, It's settled, I ordered Rorro, take her to a hotel, treat her with tender, loving care because you're looking at a real angel, she's a little upset but she'll be over that in two seconds, here, Rorro, here's my card number so you can put her up at the Wellington, they know me there and you can tell them I'll be by later to sign the bill, I want you to shut yourself up with her in a suite, give me a call to report mission accomplished, and then wait for further instructions; now take her away, but listen up, I want it to be the best suite, where she can eat well and take a nice bath and sleep off whatever's wrong with her in a good bed until she's back to normal, you take care of her tonight, Rorro my good buddy, and tomorrow, if she wakes up feeling better, bring her back here.

But the devil has his way with the best-laid plans and this was such an absolutely fucked-up day that even then I couldn't relax; despite the excellence of the Santa Marta Golden that I was smoking nice and slow, letting it filter down to the core of my being, I was tortured by remorse, unable to rest, I'd man-

aged to get you out of my sanctum sanctorum, Agustina sweetheart, and now I was doing my best to push you out of my
thoughts, too, but somehow you kept coming back. As that
golden smoke twined around me, my conscience was plagued
by a buzz of pestering horseflies, and those horseflies were particular moments from the past that seemed like carbon copies
of the moment we were living now, almost duplicates, I don't
know, Agustina princess, I guess that looking back it would be
fair to say I've always abandoned you when you needed me,
that I've let you down at every crucial moment.

The telephone rang and I answered right away, thinking it
would be Rorro letting me know that everything was cool and
under control, but it wasn't, it wasn't Rorro, it was an anony-
mous female voice speaking at the other end of the line, Mr.
Midas McAlister, do you remember me? How was I supposed to
remember anything, Agustina doll, when it was an unknown
voice, completely unrecognizable, I had no fucking idea who it
was, especially considering how high I was, and then the owner
of the voice reminded me, A little while ago I was at your Aerobics Center with my two cousins, do you remember?, and I
was thinking two cousins, uh-huh, what the fuck was this person talking about, You've got a terrible memory, Mr. McAlister,
and I struggled to pull myself together, The three of us came to
sign up and you suggested that it would be better if we went
somewhere else, is it coming back to you?, Oh yes, right, right,
I kept saying vaguely, still having no idea what was about to hit
me, and laboriously retrieving from the fog of the past the image of those three bleached blondes in shiny lycra who stepped
out of a lime-green convertible, Oh yes, I said, you were the

ones who came to ask about classes and in the end decided that you'd rather enroll somewhere else, No sir, we didn't decide, it was you who decided that you didn't want us at your establishment, well I'm glad that you remember and I'm calling to let you know that my cousin Pablo remembers, too, and when I heard Pablo's name the whole scene flashed before my eyes as clearly as if I were watching it on television, and before I could say a word, the woman swore a curse on me and then hung up. What was the curse? Well, something to make the bravest man quake in his boots: I'm just calling you, Mr. McAlister, to give you a message from my cousin Pablo, Pablo asked me to tell you that insults to his family are the only kind he doesn't forgive. Do you want to know what I did then?, well you guessed it, I started to shake.

. . .

WHEN I SAW THAT Anita had sent me a message on my beeper, I was surprised to discover that I'd given her the number; I could've sworn I hadn't. The first night that I talked to her I was so engrossed in the police-detective reconstruction of the infamous dark episode at the hotel that if I gave her my number I didn't even realize it, but now, while I was having breakfast at Marta Elena's house with my two sons, I heard again from the unforgettable Anita, whom I'd more or less forgotten in the thirty-two hellish hours it had been my fate to live since I'd left her in Meissen.

There I was heating up corn cakes and frying eggs for Toño and Carlos, who were leaving for school in half an hour, when

I received a text message from Anita that read, "I have information for you urgent meet me at Don Conejo tonight 9 pm signed
Anita at the Wellington it's about your wife and I know you'll
be interested," and my reaction was odd, because I immediately
thought, Yes, I would meet her, but I wasn't motivated by concern for Agustina, which to tell the truth was hovering at a low
point several degrees below zero for the first time since I'd
known her, meaning that I wanted nothing more to do with my
wife; after so many days and nights of thinking only of her, in
a single sweep she'd been wiped as if by magic from my poor
head stuffed to the bursting point with abuse, indifference, jealousy, and worries, Yes, I thought, I'm definitely interested in
this beeper invitation, though not for Agustina's sake but because of Anita herself.

I was at Marta Elena's that morning because I had spent the
night there; my son Toño had slept on the sofa in the living room
so that I could have his bed, and for the first time since I was separated from my ex-wife I had spent the night at her house, or the
house that used to be ours and now belongs to her and the boys.
The thing I'd like to explain is how I ended up doing something
so out of the ordinary. What happened was this: during the
whole day following the debacle of the divided house, Agustina
was sunk in a deep sleep, equal in intensity to the frenetic activity that she'd displayed during the night, but of the opposite nature, and toward evening, when she got up, she returned to the
attack, the whole thing all over again, as frantic and ferocious as
it was the first time, the imaginary border, her father's visit, and
insults, this time in every language. She shouted, Back, filthy
thing; *cosa inmunda*; Out, dirty bastard; *Vade retro, Satanas*; Out,

scum, until I couldn't take it anymore, All right, Agustina, if you want me to go, I'll go, I told her, and I left.

Expelled from my own house by a conspiracy of my crazy wife and my dead father-in-law, and without a cent in my pocket, from whom could I beg for shelter if not my children and former wife? Marta Elena, so trustworthy, so responsible, so predictable, still pretty despite the matronly look she'd acquired and despite the twenty-six years she'd spent working faithfully for the same company, without missing a single day or ever arriving late at the office, Marta Elena, the extraordinary mother, my comrade-at-arms, the person with whom I'd shared my adolescence, Marta Elena, so solid, so good, my great lifelong friend; I've never been able to figure out what could have come over me to make me stop loving Marta Elena.

When I woke up in her house I realized that for the first time in countless nights I had slept soundly, then I heard the still-sleepy voices of my sons who were beginning to shuffle barefoot around the house, and Marta Elena's calm voice starting the day off with crisp instructions, Quiet or you'll wake your father; Here's your shirt, Toño, I've ironed it for you; Carlos, take your sneakers because you have gym class today. For an instant it was clear to me that precisely these, and no others, were the voices of happiness, and that the only truly good thing in this world was hearing them when I woke up. Opening my eyes, I discovered that all around me, in the bedroom that my son Toño had let me have, there were no objects, with a few exceptions, that I wasn't familiar with or that I hadn't placed there myself, that didn't speak to me of my own history, that hadn't remained in the same place for years, Good morning boys, good morning Marta Elena, I shouted from bed.

My ex-wife asked me to help her with breakfast and for a minute I seemed to be two people at once, as if I had never stopped heating up corn cakes for my sons in the mornings, and what I saw was so pleasing to me that I asked myself why it wouldn't have worked in reality, at what point things had broken down; if this was where my children were growing up and where a woman who still loved me was keeping a place for me as if I might some day return, why in the hell, I asked myself, was I running absurdly around in pursuit of something I hadn't lost. Of course I vaguely remembered the sense of dissatisfaction that had made me leave and driven me to look elsewhere, I remembered it, but only vaguely and I couldn't see any justification for it, because at this exact moment everything was calling me to stay in this place where, despite my four years of absence, I'd always been present, and I was struck with uncommon force by the feeling that all the puzzle pieces of my life fit this house, which I had never lost despite having abandoned it; everything spurred me to return, everything except enthusiasm, and standing outside myself just then, enthusiasm didn't strike me as a particularly important factor.

The boys left for school and I asked Marta Elena whether I could take a shower. She said that I could, directing me to the boys' bathroom and then thinking better of it, The kids use up all the hot water in there, she said, you'd better shower in mine, so I went into Marta Elena's bathroom and started to undress, not daring to close the door, which would've seemed ridiculous, since after undressing in front of Marta Elena for seventeen years there was no reason why I shouldn't do it again, though I felt strange, and through the half-open door I could see that Marta Elena had finished getting dressed and was sitting on the bed, pulling on her stockings and I had the feeling, something very like vertigo, that this was the sight I'd like to see every morning for the rest of my life; now Marta Elena was adjusting her skirt and fastening her earrings, then putting on her shoes, and what's odd is that she must have been thinking the same thing I was, because she didn't close the door, either.

I took a quick shower, quick, I think, out of fear that she would finish getting ready and call to me from the bedroom that she was leaving; the idea of her going pained me. I felt good with her around, and I thought that I'd still like to be there when the boys got home from school so that I could go down with them to play basketball at the neighborhood courts and come back, hungry, to make the ravioli that Carlos likes, to ask Marta Elena how things had gone at the office and let my mind wander a little as she told me, with slight variations, the same stories I already knew by heart. So I took a quick shower, then started to put on the clothes I'd been wearing the day before, but I stopped, opening the doors of Marta Elena's closet and confirming my suspicion that much of my clothing would still be hanging there, everything I hadn't taken when I moved alone to Salmona Towers, and there it all was: my plaid shirts, my drill pants, my old leather jacket.

• • •

TODAY NICHOLAS PORTULINUS is frying sausages for dinner and he serves them on a plate to his younger daughter, Eugenia. You're a forest sprite, my poor little Eugenia, he tells her, you're a silent sprite hidden away in your cave. It's just the two of them, father and daughter, in the enormous kitchen, with sacks of oranges that the agent brought today piled against the walls and bunches of plantains hanging from the rafters. Eugenia is squeezing oranges with a heavy cast-iron juicer that is screwed to the table, from which comes not only the juice filling the pitcher but also an intense scent of orange blossoms. Nicholas Portulinus looks into the eyes of his younger daughter, Eugenia the strange, and asks her, Does the smell of oranges make you cry, too? At dawn today, he tells her, the road was carpeted with oranges crushed on the asphalt, because during the night they fell from the loaded trucks and the wheels of the cars rolled over them. I spent a long time sitting by the side of the road, little Eugenia, and the smell of oranges was very, very sad, and very, very strong. Eugenia watches him chew his food with the heavy jaw and wistful deliberation of an old cow and thinks with relief, Thank heavens Father isn't queer today.

It's July 20, and Independence Day is being celebrated in Sasaima; the servants have been given the night off, and Blanca, Farax, and Sofi have walked down to town to watch the parade and the fireworks, and then go to the community dance. They've announced that they'll be back late, which means that if the festivities merit it they might not return until seven or eight the next morning, because tradition demands that the celebration be concluded at dawn with a town breakfast in the market square, and the mayor, who is a conservative, has announced that this year free tamales and beer will be served. Nicholas and Eugenia are left home alone, Blanca having called Eugenia aside before she left to entrust her with the care of her father, predicting that this time the task would be easy. He's quiet, she said, all you have to do is keep your eye on him until he falls asleep, and in fact it is one of those rare peaceful moments when her father is all right and even talkative; since Eugenia isn't used to her father speaking to her, she stutters and doesn't know how to reply. Although it's already nine, her father isn't yet drifting in a ponderous prelude to sleep as he usually does, but instead he's awake and on his face there's something resembling a smile, today Father brims with chuckles, little gurgles, as he fries sausages in the kitchen and serves them on a plate to his younger daughter, seemingly reconciled to the simple reign of the everyday.

Eugenia looks at him and lets out a deep breath as if she really has been relieved of an exhausting responsibility. Father is queer, the girls say when they sense he's slipping toward those murky regions where they can't reach him, Father is queer, and no one knows what agony there is in the voice of a child who speaks those words. The first time that Eugenia thinks she noticed her father's queerness was when she was five or six. While she was playing with shells from the river, her father was busying himself nearby clearing away the fallen leaves blocking one of the channels down which water flowed to the big house, and since the sun was strong, he was wearing a straw hat to protect his head, but it wasn't a single hat; little Eugenia stopped playing, uneasy, when she noticed that her fa-

ther was wearing not just one hat but two, one wide-brimmed
straw hat on top of a smaller cloth cap. She thinks she remembers that it was horrible to suddenly realize that there was
something irremediably strange about her father, something actually grotesque, so she went up to him to try to take off one of
the two hats as if that would solve the larger problem, and he
looked at her with unseeing eyes, infinitely remote eyes, and
ever since then Eugenia thinks in terms of double hat when Father is queer, Father is double hat, she says to herself, and she
is seized by dizziness.

But today Father isn't double hat and after dinner they sit
together in the rocking chairs in the gallery that overlooks the
river, or rather that overlooks the hollow where the Sweet
River flows, since on this patriotic night of July 20 the river is
no more than a darkness that slips whispering along under a
quiet sky lit up every once in a while by bursts of fireworks
from the distant celebration. There, where the rockets are
thundering, her father says, that's where young Farax and my
lovely Blanca are, maybe holding hands as their eyes fill with
artificial stars, and since Eugenia is scrutinizing him, trying to
decide whether a new bout of delirium is brewing in him, her
father soothes her by clumsily and heavily stroking her black
hair. Don't fret, daughter, he tells her, the problem is that neither of them has any literary gift, neither of them has an understanding of the tragic. One must be strong, like your father,
not to want to resolve the conflict in one's own favor; one must
be generous, my child, generosity is what's required here. Eugenia, who is very pale, her skin almost transparent, fails to

grasp the meaning of her father's speech from where she sits, hunched in her rocking chair, but that doesn't alarm her, since she's used to not understanding most things he says.

On this peaceful night the cicadas and the crickets are making a racket, perhaps too much of a racket; Eugenia is afraid that her father's eardrums, already overwhelmed by the constant buzz of tinnitus, will be assaulted, and as if her father has guessed what she's thinking, he speaks to her of the eternal murmur bottled up in his ears. Your mother says it's tinnitus, but she's wrong, he says, it's an extraterrestrial noise that doesn't seem to come from a fixed point in space but from every direction at the same time. Father, the girl tries to explain to him, it's just the singing of the cicadas. These women, says Nicholas Portulinus condescendingly, shaking his head from side to side, cicadas and tinnitus are what they call the age-old echo of the creation of the universe. And then he rocks until he dozes off, big, soft, and ugly in his green silk robe printed with a tangle of black branches. Ugly but peaceful, thinks Eugenia, and her thought is borne out by the litany of German rivers that she hears him mutter. The Lahn, the Lippe, the Main, the Moselle, the Neckar, and the Neisse, recites her father, talking in his sleep now. For a moment he seems to wake up and he says to his daughter, In Germany I have a very beautiful sister called Ilse, did you know? Yes, Father, Eugenia replies, but her father has already returned to his alphabetical listing, the Oder, the Rhine, and the Ruhr. Mother was right, thinks Eugenia as she too surrenders to sleep, Father isn't queer today.

That's why the shock is so great when, a few hours later, she hears the clamor rising from the blackness of the river, the shouts of the steward Nicasio and his wife, Hilda, the long We fooooooound him echoing in the background, beneath the racket of the cicadas, beyond the crackling of the fireworks that is already dying away, We foooooound him, and Eugenia real- izes that her father isn't in his rocking chair anymore, that all that's left of him is his slippers and silk robe. She runs to look for him all over the big house, first in his bedroom, but the still- made bed makes it plain that he hasn't been there, then in the bathroom, but the towels, hanging in place, confirm that he hasn't touched them, then the billiards room, the immense, empty dining room, the kitchen with orange peels still piled on the table and the lingering smell of orange blossoms, and the silent piano parlor where Eugenia is startled when she runs straight into the steward Nicasio who appears out of nowhere like a ghost, We found Professor Portulinus in the river, the people from Virgen de la Merced found him and came to tell us, he was down there, by Virgen de la Merced, about a mile and a half from here, they found him naked and lifeless in a little rocky cove and they're bringing his body now, the river carried it away and left it washed up in a backwater.

Between cock's crow and midnight Eugenia seems to re- member a slow ceremony by torchlight on the riverbank, but the substance of that memory fades under the crushing weight of guilt, Mea culpa, mea culpa, mea maxima culpa, a voice shouts inside Eugenia, it's my fault that we're burying Father bloated and green and in secret, my fault that Father swallowed the water of all those rivers in a single gulp. I fell asleep and it's my fault that my father has drowned, I killed him in dreams and the ringing in his ears will echo inside of me forever, tor-

menting me every day of my life and reminding me of his departure. No cross, the dazed voice of her mother, Blanca, may
have said, No cross, just a stone, another stone among the
many that tumble in Eugenia's wiped-clean memory. No cross,
and there was no cross, nothing to mark the burial spot.

It's only days later that Eugenia's memory recovers its
sharpness, when she finds herself in the middle of a family
scene so static that it resembles a photograph. Sitting around
the dining-room table are her sister, Sofi, Farax, her mother,
and she herself, Eugenia, listening as her mother announces in
a cordial, reassuring voice, the voice of someone who hopes
that life will go on despite everything, Girls, your father has returned to Germany, and we don't know how long he'll be gone.
That's what Blanca, the mother, tells them, firmly and categor-
ically, offering no option for appeal. Father went to Germany
without saying goodbye?, asks Eugenia, who doesn't know
what to do now with her dream of burial and torches on the
riverbank, doesn't know what to do with the catalog of German
rivers that her father murmured that night like a funeral
prayer, If Father is in Germany then what happened to that
night when he let himself be tempted by the call of the river,
and who dreamed the dream that Father went down to the
river because I wasn't watching, that I wasn't able to stop him,
that I was the guilty one because I fell asleep; Father went back
to Germany but he left his terrible suffering here, his tribula-
tions, his muddled head; if Father went back to Germany then
maybe it isn't her fault, Eugenia's fault, if he's happy there in
his own land, then maybe Father has forgiven her for her horrendous carelessness, if Father is far away and safe, the throng

of Eugenia's guilty feelings will perhaps be quieted, reduced, extinguished, and she can rest. Sometimes Eugenia feels that she hasn't slept since that night of fireworks when she did sleep and shouldn't have. Yes, says the girl Eugenia at the dining-room table in Sasaima, Yes, yes, yes, she says, and she repeats, Father went to Germany without telling us and who knows when he'll be back, if ever.

And Farax? What happened to Farax, who disappeared almost before he completely appeared, the Abelito Caballero who shimmers in a fleeting dream that vanishes upon waking? After I'd finished reading the diaries and letters I found in the wardrobe, I didn't have a clear answer; past a certain point Farax and Abelito are wiped out as if they'd been written in erasable ink. I ask Aunt Sofi what happened to Farax, You tell me, Sofi, if you don't know then no one knows because Grandmother Blanca never mentions him again in her memoirs, she simply ignores him as if he never existed. I'd say that Farax must have stayed with us at the big house in Sasaima for three or four months after my father returned to Germany, answers Aunt Sofi, some three or four months, until one morning he was gone, taking his alpaca jacket, his old knapsack, and his lead soldiers, and heading off in the direction he'd come from, along the road to Anapoima. Maybe he didn't think there was any reason for him to stay since there was no one to teach him piano anymore, or maybe he refused to accept the too-weighty inheritance that my father had left him, maybe he never loved my mother, or maybe he loved her too much, maybe he glimpsed expectations that unsettled him in my eyes or Eugenia's, who knows what it may have been. All I can say is that

Farax was left as far behind as the days of our adolescence, and that Abelito Caballero disappeared one fine day just as my father disappeared, except that he left by the road, not the river; all I know is that we never heard a thing about either of the two, or rather, three, of them again, because my mother never offered any explanation or once mentioned their names.

. . .

I WAS PUTTING ON one of those old pairs of pants that Marta Elena still kept in her closet when I heard women's voices in the living room; one was Marta Elena's own voice and the other was also familiar but for the moment unrecognizable, then there was a third female voice, this one belonging to an older woman, like Aunt Sofi, and I thought it might be Margarita, Marta Elena's mother, although I was surprised because I knew that she was ill and housebound, so still shirtless and barefoot, I hid behind the bedroom door, and, peering out, I discovered that the woman talking in the living room was actually Aunt Sofi, and that Agustina was with her.

Standing there before Marta Elena, who had yet to recover from her astonishment, and Aunt Sofi, who didn't know what to do with herself, was my Agustina, transformed into a kind of social worker, or at best a nosy and insistent neighbor, speaking to Marta Elena in a strangely impersonal, bossy voice, giving orders and pedantically pointing out everything that was out of place according to the principles of feng shui; Agustina was an expert in feng shui and was advising a terrified Marta Elena on how she should reorganize her house. Then Agustina started wandering around without asking permission, going in and out of the boys' rooms and speaking exasperatingly fast, and my heart flip-flopped when I realized that in a few seconds she would come into Marta Elena's room and find me there freshly showered and half dressed.

At first my instinct was to hide under the bed like an illicit lover in a B movie, but I was immediately struck by a realization; what had initially been panic at the idea that Agustina would find me turned into the absolute joy of my sudden insight, into the ear-to-ear smile that must have appeared on my face when I realized in a flash what was happening, Agustina is looking for me, I thought, Agustina has come here to take me back, she missed me last night and today she's come to find me. From that moment on, I found the whole scene amusing and even joyous, despite how surreal it was and despite Marta Elena's fright and the consternation of Aunt Sofi, who tried as best she could to explain to me that it had been impossible to prevent Agustina from leaving the apartment, And how did she know I was here?, I don't know, my boy, she just knew, it wasn't hard to guess, It's all right, Aunt Sofi, I said and in fact it was more than all right, I was nearly bursting with the happiness of knowing that Agustina, in her crazy way, had come looking for me.

I stood still, behind the bedroom door, and Agustina blew into the room, passing me without turning to look at me, as if I were a ghost, because what she was doing now was critiquing furniture, objecting to vases, ordering Marta Elena to change the color of the walls, Who would ever think to paint an entire house this anemic yellow?, only someone extremely old-fashioned and boring. I'm very sorry, Señora—she always called Marta Elena Señora, not once using her name—but all the beds here are facing the wrong way, it's terrible for inner balance to set the heads toward the south, even you should know that, and it would be a good idea to increase the feng shui tein so you have some circulation of northern energy. She even poked around in Marta Elena's closet, pronouncing it untidy and recommending that she get rid of all her worn-out shoes and outdated clothes, These clothes make you look older, Señora; if you stop dressing in black, that gloomy face of yours might brighten up, Now, now, what have we here, she said when she saw my clothes, Oh no, this is no good, if your husband is gone, Señora, you should return his clothes to him and take back the space, you don't want to expose yourself to the possibility that when you find a new man he'll discover that his place is already taken.

I didn't know whether to cry or to laugh, unsure whether Agustina was raving or just pretending in order to harass Marta Elena, Look, Señora, these drawers crammed with useless junk do nothing for the place, and they block the chi and weaken the yang energy flow. Everything that was happening was so absurd, that several times I had to stifle a laugh, like when Agustina blasted an oil painting hanging in the living room and demanded that it be taken down immediately, and in the midst of it all I rejoiced, thinking that she was right, that the painting in question, which I had always hated and which Marta Elena had systematically imposed on the living room of each of our successive homes, really was appalling. I would have reveled in it all if my ex hadn't been so upset, For God's sake, Aguilar, what's wrong with your wife? she asked me through clenched teeth when we were left alone for an instant, I don't know what's wrong with her, she's just crazy, I answered, I who had never confessed to her how serious Agustina's mental problem was, at most mentioning something in passing like, Agustina gets depressed, or Agustina is very nervous, but that was all I had said, with the result that now, with no warning and in Marta Elena's own house, this whirlwind was unleashed, What's the point of a double bed, Señora, it takes up too much space and as far as I know, you sleep alone. No one could stop my rabid plaything, nor was there a single object she didn't find fault with, not even the plants, These pointy-leafed ones are no good, you'd better get some with rounded leaves, and I'd recommend that you hang a ba gua mirror surrounded by trigrams on that wall, put it up right away if you want to avoid disaster, Agustina decreed and as she uttered the word *disaster* her voice vibrated a little, as if she were predicting it. Marta Elena played along with her, taking down paintings and putting up mirrors while giving me looks of compassion, fear, and despondence, until finally she begged me, Take her away, Aguilar, I'm really sorry what's happening to you, but take her away, work things out between the two of you, because this isn't my funeral.

Meanwhile Agustina was in the bathroom, opening the cabinets one by one and calling out, Listen, Señora, this is very bad, you shouldn't have so much medicine in the house, self-medication can be deadly, this cream has cortisone in it, I wouldn't recommend it, and this one isn't good either, it's not smart to rely on antibiotics; How funny, I thought, it was as if Agustina had sensed my idle musings about moving back into

this house and had come expressly to pick it to pieces, to completely demolish both the place and the thoughts, or who
knows, it's possible that my Blimunda actually did guess that
for an instant I had begun to fail her. Aunt Sofi had fallen into
an armchair and was making peculiar motions, something like
repeated efforts to get up, though her legs were refusing to respond; Marta Elena was becoming increasingly annoyed that I
was taking everything so lightly and it's unclear how it all
would have ended if Agustina hadn't taken me by the hand,
saying, Let's go, and when Aunt Sofi tried to follow us, she
stopped her, You stay here for a while and visit with this other
lady, because sometimes it's nice to let couples do things on
their own, and all Aunt Sofi could do was laugh at the joke,
while I for my part had become a person again, because it was
the first time since the dark episode that the woman I adored
was showing signs of needing me. Before we left, my rabid
plaything grabbed a picture of me that was sitting framed on a
little table and said, I'll take this, too.

• • •

THAT WAS A HAPPY MORNING; happiness comes when you
least expect it. I'm sorry for Marta Elena, who must have been
swept away by the stirrings of hope permitted for an instant
then immediately dashed, but as for us, we left her house in
good spirits; there was a carefree expression on Agustina's face
that brought me pure delight, and I announced to them, to
Agustina and Aunt Sofi, that we wouldn't return to the apart-

ment just yet but instead would start out at once for Sasaima along the highway to Medellín: Bogotá, Fontibón, Mosquera, Madrid, Facativá, Albán, and Sasaima, That highway is under guerrilla control, protested Aunt Sofi, Yes, but only after three in the afternoon. I had been making inquiries, and apparently the guerrillas came down from the hills in the afternoon and then even the people at the checkpoints would close up and leave, but during the morning there was some truck traffic, If we leave and come back before three it will be fine.

Agustina, who was sitting in the backseat, didn't say anything or make any objection, so apparently she approved of the trip to Sasaima whatever its purpose, but Aunt Sofi wanted to know what I was planning, To get my hands on Agustina's grandparents' diaries and those letters that you yourself told me are still there, I explained, Yes, but I've also said that they're under lock and key, they've always been kept in a locked wardrobe and Eugenia has the key, Do you know what an ax is for, Aunt Sofi?, it's for hacking locked wardrobes to pieces, although in the end no ax was needed because a hard shoulder to the double door was enough to make the lock give way, and a little rummaging through the clothes inside brought to light Grandfather Portulinus's diary, Grandmother Blanca's diary, and a bundle of letters, but that would come later, because now we were just leaving Bogotá and at the first checkpoint they confirmed what I had already heard, that the army essentially patrolled until three or four in the afternoon, then retreated to safety, and at that hour the guerrillas came down, roaming around until slightly before daybreak. One round-trip ticket to

Sasaima, I said to the tollbooth woman, You travel at your own risk, she warned, and whatever you do I'd advise you to return before mid-afternoon.

Along the way Aunt Sofi continued her story about what had happened in the house in La Cabrera on the day that Mr. Londoño kicked his younger son in the back, and for the first time we talked openly in front of Agustina and nothing happened, I was watching every movement she made in the rearview mirror and I didn't notice any changes, so either Agustina wasn't listening or she was pretending not to, instead seeming preoccupied by the fruit stands that cropped up along the side of the road, by the appearance of big *jacarandas* on the last stretches of cold-country territory, by the foggy abysses that border the road down the mountain, Usually, says Aunt Sofi, when Carlos Vicente Senior hit Carlos Vicente Junior, the boy would shut himself in his room to cry and Agustina was the only one he would let in because it was she who was able to comfort him, but this time it wasn't like that. Then Agustina, who had been quiet in the backseat of the car, asked whether we were passing through Mosquera yet, and when I said we were, she wanted us to stop to eat *obleas*, the wafers spread with *arequipe*, caramel cream, at the place where the old lady was decapitated, and Aunt Sofi, who smiled when she heard what Agustina was asking, said, We always stopped there to eat *obleas* on the way to Sasaima, before they killed the owner and afterward, too, when her daughter started up the business again.

So that's what we did; the place was called Obleas Villetica and at the entrance there was an old mossy stone basin from

D e l i r i u m

which you could drink pure water, and it was beside that basin that many years ago the owner was decapitated, an old lady who wouldn't have hurt a fly, no one knows why she was so brutally assassinated but they do know that it marked the resurgence of violence in the region and that's why everyone remembers it. We parked in front and went in, and the daughter, who in the two decades since the tragedy had grown as old as her mother, asked us whether we wanted cream or jam on the *obleas* and Agustina answered for all three of us, Neither one, she said, we want them just the way they are, with *arequipe*, like always, and then when we left, as we passed the stone basin, she said, This is where they decapitated the old lady, but she said it calmly, as if she were repeating something that she must have spoken or heard many times, in the same place, all through her childhood.

Back in the car again, Aunt Sofi says that the naked photographs that Carlos Vicente Londoño had taken of her were tossed faceup on the table, I had let myself forget about them because he swore to me that he kept them in the safe at his office, but there they were on the table in plain sight of my sister, Eugenia, and the three children and there was no excuse or escape, and if that afternoon I had wished to be dead when Carlos Vicente Senior kicked Carlos Vicente Junior, now I wanted to be buried, too, and the only thing I could think of was to leave that house, hop in a taxi, and tell the driver to take me anywhere, never to return. Aunt Sofi confesses that she was gripped by the devastating certainty that her life was over, I had just lost everything, love, children, home, sister, and yet all I could think of was a story that I was told as a child about a little pig that built its house out of straw and when the wind blew, the house was knocked down; standing there in front of my sister, I was that little pig, I had built my house of straw and now the gale had blown away every trace of it, I didn't say a word, in fact I think I remember that no one spoke at all, but mentally Aunt Sofi said to her sister, All right, Eugenia, it's all yours, your husband, your children, your house, But instantly I realized that it wasn't true because when it came down to it my poor sister wasn't left with much, either; those photographs and especially that son of hers who was beaten by his father were proof that her house was made of straw, too.

Then Aunt Sofi looked at Bichi, the boy who was still standing in the middle of the room after having exposed the truth, every fiber of his body tense and waiting for the outcome, Carlos Vicente is going to finish him off now, thought Aunt Sofi, he'll beat him to death for daring to do what he did, and then my thoughts took a turn, I said to myself, Well if he wants to hit the boy again he'll have to do it over my dead body, it was funny, because if at first the revelation of those photographs stripped me of everything, the balance then tipped the other way and I felt that I was recovering the strength that had been drained from me by all those years of secret lives and hidden loves, Now that my life is in shambles, thought Aunt Sofi, I can stand up for that boy, but it wasn't necessary, the boy was standing up for himself, ready for anything, his feet firmly planted, we'd never seen him so tall, an adult at last, looking out defiantly from under the tangled curls that veiled his eyes; it was impossible not to realize that if his father had dared to lay a hand on him, this time the puppy would fight mercilessly and to the death.

So the father held back when faced with his son's newfound fierceness, I say, Maybe, replies Aunt Sofi, or maybe Carlos Vicente Senior, like Carlos Vicente Junior, was just waiting for Eugenia's reaction; the next move was hers and everyone was watching her, So what did she do then, She did the most disconcerting thing, says Aunt Sofi, turning to look back at Agustina, who is pretending not to listen. Having recovered her calm and concealing any sign of pain or surprise, Eugenia picked up the photographs one by one, like someone gathering a deck of cards, and put them in her knitting bag, then, turning to face her son Joaco, she said, and I'll repeat what she said word for word because otherwise you won't believe it, she said, You should be ashamed, Joaco, is this what you've been doing with the camera we gave you for your birthday, taking naked pictures of the maids?, and then, laying the subject to rest, she addressed her husband, Take the boy's camera away from him, dear, and don't give it back until he learns how to use it properly, What do you mean, I ask, did Eugenia really believe that Joaco had taken the pictures? Don't be naïve, Aguilar, it was clear by their format that they had been taken with the Leika camera that only Carlos Vicente used, and what doubt could there be that I was the one in the pictures; Eugenia, with stunning coolness and a perfectly steady voice, was putting on an act to defend her marriage.

For thirteen years, Aguilar, says Aunt Sofi, I've pondered the possible meanings of my sister's reaction and I've always come to the same conclusion: she already knew, she always knew, and she wasn't terribly bothered by it so long as the secret remained hidden, and the performance she improvised just then was a masterful attempt to guarantee that despite the evidence, the secret would remain a secret; what I'm trying to tell you is that she knew that her marriage would end not because Carlos Vicente was taking nude pictures of me but because it was known that Carlos Vicente was taking nude pictures of me, and not even then, but only if it were admitted that it was known. Are you sure of what you're saying, Aunt Sofi? No, I'm not sure at all, sometimes I come to the opposite conclusion, that Eugenia was surprised by those photographs and that they were as much a blow to her as the kick was to Bichi, but that she had the courage to play down the facts and behave as she did. Even more surprising was the role that Joaco played; believe me, Aguilar, when I tell you that it was that afternoon that the pact between Joaco and his mother was sealed, What did he do?, Joaco looked his mother in the eye and spoke the following sentence, just as I'm repeating it to you, Forgive me, Mother, I won't do it again.

Can you imagine, Aguilar?, that Eugenia, after a lifetime of practice, should know the code of appearances is understandable, but that Joaco, at the age of twenty, had already mastered it, that he could pick it up like that, is truly astonishing. Everything had been destroyed by a lie, my lie, the lie of my clandestine affair with my brother-in-law, and now my sister was trying to rebuild our world with another lie and preserve everything as it was before the shake-up, her marriage, the reputation of her household, even the possibility of me staying there despite everything, one lie canceling out another, tell me whether it isn't enough to drive a person crazy. What was the price of all this, besides the bottomless confusion in Agustina's head?, I ask and I answer myself, The price was the son's defeat before the father: the son had laid bare the truth and made a stand, and when the truth was denied, the son was crushed and the father saved. Almost, but not quite, Aunt Sofi contradicts me, because Bichi still had one last ace up his sleeve, that of his own freedom. When he saw that everything was lost in the house, that the morass of lies was swallowing them up whole, Bichi left by the front door, dressed just as he was, in a sweater, socks, and boots over his pajamas, and he went walking down the street and never came back, and I went out after him and I never came back, either.

By then Agustina, Aunt Sofi, and I were a good way down the road to Sasaima, and at that moment we were passing under a little cement bridge and Agustina announced from the backseat, This is the first bridge, take your jackets off now because in eight minutes, when we cross the second bridge, the heat and smell of the warm country will hit us all at once, and what she predicted came true exactly. In eight minutes by the clock we crossed the second bridge and at that same instant, like a wave coming in through the windows and hitting our noses, the heat reached us with its smell of green, damp, citrus, pasture, downpours, wild growth; we were in warm country now and it was only a little bit farther to Sasaima.

• • •

FOR FIFTEEN MINUTES all I did was shake, Agustina baby, I swear to you that after that phone call I was literally shaking, naked and helpless there like a newborn baby, until the telephone rang for a second time and I thought, Now it really is Rorro, but I was wrong again, this time it was a phone call from Mr. Sánchez, one of the security guards at the center, who spoke in gasps, unable to find the words to describe what was happening, They're here, they're here, Don Midas, and they're searching, they're tearing up the hardwood floor in the gym, they've already destroyed it and they're still looking.

The first thing that popped into my head was that after the stir Agustina made that afternoon, the police must be raiding the center and taking it apart to find Dolores's body, so I asked the guard, Who's there, Mr. Sánchez, the police? No, Don Midas, it isn't the police, it's Mr. Spider's bodyguards, Paco Malo, the Sucker, and six others, and Mr. Spider is outside with Mr. Silver, waiting in a car. I was still confused, but I managed to ask, Looking for what?, because all this came as a complete surprise, Agustina darling, if it was Spider's thugs then they couldn't be looking for Dolores, since after all they knew the stretch of wasteland where they'd left her mortal remains, so I went back to interrogating Sánchez, What the fuck are Spider's men looking for at my Aerobics Center at this hour of the night? Money, Don Midas, they say that this is where you must have hidden the stash that you . . . what do I mean?, I'm sorry, I'm just repeating what they say, Don Midas, they're looking for some money that according to them you stole from Don Spider and Don Silver, I'm calling to warn you, Don Midas, they say that if they don't find anything here, they're heading straight over there, to your apartment, these people are pissed off, Don Midas, there are lots of them and they're extremely angry, they say that if the money isn't here, it must be there, and pardon my language, boss, I'm just repeating what I've heard, they're saying that if they have to string you up by the balls to find out where you hid it, then they'll string you up.

You might ask, Agustina sweetheart, how I managed to think and respond in the middle of my intergalactic trip on Santa Marta Golden, a trip that was making my neurons, soft and spongy as marshmallows, bounce tamely around in the padded cell of my brain, and I tell you that either fear must work miracles or the double hit of adrenaline produced by those two calls gradually cleared away the fog, because at last I put two and two together and came to some conclusions, by which I mean that I assembled the previous month's sequence of events as follows: one, Pablo's cousins show up at my Aerobics Center asking to join and I rudely turn them down flat, without realizing the consequences of my actions; two, Pablo Escobar finds out and decides to teach me a lesson; three, Pablo sets a trap for me, ordering me through Mystery to ask for an excessive amount of money from Rony Silver and Spider Salazar; four, Pablo makes the money disappear and never returns it; five—and I had no way to confirm this fifth step but I deduced it logically—Pablo gets in touch with Rony and Spider and lies to them, making them think that he did return the money to me on the established date and with all the agreed-upon profits, and that he delivered it to me in full in order for me to pass their shares on; sixth and last, while I was mentally piecing together the map of the five previous points, Rony and

Spider were on their way to my apartment with their gang of thugs to snip off my balls with fingernail clippers and yank off any detachable part of me, up to and including my eyelashes, to get me to tell them where I'd hidden the money that I'd supposedly swiped, so there you have it all laid out for you, baby, in six separate steps and a single move; why did the chicken cross the road? to get to the other side, riddle solved.

I admit that I've always been a brute to you, but you have to grant me this one thing: in the middle of my panic and the every-man-for-himself thinking that came over me, Agustina angel, I remembered you, incredible, yes, but true, I remembered you, I knew that if I fled my apartment I'd never get the call from Rorro, and it really did worry me not to know the outcome of your psycho interlude, but it's also true that this was the extent of my heroic altruism, because there was no way I could sit there waiting for news of you until the Sucker and his hordes came to rip me to shreds, so with great sorrow and wishing you the best of luck from afar, I got the hell out of there, which meant that I had no more news of you; no news of you or Rorro or Spider or the pretty girls who used to sleep with me or of absolutely anyone until today, when who should I be fated to see but you, the rest never again, kaput, that's it, total blackout, all lines of communication cut.

It's as if I've already let go of everything and settled in the great beyond, and the longer I spend shut up here, the more I become convinced that the other life I stubbornly and methodically insisted on building in the air never really existed; now that I have infinite free time I've taken to philosophizing, I've become a speculative bastard, I like to reflect on the line that goes "for life is a dream, and dreams are only dreams," I don't know which poet wrote it but I've made it my bedtime mantra, Agustina doll, and I'd like to know who it's by. Do me a favor and ask your husband, Professor Aguilar, he must have the information, or maybe that's not his field of expertise. Your brother Joaco, the *paraco* Ayerbe, impotent Spider, my sumptuous apartment, the Aerobics Center with all its anorexics, Dolores and her hideous death, even my beloved BMW R100RT are all ghosts to me, actors and scenery from a play that's finished now. The stagehands have carried everything away and now the curtain has fallen, even Pablo is a ghost, the whole country itself is ghostly, and if it wasn't for the bombs and the bursts of machine-gun fire that echo in the distance, the tremors reaching me here, I'd swear that the place called Colombia had stopped existing long ago.

This is how I spent my last few minutes in that other world: after I received the phone calls from Pablo's cousin and the guard at the gym, I tossed the end of my joint into the fire, put on a random pair of pants, the first shirt I could find, my Harvard cap, and some red-and-black Nike Airs, then I grabbed the overnight bag that I'd prepared that morning to take to the Londoño estate, which was still ready and waiting for me by some trick of fate, though for a different trip than originally planned, and I slung a golf bag over my shoulder which, as a precautionary measure, I kept packed full of dollars, and without even stopping to turn off the lights or the fireplace with the remote control, I hurried down to the garage for my bike and only then did I realize that I had left it at the gym, so for an instant I paused in my flight and allowed myself a hint of sadness as I said goodbye to my BMW, and to my Jacuzzi, my twin-headed shower, my soft vicuna pup–skin blanket, my precious record collection, and my deluxe Bose sound system, then I went out into the street carrying my suitcase and golf bag and took the first taxi that came by, and checking to make sure that no one was following me, I headed toward my mother's apartment in San Luis Bertrand, for the first time in the last fourteen years.

You don't know, Agustina baby, the host of conflicting feelings that passed through my head on that nighttime trip of forced return to the womb, of obligatory reacquaintance with my origins, a trip that was either a full step backward or a vindication of my noble, saintly mother whom I'd kept hidden for so long because of those knots in her nylon stockings. I don't know whether you get the paradox, sweetheart, but as it turned out, the maternal territory that I had kept carefully secret and hermetically isolated from my worldly clamor suddenly appeared as my salvation, a refuge to which I could never be traced and that no one would ever suspect, and all because of a strange law of fate that had me doubling back on myself to bite my tail; how can I put this, adorable Agustina, that night in the taxi, hugging my golf bag tight, I felt that I was returning to the only corner where redemption might be possible, and I haven't stirred from here since, nearly holding my breath so no one can track me down, and it looks like I'll be here for as long as I have left to live on this planet, because as I'm sure you've seen in the papers, sweet Agustina of mine, or maybe not, since you never read the papers, Congress has approved the enforcement of the Extradition Treaty, and the DEA—in other words, Ronald Silverstein, my friend Rony Silver, 007, Mr. Double

Trouble—has put together a thick file on me in which sufficient and conclusive evidence is presented to accuse me of money laundering, and just as you see me here, princess, in slippers and unshaven and sitting beside you drinking hot chocolate lovingly prepared for me by my mother, I'm a criminal wanted for extradition by the United States of America and I'm being sought at this very moment by land, sea, and air by every security organization, intelligence bureau, and international police force in existence.

But of course nothing will happen to me so long as I stay locked away in my mother's apartment with my giving and nurturing little mother, who's more efficient than the remote control I left behind, because with her I don't even have to push a button, she anticipates my desires before I can formulate them myself and she hurries to please me despite her limp. Sitting on the little sofa in the living-dining room, my mother and I watch soap operas and eat rice and lentils and pray the rosary at dusk, and you can imagine, Agustina darling, that given our modest expenses, we can live forever or even longer on the dollars I brought with me in the golf bag. Because I know for a fact that there's no informer or spy or marine in this world, no hired killer of Pablo's or bodyguard of Spider Salazar's, who can find my hiding place so long as I stay here, safe and sheltered on the maternal lap; I've become a bear in permanent hibernation, a saint perched on top of my pillar, a Tibetan monk hidden away for one hundred years in a hermitage; I bet you're surprised, angel, to see your friend Midas turned into a cheap philosopher, a stoical prophet of the end of time, amen.

Only you, Agustina doll, only you of all the people on earth knew that if I had disappeared without a trace you could find me here, and you came to me to be told what happened to you that fateful Saturday, and since you have every right to know, well, there you have it; I've shown you my slice of the cake without hiding anything from you, and I guess it will be up to everybody else to show you the rest now, my little soothsayer, as blind as you are clairvoyant. I really am happy to see you looking so pretty and so well, and I swear that in these circumstances you're the last person I expected to run into. I know that you'll keep the secret of San Luis Bertrand for me as faithfully as ever, and now I can't think of anything else to tell you, well, except what you already know, which is that here I have all the time in the world to think of you, which is what I do when I'd rather not think about anything.

• • •

ANITA, THE LOVELY ANITA, is waiting for me in all her glory at Don Conejo, and she's wearing the navy blue suit that is her work uniform, the one with the little skirt that reaches to mid-thigh, but she's changed out of her white shirt into a tight black blouse that the hotel manager surely would not approve of, because it exposes some truly thrilling cleavage; my Anita is a stunner no matter how you look at it, and she's also changed into a pair of very high-heeled shoes that aren't exactly the kind you could stand in all day behind the reception desk, The girl is looking for trouble, I think as soon as I see her, and now what do I do with her.

I'd returned from Sasaima around five with Agustina and

Aunt Sofi, successfully skirting the perils we'd been warned of, and with the booty from Agustina's grandparents' wardrobe in hand, and if I hadn't had that appointment at nine at Don Conejo, which nothing could have persuaded me to miss, I would've immersed myself in the diaries and letters that very night to find out as soon as possible who the German Portulinus and his wife, Blanca, really were. Sometimes you have to wait centuries for something to happen and then all of a sudden everything happens at once; as we were entering the apartment upon our return from Sasaima, the telephone rang, It's Bichi for you, I said to Aunt Sofi without needing to ask, because who else could that young male voice with its Colombian-Mexican accent belong to, Bichi is coming to visit, announced Aunt Sofi when she hung up, he just called to confirm.

My eyes and Aunt Sofi's eyes are fixed on Agustina, alert to her reaction, If Bichi's coming then we have to clean, because this place is turned upside down, she said in excitement, but so naturally that no one could have suspected that only yesterday she was spewing hollow-voiced venom, and in fact the apartment was all topsy-turvy because of the notorious dividing line that she herself had drawn when she was waiting for that other, crazy visitor, her father, Then can we put the furniture back in place?, asked Aunt Sofi, and Agustina said yes, that there was no reason why everything should be piled up on one side, It's not like we were about to wax the floor or give dance lessons here, she said, as if she herself hadn't been the engineer of the madness, We have to put all the furniture back and tidy this up completely, she ordered, and I felt a jolt of alarm, What do you mean, tidy it up completely?, I asked, fearing that the pots of water, the purifications, and the whole ungodly commotion would start up again, Tidy it up, tidy it up, I mean put everything back the way it was, she answered, slightly irritated by such silly questions, and she set to it with renewed vigor, excessive vigor, I thought worriedly, It isn't good for her to get so worked up, I whispered in Aunt Sofi's ear, Why no, it's not, but who's to stop her, we must trust in God, Aguilar, Well, yes, Aunt Sofi, we'll have to, won't we.

As Agustina began reorganizing the house for the hundredth time, Aunt Sofi and I sat down to rest after that marathon trip to Sasaima and back, Tell me how you and Bichi ended up in Mexico, Aunt Sofi, I asked her, and just then Agustina interrupted us, saying, I don't know, I don't know, I'm not sure about these green walls, But they're recommended by feng shui, I ventured to suggest, trying to reassure her, Screw feng shui, she said, I'm thinking that this space would look brighter if we painted the walls burnt orange, Well it was like this, Aunt Sofi told me, ignoring Agustina's outbursts, after Eugenia delivered the coup de grâce by lying about the photographs, Bichi left the house just as he was, in a sweater and boots over his pajamas and nothing else, but looking so clearly as if he'd made up his mind that we all knew he wasn't planning to come back, and meanwhile, in a matter of seconds, I had gone from being sure my life was over to suspecting that the only thing that was over was life as I'd understood it up until then, Enough of these passive little moves, Aunt Sofi ordered herself, it's time for me to play my own ace. The bag she had taken to church with her was still within reach on a chair, next to the hat with a feather in it and the palm branch blessed by

the priest. And don't ask me why, she says, but instead of grabbing just the bag I ran off with all three things, hurrying up to
my room to get the money I kept in a dresser drawer, which
was $7,500 in traveler's checks and 250,000 pesos, as well as
my coat, my passport, and my little jewelry box, then I swept
through Bichi's room, snatching up the first pair of pants I saw
in the closet, and I flew down the stairs, and when I say flew I
mean flew, because my feet didn't even touch the steps, and as
I passed the television room where the rest of the family was
gathered, I could see that Agustina was still on her knees, with
a dumbfounded look on her face, and I felt a twinge in my
heart, saying to myself, That girl is the one who'll end up paying, and I promised myself to come back someday for her; as I
went out, I saw that Bichi was already a few blocks away, and
when I realized that I was still clutching the palm branch in one
hand, I threw it far away from me, Goodbye, palm of martyrdom, and I ran after the boy and caught up with him, Let's go,
I said, and Bichi answered, We're already gone.

I remember that I arrived at Don Conejo a little after nine,
and there was Anita and her amazing breasts, Anita and her
brown legs, Anita and her long hair smelling of peach shampoo;
uncomplicated Anita, determined to get me into bed with her
that night by any means possible, the two of us sitting in Don
Conejo with a couple of beers and an order of spicy beef empanadas in front of us. Anita leaned into me with her breasts
and her peach smell and said that she'd found out who had paid
for the hotel suite my wife was in that weekend, Well, paid isn't
quite the right word, actually, the hotel is looking for him because he never paid, he left a credit card number that the bank

reported as canceled the next day, and that isn't the only bill he hasn't settled with us, because between one thing and another he owes us a fortune, Anita won't stop talking and I don't want to listen, now that she's about to reveal the name of the man who was with Agustina, I don't want to know it anymore.

I don't know why, but it no longer mattered, Agustina and I had eaten *obleas* at the place where the old lady was decapitated and everything else was beside the point; she had taken me by the hand to show me the house and gardens in Sasaima, This is the orchid grotto and this is the stable and this was my horse Brandy's saddle, and this is the little clearing where we played soccer, and these galleries are where we played cops and robbers, this is the tree I hit when I fell off Brandy and I broke my collarbone, come here, Aguilar, and sit with me in the hammock, it was on these stalks of bamboo that my mother stuck pieces of fruit for the birds, there were cardinals, parakeets, bluebirds, and canaries, this is the basket that Aunt Sofi always took with her to gather eggs, and come now, Aguilar, you have to see the Sweet River, listen, you can hear it from here, you don't know how smooth and black the stones of the Sweet River are, and they heat up in the sun, let's go and sit on them and dangle our feet in the water. After those black stones, I thought, what did it matter to me anymore what the name of the man at the hotel was, let him be called whatever he wanted now that Agustina had taken me to see the river of her childhood, I don't know, in some way I'd already gotten past the pain of having been cheated on, the betrayal or the mistake or whatever it was, and hearing a name now would just bring it all back.

So while Anita was talking I let my mind wander, focusing my attention on anything else, on her improbable nails that were no longer striped but now painted with stars, tiny blue stars on a silver background, which meant that they were still flags, though not French flags but some other country's flags, flags with stars; Anita kept telling me things but I was thinking about the Cuban flag, with its single star, white?, red?, and the gringo flag, on which there were lots of stars but which was the reverse of the flags on Anita's nails because its stars were white on a blue background; the Algerian flag, if I was remembering correctly, had a moon and a star; the Argentinean flag had a sun, and after all the sun is a star; I imagined that there must be stars on the flags of many Arab countries, like Iraq and Egypt, though those stars would probably be green, and as Anita tickled my forearm with the tips of her starry fingernails, I thought, What an incredible thirst for the heavens, there are stars on almost every flag on earth and yet the earth itself appears on no flag I've ever seen, and still I couldn't help hearing the man's name when Anita's mouth finally uttered it, Midas McAlister? Midas McAlister was the one she was with?, Yes, yes I know who Midas McAlister is, he's an old boyfriend of Agustina's, and then I felt sick and it occurred to me that it had been a bad idea to have that beer and those empanadas; suddenly there was a burning in my chest and I suspected that the culprit was the hot peppers, or maybe it was Midas McAlister, and I went looking for the restroom to splash water on my face and be alone for a minute.

By the time I returned to the table, Anita was worried, I was just about to come looking for you, she said, Let's go looking for someone, but let's make it Midas McAlister, because he owes me an explanation, or rather he owes my wife one, What are you going to do, beat him up?, No, I just want him to explain what happened that weekend, then Anita offered to tell me where we might find him on the condition that things not turn violent, That is if we can find him at all, she warned, because he's vanished, I tell you, the hotel wants to kill him but they can't find him, people say he's disappeared from the face of the earth because he heard that the government was going to issue an extradition order for him.

So we ended up at a gym that belonged to him, a gym with an English name in one of the residential neighborhoods on the north side of the city, but it was already closed because it was almost ten, and the tall, dark man who was pulling down the gates and locking up was him, it was Midas McAlister, I recognized him as soon as I set eyes on him, That's the man who was with her, I said, Yes, that's him, Anita confirmed, So this is the moment of truth. And yet it wasn't the moment of truth but a moment of confusion, because there I was challenging this Midas person and he swears to me by the Holy Virgin that he's Rorro, not Midas, Rorro my ass, I shouted, although now I admit that although I was standing up to the so-called Rorro, I was doing it cautiously, because the bastard was a real athlete, one of those professional muscle men, and then three or four gym members came out on the way to their cars and confirmed that this actually was Rorro, an employee of the gym, the man in charge of weights and stretching, and that Midas, on the other hand, was the owner, but that he hadn't been seen for days, He hasn't been back here, That's right, he hasn't been back, No one knows where he is, No, no one knows, and you aren't the first to come looking for him, No, you're certainly not the first, This place has already been ransacked several times and it's likely that they'll close it any day now and seal it off, Yes, extremely likely, says Rorro, and I'm owed three months' salary.

But I saw you, I accused him, returning to the offensive, I saw you coming out of that hotel room where my wife was, Then you must be her husband, nice to meet you, I'm Rorro, said the Midas McAlister who claimed his name was Rorro, and he offered me his right hand in a way that seemed friendly and even honest; convincing, you might say. I was the one who called to let you know that you should pick her up at the hotel, he told me, And who gave you my number?, Your wife did, she gave it to me herself and asked me to call you, She asked you to call me?, I demanded, feeling at last that I was myself again, that after so many days and nights of emptiness I had recovered my true self, Are you sure of what you're saying?, Sure as can be, she gave me the number, and if she hadn't, how would I have gotten it, think for a second, pal, of course it was your wife who asked me to call you, Thank you so much, Rorro, and please forgive me, I said, but now tell me what all this was about, what happened to my wife, why was she at that hotel with you, what were you doing there with her?

Come on, said Anita, who was the only one who seemed to know how things should be done, let's all go sit at that bar on the corner and we'll buy a drink for Mr. Rorro and ask him nicely to do us the favor of explaining everything, because we're all friends here, Don Rorro, Well there isn't much I can tell you, but yes, thank you, I will take you up on that drink, because the cold gets into your bones, something to warm me up, and once they were at the bar and had downed a few shots, the man who called himself Rorro kept insisting, I wasn't doing anything, Señor, I wasn't doing anything, Señorita, I was just taking care of the lady who was so upset, a very pretty lady, if you don't mind me saying so, but not right in the head, I was taking care of her because I had received instructions to take care of her, Whose instructions, Rorro, have another shot and maybe then you can tell us, Instructions from my boss, I already told you, from my boss Don Midas, who else, there's nothing I wouldn't do for him and to think he left owing me three months' salary, And where in hell is Don Midas?, I asked him, You said it yourself, hell's as likely as anywhere, because the honest truth is no one knows where he's gone, and if I knew, don't you think I'd be there claiming my back pay.

When I was convinced the man didn't know any more than he was telling, I left the bar with the firm resolution that beginning the next day I'd search high and low for Midas McAlister until I found him, determined to dig him out of whatever hole he was in, even if it took me a lifetime, and how could I have known then that the only person in the universe who would have any idea of where to find him was Agustina herself. As I was about to get into the van, I saw Rorro come out of the bar and run toward me, motioning for me to wait, I forgot to give you this, he said, offering me a little card, your wife had it in her hand until she dropped it at the hotel, I picked it up because it struck me as unusual and I put it in my pocket, and here I am still carrying it around, the only reason I haven't thrown it away is because I was afraid it might be bad luck to mess with it, what if it turned out to have some kind of strange powers, take it, I'm giving it back to you since it belongs to your wife, she was holding it tight.

As soon as I took the card I recognized my own left hand, shrunken down and laminated in plastic, the back on one side and the palm on the other, it was the Hand That Touches, made from the photocopies that I'd sent Agustina at the beginning of our time together, so when I saw it and I heard that Agustina had been clutching it all through the dark episode, I couldn't help myself and I shouted, This is a miracle, What's a miracle?, asked Anita, looking at the card and declaring it strange, Very strange, as a girl I spooked myself playing the Hairy Hand game and now I pray to the Miraculous Hand, but I've never heard of this Hand That Touches, Come on, Anita, get in the van and I'll take you to Meissen, I offered, but no sir, Anita expected more, she'd seen me through the hard times and now she was going to demand some good times; Anita hadn't planned to show off her lovely breasts for nothing, Anita was used to people following through, pretty Anita switched from the casual *tú* to the formal *usted*, her voice turning cold when she spoke to me, and she said, No, Señor, not Meissen, now that I've helped you find what you were looking for, you have to take me out dancing for a while, and what could I say but, Of course I'll take you dancing, Anita, it's the least I can do to thank you for your sweet company in my times of trial.

So that night we ended up at a club in Chapinero where a pair of dwarfs worked the bar, and it was half empty anyway, since it was a weeknight. How infinitely graceful Anita was when she danced, what an effort I had to make not to pull her to me, what a sin it was not to kiss her, what a crime to remove my hands from her hips; smiling, willing, delectable Anita in the dim light of a club in Chapinero with two dwarfs behind the bar, But my heart is elsewhere, Anita, and even my body isn't entirely present here with yours, Goodbye, Anita from Meissen, I would have liked to say, in another life I'll come looking for you and marry you and make you happy, Anita, because you deserve it, and it's something I'll always owe you; and I would also have liked to say, In another life I'll take you to bed in the suite of a luxury hotel, Anita, it can even be the Wellington if you want, I deserve it and it's something you'll always owe me, but that will all have to be in another life because I'm going home now, pretty Anita, which is where my life is waiting for me, the life I'm living now, I mean, the life that in the end is the only one I've got and that's waiting for me at home, it will be a pleasure to dream of you, Anita, but right now I can't have things in my real life that aren't real, because there's been more than enough of that already.

When I got to the apartment at two in the morning, I was greeted by a smell that made tears spring to my eyes, and that's no metaphor, because this smell, which I'm not sure I can describe, really did make me cry, it was the smell of home, how else to put it, an everyday smell, a smell of people who sleep at night and get up in the morning, of real life, of life that has returned to the realm of the possible; how long it will last I don't know, I thought, but at least as long as the smell lingers, as long as this calm remains unbroken. Agustina was asleep on my side of the bed and she had left me a note on the night table, a note like the one she'd slid under the door of my cubicle at the university three years ago, asking for two things, a photocopy of my hand and my help in writing her autobiography; this time the sheet of paper wasn't in an envelope but folded in half and addressed to me, Aguilar. I may not know what happiness is, I suppose no one knows, but what I do know is that happiness is what I felt when I saw my name in her handwriting on that sheet of paper, with a little circle instead of a dot over the *i*, and inside it said, "Professor Aguilar, if you still love me despite everything, wear a red tie tomorrow." I read it many times before I fell asleep, and the last thought that crossed my mind that night was, I'm happy, tonight I'm happy even though I don't know how long this happiness will last.

When I got up the next day Agustina was already dressed, and she was calling the airport to confirm the arrival time of the flight from Mexico. I took a leisurely shower, trimmed my beard, combed my hair the best I could considering that it hadn't grown out enough to hide the damage done by Don Octavio the barber, put on a white shirt and rummaged through my drawers until I found an old red tie that I was sure I had somewhere. I looked a little strange, because I've never worn a tie and I don't have the right jacket, but there I was in my red tie, and for the first time I even splashed on a little of the cologne that Agustina always gives me. When I came downstairs, Agustina walked past me several times without saying anything, not even good morning, pretending not to see me, her eyes avoiding my red tie as if she regretted writing that note, or rather as if she were afraid to see whether I'd put it on or not, purposely not looking. She and Aunt Sofi were putting the finishing touches on the lunch with which we would welcome Bichi when we brought him back from the airport; they had made a turkey and were fussing with some apples and vegetables, paying no attention to me, so I poured myself a cup of coffee and sat down to breakfast, glancing through the newspaper and watching my wife as she walked back and forth past me with her eyes averted, acting as if she hadn't noticed me and yet at the same time nervous, wanting and not wanting to check and see out of the corner of her eye whether I had put on the tie or not, until I planted myself in front of her, took her by the shoulders, made her look me in the eyes, and asked her, Miss Londoño, is this tie red enough for you?